The Door in Lake Mallion

The Brindlewatch Quintet

Book 2

S.M. Beiko

Published by ECW Press
665 Gerrard Street East
Toronto, Ontario, Canada M4M 1Y2
416-694-3348 / info@ecwpress.com

Editor for the Press: Jen Hale
Copy-editor: Jen Albert
Cover design: Lisa Marie Pompillio

This is a work of fiction. Names, characters,
places, and incidents either are the product of
the author's imagination or are used fictitiously,
and any resemblance to actual persons, living or
dead, business establishments, events, or locales is
entirely coincidental.

LIBRARY AND ARCHIVES CANADA CATALOGUING
IN PUBLICATION

Title: The door in Lake Mallion / S.M. Beiko.

Names: Beiko, S. M., author.

Description: Series statement: The Brindlewatch
quintet ; book 2

Identifiers: Canadiana (print) 20240398483 |
Canadiana (ebook) 20240398491

ISBN 978-1-77041-696-3 (softcover)
ISBN 978-1-77852-254-3 (ePub)
ISBN 978-1-77852-257-4 (PDF)

Subjects: LCGFT: Novels. | LCGFT: Fantasy
fiction.

Classification: LCC PS8603.E428444 D66 2024 |
DDC jC813/.6—dc23

This book is funded in part by the Government of Canada. Ce livre est financé en partie par le gouvernement du
Canada. We acknowledge the support of the Canada Council for the Arts. Nous remercions le Conseil des arts du
Canada de son soutien. We would like to acknowledge the funding support of the Ontario Arts Council (OAC) and
the Government of Ontario for their support. We also acknowledge the support of the Government of Ontario
through the Ontario Book Publishing Tax Credit, and through Ontario Creates.

PRINTED AND BOUND IN CANADA

PRINTING: MARQUIS   5 4 3 2 1

Purchase the print edition and receive the ebook free.
For details, go to ecwpress.com/ebook.

For Wesley.
If you bring home a potential crush
from a subterranean city,
I'll support you.

A NOCTURNE IN
PIANISSIMO

The curtain pulls away to reveal a town. Not a hamlet or a village. Big enough to have its secrets. Small enough that everyone living there knows them before you do.

Knockum. Like a town you knew in a close-to-hand memory.

Knockum, a place by the water to grow up, to grow old.

Knockum, one of the many fishing towns built on the inland sea called Lake Mallion.

Enter, night.

The lake is still, eight miles of dark glass stretching, as it has since the meteor that made it slammed into the land, carving the lake from its destruction and power. The original peoples that fished here by hand with spears and nets respected its depths. Its gifts. Its dangers.

The lake is still and so is the Door at the bottom of it, precisely two miles from the shore and seven miles more from where Dunstan Cord's family home in the middle of Knockum stands on this night, the night his newborn cries will climb those walls. The night fifteen years before he will lead Knockum to lose everything.

The lake is still. It is a black mirror reflecting the black sky, solid granite, starless, when broken-hearted Reeve Gris steals his father's thirty-five-foot steam trawler *The Darling Mermaid* on a dare. His three drunken friends cheer and slap him on the back as they roar across the lake, shattering the calm for one night of revelry that will ruin things for a future generation they don't even consider.

It wouldn't be far, they'd told themselves in their teenage certainty. Just two miles. Every child of Knockum at the knee of the fishwives has heard the story of the Door in Lake Mallion, though accounts of what it looks like differ wildly depending on the storyteller's respect for what's on the other side of it:

Intricately carved from an oak that once stood where the lake is, undamaged by the water.

No, it's heavy wrought iron, enchanted, impossible to rust.

No. It's hewn from braided lakeweed that parts only for the chosen few.

On one thing, all the tellers agree: it is a door that is not to be opened. It is shut for a reason. It keeps Them out. It keeps Us safe. We respect the Door, and we leave it alone and we prosper.

Reeve Gris knows all this. He isn't stupid. In fact, he's in line for valedictorian at Knockum Upper, has always been the head of his class, has always respected the stories, the histories, the beauty of this not-to-be-uncovered mystery. *Reeve knows better* has been the smiling proverb of his fathers, his neighbours. But Reeve isn't immune to needing to prove himself, on the night that he swears his teenage heart will never mend. On this night *he* will be the hero, for once, and mark himself down in the legends older than Lake Mallion's originating meteor.

He will get what he wants, in a way. They all will, charging ahead and blasting the horn on the empty lake, usually crawling with boats before first light, when the order of fishing and catching rules these waters, and not the heady chaos of children.

The horn blast rouses Ada Cord, Dunstan's mother, descended from a long line of lightkeepers, loyal at her post on the eastern dock tower. She turns sharply to the window, squinting, sees the trawler's lights bright as a flame where a boat shouldn't be, out there on the water, at this hour. Then she stiffens as the boat's lights flicker out, the horn dying. The uncertain shouting of frightened children not much younger than her echoes back to her, though there is no wind. There's a painful silence in which she doesn't breathe, calculating. She clutches her pregnant belly full of her son and readies to scurry down the watchtower steps, land on the dock where her skiff waits, and—

A blade of green light cuts the lake in half about two miles from the shore. She only saw the flash of it, screwed her eyes shut half a second after.

Though she isn't looking directly at the light anymore, Ada wants to move, to get away from the green afterglow, but she can't. A painful hum has taken root in her molars, climbing to the nerves behind her closed eyes. A scream cut short, then silence.

When Ada opens her eyes again, the lake is still. The lake is dark. Ada takes a breath.

Her water breaks.

In the morning, at the same moment when Dunstan Cord sings his first world-entering solo, *The Darling Mermaid* will be declared lost. Grief burns like a brand on the town, the scars grown over but never forgotten. Later still, a former Brindlewatch Guard with an eye for art will set roots in the town and will use these scars as the grist for her first statue: a tragically beautiful stone mermaid to memorialize the four teenagers who drowned in Lake Mallion that night.

Knockum will count this as its greatest tragedy for the next fifteen years. They will mourn and question and take even greater care not to disturb what lies at the bottom of the lake that has always provided for them.

The stage goes dark. But not for long. The edges glow green. Where there is dark, there is always light — but some lights aren't meant to shine.

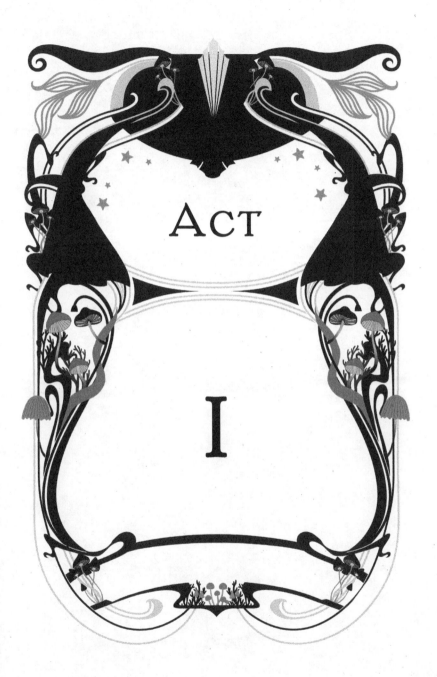

ACT

I

SCENE 1

ONE LAST TROLLEY DANCE

The stage is set. The orchestra thrums through the overture. The lights come up. This is it — *the* moment. The one where the racing mind stops, everything clicking into place the instant the curtains fly apart. The audience inhales. All the preparation, the work, the sacrifice, comes down to this one performance.

The part of a lifetime. The part that Dunstan Cord was born to play.

He flicks his fedora, suspenders sparkling red as he twirls, sauntering out the dance steps of the opening number, voice clear as he two-steps his way through a busy crowd set against the backdrop of the fishing docks. *This is where I'm from / but oh I don't belong!* The trumpets jig underneath each step as the backup dancers join. Dunstan's dreams are too big to inhabit just this stage, and so the stage becomes enormous, deeper to accommodate. It's beyond deep. We are inside his very dream.

It's a stage for the follies on film, decadent and layered as Dunstan imagines his small-town life to be. As he spins, the wingtips of his glasses glint with the rhinestones carefully glued there. The spoils of his humble beginnings in the fishing village are highlighted throughout the number: his first "aria" as soon as he left accommodations inside his mother Ada's belly, caterwauling in time with the horns. His first day at school, bedecked in a bowtie he sewed when he was only four, subsequently tripped into the mud by the other children — the Perfects. The ones Dunstan always reaches for, even when he's picked up out of the mud by the other outcasts. Maybe the metaphor is *too* on the nose, but audiences, these days, need to be pointed towards the moral. It leaves more space to showcase the production values.

Each bullying incident is given its due, but with an undercut of humour — don't want the audience to lose heart this early in the show! There are his mothers, sweet Ada and let's-get-down-to-business Lorraine, encouraging him at every birthday party where his invitations flutter in the wind, ignored. His castaway coterie of friends, each their own brand of tattered fabric, grow up alongside Dunstan, happy in their lot, but there's our unlikely lead, always looking elsewhere, dreaming beyond what he's been given. And why not? He hops down each stage-layer as each memory is played out, from Dunstan's glasses being crushed underfoot by an endless stream of bullies, growing from a lad to a teen, still defiant as the world treads on him, each night at his lonely sewing machine creating and planning for the Great Time After, when he'll have grown up and escaped.

The corps dancers flourish past him in billowing skirts of silk organza, the gents in suits of gleaming gabardine — the music swells. Out of the small town grows a metropolis of glittering buildings, flashing marquees. And in the biggest lights of all: *Dunstan Cord, hero and star.*

This is it. His moment. His leading man sweeps him away in a waltz as the city falls into a glowing green nightscape — the lead quarterback, Dunstan's chief Perfect bully who saw what was right there all along. Happily ever after, waiting in the wings!

The leading man twirls off into the darkness, leaving Dunstan behind.

The stage lights go out, but for one spotlight. Blinded, Dunstan peers out into the gallery.

Snickers. Quiet at first, as if he'd missed his cue, the entr'acte to his perfect soliloquy. But no. This isn't in the script. He squints — it's too bright.

Then the stage falls out from under him.

The orchestra falters, the horn blitzing the notes and the piano keys crackling. *No. It's not supposed to end like this!* Aren't dreams supposed to be true if you're the one steering the ship?

Finally Dunstan lands, and the lights come back up. He blinks. The ophthalmologist raises the massive clunking device he's had Dunstan staring into for years, every time he's come in for a new prescription.

He stares expectantly at Dunstan, who looks around, finds Ada in the seat next to him, a hand over her mouth, eyes straight ahead.

"I'm sorry?" The ringing in Dunstan's ears lets other sounds back in. Not an orchestra at all. Not even elevator muzak. Just the sound of the traffic in the street below the building, the comings and goings of Luxe. His dreams were just within reach, now slowly receding as the house lights of his fantasy flicker out, one by one, leaving behind an afterimage of green.

Dr. Arch slides back in his chair and smiles, all pity and *Let's talk about next steps.* What steps? Dunstan knows every popular mutton-trot out there, but not this dance. What steps are there in the *danse diagnosis?*

Dr. Arch lies and says it isn't anything to be upset about. But Dunstan can still spot a fellow performer. He isn't blind.

Not yet, anyway.

Fantasy was always Dunstan's chosen therapy. When bullies came a-knockin, or he didn't move past his thirty-second audition moment . . . disappointment could always be turned on its head. It had to. Or else there was dwelling in reality, and Dunstan wasn't much for that.

In his chiefest dream, glittering in the limelight, a big band swelled behind him as he belted the first bars of a ballad. One from that swing era vinyl Mama Lorraine loved to play when she was still here, with a daring beat and heaps of romance. Dunstan always held out his hand towards the wings of the stage, and his dance partner spun out to catch him — but even now, even when he needed to most, he couldn't see the face of his partner clearly. Someone to lean on. Someone to dance him out of his misery, this town, and every disappointment stacking up to crush him.

Ada stared at the floor of whatever vehicle they'd been on — first, the train back from Luxe, the shapes of buildings becoming the shapes of trees as they travelled back into the wide and winding country. An hour and a half later, on the platform of the Tantalon Depot, Ada seemed to be cataloguing cracks in the terrazzo. Only when they boarded the gondola that would take them almost vertically down the basin, back to Knockum, did Dunstan's mother finally ask him, "What do *you* want to do, Dun?"

Scream. Run away. Dance *away. Get away from this moment, this town, all my mistakes that I'm being punished for now.*

But Dunstan only swallowed. He had to choose his lines carefully. He closed his eyes, pressed his forehead into the steel bar he held on to as he stood while she sat. The green afterimage of his imaginary metropolis was still there, flickering — but no, it wasn't part of a dream. He'd had these little flecks of light plaguing him for months now. Sometimes he imagined it was a face, or a secret symbol only he, a fifteen-year-old going blind, could see, and it would lead him on a great adventure like the protagonists in the moving pictures and musicals that had been his closest companions. His *real* friends. Not the phonies at school, the ones he'd fought so hard to keep. Or the ones he'd left behind for brighter pastures . . .

Juvenile macular degeneration is what Dr. Arch called it. The little green spots in his vision were simply a symptom of Dunstan losing his sight — something that had already been weak to begin with, leading thicker and thicker glasses to be slapped off his face or crunched underfoot.

Dr. Arch had delivered the news so blandly, but Dunstan was already affixing sequins to the diagnosis, making it sparkle spectacularly so it was an easier pill. Like collapsing stars, the light in his vision was going out. There wasn't much anyone could do about it, nothing to blame it on, which made it all the worse.

Dunstan decided to grin, eyes still closed. "Think of all the money you'll save on glasses."

Without a response, Dunstan peeked. Ada's usually hard face was cracking. He'd never seen her cry, not even when Mama Lorraine went off to war. Ada was forthright: duty first, duty always — that was the lightkeeper way. But her mouth pinched now, and she cleared her throat too hard, and it made Dunstan feel sicker. He needed to mend this tear before the whole show came crashing down.

"Oh, Ma, you *have* to laugh," Dunstan admonished, patting her arm. "I've had fifteen years to look at everything! I've seen lots. Honestly, it's fine."

It was not fine. All the way here, he didn't think gracious things like, *I'll never look at my parents' faces again, or my friends. Or my beloved hometown.* No, Dunstan was mourning all the silver-screen spectacles he was going to miss out on, or how much harder it was going to be to become a Vanway star if he wasn't able to see the kickline. All his dreams were crumbling — the ones enshrined in fantasy and the more practical ones. Whatever his fate was, everything was going to either be ten times harder, or impossible.

He wanted to whine, *Why me?* Dunstan Cord, perennially overlooked for everything, and yet here was destiny singling him out in its spotlight. He was too young to be a real sinner . . . though given his most recent failings, ones he pushed to the back of his sparkle-addled brain, he probably deserved this as punishment. He couldn't even think of repenting. He needed to write a different ending, one where the bad choices he made still had good reasons, even if those reasons were all but evaporated now.

But Dunstan would never say any of this to Ada. He'd keep his chin up, which is what Mama Lorraine had told him to do when she was deployed two years ago. *Stay out of trouble. Cheer Ada up every now and then with one of your musical numbers. And always remember to keep your promises.* Parting with his second mother

15

was a clear memory, at least, and Dunstan would keep it safe in his heart, because he might not *see* Mama Lorraine again before his vision went totally kaput.

Well, maybe he wasn't so superficial after all.

"It's not fine," Ada said, echoing Dunstan's true thoughts. "Dr. Arch said there are treatments, new trials for surgery—"

Dunstan's hands shot up. "No thanks. I've seen way too many horror movies to want to walk into a hospital, unhaunted or otherwise."

Ada seemed shaken by this declaration. Then she frowned, looked to the side. "You don't have to do that with me. I don't need the *show*."

Dunstan's false smile dropped as the heat crept up the back of his neck. He looked away, pushed his glasses up his nose. *You need to be vulnerable sometimes*, Mama Lorraine had also warned him. *Let people be there for you. Open that locked door inside you and let them* in.

Dunstan didn't want anyone in his head on this one. Not if he was going to get what he *really* wanted. So he gave Ada a bit of what *she* wanted, to get her back on track.

"I'll . . . I'll think about what Dr. Arch said. But you know me." He chose his words — his lines — carefully, the gondola shuddering as it descended on its twanging cables. "I was never suited to be a lightkeeper like you — way too distractible. And I'd rather trawl in Myra's Records than try my hand at the net like Mama Lorraine did." He struck a pose, imagining how fine his silhouette might look if he were delivering his grand moving solo before the curtain call. "I dream big, and I am absolutely not interested in wasting my time on what-ifs. I'm finally fifteen! I can't waste a minute of this golden summer moping." He clasped Ada's hands in his, drawing her to her surprised feet. "And neither should you."

He managed to twirl her in the cramped space. There were only one or two fellow passengers, but they smiled as Dunstan led Ada around in a two-step. She was laughing then, begging him to stop, but he was just thinking of his sweet mothers, who had always raised him to look on the bright side, no matter how dim things were.

Even if those things were Dunstan's fault.

As they danced, Dunstan humming the *da-da* of the tune and charming everyone with his small staggers and burst of guffaws when they made the gondola sway, Dunstan felt his heart quickening with too many regrets for a teenager. He would go blind, and become a burden, less than a has-been — a never-got-the-chance-to-be. He'd never see the *Gris Mermaid* at the Western Dock ever again. He'd likely never leave Knockum. Never find the stage that was his and his alone. Everything was ending, and it hadn't even begun yet.

He was more sure than ever what he had to do.

Ada pulled away and the two collapsed side by side on their seats. She rubbed her thumb over Dunstan's cheek just underneath the thick rims of his glasses. He didn't look directly at her; he felt tears pricking, and though Ada wasn't a weeper, Dunstan was an excellent one. He smiled numbly. Dunstan was a born performer, sure and certain. He wouldn't let this mask slip; he could play this part to a tee. So he looked just past his mother, at the green flickering after-image dancing between the cascade of sunlight outside the gondola window, settling neatly on Lake Mallion as they drew closer to home.

"Besides," Dunstan deflected, "blind folks can do lots, like the lady running the boarding house in your cousin's town. Life's not over by half, I promise, Ma!"

Ada clucked. "That reminds me, I haven't heard from Letitia in a while. I wonder how things are going in Quixx these days, with her junk shop . . . maybe we can go up and see her this summer . . ."

Ada fished around her starched pocket for her little black book, and Dunstan was relieved that, for the moment, he could just lean back and stare at his secret little green light, his dancing time bomb, and hold it there in his sight while he still could.

When they disembarked on the platform in the townsite at Knockum proper, Dunstan locked eyes with a familiar pair just two gondolas down. She startled, like she'd been slapped, then her face rippled to utter indifference before she turned on her heel, neat black hair whipping, wounding Dunstan like it was loaded with glass from a shattered chandelier.

17

"Wasn't that Luisa?" Ada said from Dunstan's shoulder, and he unclenched his tightened fist from the thigh of his jeans.

"Don't know," he lied, turning away as quickly as his ex-life-long-best friend had. "I didn't see."

INTERLUDE:
BALLAD OF THE BETRAYED

The lights come down, cascading on a scene as the stage changes rapidly, set pieces clattering and holding together tenuously. Some scenes are better left unperformed, but Dunstan can't help but play this one out, again and again, though by now he should have forgotten it.

But you can never forget when you break your best friend's heart. And partially your own.

The scene is Knockum Upper School, in the field behind the auditorium. The familiar site of bullyings, teasings, moments both remarkable and mundane, but mostly where Dunstan and Luisa, the latter cast immediately as best friend forever from the age of three, made their plans. Their dreams. Their promises to one another.

But now they stand back-to-back, eyes stuck on an unseeable horizon, jaws tight. They each hold something to their chest. They begin to march outward, one pace, two, five, ten. They spin. Luisa holds up her weapon — a photo of their little band of misfits: Luisa, Dunstan, Arnault, Mariah. All scarred by the same rejections, finding strength in one another. Holding one another up, in the photo, and in life.

Dunstan holds up a picture of the Perfects — the children of town luminaries, raised on easy street, silver spoons in every pie. Everything is easy for the Perfects and always will be. The quarterbacks. The sock-hop society girls with glowing hair. The heirs to the fishing companies and the county generals who run the lives of the misfits' parents.

Dunstan is in both these pictures. He has found a loophole. He can exist in the world of the Perfects, maybe even become one of them, and use it as a stepping stone to his many dreams.

You have to choose! Luisa cries from her side of the stage, hands shaking. *Us or them!*

But why? Why can't he have it all? Dunstan is tired of rejection. He's tired of thinking small. The misfits rescued him from the mud, but the Perfects could elevate him far above it. It's Luisa who is narrow-minded: Luisa, always calculating but never calculable. Cautious and knowledgeable but knowing nothing about the world or what's out there beyond Knockum. Luisa, who dragged Dunstan down from cloud nine one too many times.

They aim their pictures. Dunstan fires. A stage arrow pierces Luisa's photo, shearing it in half. And Dunstan runs offstage, clutching his picture so hard he can feel it beginning to tear, with a silent audience out in the gallery unsure who to root for.

The stage lights go out.

Dunstan had sinned, maybe a little. But did he deserve to go blind over it? If this were a play, it would probably be the ultimate hubris. But for now he had to live in reality. And he would not lie down and let the black hole swirling inside eat up his glittering dreams.

So after supper, he did what he always did: cleaned the dishes. Sang a show tune or two. Really laid on the "nothing's gonna bother me" air, before climbing up the ash tree in the backyard, to the tree-house he and Lorraine had built four summers ago. Only when he was inside, pulling up the board in the floor hiding his well-packed canvas duffel bag, did Dunstan realize it was likely the last time he would ever come up here.

He pressed his eyes closed to keep the tears in. The time for sentiment was over.

19

"Inventory," he muttered under his breath, yanking the light on above his head, trying not to think about how it was Luisa who had wired the place for him.

"Seven hundred and eighty-three dollars." He counted through the carefully organized bills, saved from every odd job and home-work copying gig he could come up with over the past few months after school. "Tent, portable stove, matches, city map, sheet music, two-pound bag of rhinestones . . ."

Sure, the only wilderness survival skill he could confidently say he'd earned a badge in was sewing. But this situation wasn't going to solve itself. He'd have to improvise a little, and he was good at that, too.

The plan had been formed when all his other plans had fizzled out like the last bulb on a backstage makeup mirror. This was a last resort, running away, but when there were no parts left to play, he'd need to find one elsewhere. Ada would understand, once he was famous and sending money back home by the truckload. The sooner he got there, the sooner he could get his big break.

He would camp as much as possible on the road, avoiding public transport, where he might be spotted and dragged back. He'd travel light, as the hero twins in the Sade Sisters Mysteries did, and take work where he could. So many stars of the stage and screen started out waiting tables while their big break lurked around the corner. But he didn't have time for that. He'd get by on the passable ID Norma Wheeler had made him in exchange for his extensive algebra tutoring in the spring. He'd arrive at the Lavish Theatre, Luxe's crown jewel of the performing arts, four blocks north of the ophthalmologist, and he would be relent-less. He'd work his way up — usher, stagehand, costumes, vaux accompanist . . . one day he'd be sweeping the stage and he'd belt out a solo or throw his lanky body around the wings with deft two-steps accompanied by his broom. A producer who'd stayed past lock-up would see him, and that's all it'd take. He'd be a star, he'd be out of Knockum, and he'd do it all before his whole world faded to black.

The plan was perfect. Foolproof! And it would have to be tonight, before Dunstan had a chance to remember logic. Seeing Luisa on the platform earlier today had nearly clinched it. Nearly made him weak, desperate enough to ride his two-wheeler to her place, beg her forgiveness, and spill his entire plan to her so she could talk him off his ridiculous cloud, like she usually did.

But Dunstan would have to be stronger than that. He'd already given up everything that had mattered to him and was losing what little he had left. If he was going to seize the grand adventure he'd been waiting his entire life for, he'd have to give up a little more.

Ada was finishing her nightly letter to Lorraine, after which she'd sit by the radio to hear the news from the front, downing two cups of black coffee to keep her steady for the long night ahead. Her lightkeeper shift would begin an hour later, promptly at 9 p.m., and since it'd been understaffed lately, she'd be too preoccupied to come back to check on Dunstan. And by the time she got home after dawn, he'd be long gone.

Maybe I should leave right this second. Dunstan squinted over his shoulder at the carefully penned goodbye letter pinned near the treehouse's entrance, calculating the timing. He was already sick of lingering, heart hammering as it did when Moss Richler had dumped him two weeks ago, during the third act of *Revenge of the Flesh Rippers*.

Moss Richler. Lead quarterback of the Rampaging Roadrunners. Brutish, dark hair, thick skull. Tall as a lamppost and nowhere near as bright, but still a beacon of hope to one Dunstan Cord, perpetual theatre dork, unable to stop himself from being in love with Moss since forever ago. There were notebooks buried under crawlspaces with pages full of *Mr. Dunstan Richler* in the flowingest, heart-popping script that would never again see the light of day.

But just as Dunstan knew he would be famous, he knew he would be Moss Richler's boyfriend. And somehow . . . he was.

Until he wasn't.

INTERLUDE:
BALLAD OF THE BROKEN-HEARTED

A moving scene: the first, a stage within a stage. A bustling school performance. A poster with the title *Shambly!* across it in bold red lettering. Dunstan and Luisa working backstage, as always — Luisa with a clipboard, Dunstan sweating with fabric draped over him, a pincushion on his wrist. Before the betrayal, when they were still friends forever.

"What is it?" Luisa stage-whispers, a mad pivot, a semi-dance sequence. "Where are you going?"

"Nowhere!" Dunstan whispers back, ducking under Luisa's arm, as the corps dancers, dressed as students, flit and flutter around them. "Only . . ."

"Dun, not this again!" Luisa opens her arms, exasperated. "Please don't tell me—"

"Only maybe I locked the lead in the bathroom, and I'm about to go on for him?" Dunstan squeaks, the audience roaring with laughter.

"You can't! You'll be expelled!" But Dunstan doesn't listen — she says he never does. And in a flourish, he whips the enormous drapery off him to reveal the lead character's glittering toy soldier coat to the roar of the audience. He takes the stage for the whole play, and blows everyone's socks off, before being hauled away by the principal for the suspension of a lifetime.

The stage within a stage slides away to a school hallway. Dunstan riding the high from the best night of his life . . . and somehow, at the end of the hall, is Moss Richler. Object of his heart. Too good to even be there, let alone be true. Dunstan makes a show of cleaning his glasses, checking to make sure this isn't another wishful mirage.

"Cord, you really are something else." Moss smiles, striking Dunstan dumb with his beauty. He has teeth for miles. "It's like you were glowing up there. I guess I've seen you in a totally different light."

Dunstan stammers, all blushes and bewilderment. And as Moss asks Dunstan out *sometime*, Luisa, from the wings, looks on, with a pain the audience knows only too well.

Dunstan thinks this is destiny. But Luisa always knows better. Moss reaches for Dunstan.

The lights go down.

Dunstan grimaced. All his great, golden moments were made of chipping spackle. As soon as it had started, as soon as Dunstan had taken that outstretched hand, he'd been swallowed up. Distracted. He'd been leaning his head on Moss's warm, comforting arm, when Moss shrugged.

"This is over, y'know?"

Everything Dunstan had sacrificed to even *get* to that moment broke into him like a wave all over again. He stuffed the items he'd carefully laid out back into the canvas bag as the tears caught up. *None of it matters.* He'd make his own way in the world, see it all before it disappeared, and—

"Going somewhere?"

Dunstan froze as a head appeared in the hole in the treehouse's floor. The stupidly handsome head of his dreamy ex-boyfriend.

"Think of the devil," Dunstan blurted. As usual, Moss blinked, uncomprehending, before pulling himself inside without an invitation.

Dunstan stayed quiet, an unnatural state for him. He'd taken his spiral-bound notebooks of teenage angst and buried them, but he wanted to burn them instead and stuff the ashes in Moss's gym locker. He wanted to build a stage of milk crates in the middle of the quad and tell everyone that Moss was a beautiful, stupid liar.

But now, faced with the moment to tell Moss he'd broken his heart in half, Dunstan just stared at his jeans and willed his failing eyes to suck the tears back in. Moss lightly toed the canvas bag, letting out a low whistle as he looked up and skimmed the farewell note meant for Ada.

Moss's mouth twitched, putting the pieces together. "So you aren't just all talk, after all."

Dunstan may have not yet been successful at making the main cast list of his school plays, since lead roles went to the Perfects, but he wouldn't stop trying. Especially when it came to this gem from the directors: *he had heart, but just not what it took.* And when they let him work backstage, it was because he was, at least, a good talker.

But right now he couldn't say a word.

Suddenly, Moss was a lot closer. "I kinda regret how things ended," he was saying, but Dunstan was only half-listening, watching Moss's mouth form the words "I'm sorry, let's make up."

A green web flickered across Dunstan's vision, and he pulled away from Moss, rubbing his eyes.

"What is it, Cord?"

"I, uh. Can't talk. Leaving. I'm in the middle of it." Dunstan adjusted his glasses, tried to get around Moss to his escape hatch, his bag. But Moss was the starting quarterback for a reason, and Dunstan's strongest muscle was in his bedazzling gun trigger finger. Moss held tight to Dunstan's forearm.

"You'd go off without saying goodbye?" Moss asked before kissing Dunstan lightly. Dunstan grimaced, finally finding his voice again.

"I know I'm the dramatic one, but *you're* the one who broke up with *me!*"

He expected Moss to pout, toss his dark locks and shrug, but instead Moss leaned in with an intensity Dunstan would never be able to shake for the rest of his teenage years.

"I made a mistake," Moss said, clearly and evenly. "And I want to make it up to you."

For all Dunstan's cleverness, his talking, his ability to shape a soliloquy, he should have seen right through Moss, but he was still a teenager and a bona fide visions-of-grandeur romantic caught up in a miasma of hormones, so it didn't take much to convince him. What were a few more minutes before the rest of his life, anyway?

Dunstan glanced from his bag back to Moss, but Moss grinned and hefted the bag out of Dunstan's reach.

"There's something you have to see, before you go," he was saying, taking Dunstan's hand and guiding him down the treehouse ladder. "*If* you decide to go, after you see it."

"I don't have *time* for this magnificent tryst," Dunstan protested, landing in the tangle of the ash tree's roots as Moss walked ahead of him, dangling the bag like bait. Dunstan ducked low, as if Ada could see the two of them from the kitchen window. "If I don't leave now, I'll be caught for sure."

Moss threw the bag into the backseat of his father's '32 Comet, parked on the street. "Then you'll have to stop stalling, won't you?"

Dunstan rarely felt helpless; when you pretend to have all the answers, you can even convince yourself. Jaw clenched, he jumped into the passenger seat as the engine roared, and they took off towards Harman Tunnel, heading for the lakeshore.

SCENE 2

HARMLESS TEENAGE HOMICIDE

"This is Gladys Britehart on Radio KNCK38 bringing you the latest update from the front.

"As the battle seemingly took a holiday in a perceived armistice for this past week, tensions are running hot once again as the Brindlewatch Guard saw losses across the north, where they had been advancing with some success, and in the Witching Cross Archipelago to the northeast. Codebreakers continue to keep their eyes to the skies, and to the ground, but the assault was once more a surprise to all involved, with our forces beating a hasty retreat back to Fort Ygwaine on the Isle of Swann. Farther inland to the west, towards the nation of Ashann, the Assembly of Chiefs has asked once more that the Brindlewatch Guard supply ground troops in the deep woods surrounding their capital community of Kuo.

"Will the unseen enemy relent when the monsoon season returns to the archipelago? Who are They Who Attack, and why does it seem their salvos ebb and flow with nary a motive? We continue to pray for a swift resolution, to send supplies to our Knockum naval heroes stuck on the other side of the sea, and endure our own war at home . . ."

Moss switched off the car's radio. "Don't need to hear it," he said before Dunstan could ask. "We know how it's been around here these days."

Moss, interested in the *news*? Dunstan tried to keep himself from commenting, squeezing the handle of his duffel bag until it dug into his skin, but he couldn't help it. "Yeah, that's why I'm glad to have Knockum as far behind me as possible, starting tonight."

They'd only been driving six minutes, but each one was precious and counted. What if Moss didn't drive Dunstan back up the escarpment? It'd more than double his climbing time to get back to Tantalon Depot, not to mention extra hours in the open ground between Knockum's borders and the Eastmerlin Woods, where he'd take refuge tonight before continuing on to his ultimate destination: stardom. Freedom. Before it all went to Hades in a handbasket.

Dunstan should've kept quiet all the same because Moss pulled over suddenly and cut the engine. There was something in his face that Dunstan had never seen before, and didn't like.

"Everything that's happened lately," Moss said, "you don't care, even a bit? You'd leave everyone behind here to suffer, without trying to help?"

Dunstan was more than confused. Weren't they headed somewhere to make up and make out? It also wasn't like Moss to have an opinion, strong or otherwise.

"And how exactly would *my* staying help anyone?" Dunstan asked. He counted on his fingers. "I can't solve the fish supply crisis. Or the dropping lake levels. I can't even keep people's spirits up to get their minds off the war! I couldn't even get folks to sit for the six-page lament in the middle of *Wheels of a Salesman* before they left the Beckon Bandstand at the last Spring Festival. No one listens to me let alone likes me. It'll be better when I'm gone — for me, and for Knockum."

Wow, pitiful. Dunstan swallowed, an uneasy silence creeping between them. *Don't you dare cry.* He glanced at Moss, who was leaning back in his seat, one arm resting on the gear shift, the other tapping the steering wheel.

"I like you," he said, and Dunstan's heart surged. "I think you have a purpose here. You just don't know it yet."

Now Moss Richler was giving *platitudes*? Dunstan should've checked his forehead for a fever, but instead he nearly leapt across the passenger bench seat, grabbing Moss's gear-shift hand as he was seized with an idea.

"You should come with me!" His heart was an earnest lump in his throat. "There's nothing for you here, either! Not since your dad left, anyway. I mean, 'went off to the war.' Whatever — you never wanted to own a fishing company anyway, right? Think about it! There's an entire world up the escarpment, Moss! You could find your own way in it. We both could. *Together.* Like we talked about."

Moss blinked, as most folks did when bowled over by Dunstan's enthusiastic certainty in whatever idea he was pitching in the moment. The Richlers were as well-off as their name would suggest. Mender Richler had owned a fleet of twenty-four trawlers, and his legacy had been growing, to the point where his company outpaced all independent fishing groups combined. It looked like they would, eventually, take over all operations on Lake Mallion — the largest lake in the country. Mender even had designs on building what he called a mass fishery to end the need for trawling the once-plentiful salmon and trout that had filled the lake to bursting from the Thousand Tributary network surrounding it. Moss would have inherited all these enterprises, and this town would essentially have been his.

But for more than a decade, as the lake levels dropped, and the rains decided to avoid the basin, and the fish declined almost to vanishing, the Richlers' hold on Knockum loosened. Mender had to sell boat after boat until only a scant ten were left, two of which needed serious repair, and there were no fishers to staff it. The war put more pressure on the industry, so now the Richlers were nearly kaput.

Then Mender up and left without a word, claiming he'd been *conscripted*, when no such order existed in Brindlewatch, and Mender had feet flatter than Borgnine Benoit's pet sloth.

There went Mender. And, acutely, there went Moss's future, too. Dunstan gripped his arm tightly. It made sense. Moss seemed to be a different person tonight. Maybe Dunstan's fairy tale romance wasn't as dead in the water as he thought!

Then the Comet's engine startled Dunstan off Moss's arm, and they were turning down the fire road, towards the water.

"We can help Knockum *now*," Moss was saying, but it seemed like he was no longer saying it to Dunstan as the headlights crawled through thick brush. "I think you want to help, deep down. I think you just don't know how."

"What—" But the car jerked to a stop again, this time in front of Boathouse Drive, and before Dunstan could finish his protest, Moss had dragged him across the driver's seat and thrown him face-first into the dirt.

"But *I* do. I know how you can help." Moss stood behind Dunstan as he rose to his knees, staring into the faces of the Knockum Upper defensive line crowding him in a circle.

"We all do," Raymond Sardo said, before he and four other Perfects hauled Dunstan, feet kicking, towards the docks.

Dunstan had to give them credit for ingenuity and use of resources — good improv skills. The Rampaging Roadrunners gagged Dunstan with the very socks he'd packed in his duffel. Then, despite muffled protests of "You'll wrinkle the silk!" they tied his hands in front of him with the elegant scarves his grandma Wexler had left him — which, ironically, he'd imagined would bring him luck on his journey to fame.

Dunstan was a head shorter than Moss, and skinny, so he couldn't muster much fight against five footballers who had a plan they seemed deeply committed to. One that made them avoid looking at Dunstan at all, which made everything seem that much more sinister.

"Are you sure the gag is necessary?" Valmont Trigger said, rubbing the back of his neck from beside Moss, who was at the wheel of Mender's smallest trawler, heading at a slow clip across the water, lights out, engine low, to keep attention off them.

"Can't risk the lightkeepers hearing him caterwaul," Moss muttered, glancing over at Dunstan with a sneer. "Or Cord trying to weasel his way out of this with a flowery speech."

Dunstan's emotions were in a tumble dryer — hearing both the praise and the scorn twist together in Moss's comment sent his heart clamouring. Despite the fact he might die tonight, for reasons yet unknown, Dunstan still admired Moss for not only planning this, but being appointed the leader when he could barely guide his finger out of his nostril in fifth-period biology. Dunstan looked to the others for any clues: they were whispering quietly in a knot, bent over, out of earshot. They weren't wearing anything incriminating. All-black cotton sweatshirts and dark slacks. They didn't want to be discovered.

But then something flashed at Valmont Trigger's chest — something on a chain. Blink and you'd miss it: a brass heart, with a shard through the middle. He caught Dunstan looking, then stuffed it into his shirt as Kavan slapped him in the back of the head.

Dunstan screamed, gag or not, and slammed his feet into the deck, trying to stand, but Moss shoved him to the side, and Dunstan crumpled into a pile.

Grislies. Great. How unoriginal.

INTERLUDE:
REEVE GRIS, YOU'LL BE MISSED

This stage is a simple one, but the props give it flair. Dark, on a body of water, simulated by dark sheets shaken by dark-clad figures. A boat. A boy. And a green light pulsing.

Narrator:

In a small town, what else is there to do but cook up stories? Even better, why not use tragedy as the stock, and the grief left behind as the juiciest marrow? Reeve Gris vanished. This is fact. But so did his dad's pleasure cruiser-cum-trawler, *The Darling Mermaid*. Teams were sent to try and retrieve *something*. A bit of the wreckage. Maybe Reeve's letterman jacket. But nothing surfaced. And Lake Mallion was deep. Two miles out, there were . . . difficulties. Almost-new diving equipment that had been checked failing as they got close to the bottom. Luxe University sending experimental instruments, only for them to fizzle out. It made the locals certain that this wasn't *just* a tragedy. It was a trap.

Something had *taken* Reeve, his friends, the ship, and everything on it. Something with a hunger that couldn't be sated.

The last line is from Dunstan's own creative take on the subject, the urban legend that sprang up with newly formed teeth after Reeve and his friends disappeared, and which consumed most of Dunstan's growing years:

The Door in Lake Mallion had certainly opened. And Reeve had gone through it.

But *why* had it opened? The legend of the Door had been around long before Reeve went out on the lake. Why did it choose him? It all came down to the barest gossip: Reeve had stolen the boat in the first place because he'd just had his heart broken, and he wanted to show his ex-beloved, Bremner Allan, that he was capable of doing something ridiculous to win them back. He'd intended to circle the Knockum shore, shouting their name, so it could be heard by everyone awake and recorded in the official lightkeeper log, thus enshrined in the Brindlewatch archive.

As far as dramas went, this was one Dunstan could get behind. He'd tried to write a moving musical about the whole affair, but the Council of Mothers had vetoed any creative liberties taken that would offend the Gris family, even if they no longer lived in Knockum. All agreed: something strange had happened on the lake that night. Something only lightkeepers saw, but never spoke of. Something Dunstan had been dying to find out, had begged Ada to spill but she had spent fifteen years demurring . . . After all that, Dunstan had decided it was better to escape and never find out.

But another group of devotees arose after the fact. A group who kept vigil on the anniversary of Reeve's disappearance — and also, coincidentally, Dunstan's birthday. They wore all black, and necklaces made from scratching and soldering old pennies. Brass broken hearts, wishing that one day the Door would open again, and Reeve, the tragic hero, would come home.

Narrator: And they called themselves . . . Grislies.

"Someone's gonna miss the chatterbox, Moss. The fish disappear just fine, but not kids outta Knockum." Bless Gordo for worrying, and for stating what Dunstan would've himself argued if the sock weren't firmly lodged between his teeth. Sadly, as Moss's grin reached his eyes, Dunstan realized he'd dug his own grave.

"He was in the middle of running away!" Moss guffawed, smacking the steering wheel. "Left a note and everything! It couldn't be more perfect. It's like it was meant to be. *Destiny.*" Then Moss's face changed. "Maybe that's all the proof we need that this is going to *work.*"

Dunstan pulled his legs closer to himself as the entire defensive line turned and stared at him in unison. Even as the sun set, and darkness crept in, they all looked haunted, and decidedly not like teenagers about to enact a harmless prank.

What was so great about Reeve Gris, anyway? He *had* taken three of his friends down with him — The Sunken Three, they were called — but it was Reeve the town rallied around. Maybe it wasn't him, in particular. It's that, since he vanished, things had been going wrong in Knockum. The fish, the lake levels, the war. Businesses closing. Folk unsure of the future. They both venerated Reeve's loss and blamed him for everything. Better the scapegoat you can't see, Dunstan guessed.

He looked pleadingly at each footballer, eyes begging them to see reason. Gordo was the first to look away, jutting his chin towards the water ahead of them. "There's the first marker, Moss."

Moss brought the boat close to the buoy, then spun the wheel so the boat was adjacent before he let the anchor down. The other boys at least had something to hold on to, but Dunstan went flying as the boat came to a halt, body smacking into the cabin and knocking the wind out of him. The sock in his mouth didn't help the sudden sensation of dry drowning.

Then the sock was gone, and he sputtered, gasping.

"Hey!" Moss shouted, but Raymond pulled Dunstan to his feet, and just when he thought he had maybe willed someone to take pity on him, Raymond only smiled.

"Can't have him dying yet, right?"

Dunstan felt the blood leave his face, finally able to scream, "Let me go!" as ten hands pawed and grabbed at him, then let him fall to the deck. Dunstan felt heavy. Likely because they'd filled his jeans pockets with rocks.

The boys stood back as Dunstan struggled to stand, catching his silk-tied hands on the deck rail as he looked out onto the water. Ahead was the ring of buoys, lights slowly winking, covered in the lake brine of the fifteen years since they'd been anchored in place. Knockum Remembers had been painted on them, but the letters had long since faded. The memory hadn't.

Dunstan turned and stared at these boys, these homegrown sports stars who barely ever followed a thought when it entered their heads. Moss smiled in the way Dunstan had fallen in love with, careless and so sure of himself. "You could always figure things out, even without asking. That's what makes you special, Cord."

Surely it was the sun setting, and the panic, that scattered the green spots across Dunstan's vision like a comet. His temples hurt, and he winced. "Well it's not like the Grislies are some *secret* society, now is it? I don't need to be a detective to see what you're all trying. But human sacrifice, Moss? Really?" He tried to come off as unimpressed. "How can *you* be a Grisly? You said you didn't believe in that garbage!"

Moss surged and twisted Dunstan's shirt in his fist, pushing his spine against the railing. Dunstan squawked as the boat heaved, the waters of Lake Mallion splashing upwards.

"Knockum was a *great* town," Moss hissed, sounding almost feverish. "It was just becoming greater. Then Gris had to go on a bender to prove himself, and everything started going wrong. He angered the Door, the Lake. We're going to appease it. Because the lake provides."

"The lake provides," the others said in unison, confirming Dunstan's cult suspicions — far too late.

"It's just a *myth*, Moss!" His attackers were unmoved, but at least they were listening. "Okay, fine. You believe it. That's cool! But what about the part where you need someone with a broken heart in order to . . . to . . ."

The rest of the starting lineup looked solemnly at one another, as the realization hit Dunstan like a heap of lodestone from Dunlands Quarry. His brain went back to the day he'd met Moss. How incredibly *lucky* it had felt to be noticed by him, to have his arm around Dunstan's lonely shoulders. How it all seemed too good to be true.

Because it was.

There was no mask that Dunstan could put on now that would hide his crumpled face. "So all this time . . . you . . . and me? It was just an act? *For this?*"

Moss let him go and stood away. Dunstan went limp. For a moment he was resolved to let Moss throw him in Lake Mallion. He felt like he belonged down there. What else was he good for, going blind, forever the object of Knockum's rejection and ridicule and trapped in the chorus when all he wanted to do was *shine* centre stage? Then he came to his senses. He had fame to grab, and he wasn't going to get it dead.

He tried to make a dash for it, find something sharp to get the scarves off, or even, dignity be damned, take his pants off and dive off the other side of the trawler.

But Moss grabbed him tight on one arm, Gordo on the other, and he could barely lift his legs for the rocks weighing them down. "You can't call it human sacrifice, not really." Moss shrugged. "We aren't *trying* to kill you. You'll just sink to the Door, and open it, and go through. Bring back Reeve Gris, and Knockum will love you for it."

Gordo was a powerhouse, and all Dunstan's incensed struggling got him nowhere. "It's a hundred metres deep out here! *No one* has seen the bottom of the damn lake, and no one's ever seen a door down there! This is stupid and you'll all be arrested! Let me *go!*"

Dunstan should have known better. Moss gave a little nod, and Gordo threw Dunstan at him, like he was a tight-end pigskin on the pass. Moss was lifting him over the railing, and very soon, nothing would matter at all, because Lake Mallion would take what it was given. But Dunstan decided he wouldn't stop, not until his last breath.

"C'mon Moss, I *know* you. This isn't you!" Moss paused for a second, glanced at the others. Dunstan swallowed, aimed for the quarterback's soul beneath the peer pressure. "You've already broken my heart. You don't have to break what we had."

Then Moss let go of Dunstan suddenly. *Yes, heartstrings officially plucked! Give the boy his laurels!* But the boat rocked angrily, and the other boys cried out in the dark.

Had they hit something? Dunstan couldn't see anything, glasses askew, but they were all pointing towards him.

Dunstan turned, looked out onto the water, saw a faint green glow glittering back at him on the surface of the lake.

Dunstan rubbed his eyes with his bound hands, trying to banish the afterimage caused by his encroaching blindness, but the green wouldn't go away. And when he turned to face the other boys, he realized that same glow was rippling across their faces.

"What in the waters?" Valmont swore, and huge Gordo fell over himself to get behind something, anything, that would protect him. Kavan, whom Dunstan never had quarrel with, was cowering on the ground beneath the shelter of his own arms, praying feverishly. Valmont held his Grisly talisman, frozen in place.

Dunstan shook, stared at his hands. They weren't glowing, and when he tried to see his reflection in the water below, he swore his eyes were streaming outwards, like acid-smoke, and he covered them with his bound hands, stammering.

"I don't— it's not—"

"He's cursed! Give him to the Door, quick, before he infects us!" Valmont shouted. Moss's four followers weren't made of anything stern, and neither was Moss — but he was the least likely to think of the lot, and sometimes that was enough. This time Moss grabbed hold of Dunstan, more certain than before, and Dunstan's sneakers beat against the railing as Moss lifted him nearly over his head.

"The Door loves a broken heart," Moss said, "And now it can have yours."

Dunstan careened overboard, smashing into the water.

SCENE 3

ENTER: THE PRINCE

INTERLUDE:
A BRIEF INTERMISSION ON THE
SOJOURN TO DEMISE

Midsummer. A treehouse. Music from a record player drifts into the sweltering air. Two teens, full of their best-laid plans, before they pettily rip them to shreds.

"I don't think there's a door at all," Luisa says, reaching over her head, screwdriver in hand. "I think it's an allegory."

Dunstan squints at the sparkling soldier vest he's been carefully embroidering all summer, trying to follow Luisa's logic and pretend he isn't having a hard time seeing what he is doing. "An allegory for what?"

She shrugs. "Escape. Who doesn't want to believe there's a gateway from Here to Otherwhere just in your backyard, common disappointment the key? Transmuting a broken heart into a way out, no matter the cost . . ."

Dunstan snorts, unable to keep from smiling. "Tragical."

Luisa leans in and rubs Dunstan's shoulder. "Dun, maybe you should take a break. You strain your eyes any more, you'll be blind."

He leans back on his knees, pushes his glasses up the bridge of his nose, feeling the back of his neck burn. "I think it *is* a door, a real one, solid, something you can pass through." He needs to change the subject as Luisa works on wiring the treehouse so they can stay up later reading their adventure comics, talking nonsense theories, planning their dreams.

This conversation is familiar, the basis of their friendship; the story of the Door was what had initially connected them on a long-ago playground.

"Doors have other sides. So where does this door lead?"

Another planet, Dunstan had once guessed. *Another world. A cave full of gems. An ocean you can breathe in. A place that will have all the answers to all of Knockum's problems, to all of my problems, a place where I can be the person I'm destined to be, the person I really am, a place . . .*

"I don't know," Dunstan says this time, older now, the edges of him sharper. "But in the meantime, *I can dream about it.*"

There was something down at the bottom of the lake, though Dunstan couldn't figure out if it was a door, or just a heap of lake trash his body was about to be added to. But door or not, Dunstan wasn't thinking, *Wow, I'll be famous for discovering this, at least!* Dunstan wasn't thinking much at all except, *I can't breathe.* He struggled to swim up, but with the scarves on his wrists with their water-thickened knots, and the rocks in his pockets, all he could do was kick. Kick because his life depended on it, arms like dull swords cutting for the water's distant surface.

But Dunstan kept sinking.

He flipped over suddenly, head-first, as if some invisible net were dragging him down. No matter how he fought, this current had a plan, clutching him close as he slipped quickly into the dark.

But it wasn't dark, not for long. Dunstan landed on something protruding from the bottom of the lake. A dark plinth of rock. No, shinier. How could it be shining this deep? Shining in a green halo of fractured light . . . he pawed at his eyes, his face, the last of his lungs' precious air choked out in a gutting bubble. He slammed his hands against the shining rock, sawing, desperate, Grandma Wexler's scarf fraying . . .

I'm going to die before my big debut, he thought, grabbing hold of the plinth with his freed hands, trying with the last of the failing life in his lungs to push off it, push himself back up, to fight the force pulling him down—

The plinth, a faceted, gleaming rock made of interlocking parts, shone as brightly as an underwater star. The pieces clicked in and out of place, glowing green and dancing as Dunstan stared, his lungs filling, vision going dark.

The Door had been asleep for a long time. It was trying to stay that way, ever since Reeve Gris. It couldn't help itself, one broken heart meeting another. It had travelled so far, with its sole companion betraying it. But now it needed to sleep, stay closed, stay vigilant, because if it ever opened again, that would be the end of it.

And then Dunstan Cord rested against its dark, cold surface, carrying that companion inside him. Long lost. Never forgotten. His own broken heart answering the Door's.

So despite its misgivings, the Door knew it had to open, shuddering on its ancient hinges, pulling the boy inside its embrace, and hoping this would be the end of it.

Welcome home, it whispered, not least knowing that it was, for better or worse, just the beginning.

Luisa was not a performer.

Nor did she want to be. Order was her stage, and she shone on it. Having this certainty at such a young age was a gift, grown-ups told her. And while she had an organized mind, for once she wanted someone else to tell her the order of things. Just for a change. Being relied on made her feel good, but now, with Dunstan out of the picture, who did *she* have to rely on?

She tried not to think about much as she watched her father's chest move up and down with thankfully even breaths as he napped beneath his desk. At that moment, she certainly wasn't thinking about the Door in Lake Mallion. Or about Dunstan Cord. Well, she'd had a little slip just now, that's all. Push him to the side, like he had done to her. Think of something *else*. Luisa often had hundreds of thoughts pinging in her mind like signal flares, and there were several she didn't acknowledge for order's sake.

The truth was many of those flares were about Dunstan. She had loved him, after all. Not in *that* way, obviously. But theirs was a kinship. A type of predestined soulmates who would be on each other's side till the bitter end. As Luisa curled herself around the steaming camp mug of milky bergamot tea, staring at the enormous blinking control panel of Knockum's energy station, she couldn't help but feel sad that the bitter end had come so soon. They were only fifteen, after all.

She stretched in her chair — her father's chair, the chair reserved for the chief electrical engineer, and checked the main generator's output level for the south side of town. For a while after the Great Betrayal had happened, Luisa was certain Dunstan would come knocking on her door, sheepish at least, beating his breast at worst, and beg her forgiveness. Beg Arnault's forgiveness, and Mariah's, but especially Luisa's. Best friends always know precisely how to cut each other the deepest. That they stop themselves from doing so is what makes the bond stronger.

But Luisa wasn't a poet. She was a calculator. And she was surprised at how much worse the hurt became when Dunstan did nothing, dug his heels in, thrust his chin up at her as he passed her by in the halls with his *new* friends. He was enjoying himself, the drug of popularity. And maybe Luisa was jealous. But maybe, most of all, she missed her friend.

Her father, Hector, twitched in his sleep, half rolling over, groaning. Luisa stiffened; would he rest or would his nameless terrors come for him? She'd been covering for Hector nearly a month now, trying to keep everything smooth sailing when inside she was drowning. Hector had worked the overnight shift, watching over the generators, for well over a decade. It was from him Luisa got her sharpness, her keen attention to detail, her unfailing ability to make sense of numbers and equations and wires and methods to create light, like the generators themselves. Knockum relied on the generators. So did the lightkeepers on this side of the shore. It was a great responsibility, one that Luisa wanted one day.

But Hector had started falling asleep on the job, without warning. And he'd wake terrified, and the next engineer on shift didn't know whether to comfort or commit him. This job was Hector's life, and he had no one else to protect the job, or him, but Luisa herself. She glanced over again, saw him resting comfortably, and smiled. She loved a puzzle. She would put her mind towards solving her father, and all the flares in her brain that were dedicated to Dunstan Cord would eventually be smothered by sheer will.

The light in the generator station faded in and out, like the dip of a wake caught after a boat passes. Luisa put her tea down, and the mug shuddered. She held on to the edge of the panel and felt a subtle tremor pass through the floor, up the chief's chair, and into her bones.

As quickly as the tremor had come, it subsided. All was still. Luisa frowned, checked the levels as the lights came back on. Everything was in order. What *was* that?

Then Hector sat up slowly, turned his head towards his daughter, eyes still closed.

"The Door," he said. "It's open."

Then he lay slowly back down, and the lights came back on, and while the generators hummed, Luisa shivered. Then something crackled under her fingers, and she hissed, like someone had static shocked her.

Unclenching her hand, a little arc of green cascaded over her fingertips. Playfully, almost. Luisa felt something like a flare, lighting up the darkness of her mind, that she couldn't help but acknowledge.

I wish Dunstan were here.

Dunstan wasn't wishing for much. He was barely conscious yet, and as he came closer to waking, he could only think, *My head. My HEAD. I can't wear fabulous tiaras if my head's been caved in!*

He groaned, clutching it, slowly peeling himself from the cold surface his face was stuck to. His aforementioned head was not caved in, thankfully, just a bit of post-traumatic drama. He was shivering, soaked, and coughing up the brackish water that had been sloshing around his lungs.

When he took a breath, and his heavy eyes opened, he saw . . . *clearly.* This shocked him more than what he saw — that his vision wasn't blurred, that he could see far, see every sharp detail, and the absence of his thick glasses made his face feel light for the first time in years. *I must have lost them in the lake . . .*

But when the shock of seeing passed, Dunstan had to come to terms with the sprawling black rocks that stretched for miles below him, glowing an eerie, twinkling green. He faltered backwards, remembering fully the lake, the pull of the water, and the Door that had swallowed him. *The Door!* Staring up, Dunstan saw that a ways above was likely where he'd fallen out; a column of perfectly symmetrical, shining dark rock, shaped like a passage, whose facets had clicked open and admitted him from the other side.

Topside . . . ? Dunstan looked down again at the rocks beyond, heart racing. Squint. He certainly could see, but he couldn't be seeing *right.* Beyond the seemingly deserted landscape he found himself in were more cliffs, and plinths, covered in those dazzling lights, yet there was something uniform about it all. Clustered. Engineered.

It couldn't be, but . . . "A city?" He clutched his forearms as the chill set in — as much from being soaked as from the tangibility of this weird dream. He swore that, in that distance, he could hear music. The sounds of a metropolis. And a longing to go towards it.

"You know, this isn't unexpected," he said to absolutely no one at all, shivering and giddy and pacing — after all, soliloquies were his specialty. "Death'll do this to a brain. Generate endless fantasies, make you think you're *experiencing* them! I'm probably in my last moments. You'd think I'd be reliving the moonlight sequence from *See Ya on the Other Side*, which I'd prefer, honestly, to a wild nightmare about local Door lore and a black rock city. Well, I'd actually prefer not to die, if I get to choose, so wake up. Wake *up*!"

Dunstan stopped smacking his temples for a second to glance back up. Nothing happened. His head definitely hurt. So maybe he *was* already awake. But still in the dream? And if he was following the dream's logic, and that Moss was somehow *right*, then he'd gone through the fabled Door in Lake Mallion. So was he *underneath* Lake Mallion, now? And closer to hand — or foot — as he stared at his sneakers, he realized he hadn't been spat out onto one of these onyx cliffs, which jutted out like teeth in his immediate vicinity. Somehow, he was standing on lacquer-chipped wood — on a deck, to be precise. The deck of a trawler, balanced precariously in a broken rib cage of rock, and in the glowing dark he could see, in faded paint above the bridge: *The Darling Mermaid*.

Dunstan felt his face crack as he backed away, clapping. "Oh, sure. *Sure*. This is too good!" Then he shouted, upwards, as if he could be heard: "Ya got your wish, Moss! Here I am! Making up for Reeve Gris's many mistakes! Don't see him around, though! Would bring him up if I could! *Happy?!*"

He clenched his lake-drenched hair, looking for a way down, a way off, a way out, trying to stop the hysterical grin from climbing, still trying to wake himself up—

Then Dunstan backed up into something solid, and hardly had a chance to turn around before the something grabbed hold of him, pinning his arms down, and it was Moss and his cronies all over again, but this time Dunstan screamed, kicked out, and smashed his head upwards with all the panicked strength he had left.

"*Stalac!*" the attacker said. It came out like a swear word.

Dunstan didn't stick around to find out. The grabber let go long enough to clutch their face. Dunstan hit the ground running and raced around the bridge to the aft of the busted-up trawler, where the lake ladder would be, and unable to find it, scrambled over the rail. But something sharp had found grip in the T-shirt at Dunstan's back, swinging him in a circle and sending him crashing back onto the deck. When he tried to get up again, an enormous boot pressed into his stomach, holding him in place, its owner bent over him with a long spear pointed at his eyes.

"Okay!" Dunstan caught his breath, tried to take in his attacker, but they blended into the dark glowing haze, head-to-boot in black, no discernible face behind what looked like a mask with goggles. "I'm here, I'll stay, you could've said *please!*"

The face didn't move. Nervous humour couldn't penetrate *that* stare, the one Dunstan could only imagine. Then he swallowed, trying to figure out what angle to take here. Dunstan squinted.

"Reeve Gris?" he whispered. "Is that you in there?"

The attacker flinched, paused. Then the boot pressed harder.

Dunstan squawked. "Look, okay, it was an accident! The Door — there was this *light* — and I fell—" He grunted, trying to wrench the boot off him. "I could be much more coherent if you'd stop crushing me to death."

The face, if Dunstan could call it that, came uncomfortably closer, and Dunstan could see his reflection in the dark glass of the goggles, but nothing more.

"The . . . Door?"

The voice was muffled, a nasal croak. Dunstan felt himself nodding, one part of his brain shutting out this whole nightmare scenario, the other clinging to whatever shred of reason he had left. "Yes, it — it opened and I — *bam!*" The attacker didn't respond, save for the sound of clicking somewhere unseen. "Here I am. But I don't want to be here. Who would? So I'll go back . . . somehow. Or else I'll be dead soon, and you won't have to worry about a thing!"

Dunstan would be reduced to a carnival corn dog in less than a second with one jab of that stick. He rearranged his face, softening it as he pressed a palm into the boot crushing his rib cage. "I promise I'm not a hazard. I swear it on my stupid broken heart."

A quick tilt of the head, which Dunstan noticed was pointed. A sound like a cicada shuffling in its carapace. Then the stick was carefully withdrawn, and Dunstan was pulled gently to his feet by a gloved hand.

He shuddered, dusting himself off. "Ah, uh, thanks, I—"

Long arms snatched him, pulled him up and close, and before Dunstan could react, he was squeezed and coughing.

His attacker was . . . hugging him?

"*It worked!*" they crooned, twirling him around, the large goggled head pressing into Dunstan's shoulder as laughter came out of both of them. Dunstan was on the verge of being twirled a third time when he managed to shimmy away.

"I think, uh, you might have the wrong . . . someone," he stammered, dizzy, but the masked stranger decided to keep twirling and celebrating on their own. Dunstan started as he caught sight of a massive, scaled, spear-like tail whipping out from the split in a dazzling duster coat.

"I can't believe it finally happened! The Door heard me!" The stranger held their head in their hands, incredulous, pausing, running a calculation. "But if you're here, then that must mean . . ." The hands snatched Dunstan's shoulders, the pointed head dipping this way and that as it assessed. "You have the Meteorlight, don't you?"

Dunstan shrugged away, arms crossing an X in front of him. "I don't have anything! Literally! All my stuff was taken, then I was thrown into the water, left for dead, and . . ." He screwed his eyes shut, shook his head like there was still lakeweed sloshing around in his skull. "This wasn't destiny. It was a *setup*. Not one I had any involvement in, might I add. There'd be more dramatic flourishes, and maybe some pyrotechnics *at least*."

Nimbly grabbing Dunstan's gesticulating hands, the goggled person stopped Dunstan in his tracks. "All right, fast talker! I didn't understand a *trice* of that, but it sounds like you're lost." The croak seemed a little more even now, the shadow of a grin on the prowl. "You called me something earlier. A name. A name that isn't mine. Are you looking for someone?"

Dunstan reclaimed his hands, his heart slamming as he was gently pressed into the cabin of the trawler, the splitting wood scratching at his back.

"N-no," he said, trying to smile the lie off to make it easier to digest. He cleared his throat; if this were a near-death delusion, which it most definitely had to be, it meant he was in control — for once. He straightened his back. "Why? Have you seen anyone come by here in the last fifteen years?" Then he jabbed a finger into the stranger's chest, trying to ignore that it was rock-hard. "And who are *you*? And why are you so deeply in my bubble?"

The stranger took a step back, on the defensive. Then he clapped his own cheek. "*Stalac*, that's right! Where are my manners?"

The tall stranger bent over, the huge tail swishing so fast that Dunstan had to leap over it like a jump rope. With a flourish of gold-striped coat, the stranger yanked off their mask and goggles. Dunstan tried to close his throat around the gasp as he stared into the stranger's face.

Scaled. Elongated. A raptor. A dragon? His mind clawed for descriptors while trying not to close in on itself. The pointed face, a dusty colourful haze of purple and blue, was covered in gold-flecked markings like fireworks around glittering opal eyes. They blinked sideways around dark slits. The creature bowed, showing a head that came to a point with horns that ringed it like a crown.

"Prince Ven, at your service," he said smartly. "And you're trespassing in my geodom." Then he shrugged magnanimously. "Which is fine by me! Because I intend to shroom-nap you and use you for my nefarious plot to *get the bash out of here*."

Dunstan's cheek twitched, but he rubbed his mouth and chin in deep thought as he circled the "prince," looking him up and down carefully.

"I'm Dunstan Cord," he replied, sketching a mock bow. "Your *vagrancy*."

Prince Ven didn't seem to be expecting this turn of events, mildly taken aback as Dunstan appraised him. "Ah. Didn't you hear me? With the capturing and the languishing ahead, now that you're in my clutches? What are you—"

Ven yanked his tail out of Dunstan's suddenly grabby hands, aghast. "It really is the best costuming I've seen," Dunstan mused. "Honestly. I mean, not that I'm well-travelled. But I've seen enough monster movies, and I have a mail-order subscription to *Creature Feature Monthly*." He fingered the fabric of Ven's coat, then lightly pinched one of the lizard's cheeks, sending the "prince" yowling. "And the practical effects! What is this, latex?"

Ven's expression was incredulous — *how* was he able to make such a face under so much makeup? "It's . . . I mean it's my *face*. Scales? Mica? What's yours made of?" He grasped Dunstan's in much the same manner, eliciting a similar yelp. "It's soft and gooey. And what colour do you call *these*?" The creature gestured at his eyes. Dunstan darted away, covering them quickly, remembering the boat and Moss and something strange about his eyes that he suddenly didn't want to share.

"They're a dignified amber, if you *must* know." He sniffed, rubbing his arms as he moved to the trawler's deck rail, looking out into the far, twinkling distance. "Some delusion," he muttered. "For my last moments, it's not bad, but it sure is cold. The lake's so deep no one's going to find me at the bottom of it. View's pretty at least."

Suddenly Dunstan found himself draped in that fine coat, though it was heavy and smelled like the damp earth after the rain. His heart sped up, and he wondered how he could still feel it if it had stopped beating.

"A pretty view indeed, Dunstan Cord," Ven chirped, springing up onto the railing and curling his tail around it as he leaned towards Dunstan meaningfully. Beneath the coat he wore something of a tunic, belted with striated, crossing cords. Ven's arms were marked with symmetrical gold flecks, and he'd stripped the gloves, shoving them into the sash at his waist. The fingers were claw-tipped, yet somehow elegant.

Dunstan realized he was staring, and promptly looked away. Delusion or not, he was in *trouble*.

"Thanks for the coat," he muttered, maybe a bit delayed, but much warmer. "Are you this nice to all your victims?"

A long red tongue darted out between sharp teeth as Ven snickered. His head tilted when Dunstan didn't bother to move away, even with this display. "You're strange, you know that. Aren't you afraid of me?"

Dunstan sighed, cheeks in his fists, the coat hanging perfectly on his narrow-in-comparison shoulders. "No. You may be a lizard, but you're gorgeous. And of course you would be; it's *my* imagination." Everything was topsy-turvy. Why not flirt with the last hallucination popping into his dying brain? "I've spent my whole life being afraid of things — of missing out, missing my big break. For once I want to enjoy the magic . . . while it lasts."

He smiled up at Ven, who blinked rapidly in response, scaled brow arching. He said, "Let me reiterate: I'm here to snatch you away to my high, bright lair. To trap you in this place forever! To never let you go back where you came from — and you're brain-bellowingly all right with that?"

Dunstan joined Ven up on the railing, legs kicking. After a pause he said, "Can we get going then? Anything's better than up there, honestly." Another smile, the kind the lead would give — lopsided and self-assured, somewhat sad. "Besides, I don't mind the company one bit."

And before he really clocked what he was doing, he stretched his face up, and gave Ven a kiss on his scaled cheek, then pulled away laughing when Ven recoiled and stuck out a long, forked tongue in disgust. The prince's responding laugh was full of those sharp teeth.

"Sorry!" Dunstan held up his hands. "That's probably culturally specific. I just wanted to try it once before I died."

Ven rubbed his face. "What were you trying to do? *Eat my face?*"

"To see what it felt like." Dunstan shook his head, looked around. "Geez, this dying thing sure is taking forever."

"Why do you keep saying that?" Ven's tail left the railing, curled around Dunstan's middle, and shook him, sending Dunstan squawking. "You're pretty lively by my estimation, Higher-up. Warm-blooded and awake. Maybe dying's more like living where you're from."

"Gee, that's a great line," Dunstan clamoured, landing with a thump in the prince's lap, his hands pushing against the tunic and indulging in a quick feel of the fabric. "What *is* this? It's so supple!"

Ven peeled Dunstan's fingers away. "What if I told you I was running away, too?"

"You are? Why?"

"Let's not get into specifics. This plan is just a spore yet." He put Dunstan back down on the deck. "How about instead of me snatching you, you snatch *me?*"

Dunstan eyed Ven up and down — he was over six feet tall, taller than Moss, and made Dunstan look like a child in comparison. "I don't think the physics would balance out."

"You said you wanted to go home. Follow that impulse. Believe me, you don't want to stay." Ven leaned in, claw-tipped hands in supplication. "So take me with you!"

Dunstan sighed, slapping his arm over his forehead. "O, hand-some lizard prince, I thought you'd never ask!" He threw himself backwards in a mock swoon, and Ven caught him. He stood back up, folding his arms crossly. "If this magical meet-cute were real, sure. But this is going too well. Thus, I'm definitely dying right now."

"Maybe this will resurrect you." And before Dunstan could stop him, the prince leaned down and kissed him.

And his head lit up like a firework.

The world turned green. Well, it was bright and white, as if a short fuse had been incinerated. It wasn't hot, just pleasantly warm, enveloping his face like an oven open on a batch of fresh cookies.

Sweetness in the air. Dunstan blinked as the world resolved: a trawler, a lizard prince, and Dunstan, casting a green glow on Ven's face above him as his eyes streaked with strange ribbons of foxfire.

Dunstan landed with a thud on the trawler's deck after Ven dropped him from the shock. But Ven, unlike Moss and his cronies, didn't look afraid at all. He only held a hand to his mouth, trying to cover his giddy laughter as it bubbled out of him.

"I knew it," he crowed. "You *do* have the Meteorlight! That means we're set!"

Dunstan rubbed his eyes. "What *was* that?" As he blinked rapidly, everything came back into focus, clearer than ever, leaving behind a buzz in his skull like a very delicious sugar rush.

"That," Ven said, boots lightly coming down on the deck as he bent over Dunstan with a smile, "proves you're very valuable, Bright Eyes." He lifted Dunstan with his tail, propping him up against the trawler's cabin. "And before anyone else comes sniffing, we'd better get—"

Thunk.

Ven wilted sideways, onto the shoulder that had just been neatly impaled with a spear.

Dunstan clapped a hand to his mouth.

"Rude," Ven snorted, grabbing the protruding end and yanking it out.

Dunstan tried to shield himself. Too late. A splatter of blue bloodied his T-shirt, though Ven didn't seem to mind at all.

"That's embarrassing," Ven sighed, tossing the spear over his shoulder like inconvenient trash. "Now, let's get you and me to the Door, shall we?"

He picked Dunstan neatly up in a princess carry and took off across the trawler's deck. Another three spears *thok-thok-thokked* behind them in precisely the place they'd both just been standing.

They dodged four more before the attackers showed themselves, slithering out of the black plinths surrounding the boat and swarming it. Dunstan's dashing hero planted him behind him as they were encircled. The merciless band all wore similar clothing

50

and goggles, adorned or painted with bright colours and shining stones, but their coats were a distinctive crimson — matching, as if it were a uniform. Their heads twitched, like a film strip skipping a few frames.

Their tails twitched, too, but none were as long and distinctive as Ven's; his scales didn't just glitter, they shone from below with the same green glow that had led Dunstan down this rabbit hole. And it was only growing brighter.

"Prince *Ven*?" One of the attackers said, gobsmacked as they looked him up and down.

"I hate needy fans," Ven stage-whispered to Dunstan. "Yes? What can I do for you, oh disloyal subjects?"

The leader audibly sneered. "We saw the Meteorlight — you know how much it's needed!"

Mocking every word with a hand-puppet show, Ven sighed. "Yes, yes. But this one's mine, you see. I got here first. And I'm about to take him far, far away from Vora's clutches."

A disgruntled gasp from another as they edged both Ven and Dunstan towards the railing. "You would let Jet crumble? The very *prince* of the geodom?"

A yowl like a feral cat came out of Ven, as if the words themselves had been a spear. "And when was the last time I was prince of anything?" he hissed, his charming lilt completely struck out. "Jet doesn't want me, and I don't want it!"

Then, before Dunstan could react, Ven picked him up, kissed him, and a bright green light enveloped them both, sending a comet of sparks shooting through Dunstan's vision as the attackers bawled in their blindness.

Ven was already running with Dunstan bumping along on his back before the light even cleared.

"What — where—?!" Dunstan blurted, his vision returning to normal. But suddenly they were leaping off the trawler's cabin. Dunstan was reduced to damsel-in-more-than-distress as his protector hopped neatly from plinth to plinth like a crazed mountain goat, *The Darling Mermaid* shrinking behind them.

"Listen, as much as I'd like to go with you," Ven grunted, "we'll never shake these bashing chloradids. I'll have to stop them. You'll have to go back on your own."

Midway through the mania, Dunstan realized they were going up, towards the ceiling of this mad cavern, to the highest plinth, leading towards a slab of glittering, symmetrical black quartz, all interlocking squares, set directly above *The Darling Mermaid*. It had to be the other side of the Door.

"Sure, happy to take a rain check on the promised prince-napping." What else could Dunstan do but crack wise, confused, kissing one minute then nearly dead (for the second time) the next.

Immediately above them, Dunstan saw massive cables criss-crossing. Dunstan had no time to shriek when Ven flipped them up onto one tightrope, running across it to leap onto another plinth. Ven looked back the way they'd come.

"Head start's nearly run out," Ven laughed, then coughed. The rest of the tailed folk were scaling the plinths at top speed, and soon they'd close the distance. Ven had left a trail of sticky blue behind them, his breathing laboured. He'd stopped, directly beneath the faceted rock that had to be the Door in Lake Mallion.

"Well, if I'm going back, now would be a good time to send me off!" Dunstan cried, looking wildly from the Door to their attackers, closer now.

"Then open it!"

Dunstan gaped, wit evaporated. "Me? I don't . . . I can't!"

Ven held Dunstan in one arm, fiddling with something in his coat until finally he pulled it free. It was a mushroom, and before Dunstan could ask, Ven wrenched the stem off it, threw it towards their pursuers, and covered his and Dunstan's faces as it exploded below.

"What was *that*?" Dunstan cried, until Ven grabbed him close and pinned him down with his smoky purple gaze.

"You have to open the Door," Ven urged. "I *know* it's why you're here. You have to open it now, so you can live. So you can come *back*." Then that dangerous grin. "Come back for me, that is. Because obviously I'll miss these little stabbings of ours."

Sure, the dream had taken a deadly turn, but Dunstan's once-broken heart skittered, staring into Ven's strange eyes. He clenched Ven's coat, still around his shoulders. "I wish you *could* come with me."

Ven grit his many teeth, the sharp ones Dunstan had been trying to ignore. It was a strange expression — urgency and maybe even temptation. It had been an empty invitation anyway. Dreams can't follow you home.

"Now, let's try that face-eating thing again, because it yields *results*."

Ven kissed Dunstan lightly, and the same strange warmth in his face rose to his eyes, even though they were closed. When he pulled away, the world had turned a miraculous green.

Then Dunstan felt something slip around his waist, saw the lizard boy's clawed hands come away as he was raised up in the clutch of his enormous tail.

"I'll be here waiting, Bright Eyes!" he shouted.

Dunstan's streaming vision swam and tingled, but before he could touch his face, he was swung in a sharp circle. Then he was released, a pebble in a slingshot, flying towards the stalactite ceiling of this infinite cavern.

Only a few things registered in those seconds: below, his reptile saviour was swarmed and pulled down by the red-coated gang, and above, Dunstan felt the air catch him, flip him over, and tug him towards the hatch. Onyx locks *shunked* aside, the Door opened, and Dunstan sailed through, and up, smashing headlong into crushing cold water.

SCENE 4

BORN PERFORMER

Moss hadn't slept at all, which was surprising. Hadn't he taken care of his problem? Of *everyone's* problem? Instead he'd lain on the rug beside his bed, staring up at the ceiling, at the crack there, until he swore the crack was on the inside of his eyelids, and the sun was pressing weakly at his window. He could hear his mother banging around downstairs.

Then her head was suddenly in his doorway. "What are you doing down there?"

Moss shot up, made sure not to face her, but even this was an admission of guilt. Would she notice he was wearing the same clothes he'd left the house in last night? That his hair was damp from sweat? Would her maternal instinct kick in? Would she wrap her arms around him and tell him it was okay, even though it definitely wasn't?

A scoff. She was already gone. Then Moss remembered that Myrtle Richler hadn't had a maternal instinct since the day he was born.

"I heard you come in last night, Mossy. Tsk! So late. I hope it was for a good reason."

Moss felt cold rush all over him. *A good reason.* All night his mind had raced, first with terror, then with hope. He'd done something very, very bad, but if he'd succeeded, then everything would work out for the best. He *trusted* that everything was going to work out. Even through the panic of the other boys, he'd told them to hold it together. They'd all sworn an oath that they wouldn't breathe a word of it. They'd done what they had to; they'd finally broken Reeve Gris's curse! Moss promised them that when day broke, everything would be different . . . and it was.

He was still alive, and Dunstan Cord was—

Myrtle was already flitting off to the next thing. "The Council of Mothers is in a tizzy, but I've got to go open the salon, so I'm off." She sang all this from down the hall, and it was Moss's turn to stick his head out of his doorway to stop her.

"The Council of Mothers? Why?" Moss could guess. Next it would be a constabulary beating the door down. Moss looked down the stairs, towards the front door, but it was still on its pristine hinges. Why weren't they coming to cart him away for his crimes?

He looked to his mother, remote in her flightiness. If he told her, what would she even say? While she fastened her earrings, she didn't even look his way, and Moss could feel the blatant panic in every bead of sweat pasting his hair to his forehead.

"I heard it's that Cord boy, again. Ruining school plays, making big proclamations, dancing through life — he's always putting everyone through the wringer. I'd just call the Luxe police and have done with it, not get the entire *town* in an uproar . . ." Myrtle never was one for community empathy. Unless it served her interests. "Anywhoodle, there's a Grislies meeting later tonight that I can't miss. Oh! Is that what you were up to last night with your friends? Starting your own chapter?"

Moss's ears rang; he opened his mouth and only a sharp croak came out. Myrtle finally looked up at him and he couldn't really hide how sick he felt inside. Myrtle pivoted in her fine shoes, her beautiful day dress a slow wave. She looked Moss up and down.

"It's all going to be okay, sweetness," she said, patting him once on the shoulder and figuring that was enough comfort for now. "We've all got our parts to play if we're going to get this town on the right track again! You remember your part, don't you?"

Moss swallowed, nodding, looking anywhere else. "Sure, Mum."

Myrtle kept smiling, then skipped down the stairs like a chipper chickadee. "I'm sure whatever happened to Dunstan Cord will have its purpose! *In the end.*"

How could someone who looked like an advertisement for Lunacakes sound like the harbinger of doom?

Then the front door was closed, and even though Moss was in the hallway, that crack in his room was still there when he squeezed his eyes closed, maybe getting a little wider. It let in another image: Dunstan's eyes, streaming green and terrified, as Moss heaved him into the lake.

The Council of Mothers were always about getting down to business. Preparedness was their stage.

Preparedness, surety, remaining the foundations of the community when the fisherfolk had gone off to steer ships in the war. Knockum still needed someone at the helm, and these women were always on duty. They weren't interested in the bells or whistles that might have come with these positions. The assembly was always a modest circle of folding chairs in the community centre across the road from Chauncer's Pub. If this were the bi-weekly gathering, with nothing else on the agenda aside from which fishwife had taken up her partner's boat that week or who had been swiping Ellie Condor's windowsill pies this week, there'd be a piping carafe of coffee on a worn wood-topped table and perhaps a plate of treats from Kiki Somerset.

But there was no time for any of the usual. Not even the folding chairs. The mothers stood in a circle, arms crossed, brows knit, shifting from foot to foot as they waited for the last member to make her appearance — late, as usual, but she'd be the deciding vote on what they would do about Dunstan Cord.

"We *can* start without her," Helene Trigger suggested, looking for support in the others. "We've waited long enough."

Kiki, who had been kneeling beside Ada Cord — definitely needing a folding chair, given the circumstances — clicked her tongue. "Five more minutes," she urged, then turned back to Ada. "Are you sure you don't want anything to drink?"

Ada's face, dry and drawn, didn't change as she shook her head no. "I want to get out there. I just need *one* boat. I'll go to the marina myself. I don't need all the fuss."

Kiki's face squeezed, eyes darting to the others. "Honey, we already told you, Dunstan wouldn't have gone out on the water, his note said he was running away to Luxe . . ."

Wanda Sardo came back in, having pulled every radio she could find out of the storage cupboard, in case a search party was imminent. "This is the lot of them. We're ready to go, I think."

There wasn't much else to say to that, so the other mothers just kept their vigil, eyes anywhere else as Kiki's soft fretting over Ada filled the silence. The mothers were used to waiting before springing into action. Keeping this town from falling apart, which it was, every day, required a lot of patient perseverance. This incident would be treated with the same care. Ada had brought Dunstan's *I'm leaving* note and it had been dutifully passed around, and though everyone had their opinions on the matter, their priority in this instant was making Ada feel validated in her worry for her son, on the brink of blindness but still as prone to drama as ever. He was probably lost in Eastmerlin Woods, and no matter what his intentions had been, they needed to bring him home. The search party would start there.

But Ada was convinced it had something to do with the lake, but she wouldn't elaborate. *Must just be the panic*, Wanda had muttered. Whatever Ada meant, it was the mothers' job to keep her moored. And themselves, thinking simultaneously of their own kids. They all remembered being young and reckless. But Knockum couldn't afford another tragedy.

The community centre door heaved open, cutting off Kiki's third offer of a blanket to Ada. The clack of stoutly heeled boots rang out over the parquet as Coral Frakes strode directly for Ada, arms open.

Though she'd waved off Kiki's continued attempts to comfort her, Ada reached out to Coral, clasping her large gloved hand in hers, as she allowed herself to be pulled to her feet.

"Boy's gone awry, eh?" Coral said, her face all but hidden beneath today's head scarf, bedecked in sequined Birds of Paradise. The scarf, as always, covered her head in a turban, her mouth shielded with a triangle of fringed silk, and her eyes kept behind enormous dark glasses. *An allergy to sunlight,* Coral had told them all long ago. And the mothers had left it at that, because Coral was fearless, and they needed that more than any explanation.

Despite her off-putting appearance, and that she was a stalwart shut-in, Coral never missed an assembly. And they would never start without her (Helene had been testing the waters out of nerves) because Coral had started the council shortly after she arrived in Knockum fifteen years ago. Morag Gunn, the head of the Knockum County lightkeepers, had vouched for Coral, saying that she was a retired agent of the Brindlewatch Guard, and all her field experience would lend well to keeping Knockum on an even keel while she enjoyed her semi-retirement. And over the years, whenever there was a calamity or a quarrel, Coral was always there, emanating calm and reason. The town was self-governed, but if ever there was a leader to rise to a crisis, it would be Coral.

And if something ever happened to Coral, the mothers' rock — they hoped they'd know what to do, but they weren't about to dream of the day they'd be so tested.

Ada nodded, numb. Coral brought her in for a bracing hug, patting her soundly on the back. "Never fear, darling. He can't have got far."

"I've got the radios," Wanda repeated, hoping to avoid further delays. "They're old but they'll do. I've sent word up to Batterborne Powerhouse to telegraph notice to Luxe Police. We'll organize a search up the escarpment and through the woods, but I'm sure we'll come across Dunstan before the Luxeans do."

"I didn't think," Ada said suddenly, eyes cast on the floor, the pants of her lightkeeper uniform creased from her clenching them so tightly. "I didn't think he'd do something like this." She looked up, searching her own reflection in Coral's enormous sunglasses for the answer. "He's got a flair for drama, we all know that! But . . ." A choke, a wry laugh. "Maybe I don't know my own son at all."

Coral let out her own laugh, which somehow, as it often did, managed to settle the other mothers. "Isn't that the truth about every child under the sun?" her crackling voice grinned. "They're infected with wild ideas. And we rarely know what to do with ourselves when they become their own folks."

Hands on her hips, swathed in the floor-dusting mustard swing coat she always wore, with its wide bright auburn sash, Coral finally revealed her coveted opinion. "But I think our better plan is to do nothing."

It was Helene Trigger who finally broke the mothers' silence. "What?"

Coral flapped her hands and sighed. "Kids need to go off on these kinds of adventures. Need to find themselves in their own personal wilderness to realize what they left behind." Something behind her scarf and glasses clicked. Everyone always assumed it was her tongue, but they could never be sure. "Nine times out of ten, they go off with their grand schemes, get halfway there, and the night proves to be a tougher pill to swallow. Reckon he's already trudging his way back, so best get back home and put the kettle on, Ada."

Kiki's eyes welled up, torn between agreeing and fretting. "But Dunstan has trouble with his eyesight. And the escarpment has so many deadly drops . . ."

Wanda still held the radios, and Helene looked like she was going to pop a vessel. "No." Helene shook her head. "This is ridiculous. If it was any of our children—"

"I would advise the same thing," Coral said, shrugging. "We've already alerted the cavalry. So now's the time to wait. If he's in peril, let him learn his lesson a little bit."

Ada broke free, pacing, wringing her hands. "I can't! I can't just sit here! He could be hurt. His eyes . . . he could've fallen by the Crisp, or something in the woods, in the dark! Or he could be somewhere *else*. Somewhere he's not supposed to be. On the water!"

"Why would Dun be on the water?" Wanda tried to intercept Ada, to get her to stop, to take a breath. "If he was, surely the lightkeepers would have spotted him? Let's just have a rational discussion—"

"No!" Ada cried, on the brink of hysterics. "You didn't see it that night, the *light*! I keep seeing it, out of the corner of my eye, on the water, and I knew that someday—"

Everyone looked to stalwart Coral, who was standing very still, slowly raising her hands up. "My dear, you're not making any sense. But I promise, everything will turn out."

"How could you begin to understand?" Ada squalled. "You don't even have children!"

Ada stared at the ground, face red, eyes refusing to spill tears, as ever. In the silence that followed, Coral put her huge hands around Ada, pulled her in, and let her breathe heavily into her duster.

"I'm sorry," Ada mumbled, but Coral was looking towards Wanda and Kiki, coming forward to take over.

"Take Ada home. Sit with her a while. We'll wait to hear from Batterborne." Coral was already striding for the door.

Helene, shaken, turned to their leader incredulously. "Where are you going? We have a situation on our hands!"

"So do I," Coral said, somewhat pointedly. "I've got company. Mustn't keep them waiting." And the community centre's door swung hard on its hinges as she blew out, sash trailing like a tail.

"Funny, that," Helene said in the wave of tension Coral had left behind.

"What?" Kiki asked.

"Coral hates visitors." Then she shrugged helplessly. The mothers got down to business, guiding Ada home. They could at least do this one thing.

As they all swept from the community centre, locking the door behind them, Kiki said, "Oh, Wanda, did Raymond say he saw Kavan last night?"

Wanda squinted. "No, why?"

Kiki lifted a shoulder, helpless. "He said he was going out with friends, but when he came home, he didn't look so good."

Helene looked from Ada to the other women. "Valmont said the same thing."

They all shared a worried expression. Ada was too wound up to notice that, unable to help themselves, the mothers all favoured Lake Mallion in the distance with a dread-filled glance.

Nothing good ever came of the things Knockum teens got up to over summer break.

As Dunstan stared out of the grimy windows of Coral Frakes's studio, little more than a boathouse shack with a dirt floor filled plank to rafter with covered canvases, all he could think was, *What a morning.*

On the dock entry outside, the lake lapped peaceably, as if it hadn't recently been used as a place to put an end to him, all for the sake of an urban legend. He blinked rapidly. His sight was back to being wonky. Because of course it was; it had never changed after all. He was awake now. You can see everything clearly in a dream because it's happening inside your head. But as he squinted, glasses long lost in the lake, he noticed that everything he *could* see had a rime of green around it. An outer glow. Different from the afterimages speckling his vision that had taken him to the doctor and his diagnosis. Some things were easier to see than others now. Things in shadow. When he stared at Lake Mallion, which was just on the studio's doorstep, he swore he could see past the surface. See the things lurking and moving, and the things that didn't.

He let the stiff wool blanket fall beside the stool he'd been planted on and went to a workbench topped with brushes and sculpting tools, piles of sketches, abandoned cups of tea. Or was it paint water? Dunstan lay a finger on a blank sheet of paper, dragged it towards himself, and sketched idly with a stub of charcoal.

I'll be waiting for you, Bright Eyes.

The striking gaze. The laissez-faire casual heroics. The *scales*. Dunstan's medium was script, satin, and sequins, so sketching wasn't his forte, but he had to get something down, an impression. He thrust his face close to the page, and each line scrawled took on that green glow. The hard sharp fin on the head, the symmetry of the horns, almost a diadem. The smile. He just wanted to remember the good dream, the precious stolen kisses, and keep it with him, remembering what it felt like to be the star of his own fairy tale, for once . . .

"Enjoying yourself?"

Dunstan nearly leapt out of his skin, whirling as Coral Frakes closed and locked the door behind her. She yanked the flimsy curtains shut over the shack's only window.

"I prefer to work in the dark." She answered Dunstan's stare, striding tightly like an army general over to his side. "What's this, then, you flamboyant miscreant?"

Dunstan had already crumpled the page and shoved it into his pocket. "Oh just passing the time in your extremely well-appointed, um, shanty," he smiled, deflecting back to Coral: "Anything to report?"

Though Dunstan couldn't imagine the expression Coral was making under all the layers of fabric, he didn't look away, in case she was assessing him, trying to see through his attempt at charm. He exhaled when she drew away. All the kids steered clear of Coral's house and studio near the West Dock, as she had a certain reputation. One that had a thousand strands, all terrifying, yet when Dunstan sniffed and looked around again, he was aware of how keenly comfortable he felt in her presence. A kinship. They were both artists, after all.

She sat carefully down in a high-backed armchair, feet in their steel-toed pump boots planted flat. Dunstan swooned; they were painted meticulously with incandescent flowers and mushrooms. In a word, gorgeous.

"You can wait here a while longer, fabricate your best apology, then get home. Your mother is in a state. The others think you're dead. But I managed to call off the search party. No need to fuss when there's nothing to fuss about." She dusted off a shoulder, then snickered. "Ada yelled in my face that I had no idea what she was going through. She's a peach, but you brought her to the brink."

Dunstan's cheeks ached from the fake smile, the practised nonchalance. He scratched the surface of the worktable with a fingernail, keeping his stinging eyes on the ground. "I don't think I've ever heard her yell. Must've been a thing to behold!" The lump in his throat grew half an inch. He'd put Ada through something, and he felt mighty guilty about it. But he maybe felt just as bad about waking up from the dream of a lifetime.

"Guess you didn't think too hard about what running away would do to those left behind," Coral snarked. "Well, that's one thing *I* have an idea about."

Coral was probably the most interesting person in Knockum, but he didn't want to give this living bogeywoman any more of himself. He should have just run off after she'd pulled him off the beach, dragged him inside, and thumped what was left of Lake Mallion out of his lungs. But he'd taken the time to get his bearings, put his thoughts straight. Besides, how effectively could he run away now? He was soaked, his bag with his carefully packed supplies and scrimped money was gone, and even though his mother was at home, hoping he'd be there, too, all he could think was, *I should just go for broke empty-handed and head for Luxe . . .*

Dunstan glanced from Coral to the door.

"No," Coral said, just as Dunstan opened his mouth to form some well-practised excuse. "You're not leaving just yet. I kept you here for a reason. Then once I'm through, you'll go to your mother the instant you're out that door, if I have to drag you there myself."

Dunstan stiffened, pretense dropped. "You can't do that."

"And why not?" Coral rose, and Dunstan could have sworn he saw her eyes, then, narrowing beneath those thick dark sunglasses. "I may not have any children *now*, but I did once. You're all the same, above *and* below."

Something at the back of Dunstan's mind knocked, but he ignored it. "Well, lucky for us both, I'm *not* a child." His face brightened, but his heart raced as he leapt up and made for the shack's door. "Thanks again for having me, but—"

Coral was suddenly filling the exit, holding the door closed with one gloved finger. No way she was that fast. Dunstan had no way out.

"I think a child would know better than to run off in the middle of a conversation," she said, and her own brand of charm was sharp, dangerous, as she towered over him. "I'll let you go. But in return, you'll tell me one thing."

Dunstan swallowed as she tipped up his chin, tilting her head to the side. He knew without a doubt she was looking straight through him. "What happened in Lake Mallion last night?"

Had he heard that right? Did she say *in*, or *on*? Dunstan shook his head as if there were water in his ears, willing his eyes not to do their weird green thing as he backed into her workbench. "Don't you live by the docks? The lightkeepers watch the lake, and Coral Frakes watches the town. So *you* tell *me*."

"Quick, aren't you?" Maybe a sneer. She obviously didn't like the town's unofficial saying being thrown at her, despite how true it was.

Coral folded her arms, continuing to block the door. "Let's see. One of Mender Richler's boats left dock with six passengers and came back with five. Then I find you comatose and nearly lung-drowned on my walk to this very studio. You're right. There's not much Knockum can get up to when it thinks no one is watching. If one person turns away, someone else has an eye on things. Seems like someone has to." A tilt of the head. "Was it the Grislies?"

Dunstan needed to worm his way out of this interrogation. Would Coral take whatever he said back to the Council of Mothers, each of them parent to one of the perpetrators on last night's joyride? Some of them were Grislies themselves, believers of the curse on Knockum, and would probably just try it themselves. The minute he levelled an accusation, wouldn't he be a target all over again?

"You do know what kidnapping is, don't you?" Dunstan asked, smiling sweetly as if he wasn't screaming on the inside. "Because that's what this is turning into."

"Then keep us both out of trouble, and spill," Coral replied, intractable. "I promise I'm here to help you, Cord. If someone tried to harm you—"

"It wasn't . . . no one . . ." The lies came easily, even though a big part of Dunstan was desperate to speak the crime out loud. He bit the inside of his mouth. He still hadn't even come to terms with the events of last night, and there was a thick velvet curtain separating what had happened and what could not possibly have happened. A fourth wall, not to be broken between the show and the audience. Both sides couldn't be true, but maybe they had to be to make the story work. All that mattered in this moment was: which version of events would get Dunstan out of this room and as far away from Knockum and the Grislies and the mysteries of Lake Mallion as possible?

Dunstan was a born performer, but it was always easier to borrow from something that was real, even if it only was in his head.

"Funny thing," he began, pushing himself off the workbench and striding around like he owned the place. "I figure everyone in this town has gone looking for the Door in Lake Mallion. But I doubt you've ever met anyone who went *through* it." Dunstan spun, clicked his heels, and held out his hands, smug.

"That's right, Madam! In your presence is Dunstan Royce Cord, humble homegrown talent-cum-intrepid-adventurer, who not only *found* the other side, but walked into it, and lived! Semi-soaked, but that's the price you pay." He sprang up onto the armchair, and he took pride in the ripple of irritation that went through Coral. "And on the other side, a world beyond your wildest dreams: a glittering city, certain danger, and secrets to behold. I even found Reeve Gris's cursed boat, the very trawler he and his friends were sucked down in! And do you dare guess what was waiting for me, on that deck, beneath the lake, beyond the green city?"

Coral didn't move. Dunstan couldn't even tell if she was breathing. Well, he *was* captivating. He let his ego explain it away before he lost steam. A brief thought entered his head and just as quickly left it: *my eyes are tingling again . . .*

"But why spoil it for you?" He hopped neatly down to the tar-stained floorboards, striding around Coral to the door. "You'll read all about it in my autobiography in a few years, after I make it big. Don't worry, I won't forget where I came from! I'll even add a line in about the mysterious genius sculptor from my hometown who made my fame possible. Every bit counts." With a hand on the doorknob, Dunstan snapped his fingers. "Oh, and if you manage to find the Door, just know it packs a wallop on the way out. I mean, you saw me this morning. *Not* my best look."

Coral's huge hand in its satin glove slammed so hard into the studio door that the hinges cracked. Dunstan's performance adrenaline went out of him with a squawk.

"Who else have you told this story to?" Coral was staring straight ahead. This time, her whole body was vibrating, and there was something clicking unsettlingly (maybe her jewellery . . . maybe her teeth).

At his wit's end, all Dunstan could do was smile, the bits of the truth creeping in claw-first. "Everyone loves a story. Who would care that I was just out there, messing around with my friends, or being messed around *with*, as usual? This story is more interesting. In this story, I was the lead." He didn't care that his voice cracked. "In this story, I mattered enough to get through a mythical door to a glowing black city under the lake, where I was rescued by a lizard prince. When did it become a crime to have a good dream?"

Coral drew up to her full height suddenly, then stepped away from the door as if neither it, nor Dunstan, were there at all.

"The thing about stories," she said, maybe more to herself, to her studio filled with its shadows and dirt and scrawled canvases, "is that they grow like a fungus, and when they send out spores, it's almost impossible to stop the spread."

But Dunstan was already throwing himself out the door. "I'll remember to pack fungicide then!" he called over his shoulder, the light of another typical Knockum morning scattering any doubts Coral could infect him with. He was going to be something, tell his own story, and nothing would stop him now.

Two miles from the shore, beneath the buoys *in memoriam*, down past the depths that a seagull could snatch, the Door was worried.

Before Dunstan's dismaying entry, it hadn't been opened for some time. Things hadn't gone well with the trawler and the kids and the king. So it had stayed closed, trying not to think of the Meteorlight, trying to ignore its longing to be reunited with it, to do as it asked. Of course, it *liked* to be open, though it didn't like to admit it. But that's what a door lives for — to be opened, closed, passed through, needed, necessary. It felt the town's adoration above the water and the dark city's below it. It belonged to both of them, as it always had.

Some doors should not be opened, though, and like it or not, this was one of them — the Door itself knew that, knew its purpose. But last night it felt the key pressing into the lock, and it couldn't resist. What else can a door do but yield? But this Door had *concerns*.

Because if it was opened again, and again, then the key would get what it wanted. And that meant the town that adored the Door, and the city below that cursed it, would both suffer.

The thing about doors is that they're hard to resist. And this Door knew that Dunstan Cord wouldn't be able to for long, not with the passenger he carried — the same one the Door longed for. The Door knew that this was its own fault, too, for having its own trouble resisting — with Dunstan, with Reeve. The Door had done all it could, all these years. Perhaps it really was time.

The hinges clicked. Bubbles rose, almost a sigh. This was it then. The beginning of the end. It had finally come. All it had to do was open a few more times, and Dunstan, it seemed, would decide.

If a boat had been passing, and the pilot glanced down, pulling up her net, she would think, *Ah, must be my eyes. For I could've sworn, down in the dark, something waited. Something black and glowing faintly green.*

But surely, it was just a trick of the light.

Even though Coral Frakes was as weird as the town professed, Dunstan couldn't help but find his experience with her still clinging to him like an incessant fishfly as he climbed the hill towards home. Not her words, precisely, but her whole *thing*. Being unable to see her eyes or read her face made her harder to figure out, but there was something *else*.

When Dunstan had scrambled up the beach, fistfuls of lake sand, coughing, insensible in the pre-dawn light, there was Coral, as if she'd been waiting for him. She'd pulled him out of the water, taken him to the studio, not a word passing between them. But the minute Dunstan had told her the truth — or his dream, or whatever it was — she'd let him go. She'd called it a story, but could it be that she *believed* him?

Dunstan stopped dead in the middle of the road, turning back to look towards Coral's studio, to the lake, still shimmering green, and wondered, *Had she seen what Dunstan had seen?*

"I told you *that's enough*," he scoffed, and kept climbing the hill, putting distance between himself and the water. "You're insane, and so is every talented famous person, but you need to keep it under control." Yet his hand clenched his T-shirt, the blue blood in the fabric going stiff as it dried, real beneath his fingers.

"I love how hard you dream, Dun." He stopped dead in the road, Luisa's voice bubbling up clearly as if she was right there, admiring, encouraging. It was something she always said, when Dunstan would wax on about his longing to be ten storeys high on the silver screen with a leading man on his arm, then melt under the inevitable self-doubt when his name barely graced the cast sheet at the school play. She was always there with a reassurance. A validation. *You're not weird. What you want isn't weird. Don't let anyone tell you otherwise — you're great as you are.*

Tears welled up in Dunstan's eyes, and he got angrier just for that, swiping at Mrs. Gortum's prize hedges as he passed. Everything was a jumble, nothing made sense, Dunstan was supposed to be in the woods, then in Luxe making his big break — then he was supposed to be dead — and *then* he was saved by a door that wasn't real and a prince that was made of glittering scales and *why was everything glowing green?!*

"What are you doing here?"

Dunstan whirled. Was this just another hallucination? As if he'd conjured her, there was Luisa, standing behind him in the sidewalk. A light breeze ruffled her black ponytail as she stared Dunstan down, and he tried to casually wipe away any offending tears but wasn't doing a great job of it.

"What do you mean?" He acted offended, arms folded, sniffing loudly. "It's still a free country, last time I checked the news. I have every right to be here. What about *you?*"

Her scowl pinched into confusion. "You're standing in front of *my house*, Dun."

Dunstan blinked, turned, and squinted. Felt his chest tighten. "Yeah, so? I was heading home and I . . ." Pointed to his empty face, indicating his missing specs. "It was a *mistake.*"

Luisa stood her ground. "First time I've heard you admit you've made one." His jaw tightened. "Rough night in Eastmerlin Woods? Bet that's where you lost your glasses. Or was that thing I heard about you running away also a mistake?"

How had she heard, so quickly? Dunstan was shaking, close to crumbling. His fists got tighter and tighter — he wanted to tell her. Tell her everything. It was bursting out of him, like when he'd seen a cinema show before she had and he was dying to spoil the ending. But if he told her, he'd have to admit something he never could, which would get in the way of everything he'd planned, and—

Luisa screeched as she faltered backwards, and both she, and Dunstan, found themselves in the hedges. Car tires squealed on panicked pavement, folks in their houses cried out, and all of Knockum held its breath as the town lurched and rocked for twenty seconds, though to Dunstan, it felt like hours. The world came up to meet him in a splash of vibrating green, and both he and Luisa stared out at the place where the rumbling sound went on, long after Luisa's street stood still once more.

"What in the flying Fandango was *that*?" Luisa pointed down the hill, towards the lake, where the whitecaps were huge even though it was a clear, windless morning. To Dunstan, it looked like a geyser of green had shot upwards, maybe two miles from shore, like a cannonball had landed there, and all he could do was rattle in his sneakers.

Luisa pulled herself out of the hedges, too late to stop Dunstan, scrambling away and covering his eyes as he went. "Dun! Wait!" But he had already run full-tilt up the road, ducking around cars whose drivers stood in the street, staring, chattering, everyone's hearts individually filling with their own type of dread.

Like when someone knocks from the other side of a door that has always been shut.

Coral twitched the curtains at her studio window, eyeing the lake. She braced herself on her workbench, the green light arcing into the sky and then fizzling out. She tensed. Where had it come from? The other side of the Door, perhaps? *Beyond the green city*, Dunstan Cord had said. If he had truly gone through the Door, and wasn't just spitting local lore back at her, then that meant he had the key. And that was the greatest shock, and a greater threat, than she could've ever imagined.

Her stomach twisted. All these years waiting for *it* to return, to show its terrible glow, and now here were the signs of its return.

Just when she had felt herself settling in, found herself living instead of just watching.

The Meteorlight has returned. And it's in the hands of a sequin-eyed teenage boy.

As the ground settled, she looked down, realizing she was hunched over the crumpled sheet of paper that had transferred Dunstan's crude sketch. She ran a gloved finger over the outline, the horns, heaving a sigh for all the things in her heart she couldn't speak, had barely allowed herself to think.

How could you understand? You don't have any children!

Coral left her studio in a flurry, the door slapping in the wake of her fabulous coat, her painted boots. She needed to get to the boy, and quick, before he did further damage by opening that bloody Door, by shining himself any brighter than he already had.

She needed to stop him, before her own mistakes came back to bite Knockum into nothing.

Dunstan went into his house — he was sure this time it was his house, though he'd already been caught having a tantrum on Luisa's street — and besides, everything was starting to tilt, to melt together. Arnault had talked about something like this, at the mandatory vaccination clinic in fifth grade, and knowing the needle was coming his head went spinning (figuratively). Was this the same? Dunstan hoped it was, because then it'd be a normal reaction to stress. And it'd eventually go away. The world was shaking, and now pieces of it were sliding away, the edges glowing green.

And as Dunstan dragged his hand over his throbbing eyes, he had the terrible feeling it was his fault.

"Dunstan?"

Ada tore out of the kitchen, boots skidding on the parquet. She was still dressed in her lightkeeper uniform — the sandy denim dungarees buttoned at the hip, the smart blouse with the front pockets for her watch, handheld spyglass, golden pencil, and notepad.

Little details, all at once crisp and then blurred. Dunstan ground his hands into his eyes, taking deep gulping breaths.

Ada came towards him, hands out.

"No, don't!" Dunstan shot away, keeping distance between them. "I . . . I . . ." He just needed a minute to gather himself. To put the mask back on, the one he'd always practised, so that both his mothers would know he was okay, wouldn't ask questions. He had come home to apologize. Then he'd come home to hide. From Coral, Luisa. The lake. From himself.

"Sweetie, it's okay," Ada said, shocked but trying to hold it together for them both. "You're safe now. I'm not mad. But there's something going on and we—"

"I just need to go to the bathroom!" Dunstan shouted, already racing up the stairs two at a time, then slamming the door before Ada could interject or repeat his name and give him the space to fall apart.

In the stillness of the foyer, the front table shivered. Ada bit her lip, bracing. Teenagers were a force of nature, but this was something else.

Now in the bathroom, Dunstan felt a little safer. But the problem was, the dangerous thing was him. Or it was *inside* him. Maybe it really was some kind of infection, like Valmont had accused on the deck of Mender's boat. Or, maybe he'd swallowed something in the lake. Because it all came back to the water. He climbed into the clawfoot bathtub, pulling his knees up to his mouth. He just had to think this through. Approach it like a plot hole in one of his many hand-penned scripts that he'd submitted to the Luxe Radio Play-a-Thon.

His mind went back as he screwed his eyes shut.

INTERLUDE:
MEMORY MEZZANINE

A mini stage, bright with sunset and seagulls crying. Water made out of blue satin sheets, lifted up and down gaily in the breeze, sparkling. The essence of summer.

The water. It's where the weirdness all started. Dunstan had been down by the lake, hands in his pockets, hanging around Coral's sculpture of the *Gris Mermaid*— weeks ago now. The semester before summer break. It was after he and Luisa had had the Big Fight.

Dunstan at the water, strolling. He's gone there to think, calmed by the slow lapping against the pebbles and the docks, and he notices the green tinge to his vision. So slight, like a sliver under his eyelash. He thinks it has to be the sunset, at first, or a light off a buoy.

The wind riffles his hair. He thinks he hears . . . no, it is just the gulls above, crying out. But he swears he heard someone, far away but also quite close by, asking for help.

The effect on the audience is bewildering: green film, maybe, over the leading spot, like a kaleidoscope. The audience is taken in. The green tinges the scene. There's no denying it's there.

But the green persists in Dunstan. He moves from the beach to a classroom desk sliding across the stage, to the four-poster in his bedroom as the sets swirl in cadence to a tap dance. He throws himself through his solitary day-to-day, his interludes and ennuis with Moss and the Perfects. Everything would be fine . . . if it weren't for the green spotlight following his every move.

The sun sets on the stage, darkness and stars fade out and up. And the green makes everything glow, Dunstan rubbing his eyes under his thick glasses.

Then a boat rumbles onto the stage, captained by Moss and the footballers. He's hauled onto the deck, hands up — the music grows to an unsettling horn crescendo. The boys throw themselves away from Dunstan, whose eyes are streaming green.

End scene.

The boat. The lake. Moss and his cronies. They had seen it. Seen the green coming out of Dunstan, a beacon, and it guided Dunstan down to the Door that ultimately saved his life. Because here, in this clawfoot bathtub in his mothers' house, if Dunstan was going to preserve his sanity, he'd have to now play it out like the land beneath the lake was real. *The Darling Mermaid*, lost for fifteen years, had been solid under his sneakers. And the lizard prince Ven with his own eerie glow had bled all over him — what more proof did he need?

Never mind that the green light had glowed brightest when they'd *kissed*. Dunstan grabbed his hair.

The lake. The light. It was the reason everything was suddenly going wrong — all Dunstan's plans, his mistakes. The light was leading him somewhere. Somewhere down. Somewhere dark. He kept his eyes closed as he pounded his forehead into his knees.

This was all too much. He'd always daydreamed himself out any window he could find, into strange and fantastical worlds that could deliver him from his many blunders and rejections, but somehow he wasn't prepared for this. Dreaming was the only way he'd survived.

But this wasn't a dream. He didn't want to talk to Ada. He didn't want to tell anyone what he was *really* feeling. He wanted it all to stop. He wanted to be saved.

"C'mon," he whispered to himself, to the Light, to the Door far away in the lake. "Just take me back there. I'll do anything."

Dunstan opened his eyes when the bathtub beneath him began to vibrate, the faucet dripping, even though he hadn't turned either of the ivory knobs. And each drop seemed to whisper inside him, *There is something I want to see again, Dunstan Cord. You have the key. All you have to do is knock.*

Downstairs in the kitchen, gathering herself for the talk she'd already rehearsed with Dunstan, Ada Cord's teacup rattled on its saucer, and she caught it before it shattered on the black and white tile.

The house improbably tipped, and she with it.

Ada staggered to the stairs as Knockum heaved again. She cried out, "Dun! Hold on, I'm coming!" And threw herself onto the risers, the house pitching back and letting her regain her balance. She tripped up the last risers and caught herself on the hallway wall, rolling along like a tossed marble towards the closed bathroom door.

The edges of it glowed bright, and for a moment, Ada couldn't move.

Dunstan got to his feet, only to be thrown back into the tub, grabbing hold of the gold brocade shower curtain and holding on for dear life. His legs sprawled as his waterlogged sneakers failed to keep him upright with each concussive burst shivering through the porcelain.

Then the dripping faucet exploded, and clinging to the side of the tub as he attempted to escape, he risked being thrown out like a soon-to-be-concussed rodeo star.

But the water wasn't concerned with him. It came out of the tap, and climbed up the back wall behind the tub, and in the chaos, Dunstan blearily remembered that Knockum drew its water from the lake. Somehow, Dunstan had summoned it.

As the water climbed, its tendrils found the light fixture set in the bathroom's ceiling, and the force of it popped each lightbulb out one by one. The windowless room went dark, yet Dunstan could still see — see through the curtain of water, getting wider, higher, and though he dimly knew the rest of the house was shaking, he stood up in the vibrating bathtub, clutching the shower curtain in his hands, trying to stay moored to the world of polyvinyl and ceramic and the comforts that reality promised.

But reality wasn't what Dunstan wanted, never had been. His face broke into a grin. Another world was waiting for him on the other side. And with it, his prince.

He stepped forward. The water knew its invitation was accepted, and Dunstan saw, as he inched closer, that he was staring at the bottom of Lake Mallion, through this water-portal, just within reach. The Door was there, its shining black edges glowing, and Dunstan's reflection glowed, too. Yet there was no pull, this time.

No insistence. The first time, the Door had taken him in on its own. This time, he had to choose. To *knock*.

Dunstan had already chosen, though, and his grin broke into a laugh, knuckles eagerly rapping against the shower's backsplash.

The Door opened. The world shook. He'd dream a little longer.

Everything stopped. Ada stared at the door, knew she had to get to it, only bare inches away, but how could she? Something was stopping her, something familiar and weird and completely bewildering.

Then the glow around the door began to fade, and she lurched forward, grabbing the knob, wrenching herself into the room.

"Dun!"

The light was on. The house was still. The pipes didn't even creak and the tap didn't drip.

But the bathtub was full, the surface of it rippling, and Dunstan — and the shower curtain — were gone.

ACT

II

SCENE 5

VILLAIN VEN

H ere's what Dunstan *imagined* he would see after the Door in
Lake Mallion swallowed him for the second time: the deck of
The Darling Mermaid. Huge black cliff plinths. Some great, weird
metropolis glowing in the distance like the promise of an alien planet
on the outskirts of his galaxy. And, of course, the valiant lizard prince
and his red-clad pursuers. This time, Dunstan would be ready.

But Dunstan didn't know yet that the Door in the lake didn't
operate like doors in Knockum. He was spat out, face-first, into
an alleyway. He spluttered, because he'd swallowed some of the
errant bath-but-lake-water, and when he turned over to check the
space he'd come from, there was the onyx-glinting Door with its
many facets . . . folding itself back up and disappearing until only
a lattice of brickwork remained in the dripping wall it left behind.

Dunstan scrambled up and pressed himself to the wall. In the
Sade Sisters adventures, with their prim accents from across the sea,
this would be called a *close*, not an alley: it was tidy and neat, the
buildings built tightly together, with a set of steps leading downwards
to another street below. Dunstan bit his lip, realizing he really wasn't
armed for exploring this wildly fantastical place — all he had was the

brocade shower curtain, which he'd picked out and helped sew the grommets into, and it was truly a work of art, but it, like most of his creations, was hopelessly useless in this instance.

He also still didn't have his glasses, having lost them the last time the Door had made his plans for him, never mind that he could've grabbed his backup pair from his nightstand — but there had been no time to think.

But as he tested his eyes, first with a hand waggling in front of his face, then with a creeping look out of the close, and into the open, staring up, up, at glittering cavern-scraping buildings, Dunstan gaped. Every detail was sharp and crisp. Who needed glasses when you had enchanted glowing eyeballs?

"Like Christa Sade always says, 'Best make the most of it,'" he resolved, throwing the shower curtain over himself like a cloak. Not the most fashion-forward, but he blended in nicely with the surrounding architecture, which was all dark, gleaming like it was damp, and shimmering green.

Then he took a step, and another, down the well-hewn stairs, and walked into the street of his waiting, private world.

Lightkeepers in Knockum set themselves apart from all the other factions ringing Lake Mallion's shores. It was the nature of the job, for the job itself was an honour. An honour to be chosen for it, after years of training, of discipline, of methodology. Ada Cord always knew she would be a lightkeeper; her mother had been, her grandfather before, going back almost to the founding of the towns that grew up around the lake, taking advantage of its (back then) many spoils. To Ada, setting your eyes on Lake Mallion and spending your life noting every ripple that went across its surface was more than an honour. It was a gift.

It didn't feel like a gift just now, however.

When she was uncertain or anxious or scared, thinking about Lorraine on the other side of the world, or about Dunstan and his many quirks, Ada would revisit her training. She kept all her note-books from those times in the study and would read them over, the journals and the lessons recorded meticulously in perfect penman-ship, back when she was just learning, bright-eyed and hopeful. It usually helped put things into perspective: if you ever see something strange or untoward on the lake, you rediscover reason. You plant your foundation firmly in fact. And above all else — you don't dare to dream. Dreams ensnare logic. They make your foundation unsteady. *They set your craft off-course.*

Lightkeepers, first, are taught the history of the lake. The meteor that made it, the tributaries it's fed by. There are other lakes approaching Lake Mallion's size, of course, but nothing can compare, and so fishing enterprises on the lake have always been plentiful and have allowed a unique trade to exist centrally in Old Kiplington, the country in which Lake Mallion, and the Far City Network (Luxe, Oiros, Ferren, Armbruster, and Merry), reside. The lake also sees massive trade transit, and there have been talks of building an underwater train tunnel to connect the rail lines — an undertaking many have argued against, but which may be inevitable, given the supply chain needed to continue the Great War on the other side of the Sorrento Sea.

Local history and politics aside, a lightkeeper lives by strict tenets: Keeping impeccable time. Organization of thought and duty. Keen eyesight. And most importantly, a rational mind, one that Ada was warring with now as she hurried to the study after Dunstan vanished.

She needed to be sure.

A lightkeeper is a watcher. A student of details, a keeper of schedules. Which boats should be out, and when? What territory are they allowed to dock and anchor in? Are shipments from other port towns, like Sectur on the far east bank, expected? What will be on them? Is there a wedding barge due this Sunday going off to Pekan, and is the captain fully registered to perform both her duties and to officiate? What about the Paddlewheel Steamboat, taking city tourists and local sweethearts up and down the escarpment?

Are there children out on the water in their parents' boats, driving directly into the bright green light of peril . . . ?

Ada, rifled through a box of identical green-covered notebooks and pulled out the one she was looking for. She ran her finger across the date. *Dun's day*, she whispered in her mind, unable to say it out loud to the now-empty house. Even though she had gone through the pains of labour and the terror of new motherhood that day, Ada was faithful to her work. *You were on shift. Therefore you must have recorded what you saw.* Her leading lightkeeper at the time, and now the leader of the Knockum Quay, Morag Gunn, was a sweet woman, would've forgiven a report handed in after Ada had taken rest, but Ada wasn't the type of person to miss a deadline. A detail.

And she was grateful for that, in this moment.

Each entry is begun at every shift, with notes written throughout the night so that nothing is lost. Ada had begun writing, quite soberly, as always, though so late in her pregnancy her usual sharp mind had been wandering. That's what she had later blamed what she saw on: the exhausted mind of a body making a life. But after today, she knew she should've trusted her own eyes.

Ada Cord, Lightkeeper Excelsior
August 12, '27
Western Dock, 2100–0500 shift

The lake is quiet tonight. There had been some talk earlier in the day of the seniors from this past graduation year holding a party or some such near the Gris dock, but no commotion. Serene and dark. Weather clear. The rain seems to finally be holding off. Summer air is heavy. I feel heavy.

Ada's mouth quirked at that; lightkeepers were to always keep personal feelings or thoughts out of their reports, so that every report could seem as if it were written by the same person. The same ideal that made up the job. Never mind that these reports were later

82

handed over to be transcribed and added to the Brindlewatch Guard's extensive archives.

She read on:

> *I wonder what this child will be like. Will they be a lightkeeper, too? What will they dream of? Will it be of the lake, like me? Or something bigger than the lake? Sometimes I'm unable to sleep because of how big I am. Sometimes I'm afraid to sleep, and I don't want to wake Lorraine for my worrying. But the lake has been on my mind in a way it never has before. I feel heavy, like if I stepped into the lake now I would sink right to the bottom, this baby dragging me quickly to the rock bed, and I think that's what the lake wants. Not for me to drown, but to see what's down there.*

Ada sat down hard in the oak desk's chair, nearly missing it. She didn't remember writing this. She didn't remember anyone sending the report back to her and remarking on how strange it was, either. Morag would have, in her smiling, critical way. And she would have been right to!

> *0208 hr: strangest thing; the air suddenly feels clearer. Closed my eyes for a moment*

Ada, in the study, seeing the unfinished sentence, closed her eyes as if it were a command from the past. And she was there again, in her watch by the water, the lake lapping against the docks below, and in quick succession she saw Reeve's boat, the blinking light on its aft as it headed out to the open lake, past the markers. The scream. The green light. How it anchored Ada in place, how she felt like staring at it had drawn it into her, somehow, swallowed by her eyes and into her body.

Her *pregnant* body, shared with someone else moments before he was born. And now she was hurtled forward in time, to the close past, standing in the hallway outside the bathroom door, the crack underneath it gleaming green like an eerie beacon . . .

Back in the study, Ada clutched her belly, flat now, feeling lake-sick on dry land, closing her eyes again and now sitting beside Dunstan at the dinner table.

"I dunno," he said, rubbing his eyes. "Not like my eyesight's anywhere decent, but the green spots, like a reflection on the water . . . they're just kind of there. Can't blink them away." He smiled. "It's annoying enough that I thought I'd actually tell you about it."

Ada thrived on details. She collected them to pore over later, when her mind was quiet. She was one who stood by and watched and recorded and wrote and filed the reports away and that was how she did things. In her work and her life. But now, clutching the desk and pulling herself up, here, in her empty house, which her son had somehow disappeared from, in a town that seemed more keen on recording than acting, Ada Cord was tired. Of standing by. Of watching. She straightened her uniform, made sure she had her tools, and especially the picture of Lorraine tucked neatly into her pocket.

The lake, and the town, was in a mood — and she was going to discover what it had to do with her son.

This world was not so uninhabited, as it turned out, as it seemed in Dunstan's initial foray. Which was to say, he was nearly run over by what might have been a scrimshaw, or a six-wheeled bicycle, but it was moving so fast it could've been anything.

And it wasn't the only thing moving fast. The walkways were busy, with promenaders and artisan stalls, with folk little and big. The Geodom of Jet was alive and lively, and he needed to take stock.

Dunstan pressed himself to the building abutting the close staircase he'd just come down, which opened up into what could only be described as a high street, brimming with activity. There was ambient music playing, but it wasn't like any he'd ever heard before.

Percussive pipes, maybe, or a drum made of glass slabs. It filled him up, but he didn't stop to listen for long; Dunstan could tell he was drawing stares. Yet no one stopped to accost him; he wasn't the only one concealing his face. Everyone wore goggles and headgear, scarves and masks, every one unique, bedazzled to the hilt, and keeping every identity secret. Folk approached one another familiarly, grasping tails, the only part of each stranger that was uncovered. Their scales glinted with the viridian night-light, adorned with jewellery and colourful stones on cords. And when the tails connected in friendly greeting, they glowed a glorious, verdant green.

Dunstan felt himself blush, turning away from the displays of affection, of friendliness. It reminded him of Ven. Obviously that meeting hadn't been a dream, and he hoped Ven was all right. But with everyone so deeply disguised, how would he find him?

Not like he could advertise his presence, either. He couldn't blend in to the crowd down here. Not that he ever could above. But he needed to start somewhere. *Keep your promises*, Lorraine had warned him. And if it meant bringing his would-be lizard beau up to the surface, well, at least it'd make for one last cracking adventure before his view of life went dark.

Dunstan looked at the buildings for somewhere he might ask around, or at least skulk for information. There was an abundance of people, and an abundance of dark. The city was dark at every edge, lit by the ambient glow of buildings. From a distance it seemed like the towers jutting up from the ground had been filled with windows, but as he got closer, it wasn't windows putting out light, but giant . . .

Mushrooms?

Not just mushrooms, but hardy, swarthy fungi. Sage and mint and seafoam and acid and leafy, round and ruffled but always green. They grew in meticulous, symmetrical patterns on every surface, looking like freshly cut gems. Some were huge, creating massive, twisted bridges or platforms connecting roads and passing over them. Some were a multiplicity of dots creating a wave down a side street, merely decorative. But all were certainly part of a network: when one flickered, so did the others nearby, and it gave the impression that the city's buildings were blinking, or sighing. What he mistook for a light post was just a mushroom on a tall, ragged stem, glowing brightly as he passed, then fading again as he continued on.

And it was loud, all around him! Voices and music and noise, like any street in Luxe he'd gone down during his many doctor's appointments. The sets might be alien but the concept was the same. A world of lives intersecting, of folk going about their business. Real, constant, connected, and alive. All on Dunstan's doorstep, all along. And no human had been down here before . . . no one except Reeve Gris and the "Sunken Three" — Darla Denning, Emmerich Kohl, and Lenny Steez, that is. Maybe he should take a detour after finding Ven; grabbing Reeve Gris and his friends, taking them back to Knockum, and returning a hero.

That'd wipe the smirk off Moss's smugly gorgeous face.

Speaking of gorgeous, that led to step one: find Prince Ven, hopefully in one piece. He hadn't been in the best shape when they parted, given the blue blood still spackling Dunstan's shirt beneath the shower curtain cloak. Hopefully Ven was made of stern stuff, and wasn't bleeding out somewhere. He was a swashbuckling hero, thus he had probably been through worse, and Dunstan let himself swoon about it rather than worry. Aside from the romantic fantasy aspect of their humble meeting, Dunstan felt like he *knew* Ven. He seemed nice, at least. Nicer than Moss. Surely, he'd been joking about capturing him — who doesn't threaten that, mid-flirt? Moreover, he seemed curious about Dunstan, surprised, even. He'd find Ven, get the lowdown on this place, and . . .

Dunstan, trudging, lost in his thoughts, bumped into a table, sending the chair nearly flying, but he righted both himself and the seating before he could take out the entire patio. The smell of something wonderful bloomed out of what looked like a cave entrance, set beneath an enormous mushroom cap. He was dying to go inside, his stomach making a hungry fist under his ribs, but he didn't have any money on him to begin with. What kind of currency did they take down here, anyway? Would he be kicked out simply for not having a glamorous tail like the rest of the patrons? Would the food be poisonous to him, or would it ensure he could never leave?

That could be my in . . .

A new idea: once he found Ven, he'd simply take his great plan for running off to Luxe and plaster it over this place: find a job, find a stage, experience his big break. No nightmare diagnosis for his sight. Down here, able to see clearly, maybe Dunstan had all the time in the world.

"Did you hear? About what happened in the Hacklands yesterday?"

A pair at one of the café tables leaned in, their words clicking but clear. Dunstan took his seat, his back to them, instinctively acting as if he was part of the scenery.

"I don't believe a word of it," the first speaker's companion said, haughty. "The Door has stayed closed since Vert's betrayal. That's the deal that was made. The Higher-ups have kept their word all this time. Why would they break it now?"

Higher-ups. The word had a heaviness to it, and it tingled the back of Dunstan's mind. He named the speakers Donna and Darren, so he could tell them apart when he later jotted this whole thing down in his journal, or bragged about it to Luisa, in a reality where they were still inseparable.

"What if it wasn't in the Higher-ups' plan?" Donna was breathless, voice grinning. "What if it was *Prince Ven*? Maybe he's trying to open the Door again, in order to bring back the Meteorlight!"

Dunstan flushed at Ven's name as Darren snorted. "Prince Ven is as much a myth now as that Door is. If he got it open, he'd run off to the mythical Above. And if not, then he's gone past the edges of Jet, where there's nothing for nobody. There's certainly no place for him in Jet, not without his egg-right."

The Door — that part made sense. But *the Above . . .* are they talking about Knockum? Maybe the rest of the world? Dunstan glanced around furtively. He leaned backwards in his chair, imperceptibly, to get a better read on Darren's little diatribe.

". . . and if there are gangs hanging about the Door, praying that it opens again and the Meteorlight returns, that's business for the Stackers."

Dunstan felt his face grow warm. *Meteorlight*. He clapped a hand over his eyes, just in case they were streaming.

"Oh, you're always so gloomy," Donna complained. "Can't you let me be excited about something thrilling happening without having to worry about—"

A piercing shriek. The mushroom lights in the rock buildings, all around, glowed red. The earth shook so hard Dunstan fell out of his ornately wrought chair, cowering under the table. And he wasn't alone in that: the rest of the lizard folk were in a panic as the quake went on, all now running for cover under awnings and racing to get out of the street, as the red light strobed and the alarm went on.

Dunstan was terrified he'd set something off, some kind of intruder alert, yet when he looked around to see what was happening, he noticed all the folk who'd made for cover were staring up, at the place the sky would be, as a huge stream of water poured down, directly into the gleaming cobbled street.

Rain?

It only took a few moments for the lights to return to their original green, and it seemed like the passersby breathed again, clutching huge clawed hands to chests and patting each other reassuringly on the shoulder. Official-looking citizens wearing dark red coats cordoned off the area, namely the big puddle gathered in the middle of a road. Dunstan tensed — it was the same uniform of the group that had attacked him and Ven. Crowds were pushed back and encouraged to go about their business. So they were some kind of law enforcement? Dunstan saw a fish flopping on the cobbles, saw one of the guards grab and pocket it.

"Thank the Higher-ups!" someone nearby shouted, and there was a general cry of giddy relief as folk returned to their promenading.

"That's the second time in as many days!" remarked a tall spectator, wearing a glittering, well-tailored suit of scales, shaking their head. "It's getting worse. Will the Stackers be able to handle it, you think?"

"I heard that more homes on the leeward spike were close to being washed clean away! Soon you'll see whole tors coming down. Where will we *go*?"

"Have a little faith," the worrier's companion sniffed. "The Higher-ups will keep us safe, like they always have. *The Light has the right.*"

Dunstan tried to listen to the concerned murmurings, to pick up any more details of what it all meant, until he realized he was still on the ground when someone stopped in front of him and pulled him to his feet.

"Probably not the best place for you," the someone hissed from above, and Dunstan, frightened, tried to break away, but was held in place. "Bright Eyes."

Shocked, Dunstan let himself be steered away from the crowd, from the café, and under a mushroom bridge across the road. When they were safely away, he whispered, "Ven?"

A snicker as the prince lifted his goggles, then gave Dunstan the once-over. "What kind of bizarre disguise do you call this? I thought you were more discerning about fashion."

Dunstan clutched the shower curtain close, cheeks flaming. "I had to improvise." Then he grabbed hold of Ven's jacket, yanking him down, making the vagabond prince squawk. "Are you all right? That spear—"

Prying Dunstan's fingers away, Ven moaned, "Ohh, yes, the trials I went through to save your soft, gelatinous life, trusting that you'd return for me!" He mock-swooned, then pulled his jacket back to reveal that the wound was all but gone. "Injuries are boring, and we Jettites are far too busy to be impeded by them. Just slap a wood ear on it and call it a day."

A wood ear? Like the mushroom? "I see." Dunstan folded his arms, acting casual as he looked back out into the street. "Guess I worried about you for nothing. I'll just be on my way then."

Before stepping out from the protection of the shadows, Dunstan felt Ven's tail snap around his forearm, holding him back. A horn sounded — much more sedate than the warning klaxon from earlier. There was no alarming fungi light show.

"You picked the perfect time to infiltrate my kingdom, Bright Eyes," Ven sighed, the melodrama completely gone as he draped an arm around Dunstan, holding him close. "Ever see a March of the Truffledours before?"

"I can confidently say no," Dunstan said, craning his neck to get a better look. Then the tail went around his waist and hoisted Dunstan onto Ven's shoulders.

His eyes went wide.

The road beyond the bridge opened up, and coming down it was a crowd of lizard folk — Jettites — dressed in dazzling duds and brilliant bosh that made the glittering mushroom city dim in comparison. They swirled and swayed and sidestepped to the rhythm on a mushroom platform like a parade float. Behind them, musicians played, donning frills and fronds, and the dancers peeled back to reveal more folk bearing four standards, flanking performers on the highest platform.

Dunstan's glee caught in his throat when he realized that, stitched into the fabric of the standards, were four faces that all of Knockum knew without blinking: Reeve Gris, Darla Denning, Emmerich Kohl, and Lenny Steez. The four passengers of *The Darling Mermaid*, lost forever in Lake Mallion's dark depths.

Or were they?

There was much cheering and adulation from the watching crowd, clapping and shouting as the parade made its approach. "What is this?" Dunstan shouted over the din, feeling something inside him light up as the performers drew closer.

"Don't they have Truffledours in the High-up?" Ven laughed back. "They're only the heroes of Jet! Storytellers. Music-makers. Spectacle savers! Without them, we'd have no Light."

"Spectacle," Dunstan breathed, and as the crowd surged to get a better look, Ven lost his footing, sliding Dunstan back down to the cobbles with a thud.

Ven lifted Dunstan back to his feet, but his grip slipped as Dunstan was bumped sideways and pulled into the crowd moving towards the spectacle.

"Hey!" Ven cried, but although Dunstan tried to excuse himself, to get back through, he was having a tough time doing so *and* keeping his shower curtain disguise from slipping. The crowd was far too giddy to even notice him, let alone let him get back.

"Folk of Jet! You have seen the peril pursuing our city! Now, more than ever, the Higher-ups need Truffledours to keep our Meteorlight singing strong!"

A cheer from the crowd. The speaker was on the tallest mushroom tier, a short, stout lizard that looked more like a jungle creature from one of Luisa's monthly mail-in periodicals. Bedecked in a glittering purple cloak, his tail glowed beneath the scales, and in the air, he drew a figure, leaving a lasting impression like a sparkler.

"Since the betrayal of King Vert, we've struggled! But our hearts cannot be so easily broken!" Pops of light shone above the speaker, and more cheers rang out. "Who among you would join our troupe, and make Jet shine as it once did?"

The next clamouring of folk, raising hands and laughing amongst one another sent Dunstan stumbling. Shocked clawed hands tried to catch him, but his foot caught on his shower curtain, sending him flying through the throng and landing directly in the open street, in front of the fungi tower.

A pregnant pause took over the din. On his hands and knees, Dunstan looked up, glad that his shower curtain had held. A performer helped him up, then uttered a gasp, and he covered himself tighter.

"A volunteer!" the speaker cried. "Send him up to Bash Bellow, and we'll see what he's made of!"

Dunstan held up his hands, cowering. "N-no, no! It was an accident!" But his protests were drowned out by the din; claws and scratchy hands gripped him, passing him like a football to the top tier of the mushroom to stand beside the enigmatic Truffledour, leaving Dunstan as exposed as if he were under every spotlight in the Knockum Upper assembly hall.

Desperately, he searched the crowd to find Ven, and when the speaker, Bash Bellow, reached a four-clawed hand for him, he drew it back with a hiss.

"It . . . it cannot be," he whispered, looking helplessly to the crowd. "Get the Stackers!"

The crowd below, murmuring and now shocked out of its celebratory reverie, parted as a flank of the crimson-clad guards marched through. Their tail spears glinted in the eerie green darkness, the light of them brightest here in the wide-open space where onlookers had gathered on the fringes, bewildered by the new crisis unfolding. Dunstan swore he even saw a few taking bets on the outcome.

Leading them was a formidably tall Jettite, spikes adorning her shoulders, and a sneer plastered across her mouth.

"You there!" the leader shouted, raising a claw at Dunstan. "State your designation!"

Trapped, and utterly bewildered, Dunstan swallowed. "P-pardon?"

She swept her tail out and caught a long javelin in it. Then from the inside of her bloody cloak she produced a black sheet, and read from it: "Be you Jettite, Malachite, Dortite, or Quartz, the Light has a right, in your immediate course." Then she tipped her chin back towards Dunstan, as if it made any sense.

Dunstan felt his feet going cold with dread. "Could you repeat . . . that last one?"

"My crag's on Malachite!" a high-pitched voice from the gathering guessed.

"Bad guess. This one don't even have spikes on their elbows. It's a Quartz from Down-Chaise, the smooth beggars."

The commander snarled. "Quiet!" And with a whip of her tail, the javelin sailed neatly through a fold in the shower curtain, pinning it to the mushroom platform.

Ruined T-shirt, muddy jeans, worn sneakers. Dunstan belatedly covered his face with his hands and peered out of the split fingers, but it was no use. He was exposed.

"A *Higher-up?*"

There it was again, that word — but Dunstan still didn't know if it was a deity, an epitaph, or a curse. Below, nobody moved, or breathed. Any bets in whatever currency they used were off. Dunstan lowered his hands, his mouth twitching in a nervous grin.

Then he shuffled his feet. And started, incomprehensibly and uncontrollably, to dance.

"What's this, then?" Bash Bellow murmured, watching curiously.

"Improvising," Dunstan said between his clenched teeth.

A flourish, mustered from a place Dunstan couldn't quite register. Something was building inside him. At first, he was just trying to get the feeling back into his toes. Then he couldn't help himself. In his mind's eye he was with Luisa and Mariah and Arnault at the Normand Odeon, watching the celluloid flutter with taffeta and quick steps as a big musical number unfolded in crisp Spectracolour. Later they'd all practise the dances under the ash tree in his moms' backyard, falling on each other with giddy joy, but Dunstan, always earnest, would memorize every step, every beat, for nights afterwards. This was a stage, of a kind, and it wasn't his — but maybe it could be, in this dark, glowing world. He pivoted and spun and scat-beat, and short of a partner, he waltzed the full circle around Bash Bellow, the crowd below clapping in surprise.

He spun, bowed, and the mushroom platform below him, glowing only dully beneath his feet, surged like a star, a thunderclap of green light echoing out into the rest of the city's mushroom structures. The crowd gasped, many taking off their masks and head coverings to bask in it, until the light faded back to its eerie quiescence.

"Meteorlight," the commander below seethed. "Stackers! Advance! It's the infiltrator from the Hacklands!"

Dunstan staggered backwards. There was nowhere to go as the Stackers swarmed the float, sending the crowd scattering and giving him no cover.

Then a loud whirring took over. Astride one of those six-wheeled cyclers that had nearly bowled him over earlier was Ven, arcing over the platform from another bridge spanning the parade road. With a snap of glittering tail, Dunstan was yanked into the seat behind the prince, the bike landing with a thud on solid ground as the crowd gaped, awestruck.

"Time to make our grand exit!" Ven cried, and with a surge, the vehicle lit up and took off, leaving their pursuers in their starlit wake.

Luisa stared at her hand, willing herself not to blink. Calming her pulse. Trying to turn off the signal flares of racing thoughts pinging in her mind like flickering candles. Surely it had just been some kind of late-night hallucination. With all the strange things going on, seeing things would be par for the course. Dunstan acting strange, then the quake. The bright green light on the water. The state of panic Knockum was now in, folks terrified to leave their houses, folk terrified to stay, all in the span of a few hours. Luisa should have been out there helping, too, but she needed to be sure. *Concentrate.* Luisa took a breath, and helplessly, thought of Dunstan.

Her finger twitched under the green spark, and she let out a panicked cry, shaking her hand to turn it off again.

"Luisa?" Her father poked his head into the kitchen, glanced from Luisa's face to the living room sofa, where her book on closed circuits and the human body sat facedown beside her. "You're *reading a book* at a time like this?"

Luisa blinked, then remembered the book. She scooped it up and snapped it shut. "It's nothing. I just . . . I don't know!" She threw up her hands, then raced into the kitchen, pretending to look in the fridge. She was frazzled. Historically, she did not get this way. And it was all Dunstan's fault. But she was committed to never mentioning him again, even though his name was flying around town, despite all the other calamities sending everyone stark raving. Luisa may have been the only person who'd seen him since his disappearance . . . surely he'd gone home . . . but what if he hadn't?

She turned so Hector couldn't see, scrutinizing her hands as she thought Dunstan's name again . . . was her skin glowing *green*?

". . . needed at Tantalon Depot," her father was saying, her hearing fading back in from the aggravation caused by her former stubborn ridiculous best friend.

"What? You're going up to the gondola station?" The bullet train of Luisa's thoughts switched tracks to engineering. "Did the quake do something to the pulley?"

"Blew out the rotor on the north line," Hector finished. He was in a closet, gathering his harnesses, stifling a yawn. "It should be an easy fix. Rance and Morton are already up there—"

Luisa was already at his side, a hand on his arm. "Are you sure you should be climbing all the way up the power tower? With your condition?"

Hector blinked. "What condition?"

Luisa opened her mouth to reply, to remind, to accuse him of joking around since he'd been chronically tired for weeks now. The bags under his eyes were dark, she could see that clearly enough. And what had happened the night before still rattled in her mind. *The Door. It's open.* Luisa hemmed the recent events together with a precipitous string she had no control over: Dunstan, the Door, Hector's dream, the quakes, the electrical pulses at Batterborne, and the ones in her fingertips.

A pretty web of oddity, making a perfect circle around her heart.

Luisa wanted to say all this out loud so it wasn't just in her mind, but then her ear twitched at the sound of something dripping, and she whipped her head towards it. "Do you hear that?"

Hector stopped, listened along with her; the drip was steady and sharp. Then he shrugged, the phone started ringing. *He really doesn't hear that?* Maybe Luisa was the crazy one after all. It was one thing to have to keep everything inside about Dunstan, past and present, but now her dad? Was anyone listening to her? How much more would she have to hold in until she burst?

Luisa was already on the brink, and the only way to keep from slipping off the edge was to act. She stormed up to her room, rifled around in her desk drawer, and when she'd found what she needed — what she'd hidden — she smirked.

"You're gonna tell me what's going on for once, Dunstan Cord," she muttered, as she trudged out the back door and headed for his house.

The fastest Dunstan had ever gone was on the train between Tantalon Depot and Luxe Union. There weren't many good spots to joyride in the heavy steel cars that only the Perfects could afford — and anyway, going down the escarpment at speed had sent more than one unlucky teen into Lake Mallion, or the hospital. The car chases and motorbikes on the silver screen were the closest he'd gotten. Once, Dunstan had spotted a delivery motorbike in the busy streets of Luxe and had dreamed after it all the way home. It cut corners and wove through traffic as if pulled taut on the rope of its own rules; it was easy to imagine himself at the handlebars, or clinging to the waist of the driver as they sped off across a dusty desert canyon, chasing the moonlight.

At the present moment, he wasn't too far off. But instead of moonlight, it was *Meteorlight*, glistening and glittering as they streaked past fungi buildings, over spore-crusted bridges, and around hairpin turns that nearly knocked pedestrians off their reptilian haunches. Curses were shouted and fists shaken, but Ven just laughed at them as they raced through tight alleyways, dodging the buildings growing haphazardly out of the black sand.

Suddenly the world tilted, and Ven sped them up to a rooftop at the centre of town, the engine — or whatever propelled the bike — losing its hum as they came to a juddering stop.

"Think we lost 'em," Ven huffed confidently, lifting his goggles and pointing his snout down to look at Dunstan, who was still stiff, clutching Ven's middle. "Good thing I didn't lose *you*, Bright Eyes."

He peeled Dunstan off and helped him stand.

His knees were shakier than a loose tambourine. "From that? That was, well, to me, you know, it was . . ." He was trying to build a confident retort, but when he straightened and looked out from their little rooftop hideaway, his witty one-liners fell away.

"It's not much," Ven quipped, "but it's home."

"Some home," Dunstan breathed. Directly in front of them, sweeping from the ground level thirty feet below, to the highest point of the cavern ceiling above, was a dark tower. It was enrobed in mushrooms, the largest and most grand that Dunstan had yet laid his eyes on — not only did they shimmer green, but opalescent, turning blue and gold and pink by degrees. The tower soared into a point, touching the enormous twin stalactite above it. Dunstan had to arch himself nearly in half to get an understanding of the scope above.

A thunderous roar sent him toppling, but Ven, ever ready, put a hand out and caught him in the small of his back, a clumsy dip, as the clattering cavalcade streaked by. Though partly upside down, Dunstan recognized what it was immediately; after all, they had something quite like it in Knockum.

"A tramway?" He leapt for the edge of the roof and its banister, watching a shuttle car shiver down a line of cable. Dunstan recalled seeing similar cables on their mad escape only last night. The cables glittered like spiderwebs, crisscrossing over the whole city, occupied with individuals coming and going. A city alive, with a heartbeat all its own. This truly was the world of Dunstan's dreams.

"I suppose you don't have Stettle Beetles where you're from." Ven shrugged nonchalantly. "Critters the size of . . . well, there isn't much else bigger than them. They shed their shells every quarter or so. Shells make for perfect vehicles — quick, not easily damaged—"

"And pretty," Dunstan said admiringly, peeking below at a mushroom platform where Jettites leisurely got on and off. He turned to Ven, beaming. "Your geodom is incredible!"

Ven faltered, then picked an invisible mote off his shoulder. "It's fine." This must be old hat to Ven, then Dunstan lurched as the prince leaned in. "But I'd rather see your home. What's it like?

How many of you are there? And do you have an endless supply of rock slugs so you never go hungry?"

"Hungry for *slugs*?" Dunstan laughed, then his stomach gave him away, and it was Ven's turn at mirth. "I'm starving, as it happens. But I don't think I could handle slugs."

Ven's tail swept up and down languidly. "I suppose we can't run away to the High-up on an empty stomach," he said, rubbing his chin, and before Dunstan could ask him to clarify, the tail caught him around the shoulder, pulling him in. "By the way, what *was* that back there? Jettites are so prone to chatter; I've never seen them shut up that long, even during a spectacle!"

Dunstan blinked, his smile slow, cheeks flaring. "Oh, ah, well . . . I mean it wasn't my *best* performance, but for being put on the spot . . ." Stress had made him dance, but the manic energy of a good performance had brought the flourish — and maybe something supernatural had lent a hand. "Guess you saw it all, eh?"

Ven let out a hearty *ha!* "*Everyone* saw that. All of Jet will be talking about it for weeks, which takes the heat off me, for once."

"Right, I forgot. Not the most popular prince." Dunstan nodded sagely, then found the tail clenching tighter and steering him around in a full circle, to show the building directly opposite them.

"Not exactly, no," the prince answered, pointing at an enormous mural with a familiar face filling up the dark brickwork. Ven leaned down and put himself parallel to it. "Whatcha think? Good likeness?"

Beneath the portrait of the vagabond prince, in the odd scratchy lettering Dunstan had noticed on other buildings and signs, the words clarified: VILLAIN VEN.

"*Villain* is such a strong word. And a misnomer." Dunstan tutted. He smiled, though, because how could he know for sure. "I hope it is, anyway."

Ven cocked his finely bladed, tiara-horned head, eyes flickering their sideways blink before he let the smile creep across his scaly face. "Don't we all," he countered, before patting Dunstan's bare forearms down with his rough hands and claws, sending Dunstan's heart into spasms. "Now, let's get you some grub, give you a quick tour, and off we'll go!"

Ven was already striding back to the bike, which Dunstan noticed was hewn from some kind of twisted roots; its wheels, if they could be called that, were fluttering mushrooms on gnarled spokes. "Ah, sorry, let me just clarify. We're going where?"

"To your place, Truffledour!" Ven chirped, all cheer, mounting up. "You invited me, remember?"

Dunstan's mind whirled. Everything was happening very quickly. When he thought it'd all been a delusion, the invitation had been genuine. "My place?" He pointed upwards. "You mean—"

"To the High-up, where else? There's nothing around here for me, that's for sure!" Ven shook his head, as if Dunstan was playing a mean joke. "You and I don't belong here. We both want to chart our own courses. And you have the Meteorlight, which means the Door will listen to you, so we can be out of this heap of shrooms before the snail tea's boiled."

"Glad we'll be missing that," Dunstan quipped. "But . . . don't you think you'd . . . stand out a little bit, in my world?" Visions of the lightkeepers on high alert, bringing in the Brindlewatch Guard to ferry Ven off to a secret lab made Dunstan all but shudder. "And anyway, Jet is amazing! Really, Knockum pales in comparison. You're not missing much."

Ven blinked slowly, brow furrowing and head tilting backwards. He slid off the bike, hands behind his back, as he strode and bent to Dunstan, the pause slightly menacing. "Are you going back on your promise, Bright Eyes? After I've saved your dainty hide — twice, by my count?"

"Didn't think there was a price tag . . ." Dunstan couldn't help but mutter, his little daydream of their budding romance souring. This was starting to sound like a Moss repeat. Why did he have to go for the bad boys? "Listen, it's not that. It's just . . ." Arms open, genuinely at a loss, all he could say was, "I only just got here. And Jet's the city of my *dreams*. Can't we stay a little longer?"

"Hmph. You want me to show you around?" Ven straightened, looking down at Dunstan with his striking opal eyes. Then the assessment broke with a grin. "What will you give me, then?"

Dunstan rubbed a hand over his mouth, questing in his pockets and coming up with nothing. Then he snapped his fingers. "I can give you . . . this!" He grabbed at Ven's hand with his, took the other down and put it on his waist, then forced them both to straighten. "Just follow my lead, scale-foot."

"Scale-foot? You've got some nerve!" Ven teased. "What do I . . . ?"

"Just relax," Dunstan said, matter-of-factly. "I wouldn't steer you wrong." He nodded and began counting out the steps as he pulled them along: one two three, one two three.

Ven stumbled, nearly tripping them both on his tail, before he caught on. "Oh, this is what you were doing with Bash Bellow, right? Like this?"

Dunstan laughed out loud. "Sure, but stop trying to take the lead!"

They both laughed, grappling a bit, until Ven took over, and when they split apart, they found themselves improvising a shining new choreography. "You sure you aren't a singing prince, too?" Dunstan asked, flourishing a kick-step. "*Princes for Fools* is one of my favourites . . ."

The mushroom fronds encircling their little black sand beach swayed along as Dunstan hummed the music, leaning in and glowing bright. Ven picked Dunstan up and swung him around in a half-circle, and Dunstan cried, "You're a natural!"

Then the mushrooms' light faded as Ven slowed suddenly, putting Dunstan gently back on his feet as the smile left his scales. He turned back towards the massive tower at the centre of the city, the peak of it strobing its haunting green glow in time with Dunstan's pulse.

Dunstan blinked, lifting a hand but not reaching out altogether. "Did I say something wrong?"

The easy smile returned, and Ven simply shrugged. "I envy you, is all."

"Me?" Dunstan cried. "C'mon! You're a bloody *prince*! A runaway one, at that, which makes your life more interesting than mine by at least triple. I'm just copying dance steps from a movie."

Ven sighed, stretching his long neck to stare back towards town. Perfect, maudlin symmetry in every scale. When he looked back at Dunstan, smiling with a touching sadness only the best screen actors could muster, Dunstan felt his overactive sense of romance flutter.

"Prince in name only, at present," he clarified, then he pointed towards the magnificent tower. "The people who run things now aren't very interested in the former royal family. That's where we used to live, you know. The Tallest Tor."

Dunstan eyed it; it really was the grandest place in the city. "Who lives there now?"

The sad smile transformed so quickly into biting malice that Dunstan took a step back. "You mentioned his name when we met."

Dunstan squinted, staring at the tower again as if it'd jog his memory. Then he recalled the banners at the parade Ven had rescued him from, and the pieces clicked. "Reeve Gris? And the Sunken Three?"

"Sunken? Well, whatever you call them, that's them. Since everything went wrong, and the Meteorlight escaped . . . well, now they're running things. And Jet likes it that way. So I'm superfluous." He leaned casually against the railing, winking at Dunstan. "It's something like destiny that the rest of the Meteorlight came back, though. Inside a Higher-up Truffledour, no less." A wag of the claw under Dunstan's nose. "Just don't go supplanting me like the other ones did the second they arrived."

So Reeve, Darla, Emmerich, and Lenny were the Higher-ups that Dunstan had been hearing about . . . they'd been down here all these years, ruling Jet? Dunstan felt a sudden surge of jealousy, as well as urgency, in the swell of questions.

"Listen, I've no idea how *this* got into me. And I'd give it back, if I could." He stopped, frowning. "Wait. Can I?"

Ven shook his head. "Only the Light has the right, Bright Eyes. It's chosen you, so you're stuck with it." A flick of a forked tongue.

"But I don't mind being stuck with a Higher-up like you, so it's a bargain for me, isn't it?"

Dunstan sidestepped the flirt. "Okay, but . . . let me just think for a second." Dunstan paced, pressing his fingers into his temples. "Reeve and the others are *here*. I can open the Door in the lake. *You* don't want *them* here . . . why don't we just go to the tor, talk to them, and I take them back to Knockum?" The idea bloomed like the fungus holding the city below them together, and he grabbed at Ven's lapels. "Then you can get your throne back, and I can come visit! There. I solved it."

Ven pried Dunstan's fingers off his lapels with his claws, careful not to scratch. "We won't be doing any of that," he said airily. He didn't let go of Dunstan's hands, though.

"Why not?" Dunstan asked. "You could have your throne back—"

"But not my *freedom*." Ven cut him off, maybe too sharply, and Dunstan looked away, embarrassed at obviously saying the wrong thing.

Ven sighed, linking his hands over his scaly head. "It's not that simple. The Higher-ups don't want to leave. Don't you think they would have tried by now?" Dunstan opened his mouth to protest, but Ven went on. "And if they catch you, your freedom will be stripped away, too. Trust me. There's nothing here for me. But there's so much more out there; you're the proof of that. So let's play tourist, then get going."

He grasped Dunstan by the hand. Jerked from his reverie of swirling questions, he stumbled, until Ven spun and elegantly lifted him onto the velocipede's seat.

"Your highest," Ven grinned, and with a snort, Dunstan did a mock curtsey.

"Your vagrancy," he retorted. "But you promise to answer all my questions on our little tour, right?"

"As long as they aren't vexing," Ven promised, climbing on in front of him. "And as long as you hold up your end of the bargain and help me escape to the High-up when you've had your fill of this miserable place."

Miserable? Whatever Ven had been through, to condemn Jet like that, his own kingdom . . . Dunstan shook his head. He wasn't about to balk again. Maybe it'd come up later. "Deal."

The bike hummed back to life, and as Dunstan whooped, grabbing back onto Ven for dear life, he realized that it hovered slightly off the ground, the spokes glowing brighter the longer he stared.

"It goes faster the more fun you're having," Ven shouted, then he pointed them towards the edge of the rooftop. "Hold on tight, Bright Eyes!"

And off they sped, a streak of light and laughing wonder, into the Geodom of Jet.

SCENE 6

MUSHROOMS AND MELLIFLUOUSNESS

"Well? Where is it?"

Korman Yiles blinked. "What do you mean, Ms. Cord? It's where it's always parked. Dock 117." But as Korman pointed, his bent finger faltered, for the dock in question, viewed through the office windows, was empty.

He began nervously flipping through papers, then his cheeks went red. "I . . . Forgive me, there are all these boats that capsized during the quake and . . . yours is probably one of them."

Ada sighed, surveying the marina, which, like the rest of Knockum, was in utter chaos. She shouldn't have been so sharp with Korman. He may be enormous in both height and size, but he was a delicate oyster that needed patting at the best of times. And this certainly was less than the best.

"It's fine," Ada lied, because, while she was as rattled as everyone else, she was still aiming to look resolved. "How are things here? What's the word from on high?"

There had been a few successive shockwaves since Dunstan had vanished two hours ago, but nothing as harsh. The summer sun was still hanging high, and there was lots of light left, but Ada didn't want to try to find Dunstan in the dark, especially on the lake, when it seemed to be in a mood. She'd be no good to her son if she drowned.

Yet something inside her was pulling her to the water. And before she risked herself on it, she needed answers. She needed to see the file from the night Dunstan was born, when she first saw that green light on the lake, and to understand if it was the nucleus around which all this chaos was turning.

"This is like nothing that's ever happened before!" Korman seemed both elated and terrified and mesmerized by turns. "The chain of command is handling outside help, but we're looking for a precedent. I've been tasked with going back through all the lightkeeper Immaculata logs. I made it back three hundred years, and there has never been seismic activity in this area. It just doesn't make sense!"

Ada frowned. Surely someone had seen the green light shooting out of the centre of the lake today? Surely someone would have made the connection to her report from fifteen years ago?

"If you've gone through them all, can I pull a report? From fifteen years ago, one of my own logs—"

But Korman held up his hands. "No can do, Ms. Cord. The Brindlewatch Guard isn't involved yet, but Morag said we weren't to share our findings with anyone outside this lightkeeper unit, or let documents leave the premises." He leaned in, eyes darting. "Seems kind of like there's a bit of a conspiracy swirling, with some folk talking of Grislies playing around where they ought not to."

Ada's mouth quirked. "The Grislies? You mean the supper club that trades one urban legend for another about the supposed Door in Lake Mallion?" But even as she said it, Ada realized she shouldn't discount the local crazies and their theories. After all, hadn't her son lately vanished from her bathroom, without a trace, in an eerie glow only she'd seen?

Korman lifted a shoulder. "You never know. Strange things only started happening in this town after Reeve Gris took that boat and disappeared . . ."

Ada hoped Korman wasn't a Grisly, but she didn't dare say as much. Their beliefs were mostly benign but bordered on frantic; talk of opening the Door in the lake and bringing Reeve back to solve all of Knockum's problems . . . as if they didn't have them before he vanished. Everyone was always looking for a magic bullet. And Lorraine had warned her to stay out of it when Myrtle Richler came a-knocking with her pamphlets.

This lightkeeper station, the one Ada had worked in for well over a decade, was like her second home. It was a well-oiled machine, a large tower of multiple levels and departments, usually quiet. But today, the cable girls were frantically plugging cords in and out as they connected calls from different stations along the lake. Ticker tape strung out on the floor, and someone had pulled out an old seismograph, desperate to get it to work. From Korman's office window, Ada looked down at the marina below. Folk were racing up and down docks, checking on skiff damage, reporting on boats that had left and hadn't docked yet, gathering supplies for anyone affected on the shore and towards the escarpment.

The person she needed was Morag, her mentor. But for now, she wasn't going to leave here empty-handed. "Anyway Korman, all told, I need that file, and a boat."

"I'm sorry, Ms. Cord," he apologized again. "I'm serious about the files, even if you penned them. And boats aren't allowed to leave, either. Strict orders. Safety. Protocols. You understand." Then another lightkeeper ran up, out of breath, with a sheaf of paperwork to dump on Korman's desk.

Korman groaned. "Not the Richler boat again. Honestly, we don't have the resources right now to go and get it . . ."

Ada glanced at the pile. "What's happened now?"

Unable to filter his frustration, Korman said, "One of Mender Richler's boats turned up in Caller's Cove last night. Has to be moved. But honestly, everyone is just trying to hold things together on the Mallion perimeter with these quakes. We don't have anyone to—"

"I'll go get it for you, Korman," Ada cut in sweetly. "But I need to see my logs before I do."

Korman had been sweating before, and when a bead went down his brow, he angrily swept it away. "I really can't . . ."

Ada leaned in, glancing around furtively. "This is a matter of utmost urgency, Korman. And it may be the ticket to turn the tide on the chaos here. Morag trusted me with this mission. Will you help me?"

Normally Ada wasn't much for pantomiming, but she was desperate, and taking a page out of Dunstan's book might just lead to bringing him home.

Korman, too, took on an air of suspicion as he looked all around him, but everyone was far too distracted. "You mean, Ms. Gunn told you to—"

"Protocol," Ada hissed, and Korman visibly shrank. "You understand."

All Korman could do was nod, and Ada's heart raced as he handed her a key, gesturing with his head to the log archive.

Maybe Dunstan gets his flourish from me, after all . . .

Ada thanked him, promised again to retrieve the Richler boat, and paced off. She didn't mention her plan to temporarily *borrow* said boat, but any skiff in a storm. And she wasn't about to leave the lakeside until she dragged her son back from the depths of the mystery grasping Knockum in its claws.

Commander Vora had gone off to reconnoitre alone. As she dashed up the cliff with precise claw-strikes, coming out on a promontory to survey this side of the borough, she clenched her jaw, mind racing. She needed to gather not only her thoughts, but the last shreds of her patience. The image of Prince Ven snatching the wayward Higher-up and riding off with him made her cold blood boil. What was he playing at?

Below, the Revels went on. During Jet's time of highest hope, a fleshy fugitive and the rogue hiding him were aggravations she didn't need. The elders had suggested perhaps pausing the Revels to look for them. After all, it seemed to be a repeat of when their current rulers had arrived — invaders from a different world, using the Meteorlight. It could be their salvation, if the Light had truly returned to the city . . .

But when Vora looked to the Tallest Tor, where the Higher-ups' last remaining Light hung at the peak, dimming imperceptibly each day, she wondered if there was an alternative to bringing this Dunstan Cord before them, to pulling the Light out of him.

It hadn't exactly gone to plan with the others, after all.

"Commander?"

Vora tensed but didn't turn. She could hear Decca struggling up the rock face for a few moments now. "What is it, Stackling?"

From the corner of her eye, she saw the young Stacker wince, but she soldiered on. "I was, er, wondering something . . ." Vora shut her eyes, counting slowly in her head, taking a deep breath as she readied for one of the nestling's many wandering diatribes. "Once we catch this Higher-up, what will we do with him, exactly?"

Vora did turn then, eyes blazing. It was absurd to imagine Decca of all Jetittes reading anyone's thoughts, yet here she'd caught Vora thinking the very same thing.

"We will take him to the Higher-ups, Stackling! They will deal with him accordingly." Her nostrils flared, hoping her tone would cut off any further inquiries.

Alas. "Right, sure, of course, I was just *thinking*, since he may have Meteorlight in him, and he also seemed to be acting like a Truffledour, maybe we should just *explain* to him that he should perform a little more, and maybe that would strengthen Jet's foundations, and *then* we—"

Decca squeaked as Vora swept her up in her tail, boots wheeling, as she held the Stackling over the edge of the promontory.

"This is your city, Decca," Vora said calmly, evenly, as the terrified Stackling whimpered and clutched at her commander's spikes. "Stackers work in Jet's interest. *Not* in the interest or comfort of interlopers who hoard our ancestral power. Do you think he deserves it more than we do?"

Decca shook her head frantically, and Vora smiled. "I didn't think so. But you seem to be doing an awful lot of thinking, and not enough doing."

She tossed Decca back to the sand behind her, with barely a backwards glance as she thumped to the ground. "Now, have you swept the lower canyon, yet?" When no response was immediate, Vora spun, lit with fury. "*Well?*"

Decca scrambled to her feet, saluted. "No ma'am! But I will ma'am! Right away, ma'am!"

Vora watched her go, holding her in a steely glare. And when the Stackling was finally away, she turned back to the city, let her scales relax, and sighed miserably.

"I hope you know what you're doing, Ven," Vora muttered. "For all our sakes."

What made Luisa angrier was that the dripping didn't cease. In fact, after the latest tremor that sent Knockum reeling, it got louder. And Luisa was beyond holding it in by now. Knockumites were standing outside their houses, gossiping with neighbours, fretting about the quakes, lawns covered in all the broken bric-a-brac that had fallen from shelves, or pieces of walls that had come clean off in the aftermath. Chins wagged about *What's going on, what's going to happen next, is the escarpment going to come down on our heads?* And every time Luisa passed someone, she asked, *Do you hear that?* because the dripping refused to leave her alone. All she got in return were odd looks, nervous smiles, and a few folks taking her aside to ask if she'd seen the Cord boy.

As if that was all Luisa was good for, keeping tabs on that *brat*.

"No." Luisa smiled, teeth cracking tight. "But when I find him, he's dead meat."

When she finally neared the Cord house, she hesitated at the corner of the block. Maybe she should talk to Ada first . . . but honestly, she couldn't handle it, couldn't be fake-polite, and couldn't provide any made-up excuse as to why she and Dunstan had suddenly broken up as friends. No. She wouldn't be derailed. She was going to let it all out, and Dunstan was going to hear it, once and for all.

Determined to head straight for the treehouse, Luisa stopped dead when she saw a figure standing in the driveway already, who turned at her approach, leaving her no chance to backtrack. The mustard-yellow coat, the sash, and the silk covers from head to neck were a dead giveaway.

Coral Frakes.

"Luisa Alvarez," she said smoothly, clear enough for the street to hear, even over the post-quake chaos. "Were you here to pay a visit to Dunstan, too?"

Luisa thrust her afflicted hands in her pockets, shrugging, the lies coming far too easily despite the promise she'd just made to herself. "Yes, well, we're, um. We're friends, so, I just wanted to make sure he was okay. With the runaway rumours and all."

Coral nodded, striding up the driveway and making for the side yard. "What a business. What a strangely timed one, at that."

Luisa had only had a few conversations with Coral Frakes over the years, and most of them were somewhat riddle-like. Coral was an enigma in that she was one of the town's leaders, yet she didn't go out much. Like a sage in a mountain stronghold, everyone revered her experience and opinions, but kept their distance. Luisa often thought how lonely that must be.

"At any rate, I saw him earlier," Coral went on. "He's fine. But it seems that neither Dunstan nor Ada are home at the moment." Coral stopped at the gate that would lead into the backyard, a large, finely gloved hand poised on the latch. "So perhaps you should go home."

A pointed order. Luisa clenched her hands in her pockets. True, if Dunstan wasn't here, then what was the point? But curiosity got the better of her. "If no one's here, then why are you?"

Suddenly, inside of Luisa's ear, the dripping grew louder.

"Because of *that*," Coral said, turning her masked head sharply at the sound.

"You can hear it, too?" Luisa barked, thrusting her hands in the air. "I thought I was going crazy!"

Luisa balked as Coral stared at her, eyes unknowable behind her dark sunglasses. "You're not," Coral said slowly. "But it's odd." Something flickered in Luisa's peripheral vision, and she moved Coral's hand aside to turn the latch herself, letting them both into the backyard as she pointed. "Odder than *that?*"

A bright light strobed from the treehouse's single window. Someone was up there.

"Dunstan!" Luisa shouted, rushing past Coral as the light flickered and turned green.

"Luisa, stop!" Coral snapped, pulling her away from the ladder she was about to climb. "It's . . . it could be unsafe. Wasn't that the same light shining on Lake Mallion during the quake earlier?"

Luisa frowned, looking from Coral into the treehouse. "Maybe," she said. "But when Dunstan saw it, he took off. If it's unsafe, and he's up there, we need to investigate."

The dripping grew louder, more insistent, and while Coral took her sweet time to make up her mind, Luisa was already climbing the ladder two rungs at a time. Each droplet was now a staccato tempo, stuck in her head like one of Dunstan's bad show tunes, keeping time with memories, summers spent up there listening to records and reading comics and making costumes and—

The ladder swung hard suddenly, and Luisa looked down, seeing Coral scaling it quickly behind her. She reached for the trap door above, heaved it over her head, and burst through.

"Dunstan Cord, I'm gonna smack you so hard you end up in Oiros City—!"

But the treehouse was empty. Luisa pulled herself inside, offering to help Coral, but she waved it off, pulling herself rather lithely into the cramped space despite her foreboding height and fashionable duds.

The place looked like it had been turned over, blankets askew and hidey holes exposed. *He must have been serious about running off*, she mused, before the dripping returned, and she and Coral canted their heads up.

"What . . ." Luisa croaked. "Is that?"

On the ceiling of the treehouse was . . . a puddle? It was defying gravity, nestled amongst the many two-by-fours and juvenile dreams and whatever else kept the roof up.

Drip. Coral flinched. The centre of the puddle rippled. The dripping was coming from the other side of the massive puddle, dark in the centre, with pin dot lights glowing green as the water shifted.

"That," Coral said, "is a problem that can't easily be undone." Then her gloved hand snapped out, grabbing Luisa's. She looked it over.

"Hey!" She tried to snatch it back, but Coral held on. A green spark, large as a worm, languidly slid over Luisa's hand, then shot up into the puddle above them. In the shallows, it revealed something dark but solid, made of many symmetrical facets. The edges of it glowed green.

Beneath the roots of the ash tree, the ground shivered, and Luisa and Coral split apart.

She stared at the masked woman, perplexed, afraid, holding her own wrist. "What's happening to me? To this town?" It didn't matter that Coral had seen and now knew Luisa's secret ailment. She wanted answers more than to hide. And the way Coral's shoulders slumped as she stared helplessly up at the puddle in the treehouse ceiling told Luisa she was *in the know.*

After a long pause, she sighed. "Something I thought would never happen again. But clearly your friend had other plans."

"*Dunstan?*" Luisa blurted. "Dunstan caused all this? The quakes? The weird light? *This?*" She gestured at the puddle, her fingers sending more sparks into it. The water leapt, and Coral grabbed hold of Luisa, holding her back as the ground shook again, and the black solid thing beyond the water groaned.

"It doesn't make *sense*," Coral said to herself, then directed at the dark thing waiting in the strange shallow hanging over their heads, "You got what you wanted all those years ago! Why aren't you satisfied?"

"All those years . . ." Luisa started, but the flares in her active mind made the connections for her. "Wait. Is that the Door in Lake Mallion?" She squinted, trying to get a better look, and she had the creeping feeling that as she stared, the dark thing stared back. "But how? We're miles from the shore! And clearly this . . . this can't be . . ." But the water smelled brackish, with a tinge of motor oil, of lakeweed. Luisa knew that this was the water of Lake Mallion as much as she knew she wasn't going loco.

"This is indeed the Door," Coral confirmed grimly. "As you can see, it has a mind of its own. It goes where it's called. It goes where the Light is."

She wanted to say, *But all this is just an urban legend! A town fairy tale for bored fishkids and weirdo suburban semi-cultists.* More than that, Luisa wanted to talk to Dunstan. That she was in their childhood playground, mulling this over with the eccentric town shut-in, was by far the strangest part of this ordeal.

Instead she asked, "Does this have something to do with Reeve Gris and the disappearance? If you know something, why have you kept it secret all this time?" Then she stood up, her nose nearly at the water, her sparking hand reaching. "And what's on the other side of that Door?"

As if it knew they were talking about it, the Door groaned low, asking a question that neither could understand. Coral took Luisa's hand more gently this time, pulling it away from the water.

"I'm sorry," she said. "There are some things I just . . . can't say. But know this: if Dunstan Cord went through that Door, then the trouble has only just started." She clasped Luisa's hand with both of hers then and dipped her head. "You have to bring him back, before it gets worse."

"What? Me?" She ripped away, backing up towards the trap door in the floor. Going after Dunstan had been her original intention today, sure, but not like *this*. "If you know so much about this Door stuff, shouldn't it be you going in there?"

"Doors need keys. I don't have one." She jerked her chin at Luisa's hands. "But you do."

Her fingertips sparked, livelier now, keeping time with her heartbeat as the green bolts slid from one finger to the next, a rollicking cascade.

Drip, drip. The Door groaned louder.

Luisa clenched her fists. "There's no way in Beulah's bountiful Brindlewatch that I'm going through that — that thing!" She thrust her hands under her arms.

"You have to *try*," Coral urged. "Bring your friend back here, so we can make sure this Door stays closed." They both stared deeper into the water. "Before it swallows this entire town."

"He's not really my friend," she muttered.

"Then do it for the rest of Knockum," Coral replied. "Or you can do it for yourself." Luisa turned at that, eyes wide. "Think of the self-satisfaction you can get from dragging Dunstan Cord back to his betters. Revenge is a good motivator, or so I hear."

Revenge. That's not strictly what Luisa wanted. Retribution, maybe, for how Dunstan had dumped her and their friends with no explanation. She did, deep down, want to help him, which made her madder.

As she tied her long dark hair into a tight bun, face set, she said, "I don't want revenge. But I *do* want to tell him, *I told you so.*"

She walked past Coral, underneath the very centre of the ceiling puddle, and raised her hands. Her fingertips, brushing the shallows, lit up green, and the facets that comprised the Door lifted, swirling away, eager to open.

"And what if he doesn't want to come back with me?" Luisa asked, jaw set, not wanting to imagine the answer.

"He has to," Coral answered gravely. "If you want that *thing* out of you, and him, and put back into its box, you'll do me this kindness."

Too many questions. Too many reasons not to do this. But Dunstan's heady dreams of heroism and plays of fancy had rubbed off on Luisa; she *wanted* to go through the Door.

Luisa took a huge gulp of air and slowly plunged her whole face into the puddle in the treehouse ceiling. Then, as if someone had grabbed her by the shoulders, she found herself pulled upwards, downwards, and end over end, into the glowing water.

It's not as if they'll miss them, Ven had said about the clothes he'd planned to secret from a line outside someone's house — or what Dunstan supposed was a house as they streaked past them on the velocipede. The homes here were all built into the sides of hills, jetties, or below the ground they trod. The spires peppering the cityscape weren't often lived in, like the skyscrapers Dunstan tried to describe to Ven — *The sky? What's that?* They were for capturing and keeping Meteorlight.

"It's an energy source, really," Ven had said as they cruised, searching for a hiding spot for the velocipede, and for a requisite costume change. "But every single Jettite has a little bit of it inside them. It's what makes us . . . us! Now how you got it, well, you said you didn't know — but *I know*, and every other hatchling from here to Dark Rock Fifth knows, that it was stolen by the Betrayer King Vert and escaped to the world above."

The king? Dunstan put the pieces together a little too quickly. "You mean—"

"My father," Ven finished for him, tone sharpened with chagrin. "Long ago, the Meteorlight fell here from higher than Higher-up. And when it crashed into the rock, it went deep into it, and all the great shrooms unfurled and blossomed in its path. And that's where my ancestors came from. Or so they say. I was never much for sitting still during lectures. I was a bad prince back then." A quirking smile. "Even worse than I am now."

Ven flashed his tongue and teeth, as if he was boring himself with the history lesson, the bike streaking them through the brilliant cityscape as if they were but a firefly on its back.

"The little show you did back there? Folk haven't seen anything like that since the Meteorlight escaped! What little we have left is controlled by the Higher-ups, and amplified by the Truffledours. See that?" He pointed towards the Tallest Tor, and the throbbing beacon of light at its peak. "It used to shine so brightly, you couldn't look at it! Jet was a grand geodom. Now we live off spore-scraps the Higher-ups deign to provide." A grimace, then he arched a glance down to Dunstan that made him swallow. "But now it's back. In the shape of you."

They'd landed on a ledge of mushrooms jutting out from a cliff beneath what looked like a shopping district but smelled like an eatery. Whatever they served, Dunstan would eat it gladly, even slugs at this point. Ven had scampered off, promising food and fashion on his return, and Dunstan was left alone with his thoughts.

His whirling, swirling, impossible thoughts. *What have I gotten myself into?* mixed with *How can I stay here forever without being imprisoned or filleted?* He sifted through what he *did* know: this Meteorlight stuff inside him was a precious commodity. Maybe one he could leverage. And it was the perfect portmanteau: a light from a meteor. Higher than Higher-up probably meant *space*. And a meteorite had formed Lake Mallion, after all. Every kid in town knew that — the Falling Star Festival, which took place every summer, celebrated it.

Before Ven had run off, Dunstan had tried to explain the concept of space, of the meteor, and Ven nodded eagerly, but noted that when it landed, its heart was broken, and all that was left of it was . . .

The Door in Lake Mallion.

So was the Door . . . the old meteor? And the Light it carried . . . it sounded *alive*. It was sort of romantic, if lights and doors had feelings. Stories upon stories from two different worlds, overlapping, diverging, and intersecting again. A lost entryway and Dunstan had the key. With that kind of destiny, how could he *not* make anything of it? While he waited seated on his mushroom cap, sneakers dangling into the dark below, he traced the lines of his hands. A faint sparkle of green glistened in the wrinkles, telling a fortune that Dunstan couldn't interpret.

He had felt this Meteorlight not only moving through him on that fungi parade float, but somehow whispering, encouraging, like the acting coach he likely needed. And it had buoyed him into flashing favour with the folk all around him. *Truffledours amplify the Light to keep Jet going.* Could he use this Meteorlight further, to grasp the life he always dreamed of?

A shudder. Then a very definite shake. Dunstan tensed and looked all around, heard a concussive thudding as the rock at his back went on vibrating.

"Ven?" he said, maybe a little too quietly. Then it became seismic, like the quake Dunstan had experienced in Knockum in front of Luisa's house. He clung to the cliff, just a little too tall to scale, and when he glanced down at the mushroom ledge beneath his feet, he saw the fungi's green glow slowly going out. Turning black.

"*Ven!*" Dunstan screamed, as the mushrooms on either side of him began to fizzle, black out, and crumble off the cliffside. Just as the mushroom around him began to fall away, a familiar scaled tail snapped around his forearm, yanking him up the cliffside and dangling him in front of Ven's side-blinking, tilted face.

"Must you get into a scrape every time I turn around?" he managed, before a waving jolt went through the ground and upended them both into a heap.

Blearily, Dunstan managed to lift his head from Ven's chest where it'd landed, watching as a huge sluice of water cascaded from the dark cavern ceiling and into the space where he'd just been standing, the force of it slicing the rock directly in front of them like it was warm butter.

Even when the shaking ceased, Dunstan could still feel the vibrations in his teeth. He looked down, saw he was splayed on top of a much-maligned Ven, and scrambled off.

"Does uh, that happen often?" he managed, teeth still vibrating, as Ven sat up stiffly.

"It's a recent development," Ven muttered, then he looked between his hands, which Dunstan only now realized were each clutching something. "At least the food and the disguise made it through."

He handed both over to Dunstan, then crawled to the edge, surveying the damage. "We'd better hightail it out of here, before the Stackers come for damage control . . ."

Although he'd been down here a while, Dunstan glanced nervously upwards, remembering that above this gloriously glittering metropolis was several quadrillion gallons of water. But maybe Jet, and the unsuspecting citizens living in it, weren't aware of that. "That happened in the square earlier, too, after I arrived . . ." He didn't want to imagine that it had been *his* fault but didn't want to discount it, either. "Do you know why the cavern is suddenly springing a leak?"

Stretching, Ven shrugged. "The Elders seem to think it's the foundations weakening. The city is built on the root network of our mushrooms. The mushrooms rely on the Meteorlight . . ."

"And the Meteorlight is inside me," Dunstan finished. "Well, not all of it, right?"

"Quick study." Ven grinned, then he gestured to the bowl in Dunstan's hands. "Now, eat up, suit up, and we can take a tour before it all comes crashing down around us."

Dunstan stared into the warm, hollowed-out rock in his hands. "I'd ask what this is, but it smells good, and maybe I don't want to know." He tucked in tentatively at first, then inhaled the bowl's contents, glancing at Ven with a whiff of consternation. "Aren't you going to have any?"

"Oh, I wouldn't touch that stuff, but it seemed up your alley." His face only stayed mild for a second, though, until he broke into laughter. "Don't worry about me, Higher-up! I can eat *plenty* when we get to your world!"

The earlier creeping chill became a smaller, but not easily ignored, wave of panic. "Right. I suppose a prince wouldn't mind eating hot dogs if you didn't know they weren't haute cuisine."

"I'd eat that, too," Ven sniffed.

They both turned, startled, at the sounds of folk racing towards the cliff on the other side of the canyon, to assess the damage. Amongst them were the flashing red of the Stackers, and Dunstan immediately dropped his bowl, snatching up his disguise as Ven threw himself in front of him.

"Quick, get changed!" he urged, and Dunstan faltered.

"Right here?" he squeaked, looking around for somewhere darker, a little more private. "I'm not going to *get changed* in front of you!"

"Why not?" Ven countered, head tilting, and Dunstan didn't want to know what the prince was thinking as he scrambled out from under him and went behind a clot of frothy mushrooms climbing up a nearby building.

"Because!" was all Dunstan managed as Ven moved to follow, until he blurted, "It's not like you're my *boyfriend*."

Dunstan immediately regretted that, because it unleashed a new cavalcade of questions. "Boyfriend? What's that? Does it mean *valiant and very svelte protector and also feeder of Higher-ups*? If so, then yes, fairly sure I am, given the volume of scrapes I've pulled you out of." Then, with one last click of his forked tongue, Ven covered his eyes and turned away, smirk contagious and cheeky. "There. Privacy. I'd say I'd keep watch, but you have your priorities."

Huffing, Dunstan hid himself as much as possible, kicking himself internally as he shimmied out of his jeans and crusty T-shirt. *Boyfriend? What in the waters did I say that for?* He cast a glance over his shoulder, caught Ven peeping through his claws, and tripped further away to save what little pride he had left.

He re-emerged after he was changed. Lita Living, it was cold down here, and Dunstan was grateful for the coat, dark royal purple and sparkling with mica crystals woven throughout the fabric. The goggles he kept on his head for now, offsetting his messy red curls as he admired himself in a partial twirl. In the glowing light of his fungi change room, the crystals did a shimmering wave.

"Even the clothes in Jet are spectacular!" Dunstan crooned, but when he turned towards Ven, the prince was standing at the edge of the cliff, hands behind his back, staring down at the destruction. He'd seemed nonchalant about it before, but now he had a look of concern, maybe even devastation, as Dunstan joined his side.

He cleared his throat. "Things aren't going well down here, are they?"

Ven jerked slightly, surprised, then snorted. "Nope. Haven't been for a while." Jettites and Stackers below were looking for a way down, but the water had washed into the canyon floor, and some folk, soaked head to toe, were being lifted out in bewilderment. Had there been homes down there? This was Ven's kingdom, after all. He may not currently be in charge of it, but Dunstan wondered if a part of him wished he could be.

Then he shrugged dramatically. "Oh well! It's the Higher-ups' problem! As for us" — a tail and an arm scooped Dunstan away — "we've got a tour of magic and misadventure to get on. And look at you! Not as high dazzle as me, but it'll do in a trice." A quick check of Dunstan's backside. "Sorry I didn't have the materials to fashion you a tail. If anyone asks, you're mid-moult."

As they climbed back onto the velocipede, Dunstan hazarded, "It seems like Jet needs a hero. And you're pretty heroic. Why don't you use this whole situation as a way to get your throne back?"

Ven turned his purple eyes on Dunstan, the centres flexing. A tongue flick. "You won't let it rest, will you? Like I said. Jet will be better off without me."

Dunstan looked back at the people being guided out of the canyon, knowing now that the Meteorlight he carried could maybe help the folk below.

But will it be okay without me?

The bike hummed, and they were off. "That reminds me, I saw the beginning of the Revels in Vonda's Viridian while I was grabbing libations. Let's go there first. You'll love it!"

Dunstan bit off any reply as they skated around buildings, the glamour of Jet filling his every sense. It was massive and marvellous and everything Dunstan ever dreamed of. A pang of responsibility nagged at him as they soared from one transit station, across the cables connecting them, and landed on the other side: Jet needed Meteorlight. Dunstan seemed to have it in abundance. These Truffledour people made Jet shine all the brighter with their performances.

Little broken-hearted Dunstan Cord. *Could he save an entire secret city from the stage he always wished he could grace?*

It was too good a logline for a playbill. More like a feature presentation, plastered on a glowing marquee outside an odeon. An idea was blossoming inside Dunstan, the way all his best pantos and fever-pitched notions did.

As they snuck into the *Revels*, as Ven called them, the two shared witticisms and observations and cracked jokes that didn't quite land for the cultural barriers — but made them laugh anyway. Dunstan didn't want it to end. The entire city was throbbing with life, colour, music, and, as Ven promised, magic. For a while, Dunstan forgot about the black, crumbling mushrooms. Forgot about Knockum, his mothers, his bullies, and his mistakes. All he saw, all he was filled with, was the effervescence of black and green, mushrooms and mellifluousness. Jettites using their prowess on their mushroom stages to wow the crowd, to make the city brighter, make the fungi stronger. Truffledours — performers — were the real heroes here. Which made this seem more and more like a destiny Dunstan couldn't ignore, even if the prince seemed keen to get gone from the kingdom that didn't need him.

The proud reptilian prince. His legacy taken from him. His world crashing down. But he'd saved Dunstan so many times, and the longer they were together, the more Dunstan couldn't help but add that dash of romance to reality that often got him into trouble. Ven had a kind heart, he was sure, buried beneath layers Dunstan had yet to knock away. He put on a good performance: the prince turned vagabond with selfish dreams, unfettered by obligation, and dodging the authorities to get what he wanted.

Villain Ven. Maybe he needed a recast. And maybe, as Ven grabbed Dunstan for the umpteenth time, preventing him from being knocked down or bowled under, their connection producing its own shining light in the darkness, the idea just wouldn't go away.

If Dunstan was going to stay in Jet, he'd have to save it first.

"What part of Jet do you live in?" Dunstan shouted, pulling himself away from the Revels he very much wanted to continue watching.

Ven looked down, halfway from tossing a glazed centipede from the bag in his hand into his maw. "Why? Have you seen enough, Bright Eyes?"

I want to see more. Always. Forever. And even though above, his sight had been afflicted with a green harbinger of doom, down here he could see it all clearly. Jet was Dunstan's second chance, and it seemed more real than Knockum itself.

He'd just have to convince Ven to tarry a little longer . . .

Dunstan shrugged, putting on his best mask. "Wouldn't mind heading somewhere, you know, quieter?" He had a pitch to make, after all.

Ven pocketed his snacks and led the way back to the bike. "You're right. We've lingered long enough. It's time to pack!"

Dunstan barely managed a snort before they were wheeling away, sliding up a steep incline and heading straight for the Villain Ven mural they'd seen earlier.

Then Ven turned sharply and tucked them through a huge rent in the building, riding upwards on an interior corkscrew of spongey mushroom, sliding neatly under beams and over rough staircases, until Ven pulled them to a stop in a wide, empty corridor sliced through with shafts of light.

He helped Dunstan off the bike, ducked him down, said, "Mind your head," then tossed him upwards into the ceiling, and, thankfully, through a porthole where he landed on something soft in the loft above.

He caught his breath as Ven leapt through, sliding a slate over the hole behind him. "That was not enough warning," Dunstan muttered.

Ven shrugged, helpless. "I don't often have guests."

Dunstan blinked as Ven touched his tail into a dim tongue-looking mushroom in the wall, the room's fungi lighting up in sequence to reveal what looked like a spacious bohemian apartment. The dripping rock walls were draped in shimmering fabric, the floors covered in woven rush rugs, and when Dunstan stuck his head out the single window looking out into the city below, he realized that it was the eye of Ven's very misleading mural.

Dunstan pulled himself back inside. "Don't you think it's a tad obvious to be hiding inside your own face?"

"They haven't caught on yet," Ven said, deep inside a crevice in the wall. And behind him, another mural. Dunstan let out an enraptured *ooooh*.

"What's this?" He approached the wall, reached out, and had his finger slapped away before it made contact with the vibrant colours stretching over the wall.

"It's very carefully placed moss and lichen, thank you kindly." Ven sniffed, though he looked somewhat self-conscious. "It's . . . not done."

He returned to yanking out clothing, and maybe supplies, and piling them in a heap at his back. Dunstan backed up a few steps to take this picture in. Indeed, it was delicately wrought and detailed.

A painting etched in plants, of the Tallest Tor and the stretching beauty of a completely alien world above it. A dreamscape. And, more to the point, a masterwork.

"You're an *artist*," Dunstan breathed, a hand to his mouth. "Wait. Did you do the one outside?"

Ven snorted. "No one else could get my frills right." He flourished a hand around his head, its diadem of horns, its sharp point. "I used moth wings for that one."

"Well it's . . . it's beautiful. They both are." Comparing the two images, Dunstan felt that same familiar tug — loneliness and longing, the dream to be somewhere, anywhere, but here. He took another cursory look around the flat. It was cramped but well-appointed. How long had Ven lived here, alone, in a city that had no use for him? No parents, no family, no friends? Looking at this mural, it was certainly a city he loved . . . but in the space above it, the lichen created a blue, wavering mirage of another place. A place where things were better. Dunstan knew this dream all too well. No wonder Ven was excitedly packing.

Packing. Dunstan faltered. The timeline was speeding up, and the longer he lingered, the more torn he was getting. How desperately he wanted to repay this put-upon prince. How ardently he wanted to stay in Jet with him and write their own happily ever after.

Heartstrings. He'd hit those first — presuming Ven had them. Dunstan cleared his throat and looked out into Jet from the eye-hole window. An enormous moth, wings glittering with radiant fuzz, soared by like a streak of inspiration.

"This place . . . it's everything I dreamed it would be." It wasn't a lie. But it *was* a test.

The tiny lights of the Stettle Beetle cars whizzed over the city on their cables, little shooting stars, arcing in precision. Dunstan made a wish on all of them. He needed to go for broke.

"I'm glad I got to finally see the city of my dreams, before I can't see anything at all."

"What do you mean by that?" Ven's face was suddenly inches from his, interrogatory. "What's wrong with your—" Then the prince jerked back as Dunstan let go of the tears he'd been holding in for weeks.

"Oh, uh, yes, I do see the problem. You're *leaking*." Ven reached out a tentative, sharp claw, but Dunstan just turned away, waving his hands.

"Sorry, don't mind me. It's something my people do when we're feeling like the world is coming down on our heads." He dug his knuckles into his eyes, cheeks radiating with shame. He was feeling a lot of things at once, mostly that he didn't want to leave. More that he didn't want Ven to leave him. This was his chance to have it all, so he'd use the pain he'd been holding in — from losing Lorraine to the front, then losing his eyesight; from breaking what he had with Luisa and his friends; and from Moss destroying him in every way a boy could. Dunstan let it all wash over and out of him, miserable, yet hopeful it could be good for something.

He paced the room, trying to make each step have meaning. "I just feel that, with this *light* inside me . . . I should do something for Jet. There's so much I can do . . . to repay this place for making my dreams come true. Like the Truffledours out there. I think we could really make a difference together! You and me!"

Ven stared. Then he smiled.

"The world *is* coming down on Jet's head. But you don't owe this city anything. Let it crumble. We can build our own." The humour still played in Ven's grin, but it had gone out of his eyes. Dunstan swallowed as the prince went on. "Save your eye-waters. Jet will only break your heart. I won't." He tilted his head slyly. "Besides, isn't your heart already broken enough? That's what you swore on when we first met."

Dunstan looked away quickly. "It's mending," he sniffed. He had one last card to play.

"Don't you worry, though!" Ven said brightly, squeezing Dunstan's shoulders as he moved away to continue his whirlwind packing. "Once we're in your world, we'll see plenty! Together!"

"I won't see much of anything," Dunstan blurted, "Since I'm going blind."

Ven stopped sharply, staring. "You can't see?"

"I mean, I can *now*. I can *here*. It must be the Meteorlight . . . " Dunstan paced, and when he chanced a glance at Ven, something a little sharper seemed to be dawning on him.

A tongue flick, a malevolent sneer. "That's why you don't want to leave." Ven suddenly seemed torn, then he shook his crowned head. "We'll find a way to fix it! Or the Meteorlight will over time! We just have to get out of here now—"

"It's not just that!" It was now or never. Dunstan needed to put on the best performance he'd ever managed, and his earnest, glistening eyes dialled it up to absolute maximum. "Because I've been sent to Jet — with the Meteorlight — to save it!"

Dunstan had spent his life trying to sell ideas to folks who would listen, and many who wouldn't — Dinah, isn't that what a performer did? They told beautiful lies to transport you into a glorious story. How was this any different? Ven's dingy hideout was Dunstan's stage, and with a quick glance, he pushed himself out the window, hefted deftly onto the precarious mushrooms growing sideways from the dark brick, and perched on the edge of the roof, hoping Ven would follow.

And he did — almost too quickly, furtive. Furious. "What are you going on about?" he hissed as he leapt up and after Dunstan, his bag slung over his shoulder and his opal eyes blazing. "You said you'd—"

125

Dunstan spun, heart thrumming. This time his eyes were dry, and the thing inside him moved, grew warmer . . . and his dry eyes streamed green. He needed all the help he could get.

"Picture it!" he beamed, arms open. Behind him, the Tallest Tor and its strobing light at the top lit up his back. The perfect spotlight. "Villain Ven, recast as the legendary hero that rebuilt his city — his *legacy* — and connected two worlds! Whoever has the throne now will be quaking harder than the city's faltering foundations! The geodom will be yours again! The past washed away! King Ven the Revered!" And clasping his heart, Dunstan bowed. "With the help of the humble Higher-up Hero, sent here from regions beyond by direst destiny." A flourish of the borrowed coat as if it were a pair of wings, as Dunstan raced across the rooftop's edge. "I always knew there was something beyond Knockum, beyond the waters of a humdrum hometown! The Door *called to me*. It opened *for me*! And now is the time, Villain Ven, to seize your part in the greatest spectacle of all!"

He leapt down, five steps in front of Ven, chest heaving, eyes full of green and grandeur as he delivered the final pitch: "The redemption of the vagabond prince, the saving of this radical rock city from its mortal plight!"

Ven, deadpan, added, "With the Higher-up Hero that made it happen?"

The Meteorlight streaming from Dunstan's eyes melted away, surely revealing the chagrin all over his freckled face. "Would that be so terrible?" he asked, boldly honest.

"I think you made a promise," Ven said, somewhat dangerously, "and you don't want to keep it."

"That's not—" Dunstan yelped as the tail, strong and quick, snatched him around the middle, and pulled him close to Ven's predatory face.

"I saved your life." Ven repeated the claim in a low tone, the tail squeezing like a hungry snake as he went on. "I showed you the city. I kept you safe. I did *boyfriendly* things." Dunstan held down the scoff at the last part; he'd need to save the oxygen. "And now you're going back on your word to take me to the Above?"

A thread of betrayal went through his menacing gaze. "All you Higher-ups are the same!"

Dunstan winced away. "I *will* take you there! I swore it, and it's true!" He coughed, grabbing hold of Ven's lapels. "But you know that if you leave here, and my mission fails, and Jet crumbles into the earth — you'll regret it forever!" With fading lungs, he snorted, "*The Light Has the Right.*"

Ven's eyes widened, tail loosened. Dunstan spluttered, giving Ven a light smack to the chest. "Bit dramatic, your vagrancy."

The dangerous look faded somewhat, the slit pupils expanding. Ven rolled his eyes into his reptilian skull. "I could just drop you and go about my life, you know."

Dunstan immediately wrapped his arms around Ven's neck. "I'd rather you didn't, thank you."

Ven chuckled, then sighed moaningly. "Save Jet? What has Jet ever done for me? The Higher-ups on that throne that I don't have — they have the most Meteorlight of anyone. That's why they're the rulers, and I'm not. What makes you think *your* Meteorlight won't turn you into *them*?"

Dunstan looked towards the Tallest Tor, imagining Reeve Gris and his friends ruling over this place, never returning to Knockum. They'd had the chance to go back, but they'd stayed. Now Dunstan had to make the same choice. "Are they really so bad?"

Ven set his jaw, then righted Dunstan carefully on his feet. "Too bad there's no way to take the Meteorlight out of you. Then we could've been long gone from the start."

"Oh." Dunstan rubbed his arms, looking at his sneakers. "I guess that would've made things easier for you if . . . I wasn't part of the equation."

They stared out into the city in silence, the noise and music floating on the moist air, a vent belching mist over the borough. Dunstan wanted to stay. Ven wanted to leave, but he couldn't without Dunstan's help. They were at a stalemate.

Dunstan sighed. "Well. It was nice while it lasted." He started making his way back down to Ven's apartment, feeling a sadness he hadn't accounted for. "I'll take you to my world then. You can go your way. But I think I'll come back here, have a word with the Higher-ups, and I'm sure . . ."

A claw on Dunstan's sleeve. "That's it?"

Dunstan looked up into Ven's face, which was openly questioning, head tilted, opalescent gaze shining. "What do you mean?"

A grimace or a grin, Dunstan couldn't be sure. "You'd give up your mission that easily? To save this city together?"

Dunstan pulled away, hands on his hips, keeping his gaze on the ground. "You don't need me. We can . . . both get what we want. Go our separate ways." Dunstan had been used before. What was one more time?

Ven sniffed, folding his arms. "Well, I wouldn't be much of a former prince if I left a bona fide hero here without vetting you myself. Besides, you don't know the Higher-ups like I do. Or the Stackers. They might try to get the Meteorlight out of you using not-so-nice methods; they're that desperate."

Dunstan flinched, remembering the spike that had so neatly sliced into Ven. Jet was beautiful on the surface, but he could be sashimi before he knew it.

"I thought you wanted to get out of here as fast as possible?" Dunstan tested. It was Ven's turn to look away, to hide his face.

"I'm sure you can tell I don't have many friends." Ven stared out at the city, tried to laugh it off. "Vagabonding is lonely. And I've grown attached to having you around, Bright Eyes."

Dunstan's heart sped up, his eyes tingling, streaming out before he could clap his hands over them. He felt Ven's hands on his wrists, pulling them away, leaning in. Was he about to . . . ?

"But if you're the Higher-up Hero you claim to be . . . then you'll have to prove it."

"Ah . . . sure," Dunstan replied uneasily, as Ven dragged him back to the velocipede, deposited him into the seat behind him, and revved the engine.

"Where are we going now?" Dunstan bleated, the bike's hum vibrating his last nerves.

"To a show," Ven smirked, and they took off in a streak of light and lament.

There were suitable words to describe the place where Luisa had landed, but she was having a hard time finding them as she sat up, testing her boots against the glowing, spongey surface she'd slammed into, bounced lightly against, and came to a rest on. Crawling forward, she looked over the edge and found more spongey ledges, which she shakily slipped towards until she was on solid black sand surrounded by high cliff walls.

When she looked back up, she saw that the spongey platforms were enormous dwarf-ear mushrooms, Mariah's mushroom terminology flooding her brain. They were glowing the same eerie green that her portal had, which she realized had completely vanished. *The Door has a mind of its own*, indeed.

Now, all she had to do was find Dunstan. But as Luisa wandered farther into the canyon, clutching her arms around herself to keep warm, the adrenaline of her destiny was wearing off. Above, tiny lights arced, and there were the sounds of a city somewhere in the distance . . . but the canyon walls were high, and she didn't seem to be getting anywhere. More mushrooms glowed dully, and she realized she didn't even care if there was a monster down here, waiting to snap her up. At least she wouldn't be *alone*.

Then she spotted a ledge leading upwards, and she raced towards it, starting to climb.

"Stupid Dunstan and his stupid misadventures," she muttered. "Couldn't he have gone somewhere more hospitable?" As she pulled herself over the lip, where the sharp black rocks glowed more keenly, Luisa caught sight of the promised city just over another rocky rim.

Then, a screech. A rumbling. Luisa tripped and skidded backwards, end over end, back to the canyon floor as the world shivered and shook. *Not again*, she thought, the quakes in Knockum an echo of the force juddering the world around her now. She crawled to the canyon wall to help her stand, get a foothold somehow. The mushrooms above her strobed red, then fizzled to a disconcerting black—

And fell straight for her head.

Before she could react, Luisa found herself flying across the canyon floor, and out of the path of the falling debris, as something crashed into her. Rough hands grabbed her, took her hand, and they raced together for cover. Luisa just looked at the ground and kept moving, as something wrapped itself firmly around her like a cable line, and pulled her into a crevice away from raining rock debris, followed closely by a gush of water.

It hit the dark sand in a thundering rush, racing downhill and washing everything away in its path as the quake ebbed off, taking the water farther down, and away, into the darkness.

Luisa pressed her hands into her chest, heart slamming against her ribs like it was trying to escape. When she finally caught her breath, she managed a broken "Thank you," to her rescuer, then turned, looking into the face of—

A lizard. With blazing golden eyes, dark slits in the centres, lids blinking sideways rapidly. The scales were a speckled rose with frothy white whorls, and they wore a crimson cloak. The cable Luisa had felt sliding around her, holding her firmly, was attached to the reptilian rescuer. Not a cable, but a *tail*.

Luisa stumbled backwards, landing hard on the wet ground, as the lizard held their hands up, almost in apology.

"I-I-ah, w-wait one moment, please." They rummaged through their coat, nearly tripping out of the crevice they'd hid in. Their tail scooped up a javelin that had been dropped in the rush, and Luisa swallowed when she noticed its sharp tip. Coral hadn't mentioned an armed response coming after Dunstan.

The guard, for surely that's what they were, produced a little scroll from an interior pocket of the red cloak, yellow eyes dashing back and forth as the lizard muttered under their breath. Shoving it back into the coat, they stabbed the javelin into the sand, and cleared their throat.

"Halt, intruder!" They levelled the javelin on Luisa, shakily and prematurely, as Luisa groaned and got back up. "State your designation! The Light has the right!"

"I'm sure it does." Luisa held up her hands. "What do you mean by designation? Human? It can't mean nationality. I doubt you know Brindlewatch." Still shaken from the encounter that brought them together, Luisa uncharacteristically yammered on. "And I'm not an intruder! Or, well, maybe I might seem like one. But I'm not looking to stay long. I'm looking for . . . for my friend." No time for grudges now. Must press on. "Then I promise I'll get out of your hai— I mean, scales."

The lizard blinked rapidly again, perplexed. "No, you're supposed to come with me!" Then the barking demand fell out of their voice when they whispered. "Did you say *human?*" A terrified once-over. "You're a Higher-up, aren't you?"

Luisa tilted her head. "I, um. I don't know. Maybe that's what you folks might call me." Then she pointed. "Not to be rude but . . . what, or who, are you?"

"Oh." To Luisa, this unsure lizard person looked like they didn't quite fit their uniform, but they were trying very hard. They parked the javelin in the ground at their side again and left it there, hands open in unsure greeting. "I'm Stacker Decca! Er. Stacker is my role. Well, Stack*ling* technically. Decca is my name. And, er, what's your name?"

"Luisa Alvarez." Luisa stuck out her hand, then tentatively shook Decca's tail.

The flare rocketing up Luisa's arm took her by such surprise she let out a gasping scream. Decca did the same, and the two of them fairly burst apart, Luisa holding her wrist, the Stackling holding her tail.

Decca's jaw dropped, revealing rows of pointed teeth. "You have . . . Meteorlight?"

Luisa thought about it, then slowly nodded. "I guess that isn't normal, is it?"

Decca shook her head, crawling over to Luisa's side with a curious sniff of her hand. "The only Higher-ups that have it are, well, the

Higher-ups!" She pointed with her tail towards a sparkling black spire in the distance, as if her remark made a lick of sense. "They use their Light to keep Jet bright. But . . ."

The ground shivered. Luisa was jolted into Decca's arms, and they held on to each other until the aftershock passed.

Luisa sat up uncomfortably. "Sorry about that."

"S-same," Decca stammered. "I don't like the shivers, either. But even the elder Jettites say there's not much we can do about them, except encourage the Truffledours to amplify the Light we have."

Dusting the black dust farther into her trousers as she stood, Luisa surveyed. "We've been feeling the 'shivers' above, too. Do you know what's causing them?"

"That's easy!" Decca leapt up, grasping Luisa's hand and rushing her up the rest of the incline. They reached a short promontory, which gave them a view of the city — Jet — leaving Luisa all but breathless.

"See how the city glows, in the heart of the mushrooms? That's the Meteorlight. It's where all this came from. It's where *we* came from." Decca touched her chest, then pointed towards another spire covered in a spiralling haze of mushrooms. "The root network of the spores are in every inch of Jet. All its hovels and tors rely on the mushrooms' roots to stay upright. The mushrooms rely on the Meteorlight. But it's been fading more and more — the Higher-ups just don't have enough. They just have a little bit left of the original source."

Luisa, nodding along, asked, "And where is the original source?"

Decca's eyes darted nervously. "The betrayer king sent it away. But it seems like . . . you . . . and the other infiltrator . . . have it."

Luisa connected the dots, looking from the city to the cavern above, the destruction that had just rained down on her head. "So your city — Jet — needs the Meteorlight to stabilize it. Got it." She held out her hands. "Just take it out of me, and then we can find Dunstan, and do the same to him. Everything goes back to normal, and no one has to know about it. Above *or* below."

It all seemed fairly logical, but Decca was shaking her head. "Oh no. The Meteorlight can't be removed. Once it takes root, there's not much to do except use it. Only the betrayer king knew how to move the Meteorlight, and look where that got us! And *him*."

Luisa felt chilled. This thing inside her, and Dunstan, was irremovable? *Perfect.* "And where . . . did it get him?"

"Dead as a doornail!" Decca said cheerfully, until a clarion call sounded across the rock, and Decca winced mightily, burying her face in her claws. "Agh, that's my unit! Commander Vora is going to have my hide." She started pacing. "I was sent out to find a *different* Higher-up, but you're clearly not him. And now I've gone and told you maybe too many things. No matter what, I'm going to be roasting on a spit back at the barracks." She bonked her javelin into her forehead, which had an assortment of horns shaped like an upside-down heart. " *Think*, Decca."

Luisa put a reassuring hand out, then withdrew it. "Listen, I can help you find Dunstan. I think I can, anyway."

"Really?" Decca beamed.

Then Luisa backtracked. What would happen if she did find Dunstan? This place needed what Luisa and Dunstan had. Would they even let them go?

And could she trust this nervous little Stackling, who seemed eager to follow the rules and please her superiors? Surveying even this small area, though, Luisa knew without some guidance, she was surely going to get lost, caught, or worse.

Luisa held out her hand. "I just wanted to say thank you for saving me." She smiled. Dunstan was a performer. Luisa would have to take her cues from him, despite wanting to smack him upside the head on the regular.

Surprised, Decca blinked, grasping Luisa's hand gently. Had her scales gone a little ruddier? "Oh. Well. You're welcome." She took her hand back quickly, shaking it off. "But I really must get to arresting you . . ."

"Sure, of course, lead the way," Luisa agreed, waiting. Decca wrung her hands, but taking up her javelin in her tail, she began walking, and Luisa innocently followed. Luisa attempted small talk, getting the acute feeling that Decca had a lot on her mind. "It's . . .

nice here. I'm sorry that my and Dunstan's infiltration is causing you so much trouble."

Decca smiled sadly. "You have to understand: things really aren't going very well here . . . though when we last saw your friend — Dunstan, was it? Stalac, he really can shine! I think there's another way he could be of use to Jet. He really seems like the performing type, and that's just what we need—"

"What did you say?" Luisa carped, gobsmacked. "Dunstan did a *performance* here, in front of everyone?"

Decca ducked her head, like she'd been hit. "Oh dear, I really am talking too much. I can't . . . well, I mean, yes! He did! And it helped a little bit! So I figured—"

Luisa grabbed hold of Decca, swinging her around. "Do you have any theatres around here? You know, a stage where folk perform . . . music and pantomimes and whatnot?"

"You mean spectacle halls? That's exactly what *I* thought! I wanted to go and search them all, but the commander—" Decca shuddered. "She wouldn't listen. And she wouldn't want me fraternizing with you, either, but . . . oh I can't help but think about these things, you know?"

Luisa, disarmed, found herself agreeing. "I know what you mean." Luisa rubbed her chin, trying to find the angle. "Your commander sounds like a tough one. But wouldn't it help you if I helped you find Dunstan — then you can arrest us together! Better to do it all at once, right? Your commander can't argue with *that*, surely?"

Decca blinked, her golden eyes glittering as she reassessed Luisa. Her long mouth pressed in a line. "That does sound logical." Then her face twisted, mouth opened, as if she really wanted to say something else, then shook her head. "Anyway, just remember that me helping you is so that I can help Jet. That's a Stacker's core principle! Protect the city, protect the people."

Luisa nodded. "I understand. I came here to help my town, too. But now that I'm here, it's a bit more complicated than that, isn't it?"

Decca sighed heavily. "I know. I wish it wasn't. But I'm not clever enough to come up with a plan to save anything. You're just lucky

I have a hard time saying no!" Her pale scales seemed to go a shade lighter as she shook her head. "That's how I got talked into joining the Stackers in the first place . . ."

And grasping Luisa's hand, she pulled her through the split in the canyon where they'd been hiding. When they climbed out through the other side, Luisa now had a much better view of the city — all its spires, its lights, and music, fringing every glittering mushroom.

It took her breath away.

"Jet," Luisa said. Her wonderment as she took it in felt familiar, like she'd seen this place before . . . perhaps in her mind's eye, when her best friend shared his best dreams with her. "I can see why Dunstan came."

"I wish he hadn't," Decca muttered, keeping her javelin tight to her back with her tail. A furtive sideways glance. "But it was nice to meet you, Luisa Alvarez, because of it. Even if you're both kind of doomed."

Caught off guard, Luisa clenched her hands at her sides. "Why do you say that?"

"Because ultimately, Jet needs the Meteorlight back," Decca said grimly, walking ahead of Luisa and leading the way. "And they might find a way to get it out of you . . . that isn't very nice."

Jet's beauty faded at that, and Luisa walked a little faster, eyeing each mushroom a little closer. She prayed that Dunstan would keep himself from doing something incredibly stupid — at least until Luisa got a hold of him.

SCENE 7

A TRICK OF THE LIGHT

INTERLUDE:
BORN PERFORMER

Scene: a dazzling little cradle in a humble home.

When Dunstan was an infant, he learned quickly that the louder he yowled, the quicker his needs were met. Ada and Lorraine knew that this was probably normal with most babies, until Dunstan began to develop *flair*. If he yowled with panache, or did so in a fabulous get-up, then usually his childhood stumbles would be forgiven. And he developed an earnestness; he had to make his audience believe that he would be good, even when all he could think about were forbidden cookies after lights out.

All these tools were at Dunstan's disposal, honed and ready for his first-ever stage performance at the age of four: a flower in the Knockum Spring Revue. It was an ensemble affair with a few kids chosen to solo, and after seven-year-old Constance Ivyweather's tremendous Fandango number, Dunstan was inspired. He left the floral kickline and belted out an original medley of all the bedside songs Lorraine had fed him over the years. It was a hit with the crowd, but not with the organizers.

From then on, Dunstan weaselled his way onto every stage he could. He took up the keytar, percussion, the concertina — anything to find his way onto a cast and crew sheet, even if his overzealous auditions tanked him. From community plays to the school musical, Dunstan was always there, bursting with hope that this might be his chance.

But no matter how hard he tried, it'd always be the same pat on the shoulder by teachers, mentors, his parents: *You don't need to try so hard*, they'd say. *This isn't the big time.* But they didn't get it. Dunstan's ambitions seemed to outstrip the energy of those running the plays, their patience growing thinner each rehearsal as Dunstan came up with newer, wilder ways to "engage the audience," or made script edits without telling anyone, swearing up and down they were for the best. He was kicked out of as many productions as he got into for begging someone to see his vision. This often left him relegated to stage management. The silent role.

The stage darkens, one light at a time. Dunstan darts from each one, all of them snapping off and leaving him in the dark . . . until a green light flickers on, with Dunstan standing centre stage. No one else in the limelight. It's all for him. He has his chance.

Maybe his only chance.

If Luisa were here now, what would she say? Would she tell Dunstan he was crazy? Ven nearly flipped them over, course correcting as he landed beside a smokestack steaming with glittering purple fumes, parking it in the shadows of the theatre's marquee. From afar, the sign depicted a giant closed eye, and as they got closer, the lid lifted, and Dunstan realized the effect was caused by shivering mobile mushrooms growing into the rock of the stalactite the theatre was built into.

"Welcome to the Look Alight!" Ven preened. "Jet's premiere stage, where every Truffledour from Kanden to Grout are tested."

He chucked a knuckle under Dunstan's chin and smirked. "It's your time to shine, Bright Eyes. Literally."

As Ven navigated to a hatch in the roof, kicking it in and guiding Dunstan towards a set of spiralling stairs in the rock leading down, down, down, Dunstan clamoured. "Wait. I thought we were coming to *see* a show?"

"We sure are. Yours."

Ven pushed Dunstan in with gentle force and slammed the hatch behind them shut. "Just think of it as a test. Your little light show before demonstrated that you have the stomach for the stage. But do you have the guts to be a Truffledour?"

A test of my Meteorlight . . . Dunstan seemed to have more than the average lizard. More than the rulers of this place, too. And he knew it was the key to making his lie ring true. It would be now or never to prove himself — but this was a play he definitely hadn't rehearsed, despite it being a part he was dying to perform.

Dying being the key word. But Dunstan stuck out his chin. "Luckily for you, I've been in more shows than you can shake your tail at. Maybe you're just nervous that I'll do so well, you'll have to be the hero, too."

Ven rolled his wide eyes, tossing his pointed head. "You'll see. Jet will break your heart just the same, if you can't deliver. Even *you* won't want to stay."

The stairway leading down was lit by tiny white *Mycena*, flickering like fireflies as they passed. From the outside, the Look Alight loomed large, and Dunstan tried to gather himself, to work on this hero character he was suddenly playing. With each careful step, he straightened his spine, clenched his fists. It wasn't only the prince that would need convincing — it was himself.

"Of course I'll want to stay. It's my purpose, my mission." Dunstan swallowed, kept his eyes forward, Ven's solid body at his back with a hand on his shoulder as they descended. It squeezed tight for a moment, then relaxed. "It makes sense that everyone in Jet has a little Meteorlight. It's yours, after all. Which is why I'm so determined to bring it back."

"Is that so?" Ven asked lightly. "But you still don't know how you got it, do you?"

"No." That much *was* true. "But I could always sense it was there. It seemed to become a bit . . . stronger lately? And I felt it pulling me here. To the Door." It wasn't really a lie — maybe patched-together semi-truths. After all, Dunstan hadn't been pulled here, per se, but pushed. But the Door *did* pull him in, and the Light *had* been the key . . . the more Dunstan told the story, the more he felt it had legs.

Maybe he really was telling some kind of truth. Maybe he was chosen to do this. Fake it till you make it, or lie so well it becomes the truth. Either way, he was committed to the role.

"I can see that Jet is suffering. I know you do, too. All those quakes . . . we've been feeling them above, in Knockum. Our town is just as much dependent on the lake staying where it is as Jet."

"Lake?" Ven asked, then they both heard a scampering in the small space, and he grabbed Dunstan back, holding him close until the sound passed.

Dunstan's heart sped up in the quiet dark.

"Must've been a borapillar . . . at any rate . . ." He cleared his throat, and ushered Dunstan forward. "What's a lake?"

"Ah. Well . . . you know the water that seems to be falling on Jet's head in big gushes?" Maybe now wasn't the time to tell Ven this specific bit of geography, but it could do wonders for his desire to save his home world.

"That's a lake?" he croaked, and Dunstan felt him shudder. "Jettites don't do well with water. I hope there isn't too much more of it up there."

Dunstan clamped on to this fact, perhaps with a little too much morbid cheeriness. "A lot more, I'm afraid. And if something were to happen to the ceiling of this cavern . . . everything and everyone in Jet would be washed clean away. Besides, we have to go *through* said lake to get to my town at all. Hope you know how to swim."

Ven grabbed Dunstan. "You're lying so I won't leave Jet, aren't you?"

Dunstan frowned. "That'd be a good angle, wouldn't it? Except I'm not. I had to sink to the bottom of that lake just to get here."

He shrugged out of Ven's grip. "Not by choice, mind you. None of this was my choice. And yet here I am. Trying to help Jet. Help *you*. I'm here to do your test."

Ven blinked rapidly, then a grin broke across his face, and he covered his mouth to stifle the giggles. Dunstan sighed, turned, and continued down the stairway.

"All you do is laugh at me," he muttered, until he found Ven's tail wrapping gently around his hand, beckoning him backwards.

"I'm sorry," Ven said. "You always catch me off guard, Dunstan Cord. So let me show you something. A sign of mutual trust." He jerked his chin towards tail and hand. "Squeeze it."

"W-what?" Dunstan nearly choked, the gesture a little too intimate. "Why?"

"Trust me," Ven said. And with only a slight pause, Dunstan squeezed. At first nothing happened, then with a glance to Ven, checking his face for signs of jest, the scales began to glow. Dunstan felt like he was holding on to a live wire.

The shock rocketed through him. He didn't want to let go. It was like something inside him was answering something in Ven. They stood like this a while in their little alcove, the air around them buzzing and glowing. The electric wave became a mild pulse, and when Dunstan released, he found he wanted to grab hold again, and not let go.

All around them, the stairway lit up, showing the way to an opening in the rock, and Ven pushed his way around Dunstan towards it, tail trailing.

"Here we are!" His voice was low, and he beckoned Dunstan inside. The doorway led to a gangplank, a cacophony of music and voices drifting towards them.

"What *was* that?" Dunstan breathed. "The Meteorlight, it . . . it's like we made it stronger. By sharing it?"

Standing side by side on the swinging bridge, Ven's tail flicked Dunstan's ear. "Exactly. It amplifies it. But it doesn't last forever." He spread his hands out. "Now imagine if that Light you have inside you, could spread through the entire city. All Jettites share it. All Jettites need it. And all of Jet runs on it. If you want to save the city, and keep your lake from landing on top of us, you're going to need to figure out how to share it with everyone."

"Right," Dunstan replied, trying not to feel like what he'd promised was the tallest order he'd ever imagined. Then, he helplessly added, "It felt nice. Sharing the Light with you. It made me feel stronger, and also . . . protected." Then Dunstan clamped his mouth shut, looking at Ven. "I mean, ah, erm, it'd probably feel good to share with . . . everyone. Is where I'm going with this."

"Stronger together, protecting each other . . ." Ven mulled, then thrust a claw in the air. "Ah! So that makes you my boyfriend, too, right?"

Dunstan usually would've ducked like something was being thrown at him, but he was really practising his straight face. The corner of his mouth twitched, but that's all he'd allow. Here was an impasse he didn't know how to cross, or if he should. Then he remembered why they'd done Ven's little light show in the first place. "But how was that an act of trust?"

Ven blew out his cheeks, then turned, leading them farther down the plank to another set of stairs — shorter this time. Dunstan realized that beneath them were crowds of lizard folk, performers . . . and the stage.

"You were telling the truth, about the lake. I could feel it." Ven pulled Dunstan down to a crouch, and he realized this must be their destination. "What did *you* feel?"

Unsure how to answer, Dunstan looked down at the hand, the ghost of Ven's tail still wrapped around it. He squeezed, the afterglow remaining beneath his flesh. "Loneliness," he blurted, then he clapped a hand over his mouth. "I mean, and, er, like I said. A protectiveness."

It was a little brighter here; Dunstan was sure Ven could see his flaring cheeks. After a pause, and staring at his hands, Ven nodded. "Yes, well." He looked away. "As I said. I've always been alone."

He seemed surprised when Dunstan said, "You're not alone now."

Taken aback, Ven laughed lightly, then pointed down, to get away from the moment. "So what do you think, Higher-up Hero? Best seats in the house at the Look Alight."

Dunstan, eager to get off the awkward subject, surveyed the view below. The music trailing up was rhythmic and full-bodied, sliding out of pipes and drums and strings over crystals in the deft hands of their musicians. The air was peaty, cool, like the earth after a long-awaited summer rain. They were seated in the upper wings of the stage, far away from riggers sliding down ropes — vines? — that mastered a massive curtain of glittering silk. And above the stage, a deliriously glowing arch of mushrooms, filtering every colour to the beat of the music below.

"It's incredible," Dunstan sighed longingly. "Perfect stage to prove myself, right?"

"Exactly," Ven nodded smartly. "Now, here's a history lesson. Truffledouring is Jet's greatest and oldest tradition." Ven leaned over the rock ledge that kept them from careening into the audience. "For generations, Truffledours have attempted to amplify Jet's Meteorlight, even before it started fading. The Revels get bigger, and more desperate, every year. The Meteorlight is in limited supply, but it needs to keep glowing. So if you're a Truffledour, you are *revered*." He elbowed Dunstan affably. "Which means if you put on a good enough show—"

"Jet will owe me," Dunstan finished. He felt his eyes, his body, filling up with something like hope. It made a kind of sense. When Dunstan had done his little ditty on the mushroom float, the crowds had all stopped and stared, pulled away their goggles and *basked*. Not to mention the nearby mushrooms glowing in response. Dunstan stood up abruptly, and when Ven tried to pull him back down so they wouldn't be discovered, he grasped hold of his coat and pulled them face to face. "So that means Jet itself runs on . . . entertainment?"

Ven raised a brow. "Your world really is different from ours, huh?"

"Not at all." Dunstan grinned madly, and in that moment, all the mushrooms scattered on the damp walls around them flickered in harmony with Dunstan's heart. He caught his reflection in Ven's goggles. His eyes were streaming green, but this time, Dunstan didn't clap his hands over them. The Meteorlight was his ticket, and he was going to take it.

Even if it felt a little that *it* was taking him. Dunstan knew it was destiny. It had to be. This is where he was meant to be all along.

Dunstan clapped. "No time like the present." He leapt up, squinting into the dark, and pulled away from Ven to find his way across the gangplank. "You lead, I'll follow!"

"Stop!" Ven hissed, scampering after him and grabbing Dunstan back with a claw snagged in his coat. Backstage hands on the other side twisted their heads towards them, and Dunstan snapped his goggles back on, waving sheepishly, as the confused Jettites started towards them with rough words on their forked tongues.

"Come on!" Ven grabbed Dunstan and pulled him the other way, muttering. "Why did I listen to you in the first place?"

"I get that a lot," Dunstan said, then they stopped, crammed against one another, as more stagehands from the other side blocked their way out.

"Stalac," Ven uttered, just as Dunstan took a single step backwards, towards the centre of the scaffold, and heard a disheartening *crunch*.

No matter how full of theatrics Dunstan was, he wasn't ready for the platform beneath him gave way, and he fell, squalling, onto the stage and into the very limelight he'd been boasting was his and his alone.

When Dunstan got his breath back, he realized that the thing that had broken his fall was an enormous pipe instrument, its player standing aside with matching paddles and a crumpled expression as he looked from Dunstan to the shocked audience to the mushroom arch above.

"Poor Fora," someone from the stage wings muttered, covering their face.

Dunstan, and the audience, looked up at the arch. It had been glowing in time with the music before Dunstan's interruption; but now, the Light didn't quite reach the bend of the arch. The Jettite, Fora, hid behind his paddles, cringing, as the crowd whooped and clicked and made all manner of noises ranging from shock to hysteria as a tendril shot down from the arch, grabbed the musician, and threw him shrieking from the stage. He sailed so far out of the theatre, his screams fading to nothing. Dunstan couldn't see where he landed.

Someone in the crowd leaned their cupped earhole to where he'd vanished, a distant, weak murmur of, "Thanks for the opportunityyyyyy," causing a smile of relief on the spectators' faces. The would-be Truffledour was still in one piece. Dunstan remembered Ven's bloody injury and clutched his heart. Jettites seemed to be made of tougher stuff.

But was Dunstan?

The mushroom tendril coiled up and returned from whence it came, and Dunstan swallowed. From the stage wings, a Jettite with a clipboard made a decisive strike with a pen, then nodded at Dunstan.

"Hope your act is ready," he grimaced, then barked, "All right, people! Stage reset! Get this Truffledour prepped for the next trial!"

Dunstan was snatched up in stagehands, blearily searching the gangplank debris above for the prince who claimed he didn't want to leave Dunstan behind.

Except he had, and Dunstan, watching the curtain steadily fall, knew that his fate would be made when it rose again. Do or die.

Shine or go blind.

"Where is Stackling Decca?" Vora barked as they emerged from the canyon, the refugees shuffled off to other dwellings. Their homes had been decimated, and with another report of a gushing near the eastern bulwark, Vora needed all claws on deck — even if they were useless.

The captain narrowed his eyes, then scanned the unit nervously. "We haven't seen her since the canyon call went up," he answered. "She was sent in initially, before the wave . . ."

"Surely recruits aren't stupid enough to jump in front of these raging waters?" Vora sighed. It would be inconvenient if she lost a Stackling in addition to everything else piling up on her plate.

"Search the canyon again. I'll head to the bulwark and see if I can spot her from above."

The captain nodded nervously, and Vora leapt up a few fronds until she was far and away above the canyon, working her way back towards the next crisis.

Then, heading towards the Palisade Truffledour celebrations . . . a flash of green.

She pulled her crystal gazer from her belt, pressing it into her eye as she adjusted the focus. There — two figures emerging from Verdant Park, heading towards the Look Alight.

Stackling Decca, confirmed. And with her . . .

Vora pulled the gazer away, rubbed it against her coat, then looked again, but they'd moved beyond her sight. She raced higher, through an enclave of hovels and up a cliff that had once held some of the more prominent homes this side of the Hacklands, shorn away now with the water and the quakes. But she needed to shake off the sentimentality — she needed to *see*.

There! Spotted again, closer now and across the road from the spectacle house . . . crouching beside Decca, flesh smooth, no tail, and soaked.

A Higher-up. And not the one the prince had snatched from the parade. A second one. And Decca was taking her to . . . a Truffledour Trial?

And as Decca took the Higher-up's hand, a green glow arced between them. *This one has the Meteorlight, too!*

"Looking for your companion, are you?" Vora swore under her breath, hackles rising with an irritated click. "You'll either get a commendation or a demotion for this, Decca."

The reasons didn't matter. Vora had one job to do: protect the people of Jet. Whatever Ven was planning, she was going to put an end to this.

She was not going to repeat the Betrayer King's mistakes and let the Meteorlight escape.

Dunstan wasn't prone to stage fright. But this was different. The stakes were much higher. Ven had left him behind. Dunstan's mind raced from one agitation to the next.

He bit the inside of his cheek. Ada and Lorraine were usually in the front row. Sometimes Luisa, if Dunstan hadn't already dragged her to help out with the show. Whenever he performed, they were his sight line, his guides. But Dunstan was in a strange land on stranger tides. He felt himself shaking. He'd wanted this, and yet . . .

I'll help you.

Dunstan opened his eyes, blinking rapidly as he searched for the source of the voice. "Who . . . ?" But then he looked down at his hands, fingertips streaming with the same green his eyes always had.

You can shine, Dunstan Cord. You can shine for all of them. There's nothing we can't do together. Let your sight line come from inside. You were always meant to do this. It's why I chose you.

Dunstan was truly going crazy. Or maybe he always had been. "Is this . . . the Meteorlight talking to me, right now?"

He didn't need an affirmation to know it was true, but still Dunstan crossed his arms, hugged himself close. His throat was dry, his usual stream of inciting monologues fleeing from his grasp. All told, this performance, so far, was an actor's worst nightmare. If the coat weren't so thick, he'd pinch himself to wake up.

You're meant for this stage, the Light whispered. *We both are.*

". . . on!"

Dunstan whipped his frantic, begoggled face towards the bookie in the wings, his clipboard at the ready as he shouted, repeating himself. "You're on!"

Then the curtain rose sharply, the stage cleared away of the previous tanker and his busted instrument.

The expectant silence was so rough it almost rang. The velocity of Dunstan's blood racing back from his extremities, to his brain, couldn't be measured.

The hissing was already starting.

146

"What is this, nestling hour?" someone shouted, and the rest of the gallery guffawed.

"Let them say their piece," one retorted, then after the wave of confusion broke, snickered, "so the arch can tear them to pieces!"

Fists slapping on the table, more howls. *Tough crowd* didn't cut it. Dunstan squeezed his fists harder. He'd foolishly thought that Jet was different, that all the taunting he'd endured year after year was behind him. Something that didn't have anything to do with his blood pressure writhed in his belly. It wasn't stage fright or terror at the consequences of bombing here.

In response to the Jettites heckling, Dunstan howled back.

It was a mammal howl, a wolf howl, probably something they'd never heard before. A howl to curdle marrow and to immediately bring up campy werewolf *Night of the Living Moon* vibes. Back when Dunstan had friends, it was a collective battle cry against the people who didn't believe in the outcasts.

Dunstan ran out of breath. The room was silent. That shut them up.

"Nestling hour is over!" he yelled. The boiling thing in his belly had teeth, and a voice, too. Dunstan lifted his goggles up, and a collective gasp rang through the crowd. The dim glow of the theatre's mushrooms had nothing on his eyes, streaming green, obscuring his face better than a goggle-mask ever could. And Dunstan grinned again, opening his arms.

"Have any of you heard the tale of . . . *The Watery Wreckage?*"

A murmuring. An impression that the rowdy rabble-rousers were leaning in. From the back, someone said, "No?" as if scared of giving the wrong answer. The mood had turned decisively in Dunstan's favour. All he had to do was fake it.

He didn't even have to look up. The room became a little brighter. The mushroom arch above was intent, too, on hearing this.

"Once, long ago," Dunstan began, drawing his body across the stage like it was a pen, relishing each Jettite's rapt expression and twitching tongues. The glow wasn't enough to light every corner of the Look Alight, but Dunstan's Light let him see it all. Every scale, every claw-clench. He had them.

"In a town not far from this one, lived a boy without joy, living like that from day one." He thrust his gloved hand skyward — cavernward? — and intoned heavily: "But something was not right."

Of course, Dunstan was cribbing entirely from *The Sade Sisters Mysteries #12.* This is what brains did when they were in panic mode — leaf through all your archives and pull something out. But also, how could he lose? It was their greatest act yet: the sisters, after having an argument that had driven a wedge between their sisterhood, get drawn back into working together when a full-scale replica packing ship, *The Neversuch*, goes missing from its permanent exhibit in the Neranda Nautical Museum. The suspect? A would-be boy magician from the local high school who has found a way to resurrect the grim ghoulish souls of the very packing ship the replica was based on. It gave Dunstan nightmares for weeks.

It was perfect.

And there was a buzzing, something tickling in his stomach, rising up his chest. He smirked at the expectant faces of the crowd, and around to the wings where the bookie waited, arms folded, eyes wide.

The buzzing turned into a hum. Dunstan's face grew warm. And he lifted his hands up, as if he were bringing an orchestra to the tip of a crescendo.

Someone in the audience screamed.

"The Great Vessel!" they yowled. But it wasn't *The Darling Mermaid.* No; it was far bigger; an entire ship, made of the Meteorlight coursing through him, sailing through the back of the stage and into the audience, who all leapt out of the way in a frenzy.

And Dunstan intoned:

> *In all the wide world, on the land and the sea,*
> *(That's a body of water, you gotta believe me),*
> *Sailed a ship, like the one you've seen in the Hacklands —*
> *But massive, and brutish, faster than that tin can.*

The magician boy, the saddest of all,
Prayed to the sea, heard the clarion call,
And down from the depths came the rusty old sailors,
Longing for the decks of their miserable trawler!

The Meteorlight burst out as the ship vanished, coalescing in the figures of the ghoulish zombie sailors shimmering amongst the audience. Jettites, who earlier were so vicious, violent, and terribly critical, were holding on to each other for dear life. Some of the performers waiting for their turn gaped, bewitched, some with instruments still in hand. Dunstan nodded at one, and he slung a stringed rod onto his chest, started plucking a bass beat. A percussionist on a mushroom hand drum joined in. *Oh my Dinah, it's happening.* They were all *riffing* together, and it made Dunstan glow brighter, from the inside out.

Dunstan jumped out at the crowd but pulled back, testing to make sure they were still on the edge of their seats as the music swelled. The zombies all got to their feet and began to dance in time to the music, to Dunstan's commanding conducting. He could feel the warmth behind his eyes and saw the stage all around him lit with his neon aura, as the dancers wove in and out of the dumbstruck theatregoers.

Just as much as Dunstan could summon props and costumes from the bare minimum, so too could he wield the energy of a room — of an underground city — if given a chance. Had the Meteorlight been working through him all along? Was he really doing it, grasping destiny by the scales?

The music drew the words and story and song out of him, capering as the tale went on, suddenly hitting a bit of a wall, but staggering over it with the help of a crescendo. The drumbeat kept up, but he saw the musicians look nervously at each other. Things had been going so well . . . why was he suddenly blitzing out now? Dunstan felt his fingers quake. The thing about the *Sade Sisters Mysteries #12* is that he never knew the ending. He'd started reading it with Luisa. Then he'd given her his copy . . . the image spooled out in front of his green streaming eyes, unbidden, making him feel like he was blacking out. And suddenly it was happening in front of him, in front of the entire audience, rendered in ghoulish green:

An argument, their worst one yet; Luisa's hands ripping the show poster for *Terrazine and Me* into shreds, a tangible expression of their friendship ending as the wilted pieces fluttered to his feet. She wouldn't forgive Dunstan this time, and her face was steel. *You want to know what makes you such a great performer?* she snarled. *You're a liar, Dunstan Cord! And one day your lies are gonna bite you square in your stupid face!*

Pounding in Dunstan's head. He came back to the present full force, as if thrown there. The pounding of fists on tables in the audience. The booing and the howling. Dunstan's energy had dried up, the warmth of the Light fading from his eyes. Soon they'd see him for exactly what he was . . . a soft human fraud.

Then, a tail snaking through his hand. Scaly and glittering and warm. Claws at Dunstan's waist as he was pulled in, his other hand clasped tight. Dunstan looked up into Ven's face, which was tight from its own kind of managed panic. But still, all the same, he smiled.

"It's the *prince!*" someone cried, the audience a mingling of shocked silence and excitable murmuring. Some folk took off, and Dunstan knew it was a matter of time until the place filled with red coats.

But for now, Dunstan breathed, one layer of panic ebbing away. "You came *back*," he whispered.

Ven shrugged, then shook his head. "You lead. I'll follow."

"Well?" Someone from the gallery screamed. "How does it end?"

Dunstan shuddered, feeling the Light from Ven's tail glowing into his skin, then under it, shutting his eyes and opening them again to their refreshed, haunting green.

"With a *dance number!*" he shouted back, and he led Ven across the stage to the music that the uncertain accompaniment below generously flooded the Look Alight with. The zombie dancers mimicked their every move, and all at once, the Look Alight became an undead ballroom.

A quick step. A horn section. Dunstan swore he felt it all, as if he were both within the audience and on the stage at the same time. Whatever step he did, Ven mirrored it, and the look on his face was one of mixed surprise and unexpected joy.

But the Meteorlight they were sharing made a connection between them; Dunstan felt a renewed sense of confidence and an understanding of Jet that he didn't possess before. As they swing-stepped and fox-trotted, bopping along to the beat in perfect harmony, there was something else there, too . . . it was familiar, sure, but it didn't originate in Dunstan. It was that profound loneliness again. Dunstan had a taste of it after kicking the strongest friendship he had to the curb because of his ego. But *this* feeling? It was the darkest dark hole, probably what it looked like outside Jet's city limits, if there was anything out there.

And it seemed like that place is where Ven has lived for a very long time . . . yet now, they were lighting it up, together.

Because right here, right now, Ven and Dunstan were the opposite of lonely. They were shadowing one another, delighting in their togetherness to the cheers of the audience below. And if *that* didn't make for a great performance, then Dunstan didn't know what could.

Dunstan grabbed Ven's hands, slipped between his legs, and was thrown helter-skelter above his head, landing in his arms with his own crossed over his chest, and when Ven tipped him back to his feet, their connection breaking with the distance, the zombie dancers falling into line — all the Meteorlight came crashing back into Dunstan, the perfect, raucous finale.

Then darkness. Dunstan blinked, spots racing across his vision. The mushrooms dimmed back to their unearthly glow. His head canted automatically up, to check the arch, the arbiter of his success . . .

It strobed a multiplicity of coloured light, showering him and Ven with exhilarated sparks, and the city beyond the theatre surged with a brightness he knew it hadn't experienced in years. The applause was a greater rush than Lake Mallion on a whitecap Wednesday.

Ven laughed loud enough to be heard over the cacophony, lifting Dunstan up and spinning him around in a bear hug before putting his shaking sneakers back onto the ground. Dunstan laughed, too, wanting to celebrate with his whole body and brain — *I did it! The stage was mine for once! It was everything I ever dreamed it would be!*

But the spots were still flickering in his eyes, like rattling film strip racing around the cassette of his brain, and Dunstan saw something beyond the Look Alight club: his mothers in the audience, clapping encouragingly even though he was only a bit player in the chorus . . . Hector Alvarez, leaning in and smiling to Lorraine about how lucky she was. And Luisa, guileless in her manner and merciless in her criticism, clapping, too, because it didn't matter to her if he was chorus line in the play — he was the lead in her heart.

Then Dunstan blinked, and he was back in the underworld, enthusiastic Jettites clamouring to ask him questions. He grabbed for Ven's hand, for reassurance, but also for the flickering shadow of that connection they'd shared. He wondered if Ven had felt it, too, or if it had just been a trick of the light.

"Where are you from?" One Jettite looked Dunstan up and down, appraising and yanking on his sash. Dunstan pulled back, made sure his goggles were firmly in place. So far on the disguise, so good. "And those moves!" She snapped her scaly fingers. "Will you teach us?"

"I've never seen Meteorlight do that before!" someone crooned, voice high and excited. "Will you be putting on more spectacles?"

"Like a tour?" another cried, and the crowd clapped giddily, as if Dunstan's praise-replete beaming had all but confirmed it.

"Please do a tour!" someone crooned, then they caught sight of Ven. "And the prince, of all people! Who knew he was secretly a Truffledour all this time!"

Ven rubbed the back of his neck, unable to shrink any lower than his massive height. "It wasn't really . . . planned, per se . . ."

"Do you need a Truffledour troupe?" one of the musicians piped up, waving his mushroom drum. "We're available!"

"And how did you come up with that story?" It was a huge Jettite, burly, clasping the sides of his face in concern. "I'm not going to sleep for weeks!"

Dunstan smiled, ready to rebound with the energy their attention gave him, until another voice piped up. "I think I've heard that story before."

Suddenly, the vision of Dunstan's friends and family, and all the applauding audience members from plays gone by, faded. There was only one familiar face now, and she wasn't clapping. She was folding her arms, as the crowd of Jettites parted to reveal a girl about Dunstan's size, long black hair scraped back from her face in a tight, businesslike bun.

Luisa Alvarez, the Unforgiving.

Dunstan's two worlds collided. Unbelievably, there she was, scowling at him from the front row. "You know what *copyright* is, don't you, Dunstan Cord?"

Beside Luisa was a Jettite — a Stacker in a crimson coat, but she was looking about nervously, a hand on Luisa's shoulder as the two of them climbed and joined Dunstan on the stage. "I don't think this is the place to do this. We should go somewhere quieter, before . . ."

Ven grabbed Dunstan by the forearm, hard, and dragged him across the stage. "We need to leave — *now!*"

The air went out of Dunstan — not just from the shock, but because Ven had wrapped his arms and tail around him so tightly, his lungs popped. "W-wait, that's . . . that's my—" He looked at Luisa, and then to the crowd of Jettites who'd only just been clamouring for his favour. He knew things were about to go pear-shaped as an adoring fan whirled on Luisa, screaming, "It's a Higher-up! Get the Stackers!"

And sure enough, the theatre doors burst open, streams of red pouring in. The Stacker beside Luisa reached for her, and without thinking, Dunstan wriggled out of Ven's grasp and dragged Luisa across the stage with him.

"Dunstan!" she managed, but he shoved her into Ven's arms, turned towards the Stackers, and let his eyes stream wild and ready as the commander broke through, sneering, javelin clutched close.

"Time for the encore," he said, clapping his hands together and summoning the great zombie ship back, but this time, the audience wasn't prepared for the creatures pouring off it. Stackers dove out of the way as the huge ship with its tattered sails roared into their ranks.

"You idiots! It's just a Meteorlight illusion!" Commander Vora shrieked, but by the time it cleared and the Stackers realized their mistake, it was too late.

Dunstan, Ven, and Luisa were already gone.

SCENE 8

ANY SKIFF IN A STORM

A da had followed the rules her entire life. Lorraine had chided her for it, every time she straightened the row of pencils on her desk in front of her wife. And her heart caught in her chest whenever Dunstan broke the rules, creating a divide between them that only seemed to grow in Lorraine's absence.

But rules weren't getting her anywhere.

She steered clear of the Council of Mothers — she knew, if questioned, she might break down and foolishly trust they'd understand what she was going through. Ada doubted anyone would. They'd call her hysterical, and if Kiki offered her one more blanket she'd stuff it down her throat. As she skirted Chauncer's Pub, where the ladies were trying to get their bearings after a day of cleaning up Knockum's chaotic mess, Ada realized the only person who would have the answers was Morag.

Morag Gunn had overseen the Knockum lightkeepers for nearly thirty years. It was her job to write the Viewpoint report every year, to describe the conditions of Lake Mallion from the east to the other three lightkeeper appointments in each direction. These reports were confidential, kept in a central county archive. Lightkeeper Ada would need to access the other stations' archives, to see if any other lightkeepers from the other directions had seen what she'd seen — and if it was marked down in an official capacity, or "redacted," as she'd discovered from her own archive dive earlier.

Of course it was a touchy subject. Dunstan's birthday, the night that Reeve Gris and the Sunken Three vanished on a boat never recovered, was a dark spot in the lightkeeper reputation. The Brindlewatch Guard forgave it, just a blip in a stellar record. But Ada took it to heart. She had been on duty that night and hadn't seen Reeve's boat until it was too late. Had it been her fault?

Morag never blamed her. No one did. She was on the brink of delivering a baby. *Just bad luck.* Then, as Ada drove tensely down to the shoreline, wringing the steering wheel like a saturated towel, she slammed on the brakes, a memory drifting to the surface.

She reached into the backseat for the file box with her hand-written journals, snatched the one she'd earmarked from that night, and flipped through it.

There it was, a throwaway bit of text written in a margin. Proof of what Morag had said to Ada in her own bedroom after giving birth, and Ada had expressed her regret in not being able to stop Reeve before it was too late.

"Don't worry, dear," Morag had said. "It was probably just a trick of the light."

A trick, yes. Of a green light taunting her, removed from Knockum's history . . . until today. It could have just been a platitude spoken to ease her guilt, but, considering what Ada had seen, it felt more like a confirmation she wasn't crazy.

Climbing out of the car, she scanned the shoreline, and there it still was, safe and unclaimed. Ada had never stolen a thing in her life. Lorraine was the wild one, the outgoing, brash girl who had nicked sugar drops from the corner store when they were teenagers, Ada begging her to give them back before they were arrested. Ada's constant living by the straight and narrow always left her feeling an outsider to the free-spirited Dunstan and Lorraine waltzing to radio plays into the wee hours. Yet she still would laugh as they twirled around the living room carpet, would sometimes join in, off-key and reticent. Her wife and son had made her test her limitations, but pulling this off would break more than Ada's personal governing rules. *I'm just borrowing the boat. I'm just going to be out for an hour or two. I'll return it completely refuelled with a thank you note . . .*

It was docked haphazardly where Korman had said it would be: at the abandoned wool mill four miles from the marina up the shore. She suspected that Moss may have taken it for a joyride recently, its loss roped into the mystery of the other missing boats. Carefully scrambling down to the water and over the rocky shore, the sun casting the escarpment's shadows on the water and the day, Ada climbed neatly over the rail, not wasting a moment or a breath. She found the gas tank was full enough to do a few cursory laps. The lightkeepers would be on full alert, and her escapade would certainly be noticed, but at this point, it didn't matter. Ada was bucking every rule and reason, because it was her son on the line. And she'd write that down in any official report required.

The back of her neck itched, as if someone were watching her. She looked all around, eyes keen, ducking at the railing . . . but after a few paused breaths there was no one. If a lightkeeper saw her, it would be marked down and reported to the boat's owner, and Ada would fess up. She'd return it when she was done. But for now, she didn't care. She needed to find Dun. She needed to bring him home, whatever trouble he was in, whatever was happening, and whatever this green light had to do with it.

If lights could speak. And Ada didn't want to wonder if *this one* could.

"Fancy a sundown cruise, do you?"

Before Ada turned, she clocked the emergency oar at her right hand, yanked it out, and came out swinging.

"Whoa, easy there!" Coral held up her hands, backing up and away from the deck, boots catching on the rocks that Ada had just mountaineered. "I'm not interested in taking a dip, Ada."

Ada kept the oar between her and one of her most trusted friends. She wasn't feeling very trustworthy right now. "Did you follow me?"

"I've been a few steps behind, but not that close," Coral sighed, as if it were more than obvious. "After a stop at the lightkeeper Station and a brief tête-à-tête with your not-so-loyal co-worker Korman, it wasn't difficult to find you on your own reconnaissance." With a gloved hand over her double-breasted mustard coat, she gestured to the cruiser. "Permission to come aboard?"

"Permission denied," Ada said immediately. "You should go. Help the Council of Mothers. I'm . . ." She glanced suspiciously out at the water. "I'm busy."

"Boy still away? Think you'll need to nail him to the floor so he stops slipping through your fingers." Coral's amused tone died in a throat clearing as Ada's face hardened.

"Coral," she said slowly. "If you don't leave now, I'll . . . I'll—" But Ada wasn't as good as Dunstan, or Lorraine, at improvisation. She shifted her feet uneasily, keeping the oar steady. "I'll report you to Morag Gunn for obstruction of an investigation!"

After knowing Coral for many years, Ada had a knack for telling just what was going on with her, despite not seeing her face. Her tall frame sagged a little bit, her fingers twitched in their gloves. "And what do you think Morag Gunn has to do with your son's antics?"

"I don't know," Ada said, starting to lose steam with intimidation. She was a slight bird of a woman, but when it came to her son she was made of sterner stuff. "All I know is that him running off has something to do with the green light. The one I saw on the lake the night he was born! It was in my report, but no one ever . . ." She thought back to Korman's face, the conspiracy seemingly unfolding before it got stranger. "I'm not crazy! This light — it has something to do with Reeve Gris and everything that's been happening today. And most of all, it has to do with Dunstan!" She didn't care how high her voice was now, she just wanted to get it all out, into the open air, so that the theory could breathe and so could she.

"What if I told you I knew precisely where he was?"

Ada didn't blink, but she stood back a bit, not sure of Coral's intentions. "How? Have you seen him? Did he talk to you?"

She didn't stop Coral when she strode aboard, but she did take a hand off the oar to steady her friend as she wobbled on the deck.

"I, er, am not too fond of the water," Coral muttered in an uncharacteristic show of apprehension. She jerked her head towards the steerage. "Key's still in the ignition. I recognize this boat. Saw it the other night. Saw your son on it with some of his supposed friends." She sighed at Ada's look of total incomprehension. "We'll get into that later. For now, I can tell you you're right, Ada. Your little theory sounds weaker than an aluminum racer in the Luxe Grand Prix. But it's about to get wilder."

Ada followed Coral across the deck and looked out where her long arm pointed — to the Knockum Remembers buoys. "Start there. Anchor. Your boy is definitely on some kind of teenage rebellion escapade, but it's the kind he'll need pulling out of by the people who care about him. At least he's got Luisa." She clucked her tongue; something else may have clicked, too. "I hope he does, anyway."

"Luisa?" Ada parrotted. "Coral, please, what is going on? Does it really have something to do with that green light, all those years ago?"

Ada stared deeply into the darkness of Coral's swathed face and swore she saw recognition swimming in the folds of bedazzled fabric. "It has everything to do with it," she answered. "I just can't explain it all at the moment. I need . . . I need to talk to Morag, too. And to make preparations, in case the Light returns truly, and . . ." Her voice went lower, as if Ada suddenly wasn't there. "It's too much, too fast . . . it's still broken . . ."

Ada put a gentle hand on Coral's shoulder. "Are you all right?"

Coral seemed to see Ada then. They stayed like that a while, the water lapping gently against the trawler's hull, the silence seeming to build towards something, until Coral pulled away.

"You're smart, Ada. I've always liked that about you. Quiet, but in a dignified, calculating way. Those types are the most dangerous.

And the most needed when it comes to it." Coral made her way to the gangplank, then back to dry land.

"Wait, you're not coming with me?" Ada clambered, following Coral as far as she could.

"Not now," she said. "Not yet. There's more to do and too much at stake. Take your son home. Lock him in his room if you have to. And for Knockum's sake" — she stopped mid-stride, chin turning in profile with the sun lighting her in a gilt edge — "don't let him anywhere near water again."

With a few more steps down the rocky embankment, she was gone from sight.

"Coral!" Ada's voice ricocheted back to her off the rock and woods of the Crisp, but Coral did not come back. Ada wanted the answers *now*, not when someone else determined she was ready.

All she could do was clench the oar to her chest, resting her forehead against the smooth paddle. Coral knew . . . whatever it was that Ada was searching for. Morag was a part of it. Everything came back to this light. And at the centre of it, Dunstan, whose dreams seemed to shine brighter than any lightkeeper station. That light had led him into this world and led him away from it.

"Fine." Ada jammed the cruiser's keys into position and pulled back on the accelerator as the engine burst to life. Tossing the wheel starboard, she turned the craft and headed two miles out to the markers.

Ada would find the answers, and Dunstan, on her own. She would follow whatever voice there was. And she would wait.

After fourteen closes, two market squares, and more flights of mushroom stairs than Dunstan cared to count, Luisa faltered and leaned against a wall of glittering oyster fungi, unable to keep up the pace. Dunstan was glad she did because he felt like his chest was going to burst.

"We can't stop now!" Ven hissed. He threw up his hands and peered around a corner to see if they were followed.

Luisa slapped the side of Dunstan's head, and he nearly bowled over sideways.

"Hey!" Ven yelped, but Luisa kept coming, Dunstan covering his head as she let it all out.

"You *idiot*, Dunstan Cord!" she cried, the adrenaline making her stronger. "How could you just jump into the Door in the lake and drag me down with you?"

Dunstan managed to finally stand up straight, and he shoved Luisa back.

"First of all, I didn't just *jump* into anything! Moss and his Grislies threw me overboard! Secondly, nobody asked *you* to come and fish me out!"

"Coral Frakes did!" Luisa shrieked. "Whatever you've gotten into with this Meteorlight business, I didn't ask for it, either!" Then she jabbed Dunstan so hard in the chest that the green bolt slithering off her finger shocked him backwards into Ven's waiting arms.

"You . . . have Meteorlight, too?" Ven asked. Dunstan recognized the slight danger in the question as Luisa folded her arms, looking uncertain herself as she paced, eyes welling up.

"It's how I got down here in the first place! I don't understand *anything* that's going on, or why this is happening! This city is falling apart; Knockum is in trouble; the weird townie cultists were right; I have no idea if Reeve Gris is around to explain it; Coral Frakes knows *way* more than she's letting on; these Stacker people are after us; and I just—"

Luisa's speech stopped suddenly as Dunstan put his arms around her, holding her close in silence for a minute. Then, unsure what else to do, Dunstan took off his coat and put it over her shoulders. "You must be freezing."

Luisa pulled it in closer, staring at him. She sniffed. "I . . . guess."

"And I . . ." Dunstan wrung his hands, staring at his sneakers, biting his tongue. The truth was that when he saw Luisa at the Look

Alight, he felt something more than shock. "I'm glad you're here," he said. "I'm sorry."

Luisa blinked, then she looked from Dunstan to the very agitated prince. "Seems like you had someone watching your back in my absence."

"His back, his front, and now I think all of ours are on the line." Ven showed his teeth, and Luisa raised an eyebrow as he said to Dunstan, "I didn't realize there were more of you with Meteorlight running around."

Dunstan shook his head. "Neither did I."

Then, the sound of shouts, clattering. The three of them took off in the opposite direction as a mob dressed in red flanked the road behind them, one of the Stackers pointing and shouting, "They went that way!" as they raced for a switchback of multiple stairs, leading them from the ground and beneath the city's glittering web of cables.

On the next platform, exposed but at least on the move, Luisa flinched into Dunstan as a zooming cable car thundered by.

"Should we hop on one?" Dunstan turned to Ven, who seemed to be making a calculation as the Stackers drew closer, Commander Vora at the head. All around them were passersby, folk going about their business on each level, but every single one of them turned to see what the commotion was about as Ven, Luisa, and Dunstan made it up the next flight of stairs.

"No matter where we go, they'll find us. They want the Meteorlight, and they won't stop until they get it. Which means you two need to go somewhere they can't follow."

Dunstan grabbed hold of Ven. "I'm not leaving you behind this time!"

Ven dipped his head. "Why do you think I came back?"

"For the chance at heroics," Dunstan teased.

Luisa shouted, "Enough flirting!" Because just below them, the Stackers were coming, and the platform they'd found themselves on was devoid of an escape vehicle.

They needed a distraction. Dunstan had an idea. The gawking Jettites could be their ticket out of there.

So he turned to Ven and smacked him hard.

"How could you *do* this to me? After everything I promised you? You'd let me get dragged up to meet my maker?"

The commander halted the unit in their pursuit, and every slit eye and ear dialled in.

Ven's eyes darted as he whispered, "What are you doing?"

"I thought we had a connection!" Dunstan cried, laying his hands across his forehead. "I really genuinely thought we shared a moment back there, in the Look Alight!"

Ven, perplexed, blinked so quickly his eyes could have been a shutter-crazy camera. But then he read between the lines, the corner of his mouth twitching. His face changed to an expression of incredulous betrayal. "So did I! You said you had brought the Meteorlight back to Jet, to save us all!"

Their voices rattled loudly, carrying across the rock and mushrooms that made this part of Jet the perfect echo chamber. At another station a few feet down, where Stettle cars were stopping to let off passengers, the crowds turned towards the commotion, and Ven went on.

"All my life I've spent in hiding — hiding from what my father, King Vert, did to this geodom! But no longer!" Ven pushed the Stackers aside and managed to move farther onto the mushroom platform, into view of the crowd gathering above . . . and those below pointing and watching in awe.

"This Higher-up Hero has come to save us . . . and Commander Vora would put us under arrest, on this, Jet's highest celebration of sharing the Meteorlight in the Truffledour way!"

"Contain them!" Vora barked, but the crowd booed, surging towards the Stackers and knocking some of them aside as cries of jeering support rose up.

"They were at the Look Alight!" Someone shouted. "Best spectacle the arch has seen in an age!"

"Didn't you see the surge they generated?" another voice clamoured. "Leave them be!"

Soon the chorus of *let them free, leave them be* rose from the masses, and the Stackers seemed unsure of what to do. Vora attempted to quell the crowd, while Luisa looked down the cable line at the oncoming car streaming their way.

Then Ven wrapped his tail around Dunstan's hand, and Dunstan grinned madly, grabbing for Luisa's, adding her to the fray.

"What now?" Luisa cried, then she balked as the Light streaming from Dunstan's eyes flittered across her shocked face.

"Jump!"

The mushroom below them shivered, glowed, then shone so bright that all of Jet turned a searing viridian, and the clamouring crowds cried out.

When the Light faded, they were gone.

Well, not gone, precisely. Ven had grabbed up Dunstan and Luisa in his claws and tail, and once they had slammed into the Stettle Beetle car, the flash they carried seemed to ignite it from within, and it took off like a sparking green rocket across the geodom.

Dunstan dared to peek out from Ven's coat, the gushing air thrashing his hair into his eyes as he shouted, "I can't believe that *worked*!" A stunt fit for the stage, but it, like everything else so far, had been more than real.

Ven grinned down at Dunstan as Luisa held on to the cable pulley hook for dear life. "I'm really getting the hang of this improvising stuff, don't you think, Bright Eyes?"

"Improvise yourself *down*!" Luisa said as she shoved the two of them flat just as the car careened under a bridge, stunned onlookers screaming as they passed. "Where are we going?"

"Exactly where I promised," Dunstan said, pointing to the Hacklands. "Home!"

Luisa held tight to the cable car's pulley, staring open-mouthed at Ven. "We're taking *him*? Don't you think he'll be in more trouble in Knockum than here?"

"I doubt it!" Ven replied, tail wrapped around Dunstan. "Besides, you lead, I follow, right?"

Luisa rolled her eyes. "Well I don't see a steering wheel on this thing!" She *would* point out that minor detail.

Suddenly, Ven grabbed hold of them both, gritting his razor teeth. His tail wrapped around the cable car's pulley. "Hang on!"

Dunstan's confident expression slackened as they caromed towards a sudden, deadly drop.

Down they fell, then up, around more hairpin turns that looped around buildings, dwellings, rooftop cafés. Luisa was laughing. Dunstan felt like he was going to hurl. To get his mind off this carnival ride from Hades, Dunstan peeked below and into the skylight of the cable car. A rider in a pinstripe overcoat and gold-rimmed goggles looked up from his newspaper, stared a few moments back at them and shook his scaly head.

"Fare dodgers," he sighed, adjusting his paper and ignoring them once more.

The intense speed and swaying went on for five minutes more, until Dunstan cried, "Maybe we should get a transfer?"

"Not yet!" Ven shouted back over the rushing air and the scream of the cable on the line. He pointed, and Dunstan realized that the buildings were thinning. They were going to pass right through the Hacklands. Had their use of the Meteorlight somehow helped them get there? It didn't matter now; coming into view, a trawler that shouldn't be there.

"The Door!" Luisa barked, squinting at it in the cavern ceiling. "But how are we going to open it from *here*?"

"We'll just have to—" but before Dunstan could improvise further, a horrible grinding shot out behind them, throwing sparks and a screech that echoed over the borough they were stalling over. The cable car shuddered to a stop, swinging wildly on the line. *Now* the rider inside was incensed.

"Bloody transit commission!" he growled, sticking his head out of the window and berating the three of them. "Are you happy now?

Was your little joyride worth it? I have a meeting I'm going to be late for!" Then he stopped himself and looked closer at Luisa and Dunstan. "Wait . . . are you . . . ?"

"Prince Ven and the Higher-up Hero." Dunstan shook the passenger's hand. "But you should exit here. The best part of the show is about to start."

"It is?" Ven raised a scaled brow, and Luisa yanked on both of them, pointing behind their car.

"There they are!" It was far down the line, but with his Light-renewed eyes, Dunstan spotted three Stackers at a control booth sticking out from the rock face. There was the nervous Stackling, Decca, hovering over the controls, which were soon in the claws of Commander Vora as she, and the rest of her unit, spilled out of a Stettle Beetle car.

Vora's face was a triumphant grin. She grabbed Decca, pointed, and with a reluctant nod, the Stackling swung upside down from the line and began hoisting herself towards them.

A spark of green shimmered across the cable. The car hummed back to life, but it sped to a switch track, turned, and started heading away from the Hacklands and towards the control booth.

"*Stalac!*" Ven cursed.

As they were slowly dragged towards their inevitable capture, Luisa said, "We have to try to use the Meteorlight! Maybe it can let us . . . control the car manually!" She was crouched next to the pulley that yanked the car along the line. They would be in the Stackers' claws in mere minutes. Her fingers hovered above it, but when she got too near, a green spark arced into her fingertip. She yelped, shook it off, and the car shivered, slowed down slightly . . . then continued its trek towards their doom.

Then Dunstan grabbed hold of Ven's tail. "I think we could — with the right amount of power!" He jerked his chin below. "As well as audience participation."

Ven glazed over from panic into hopeful glee; he looked sideways and rightways before grasping Dunstan's hand with his tail, like they had during their dance number.

166

The rider inside neatly folded up his paper, groaned, then leapt out the window, entirely fed up with his commute.

"The Light has the right, Prince Ven!" Commander Vora shouted as they came closer, closer. "The Higher-ups will be more than happy to see you and some of their fellows! I'm sure you'll be handsomely rewarded for handing them over to us!"

"You really were always one for drawing out a play, Dunstan Cord," Luisa seethed, holding tight to the pulley and snapping her fingers like a lighter shedding green sparks. Ven wrapped his tail around the pulley with Dunstan's hand pressed into it. They felt a jolt, like static.

Then with a massive screech, the Stettle car came to a stop, twenty feet from the commander, but close to Decca, who was scaling the line with precision.

Vora sneered, her eyes a smoky quartz of malice.

"So you liked the show?" Dunstan shouted, as the Stackers piled onto the platform and, one by one, wrapped their tails around the cable, beginning to shimmy out to meet them on the stalled cable track. "Really, your reviews mean the world to us! Anyone else catch our matinee at the Look Alight?"

The Stackers paused. Dunstan wasn't addressing them, but the crowd below. Applause rang up, and it made Dunstan's broken heart soar.

Luisa clapped her hands over Ven's tail and Dunstan's hands, squeezing the pulley, which was strobing under the glow. "C'mon," she muttered, "just a little more . . ."

"You reprobates will never perform on a Jettite spectacle stage again!" Vora crowed. "Not if I have anything to—"

"But you have to admit, ma'am," one of the Stackers on the line said, turning his head, "it *did* give Jet a good surge."

Vora, looking murderous, lashed out her tail and smacked the offending Stacker off the line. He tumbled like a pill bug and landed neatly on the ground. They needed the Light to get away, but Dunstan found himself faltering, like he had on the stage at the Look Alight until Ven had saved him. He looked to the lizard prince, who was relying on Dunstan to keep his promise, even if it was born from a lie.

Then he looked back at the Stackers making their progress towards him, and the Meteorlight inside him hissed, *Don't let them take us! We must shine!*

He squeezed Ven's hand, and to the waiting crowd below, cried, "People of Jet! Hear me now!"

The crowd seemed to let out a collective gasp as Dunstan let the frightening thing inside him out, the Light streaming, incandescent, from his eyes.

"I have come from the Above, the same as your humble leaders. But I have with me the Meteorlight you're missing! And the only reason I'm here . . . is because of Prince Ven!"

Shock, drama, someone fainting. Luisa hissing, "Keep going!" as the pulley sparkled.

"Your prince brought me here with his single prayer to help Jet. And I've come, with my Higher-up Truffledour training, to bring the Light back to you! To all of you! Our performance in the Look Alight was only the beginning of . . . of . . ." If there was one thing Dunstan could manage, it was good titles. "Our Timely Tenacious Truffledour Tour!"

"A tour?" echoed through the crowd, the excitement ramping up.

"A tour!" Dunstan confirmed, and pointing towards the commander, he sneered. "All we wish to do is to return Jet's Light — but the commander here thinks we're intruders! She would snuff out the Light before it can be shared amongst you!"

A raging cacophony of boos followed. Although Vora herself was purple, her rage seemed to shiver puce as she mounted the cable and began working her way towards them, nearly outstripping Decca in moments.

"It seems I must take the prince topside to protect him, for he is *vital* to our double act! As is my beloved stage manager. But never fear, we'll be back! And Jet will quake no more!"

"The Light! The Light! The Light has the right!" the crowd chanted, giving Vora a half-second's pause as she looked down at the roiling masses ready to riot.

And in that instant of indecision, Dunstan turned to Ven, pulled him close, and kissed him.

It was the massive surge they needed, throwing the shuttle back to life. Dunstan pulled away and watched the brightness ricochet in Luisa's eyes, charge through the pulley, the car, and then the cable, ping-ponging between Ven, Dunstan, and Luisa.

The light flashed over Commander Vora, too, etching in grand detail her enraged upside-down expression as, inches from her and Decca's outstretched claws, Dunstan yelled "Reverse!" And the car, obedient, zipped away, and back towards the Hacklands.

Ven pulled Luisa up, holding her steady in one hand, Dunstan in his tail, all three holding fast to one another.

As they raced blindly on the cable line, Ven shouted, "You sure about this?"

Dunstan, eyes streaming green, smirked upwards, the Door appearing quickly overhead. He could see it shivering, feel its pull. *We need to shine. We can do that better in the Light.* The thing whispering behind Dunstan's racing mind of dreams and fantastic adventures was getting louder now. It had given him a voice, so he'd let it have one, too.

"I always keep my promises!" Dunstan cried, grinning at Ven, who, unable to help himself, grinned back.

As if the Stettle car was one with Dunstan's thoughts, it pulled itself up against its cable, easily snapping it as it careened heavenwards, leaving chaos, destroyed transit lines, and disgruntled commuters in its wake.

Above, Ada cut the engine, just as the quake sent rippling waves that crashed on the shores of Knockum, the boats docked at the marina cresting high, some of them making landfall, destroying docks. Even two miles from shore, Ada heard the screams. This was far worse than the first quakes. Ada was waiting for the world to crack open and for Lake Mallion to drain down into the abyss.

She wasn't too far off.

Ada held on to the helm for dear life as the trawler rocked and rolled, her lifejacket digging into her cheek as she looked out into the dusky waters to see what looked like a drain opening: an inverted cyclone, spinning faster and faster, and at the edges of it, a green glow that made her chest catch. The glow grew brighter, almost blinding, until from the mini maelstrom three figures shot out of the water, landed back on the surface with a disgruntled splash, then took massive breaths as they gulped for air.

The quake settled. The cacophony on the shore did not. When the waves died down, and the trawler slowed, Ada peeled herself from the steerage to look over the side at the figures splashing violently in the lake near the prow.

"Dun!" she cried, and then, narrowing her eyes, "Luisa?"

The two of them were fighting with something large, dark, whipping arms and legs. A person.

"Ma!" Dunstan shouted. "Hurry! He can't swim!"

The questions could keep. Ada threw a life preserver overboard, then dove in herself, cutting the water clean and away as she reached Dunstan and Luisa, grasping hold of the third person and guiding them all back to the trawler by the light of the bobbing boat, still recovering as the waves subsided.

Once they hit the deck, the teens sprawled and panting, Luisa smacked Dunstan a few times mid-recovery, and Ada had to pry them apart.

"Stop it!" Ada said, getting between them. "What's the matter with you two? And what in Dinah's name is going on?" She looked back over her shoulder at the buoys, no sign of that sickly light now.

"And who is this?" The one she'd pulled from the water was crouched in a corner of the deck, a dark heavy coat covering him. He was covering his head, shaking, probably still traumatized and in a state of shock.

170

Ada approached slowly, a hand out. "Listen, are you all right? Here, let me—"

Then he turned towards her, the goggles clattering to the floor, and Ada recoiled.

"Mum," Dunstan said, using that special tone of *please hear me out before you blow a gasket I promise I have a really good explanation for this*, "this is Prince Ven. And he needs a place to crash from the cops tonight."

Ven blinked up at Ada, his eyes pearly in the semi-dark as he smiled. He got shakily to his feet, tripping and catching himself on the trawler's railing not just with his hands, but with his massive tail. He was big, but his voice seemed small, as he held out a hand, claws and scales gleaming in the twilight, and said, "It's a pleasure to meet you. You must be my boyfriend's mother?"

ACT

III

SCENE 9

STAGE MANAGED

Coral had holed up in her studio since departing from Ada's company. There had been a few aftershocks in the area, but nothing significant. Knockum slept, serenely oblivious to what was lurking in the lake it was built around.

They were able to live that privilege because Coral had been keeping an eye on the town all these years, the lightkeepers keeping theirs on the water.

Many hours for many years Coral had sat in this chair, lost in thought, going around and around in her head. Sometimes she wondered what the point of her silent, lonely vigil was. It seemed like the Meteorlight was long gone — maybe back to space where it had come from. It had been imprisoned where it'd landed, then grown hungry for more. Coral gave it what it wanted. Or so she thought.

She daydreamed about leaving Knockum, perhaps retiring to a quaint place in the Hamilhess Desert where she could steep tea, traipse across dunes that would erase her passage . . . and take off her many layers of misdirection.

But the Door was in Knockum and there it would always be. And on the other side of it . . . she sighed heavily. No, she could never leave. Not until the Meteorlight was sent back to where it belonged. Where she'd intended to send it the first time.

She lay her head on the recliner, settling in for another lonely, restless night. Then, just as the sun was setting, another massive quake jolted her out of her chair, her piles of canvases and half-finished sculptures juddering to the floor despite her many attempts to rescue them.

This was getting to be too much.

She sat there a while, waiting. Ada Cord would come knocking sooner rather than later. Maybe she had the boy back already. Coral would have to go to the house and see for herself, contain this mess — and, likely, explain everything. She wasn't ready for that yet. For the consequences of her mistakes to be laid bare. *I never should have sent that boy home when I had him*, she'd admonished herself, over and over, but as she lifted her boot, and came face to face with the little drawing Cord had left behind, she knew she'd been distracted.

Because there on the sheet was Prince Ven. Older now, but alive. Cord had seen him. Maybe even spoken to him. And Coral realized that she cared more about hearing how the prince was than about saving both doomed towns.

She jolted when the phone rang. Cursing, she searched for it. Buried beneath canvases and drop sheets, she finally picked it up. "Yes?"

A shock went through her. "Unidentified craft came to shore at 22:10, west dock, Knockum — might be what you're looking for. Top brass says we'll stay out of it. For now." Coral hung up; obviously Morag had been checking in, at least, even if she hadn't been returning Coral's calls. For now it didn't matter. She raced out the door, then doubled back as the shock of the night air touching her face sent her scrambling for her kerchief, her sunglasses. You never knew who was watching.

When Coral got there, she nearly crumpled in the sand, uncomprehending. What in the waters . . . was a Stettle Beetle shuttle doing here?

Coral leaned down, checking the interior. It was empty. In fact, the door was wrenched open on its hinges, with distinct claw marks on the exit handle.

Coral cursed herself. The one time she had slipped her guard and indulged in her own petty thoughts . . . and now a Jettite was loose in Knockum.

All told, their return back to the Cord household had been very . . . one-sided. Dunstan had rushed through the tale of his epic and grand adventure — glossing over Moss and his buddies' attempt at murder, and some of the more dangerous scenarios Dunstan had found himself in.

All the while, Ada merely drove in total silence, and the tension ratcheted from there. Dunstan had been certain if he demonstrated he was completely fine, they'd be in the clear for their pitch to aid Jet in its moment of peril. After all, here was their deposed prince — an ambassador, really — who needed a place to stay. Didn't it all seem very reasonable?

". . . and the *show*! Oh, Ma, it was a stunner!" Dunstan slid out of the car, pulling Ven along with him, shaking his hand excitedly. "We lit up every corner of the city! And Ven, well, he's a natural on the stage."

"I am, aren't I?" Ven chuckled. "And the show didn't end there! That Stettle car caper was something else entirely! Oh, but I assure you Ada, we—"

Luisa cleared her throat and slid a finger across it. Dunstan and Ven halted, staring at Ada's back as she stood on the porch stairs, unmoving. Only then did Dunstan realize that simply surviving wasn't worth much, since he'd spent the entire ride home extolling the virtues of adventures far away from home.

"Ma . . . I'm sorry I . . ." He pushed his glasses up his nose, the spare pair she kept in the glove compartment, and scuffed the front path in its halo of porch light. "I didn't want to worry you. It's just—"

"It's just that you thought running away to a secret lizard kingdom was a completely rational way to tell me you're unhappy here."

That hit, and the thing Dunstan'd been carrying around that had bolstered him through his adventures cowered at the blow.

"That's not it—"

Dunstan felt a gentle pressure on his shoulder as Ven pulled his hand back and stepped forward. "Ada Cord, this is all my doing."

Now Ada turned, eyebrow raised. Her reaction to Ven had been curt courtesy so far, with no question to his appearance. She seemed willing to hear him out.

"My Geodom, Jet, is in peril. I know you've felt the quakes here, and so have we. Whole spires are being washed away by the lake we didn't know was over our heads . . . but it was Dunstan who came to us, to *help* us." He looked meaningfully at Dunstan then. No more act, just genuine gratitude.

The thing inside Dunstan squirmed again.

"Dunstan brought the Meteorlight back to Jet at his own peril. And he agreed to bring me here, to your world . . . something I always knew I had to do. And now I know why." He clasped his scaled hands, claw-tipped and fierce, in a penitent plea. "Thank you for letting him come to Jet. Because Dunstan is our only hope."

Dunstan blinked slowly, heart thrumming. Ven looked . . . serious. Head bowed, expression drawn. Dunstan knew he wouldn't *really* abandon his kingdom to go lollygagging around Brindlewatch like an itinerant scoundrel. Yet Dunstan knew that only a few hours ago, Ven was itching to get gone and not take a second glance out the rearview mirror of his velocipede. Was this just . . . another performance?

Then he looked quickly at Ada. Poor Ada, who had probably been fretting for days about Dunstan's body washing up on the shore, or finding him ripped to pieces in Eastmerlin Woods. Lorraine used to say that Ada worried enough for everyone in town, and her face, carved in the porch shadows, showed it.

She let out a great, body-wracking sigh. "You can stay the night, Your Highness. I'm not going to leave you out on the streets where someone will sell you tooth and scale to a laboratory." She pulled the front door open and gestured for everyone to get inside. "But before you get too cozy . . . Ven, do your parents know you're here?"

Dunstan had gone through the door partways but stopped, shoulders hunched. He took a quick look at Ven, whose eyes blinked sideways. "My what?"

With a tug on Ada's sleeve, Dunstan shook his head rapidly, wincing as if to say, *don't ask*. And Ada cleared her throat.

"I'm sorry," she recovered. "I suppose . . . do you have anyone who is your, ah, guardian? Are they aware of where you are? That you're safe?"

Ven swallowed, looking away with a half-smile. "Don't worry about me; I'm the only one who does." He went tentatively into the house then, looking around with avid curiosity and nearly poking a lamp right off a table until Ada caught it swiftly.

"Well, you're in my house. Which means you're under my care. And under this roof, we all take care of one another. Is that understood, Highness?"

Ven turned slightly solemn then, nodding, voice low. "Yes, ma'am."

"Good." Then she turned to Dunstan as she righted the lamp. "Show Ven the spare bedroom, please. I'll have a better head and stomach for dealing with all this in the morning."

Ada nearly dropped the lamp anew as Ven clasped her up in a hug. "Thank you, Ada Cord! You won't regret it, I promise!"

"Don't make promises you can't keep," she muttered, as Dunstan pulled the prince away, yammering, "Oh, are you used to sleeping on beds? Maybe you'd be better suited to the floor? It's more rock-like! The floor in my room is particularly great!"

They were already at the stairs before Ada could shout, "You are sleeping in separate bedrooms, Dunstan Cord!" but she let them go up the dark hall, too many warring thoughts smashing into one another, until she looked back at Luisa, who was still standing at the foot of the porch, unsure where she fit into all this.

Ada went down to join her. "Hector must be worried sick, Luisa. Should I call him?"

Luisa waved her off, backing away. "He's been on the night shift lately. He's probably all turned around from everything going on in town. It's all right." She twisted her hands, lost in her own worries, as she turned for the front garden gate.

"It's not all right, is it?"

Luisa paused, hand on the latch. Ada turned her eyes heavenwards, then shut them, as if making a prayer.

"Thank you," she said suddenly, opening her eyes and smiling at Luisa. "For bringing him home. Coral told me that you went . . . there. To get Dunstan." A weak shrug. "You're the level-headed one. Is everything that Dunstan said . . . is it . . . ?"

At that, Luisa looked back at the house, expression a bit sadder than Ada had expected. "Yes. All of it. The city, the people, the problems. I hope we can help, like Dunstan promised he would." A faraway look. "Anyway. Happy to drag him out of his usual flamboyant disregard for reality. Just like old times."

Ada took her chance to ask, "I know it was probably hard for you to go get him. And I'm still very grateful, but. What happened? Before all this. What happened between you and Dun?"

It was dark out, and Luisa had gone past the porch lamp, but Ada was certain her eyes were glassy. Luisa turned away again quickly.

"Water under the Door," Luisa said, waving her hand. "I have a feeling he's gonna need to be stage managed for this next performance. I'll see you later, Mrs. Cord."

Then she took the corner at their front garden fence and was gone.

Ven lay on the cushy surface of what Dunstan had called a *bed*, in the room that he had mentioned was *spare*, and did not know what to do with himself as he stared at the — well, it wasn't a hovel roof, not like back home. And his chest ached like it had been scratched hard with fifty claws at the thought. *Home.* The world spun around and around in his mind. *This* was Dunstan's home, a world away. And this *had* been what he wanted . . .

to come here. To see it for himself. To get out of Jet as soon as possible. So far, the margin beside his carefully crafted plan was filled with checkmarks.

So why did he feel so . . . unsettled?

He shifted on the bed-thing. It was soft. He didn't like soft. No real Jettite worth their scales did. If one of them walked in here right now, he'd get a hornful! Ven grimaced. *You don't have any friends in Jet to scold you anyway.* Being a vagrant all this time sure had been exhausting; in fact, this was likely the first time in a long while that Ven could remember relaxing. His cause had been a lonely one. That had always been the plan. And when Ada Cord had asked him about his parents and his well-being . . .

No one ever asked him that.

Ven sat up suddenly, dark-adjusted eyes pointed towards the door. On the other side of it was the hall, where Dunstan's room was. He was tired but couldn't very well sleep . . . these house-things were crowded. He needed to stretch his legs and think.

The window, then. Dunstan had left it partways open to let in "the breeze," the soft whisper of air that came from outside. Ven pushed it open, examined the distance to the ground, and leapt.

It was like wandering in one of Dunstan's dreams. The world was dark, like Jet, and had its own little pockets of glowing. But these were yellow, and when Ven got snout-close, tapping a claw on them, their shells were hard. Maybe they used insect carapaces up here, too? Whenever he heard a noise, he dove into the deeper shadow dark, and when he was sure the coast was clear, a smell invaded his nostrils on the night air.

The lake.

He turned and made his way to the place where the water met the ground. Where they had disembarked when Ada pulled them from the wet. Ven shuddered. What an awful experience that had been, feeling the water all around him, slicing through it but getting nowhere. He clutched his arms close. No Jettite would ever have jumped into so much water, enough to cover themselves. It simply wasn't natural . . .

Yet when he stood there on the shore again, staring out into the lapping blackness of the lake, the brine of it, the mud and sand beneath his boots, he felt small. This world was wider than he could have imagined, and the lake itself was a hungry portent of it. He thought painfully of his little home, his feckless lichen painting of what he'd imagined it all to be. His blistering mind only had space for two things: *All this could wipe Jet away to nothing. And, it was Dunstan who pulled me from the water and saved me.*

"Now we're even," he said quietly to himself, kicking a stone into the water with a somewhat satisfying *plorp.* He turned to leave, to muzzily make his way back, when he came face to face with another Jettite.

Ven nearly backed up into the water, but caught himself, heart racing. It wasn't moving; it was standing perfectly still, raised up — or was it flying? He picked up another stone and hurled it in the Jettite's direction, but it bounced off and came to rest once more on the ground.

"A statue?" Ven got closer, staring up at it and running a scaly hand over the smooth surface. Upon inspection, it *did* look very similar to a Jettite . . . with exaggerations. The tail was different, wide with a flourishing fin on the end. But it had the characteristic great coat all Jettites wore to keep themselves warm in a city losing its light. Hard to see it in the dark. Harder still to understand how a likeness of his people was here, in this place where none of them had ever been.

"It's not bad," came a voice. "But it *is* proof they know about us already."

Ven whipped his tail up, tensing for the attack, then he relaxed. "Oh. It's just *you.*"

"'Just *me,*'" Commander Vora mocked, waving her hands. "And what are you doing? Taking a stroll, or completely undermining the plan?" She flicked Ven's head from side to side with her tail, looked him up and down. "You're not hurt, are you?"

"No," he answered, dry and annoyed and shaking her off. "I'm perfectly fine. Like I told you I'd be." Then he tilted his head. "You made it here in one piece. Didn't think you would. How *did* you get here?"

"Don't ask," she sniffed. "The Stettle Beetle car wasn't my brightest move. It filled up with water immediately. We nearly didn't make it out."

Ven felt dread slide over him as he glanced around the empty street, up the shore, and behind the statue. "Who's we?"

Vora, pinching her snout, sighed. "The Stackling. I sent her on reconnaissance so I could get her to shut the bash up. I wouldn't have chosen her for this particular mission but . . . right place, wrong time."

Ven nodded, pretending to be at all interested in the commander's complaints. Vora had pushed him in every direction for years, ever since King Vert had ruined everything. But coming up here had been *his* plan. *His* lead. And he'd been the one to come up here on his own. The lake may be a threat, but he'd conquered it. For now, at least.

But Ven wasn't through with the statue, knocking a knuckle against it. "What do you think this means?"

Vora joined him, arms folded, tilting her head. "It means there's someone here who knows about Jet." She shook her head. "It also means we need to act carefully, and quickly. Which begs the question — why are you out in the open, alone? This place is crawling with Higher-ups who could—"

"It's *fine*," Ven replied testily. "Dunstan told me everyone is asleep. They don't get up until sunrise. Whatever that is." He began walking back towards the Cords' house, staring at the ground. "I just needed . . . to think, that's all."

"Think about what? Going back on the plan?" Vora only had two speeds: utter adherence to rules and reality, or bland sarcasm. Sometimes it was hard to tell them apart. "Remember it was your idea to let your little Bright Eyes come back to us on his own terms. You know what I would've done if it were up to me . . ."

Ven turned towards her fast; she stopped walking. "But it's not up to you. I'm the prince. We agreed. Besides, we tried it your way, with Reeve Gris and the others. And you know how that panned out."

Vora recoiled, looking away. "I didn't have a choice. The Higher-ups were . . . well, they weren't doing well. Why do you think this one is going to fare any better with the Meteorlight inside him?" She shook her head. "These humans. They're not made to carry it like we are."

Ven set his jaw, then continued up the hill. "Dunstan is different. He's stronger, more . . . I don't know. *Inspired.* He and the Meteorlight work well together, and we need to keep that in our favour. Keep him thinking this is *his* idea."

"It's not just because you've grown attached to him, is it?" Vora asked, a touch of venom in her tone.

Ven whirled, shouting, "I'm not heartstruck!" Vora clapped a hand over his mouth, dragging them both into the shadows as a precautionary measure. He shook her off, leaning against the hard wall that blocked the lake from their view. "I'm as sure now as ever that this is what we need to do. It's just that . . ."

He shut his eyes. He had come out here because he hadn't wanted to think about what had happened, to lead him here. His tail twitched, though, remembering clearly Dunstan's hand on it. The connection it had sparked. Along it, Ven had felt something he recognized, something that made him hold all the tighter to Dunstan and refuse to resign him to the fate waiting for him in the Tallest Tor. If it were up to Vora, he'd already be there, *plugged in*, and Ven knew it'd be a waste.

Could there be a way to get everything he wanted?

Squaring his shoulders, Ven snorted. "I've been waiting for this moment for too long." He looked down his snout at Vora, even though they had always been the same height. "I've got it all under control."

She snorted. "See that you do. Keep that little Higher-up and the Meteorlight he possesses close to you — whatever it takes. Let him believe he's going to be some kind of hero. This spectacle tour could be spun to our advantage. To keep the Door open . . . and keep Jet alive."

A quick nod. They each took one another's shoulder, squeezed.

"Good luck," Vora said as she turned to leave, then, after a pause, she added, "little brother."

Ven made his way back up the road to Dunstan's hovel. He felt brazen now. Realigned. If anyone saw him, he'd take care of it, Vora be bashed. He was the prince of Jet, the true heir to the geodom's throne. No one was going to take that from him — not again.

When he took the corner, Ven noticed another glow coming from behind the house. Curious, he approached in a half-crouch, until he realized there was another, smaller hovel — house, he corrected again — up in . . . what had Dunstan called these things? Trees?

There was a hole in the floor he could see through, and suddenly a great clattering that sent him twitching out of the way as something sailed past his tail. He caught it by the hole cut in its centre. Then, from above, Dunstan's head appeared. "Oh! Thank Dinah, you caught it!"

Flicking his tail, Ven caught the black disc between his claws, turning it this way and that. "Is it some kind of treasure?"

"Worth more than that! It's a first pressing of my uncle Slanner's EP! Bring it up here, will you?" And with another clattering, Dunstan vanished.

Keep him close, no matter the cost. Ven's tongue flickered as he neatly climbed the ladder up the tree, poking his head into the little high house. Higher-ups must always have been obsessed with being on top of things . . . though Jettites weren't any different with the Tors. "What is this place? I thought you were sleeping inside the other one."

"Guess you don't have treehouses in Jet." Dunstan chuckled, sifting through a pile in the corner. "What about mushroomhouses?"

Ven blinked, pulling himself inside. He placed the EP gently on the floor, looking back down the way he'd come. "Are trees like mushrooms?"

"Sort of," Dunstan shrugged. "But enough about biology! Come here!" And holding out his hand, Dunstan led Ven further into his world.

He shouldn't have gone so willingly, but Ven couldn't help it. All these years looking over his shoulder, unable to trust anyone . . . he needed Dunstan to continue trusting him. And a part of him really *wanted* him to, even if it was based on a lie.

We're lying to each other, an imp inside clucked, and Ven spoke over it: "It reminds me of my place, back in . . . back home."

Dunstan had apparently been on the verge of an apology. "How did you know I was just going to regretfully admit it isn't a palace? Though I suppose you haven't lived in one in a while." Then he waved and rolled his hands, scraping a bow, "Your vagrancy."

Ven didn't want to admit how good it felt that Dunstan was treating him like the prince he often forgot he was. He let himself laugh, though.

"Oh, don't worry. Everything about your home is wonderfully vivacious, like you are." Ven poked Dunstan in the ribs with his tail, then flopped down, swishing his tail over the bumpy texture pleasingly. "It's so full of warmth, your world. I'm not used to that."

Dunstan, this little Higher-up Hero breathless for adventure, was brimming with a contagious chaotic energy that Ven decided to latch on to, to keep his thoughts in one place. After all, Vora said to keep him close. Spending time with him, therefore, was part of the plan. So he wasn't deviating from it . . . much.

"What are you up to in here, then?"

Dunstan blurted, "I'm planning our tour!" He was already lit up from the Meteorlight's glow, streaming out of his eyes in thin ribbons, but it was an expression of such sheer delight that Ven couldn't help but be ensnared by it. "I couldn't sleep, thinking of all the shows we're going to have to put on."

This spectacle tour could be spun to our advantage . . . Ven flicked his tongue. "So we're really doing that, are we? I thought that was a clever distraction to make good our escape."

"It can be both!" Dunstan pulled from three piles that he had in front of him, arms full as he paced and explained. "We've got the public on our side. You saw those crowds! I doubt the Stackers will be able to put us behind bars now that we've proclaimed to the whole city our plan. See, we spend the summer putting on shows, using my Meteorlight to keep Jet glowing, keep it from quaking off its moorings. See if that helps with all the surges we can create. And then, who knows, maybe it becomes a full-time gig! I can live in Knockum, work in Jet. Once the City is restored, you'll get your throne back! And since I can open the Door in Lake Mallion now, maybe Reeve Gris and the Sunken Three will finally want to come home!"

Dunstan dropped the pile of papers between himself and the prince, kneeling down, hands on his shoulders, quivering with excitement.

"It will *work*, Ven. I know it will!" A moment's spark between them, Dunstan's ribboning eyes fluttering, then he backed off, rubbing his chest. "Anyway, I have oodles of material, original and licensed, as you can see. And I'm sure that tube band we met at the Look Alight will be on hand to add the accompaniment. You said there are dozens of Jettites looking for their chance to be Truffledours. We'll hold auditions! I've done this all before — I can make this happen!"

Ven didn't doubt it for a second. "You always have things all figured out," he said, legs crossed, leaning forward with his hands on his cheeks. "But if that's your plan, then why did you bring me all the way up here?"

Dunstan faltered at the question. "Oh. Because . . . I promised you I would, didn't I? I didn't want you think I was just using you to get a gig in Jet."

Ven didn't blink, or tilt his head, or move for that matter. He felt his heart jerk, which was never a good sign. "I see," he said quietly. *Maybe you're the only one who's lying,* his impish conscience said. Ven didn't do anything to silence it this time.

"Tell me about all this, then," he asked, leafing through the hard round discs fanned out before them both, goggling at the piles of thinly sliced . . . fungus? He picked up a sheet and sniffed it. "How can your spectacles be on these?"

"Those are plays. What do Jettite Truffledours write all their spectacles down on?"

"They don't," Ven answered. "The mushrooms have excellent memories. All our spectacles, and our histories, are stored in those."

"Far out!" Dunstan crowed, adjusting his glasses and almost muttering to himself as he shuffled the ephemera. "Ah, here we have Burl Hely's *Kiss in the Moonlight* LP, a seminal recording of the Vanway show . . . a little Debbie Oakenak, that crooning set I recorded from the radio a few years back. Oh! And then there's that EP you brought—" He flashed it at Ven, full of pride. "He's technically my mother's cousin, but this is his band, the Kadaver's Soiree. They've got the best jazzy sound . . ."

"So these are all spectacles?" The pile was getting larger by the second. "Why do you have them?"

Dunstan stopped, staring at his knees. He lifted his hand to his eyes but let them fall. His smile seemed sad. "You call them spectacles. Here, we call them *shows*. Musicals. They've been really important to me and my . . ." A stifled chuckle. "Hero's journey, I guess you could say."

He moved to sit next to Ven, who still did everything to control his racing thoughts. He'd been free in connecting with Dunstan, maybe a little too much. When he had at the Look Alight, a flood of truths and big feelings surged into Ven's mind. It'd made him second-guess everything. It's what stopped him from doing what Vora had wanted. He didn't mind this detour, so long as things turned out the way they were supposed to . . . but the barest admission squeaked through his control: *I don't care about the Higher-ups who took over Jet. But I do care about* this *Higher-up.*

He let Dunstan lean over him to organize the piles of precious spectacles. "It's music and words and stories. I connect with them." Dunstan held up something else made of colourful paper and handed it to Ven. "Comics, too. All of it inspires me to dream my big, weird, stupid dreams . . ." He lifted a shoulder. "This summer is probably my last shot to really to make them happen."

"Because of your eyes?" Dunstan looked away, but Ven persisted. "You have the Meteorlight! You don't have to worry about any of that. And most of all you have" — he moved to grab Dunstan's hand but pulled away, looking sideways — "me."

Dunstan didn't answer straight away, just looked directly in Ven's eyes. Dunstan's lit up green and glowing like a sudden shroomfire.

Ven laughed. "You must be excited."

"I guess the Light gets stronger when you're . . . I'm . . . people are . . . overwhelmed." Dunstan coughed through the speech and tried to cover his face, but Ven pulled his hands down playfully with his tail.

Which was also glowing.

"What do you call this . . ." Ven pressed Dunstan's hand to his chest, with his glowing tail. "This feeling? What do you call it here?"

"Love." Dunstan said it quietly, as if saying it any louder would scare it away. Then his eyes dimmed. "I don't think I'm compatible with it, though. Every time I try, I just mess things up."

Ven frowned, knowing exactly what he meant. "We call it *heart-struck*. It's a closeness, to Jettites. It's fragile, and it can also be dangerous. Is that why you . . ."

Dunstan waved his hands. "No, no. I mean, it's the same here. Love is, uh, complicated." He pulled his legs up and wrapped his arms around them. "I think I've been in love too many times. It hasn't done me any good, that's all."

"Mm." Ven leaned back, taking a moment to really think about it. Then he surveyed the piles of papers, the treehouse. "I've never been heartstruck before. But you seem to be chronically so. What a pair we make." He smiled, and this time it wasn't the easy, placating one he saved for Vora and everyone else. This was his alone. "I wouldn't mind being heartstruck with you, I think."

"Oh?" Surprised, Dunstan seemed to shrink a little bit. "I, uh. I guess I thought that Jettites . . . don't . . ."

Then Ven snapped his fingers, the pieces clicking together. "Is that what that thing was? You mushing your mouth onto mine? Is that because you're heartstruck with me?"

"Ughhhh." Dunstan buried his face in his knees, not dignifying it with a response.

"Well, you brought me here, so you must be. Not like it's difficult or anything. I'm a catch." He dragged Dunstan closer with his arm, and it didn't feel at all like an act as Dunstan leaned his head on him — gently at first, then fully relaxing.

It seemed odd that this little pink creature made Ven want to spill all his truths. But he'd have to be careful, and pick which ones. He started a little closer to home. "I haven't had a caretaker . . . not for a very long time, anyway." Ven's voice ebbed in the quiet of the treehouse. "But your caretaker — your *mother* — she seems nice. I don't remember much of King Vert. I just know I've been paying for his mistakes for longer than I should have." He jerked his head. "Your home makes me feel heartstruck. If I had a place like this waiting for me, I don't think I'd want to leave it." He rested his chin on Dunstan's head. "But you did. For Jet."

Dunstan, his exuberance tampered down, just swallowed.

"It's just that you're really, really kind," Ven said quietly, staying absolutely still. "And you're trying to do the right thing. So now it's my turn to thank you. For pulling me out of Jet, and out of the water. And for bringing me here."

"The right thing . . ." Dunstan muttered, toeing the piles of inspiration, as he'd called it. Then he shook his head, and dove back in. "The right thing to do would be to find your colour palette," he said, picking up slips of fabric pinned to paper and holding them up to Ven. "You'll need the perfect ensemble when you get up on that stage with me."

Ven half-laughed. "I think I'll retire early. Diplomacy is my department."

"Oh, c'mon, you shone up there! Just think of it — the first Truffledour Prince the geodom has ever seen!"

That had been one dream, long ago, when Ven could afford to. Something sliced across his mending heart at Dunstan's words, his promises; an ache of duty. He *was* a Truffledour now. A fine one that could fool anybody with any story he concocted.

Except, seeing Dunstan's earnestness, he didn't know if he had the heart to fool him to the inevitable end.

"Show me more of your spectacles," he smiled. Easily. "Then we can refine our heroic plans. Together."

For as long as it takes.

For the Meteorlight to be mine.

Luisa's night hadn't been restful, and she knew it wouldn't be. Not after what she'd been through.

Hector had taken another night shift after sleeping the day away; the note he'd left was more an apology than a statement of his whereabouts, couched in a warning: *There are weird things going on,* it said. *These quakes. No one can explain them. Some think they're gonna crack the basin and sink the town. Messages going out to all the lightkeeper stations. I'm just having a hard time staying awake, baby girl. Having weird dreams lately. And maybe I'm crazy, but you're in these dreams, in a city at the bottom of the lake. I'm on the night shift tonight, because I need to keep an eye on Knockum, for my part. Just hope you're okay.*

Luisa was not okay. She was exhausted. And worried. The night Dunstan had vanished through the Door in Lake Mallion, she'd heard a snippet of Hector's dreams: *The Door. It's open.* How had he known?

Unable to sleep — or perhaps unwilling to — Luisa left the empty house and sat on her porch. She needed to take lungful after lungful of fresh summer night air, trying to come to terms with the little escapade Dunstan had dragged her on. The air in Jet had been moist, earthy. Teeming, somehow, with promise. But it was a very real smell — and the place itself was real. The people, too, in the countless crowds chasing them or cheering them on. Jet was real. And after witnessing part of it be washed away, she found herself knotted with worry.

The quakes could crack the basin and sink the town. Luisa wondered where that portent had come from . . . just a rumour, or a surety? Because if the basin *did* crack, it wouldn't just be Knockum that would be afflicted. Every town around the lake, and the city beneath it, would be gone.

She buried her face in her hands. At the heart of it all was Dunstan. Why was Luisa always being called upon to sweep up his messes?

Why wasn't there anyone to rescue *her* for a change?

A huge crash echoed from down the road, and Luisa leapt up so quickly she nearly fell down her own front steps. Still sharp as a live wire from today's many surprises, she found her clenched fists sparking green in time with her heartbeat, but she didn't care. She could use it to scare who — or what — had lurched out of the shadows and under a flickering garage light.

Luisa's fists relaxed; they weren't lurching, they were cowering, and somewhat whimpering. She jogged up the street, sneakers scuffing the gravel and sending Decca wheeling onto her tail, shakily hoisting her busted javelin in Luisa's direction.

"Oh!" she cried, dropping it with a clatter, and throwing herself into Luisa's arms.

Luisa staggered, unsure what else to do but catch Decca and pat her awkwardly between the shoulders. "Didn't expect to see you here," she said, unable to stop herself from smiling.

Decca was *not* smiling. "This place! The High-up!" Her spiked head darted, as if she saw ghouls in every driveway. "It's . . . it's . . . *awful*!"

Luisa half-laughed. "Well, I guess you've never left home before . . ."

"No! I haven't!" Decca's shining golden eyes sprung wider, chin wobbling. "I was supposed to be doing reconnaissance, and I really thought I could do it, but I can't! And the commander is expecting me—"

"Commander Vora is *here*?" Luisa hissed. She grabbed Decca's arm and started dragging her back in the direction of her house. "Come on. Let's get you inside. You'll feel a lot better once we're out of the open, trust me."

Decca was a Stacker, and Luisa was sure that came with at least some basic training about survival, but Decca didn't seem to have the constitution for the emotionally demanding military life. She blubbered on their way into Luisa's house, through the door, and up the stairs, and didn't seem to realize she was indoors with a warm cup of tea in her hands and a wool blanket over her shoulders until she paused her lamentations to take a sip.

A quick sideways blink. "This is very good," she said, U-turning the conversation into a somewhat civilized direction. She then had the grace to look abashed. "I'm sorry. I think I had a, um, bit of a worm-out on you just now."

Worm-out? "Don't worry. I'm used to it." Luisa had earned her stripes dealing with Dunstan's melodrama. Decca's panic attack was nothing. "I know Jettites don't like water . . . coming up here through Lake Mallion must have been very hard for you."

Decca carefully put her teacup down, nodding. "I've never seen so much water in my entire life. It just makes me scared for what could happen to Jet . . ."

"Me, too." Decca lifted her rosy head and scaled brows in surprise, and Luisa clucked her tongue. "I may not have been in Jet very long, but it's a very real place, with very real people who could get hurt. People like . . . well, you, I suppose." Luisa rubbed her eyes hard, trying to stave off the growing headache. "Anyway, I'd ask you what you and the commander are doing in Knockum, but it seems pretty obvious. You're *that* keen on arresting us?"

Decca put her teacup down with a clatter. "I'm not at liberty to . . . to divulge further information than I already, regretfully, have."

"Of course not." Luisa huffed, getting her answer. "So, what? You want me to take you to Dunstan and the prince, then? And where does that leave us all with the predicament we're in?"

Luisa held up her hand, the fingers sparking, except now it seemed she was able to control their arcs, send them across her nails like tiny green sprites at her command. Decca was mesmerized, swallowing.

"Do you think they'll do what they said they would?" Decca asked suddenly. "With the spectacles? The show they put on at the Look Alight . . . it was so wonderful." She was reaching for Luisa's hand, but she pulled it away before they could touch.

"It certainly was something else," Luisa said carefully. She and Decca had snuck inside, beneath an eye of winking mushrooms and waded carefully through the back of an enraptured crowd. And on the wide stage, Dunstan Cord, his apprehension obvious beneath his disguise. Luisa had been seized with the impulse to break through the crowd, grab him, and pull him out of the limelight . . . until he started generating it himself. The story. The ships. It was like Dunstan's imagination, a thing alive that always ran away with him attached, had been cracked open, pouring out over the audience. And something inside Luisa, something separate from her history with Dunstan, had tugged hard, wanting to get closer to that Meteorlight.

She held her glowing fingers close to her eyes, considering. "Here," she said, getting up and digging in her closet until she finally found it, long-buried in the back where she'd angrily thrown it weeks ago. She dragged the heavy duffel bag towards Decca, who looked on curiously.

"I've known Dunstan my entire life. And he's been doing 'spectacles' for about the same amount of time." Decca leaned in to inspect the bag's contents as Luisa sorted them. It was, mostly, a bag of memories: neatly tied electrical cords, a pedal to modulate cues, a sound and lightboard Luisa had proudly wired herself. Luisa had never intended to open the bag again, but she couldn't help it.

"See?" She held up fake playbills, the ones the artistic Arnault had drawn up. *The Flying Knockarounds* — that's what they'd called their little troupe. "These are all posters from shows we tried to put on. We . . . we had fun. But they weren't anything like the show in the Look Alight."

Decca took them carefully, turning them over, trying to understand what they said or meant. "And you? Did you perform with him? Are you a Truffledour, too?"

Luisa shook her head, smiling nostalgically. "Stage manager. I like that role, though. I made sure everything ran smoothly, even if we didn't have particularly captive audiences." She pulled out the pieces of the last poster Arnault had made, before the end of term, smoothing out the crumpled creases on her leg.

Decca snatched it before Luisa could stop her. "Is this another spectacle you put on?"

Luisa clenched her fists. "No. We never put that one on. We were supposed to, for this year's Falling Star Festival at Beckon Bandstand but it . . . didn't work out that way." She grabbed the flyer for *Terrazine and Me,* Dunstan's fantastical seminal original work started in middle school, and stuffed it angrily back in the bag.

"You said he was your friend, but . . ." Decca rubbed a claw over her upside-down heart horns, looking a bit embarrassed.

Luisa let her shoulders drop. "It's that obvious?"

Decca shook her head, recalling. "I felt something when your light and mine interacted. It was sort of like a grudge. But also like a regret. Sorry. It can feel intrusive, but it's how Jettites relate to one another."

Luisa didn't want to get into it, but Decca was as objective as it came. She looked out of her bedroom window, pulling her knees up. "Our first meeting was an argument about what was on the other side of the Door in Lake Mallion, back in kindergarten."

Decca sat up excitedly. "Did you know about Jet?"

"No," Luisa said. "We thought the Door was just a story. It was fun, dreaming with him." She looked back to the duffel bag, biting her lip. "It's not that anything terrible happened between us. We just . . . had an argument. He was always wanting to get out of Knockum as soon as possible, coming up with wilder and grander schemes. And maybe I . . . envied him. Because I don't dream as big as he does. I don't know what I want, really, and I was mad that he did." She shut her eyes, remembering their pettiness. "He missed rehearsals to hang out with his more popular friends. He didn't apologize. And I didn't, either. And suddenly he wasn't our friend anymore and was hanging around with the people who had tormented us all our lives! I hated him for that. But I also still envied him."

A gentle claw scratched through Luisa's shirt sleeve as Decca rested her hand there. She didn't say anything, just nodded and said, "I'm sorry."

Luisa shook her head. "Even now just saying it out loud, it sounds stupid. Especially given the situation we're in . . ." She tried to rub the hurt out of her voice. "Anyway, if anyone is going to save a city with a stage performance, Dunstan Cord is your guy. So it's probably best not to arrest him if Jet wants to be saved."

Decca leaned in, maybe a little too close. "And will you manage the stage for him?"

Luisa's heart sped up under Decca's scrutiny, as well as at the question. "Why should I?"

Decca coughed, then spoke from the other side of her scaly hand in a stage whisper. "So you don't get arrested, too."

"Good point." Luisa rubbed her hands on her thighs, then looked around the room. It was both a nice feeling and an odd one to realize she'd just wished for this — for someone to make her feel less alone in this adventure she didn't ask for. And to realize, for the second time, that Decca was saving her, even if it was in small increments.

"I guess that means I have my work cut out for me." Luisa smiled, and Decca did, too. "And what about you? Should I show you the way back to your commander?"

Decca had been mid-tea-slurp, and she choked a little. "Ah, um, maybe I should, er, refresh myself until I . . . regroup and talk to—"

"You can stay here tonight, don't worry." Luisa got up to gather blankets and pillows. "Is the floor okay?"

"Oh yes, it's very comfy, thank you!" Decca had already rolled herself up in the wool blanket, as if she'd made the decision to sleep over before Luisa had brought it up. Luisa laughed and turned the light out, and before she settled into her bed, Decca's soft snores filled the room in a way that didn't make the walls feel so close anymore. She was finally feeling slightly better about everything, her mind starting to send out flares of ideas. Tomorrow she would give Dunstan a piece of her mind, and if the topic came up about her helping . . . well, she'd think about it.

Luisa looked out her window and into the quiet Knockum night, as if nothing had changed, even though everything had. There were still questions to be answered, and she was certain there were people in this town, people like Coral Frakes, who were keeping secrets as deep as the Door in Lake Mallion.

Rolling over, Luisa scratched her shoulder, then faltered. There was a lump there beneath her T-shirt, one that hadn't been there yesterday. Tentatively, she slid her hand under the fabric to touch it, wondering if she'd injured herself in her Jettite escapades. She was more than startled when she pulled away something unexpected — *impossible*.

She turned on her bedside light, to make sure, but she quickly realized she didn't need it. Pinched between her fingernails was a small green mushroom, glowing brightly before it shimmered dimly, turned black, and disintegrated.

SCENE 10

DREAM A LITTLE DREAM WITH ME

A da slept fitfully all night. She usually had a hard time getting a decent rest. Put rescuing two teens and a giant lizard person from the lake on top of her daily burdens, and she'd fired on her last cylinder.

Her dreams were strange, though stranger still that she dreamed at all, because she often didn't. There were so many doors in these dreams — doors in the Knockum Lightkeeper Station, the doors in her house, all of them swinging wide open and closing again, admitting her then disappearing behind her. Unfamiliar doors, too. Doors that led to strange places that her logical mind refused to translate, doors she passed by and doors that didn't like to be ignored. They hunted and chased her, down to the edge of Lake Mallion, where a door at the bottom was calling her. *I am a door but I should not have been opened. Not then and not now. But I cannot resist. I cannot hold things together much longer, and soon I will be open forever. Please put the Light back in the Darkness, where we both came from. Where we both belong.*

The ground rumbled.

And Ada woke up.

It was morning. Her head felt heavy, and her mouth was open, as if she'd just spoken something aloud but couldn't recall if it was part of the dream or a warning to herself. She sat up, still wearing her rumpled lightkeeper uniform as she tried to will away the buzzing in her head . . . and the frantic feeling that she may have left a door open somewhere.

As her brain began to wake up, she was reminded that this had already happened: a door had been opened. By her own son. And the creature that had followed him home had a name. And a mission. And they were all tied up in it now.

As she stood up, Ada rubbed the back of her stiff neck, felt something alien there. As she pulled her fingers away, they were covered in a glowing green dust. She shook them frantically, staring at the pile left on the floor, horrified to see the sparkling spores turn black.

Was the green light . . . *contagious?*

Ada immediately left her room and cried out, "Dun?"

No response.

Yet when she checked Dunstan's room, she saw the sheets untouched. The window was thrust wide, his usual route for sneaking into the treehouse after lights out . . . but it, too, was as empty as Dunstan's bed.

And Ven's.

Ada dragged her hands across her face, then jumped down the stairs, and raced out the door into the morning.

Ada wasn't the only one suffering from bad dreams. Moss had had so many that he decided the only course was not to sleep at all.

He didn't deserve sleep. Not after what he did. Even though it made sense at the time; he really believed he was doing something to help Knockum for once. All the trophies and accolades from faceless friends and every adult in his orbit had been fine, but this was the chance to save the town from the impending doom the Grislies had talked about. To be the real hero. Myrtle had dragged him to so many meetings in their neighbours' living rooms, he could hardly help but listen in, and the older he got, the more their fretting made sense. No one in Knockum deserved to suffer because of the water levels, or the lack of fish, or the war. Mender had left because his business went downhill, too, but if Reeve Gris came back . . .

Everyone in this town worked hard. So it must be something supernatural hanging over them all.

Myrtle had only started hosting the meetings in their own living room in recent months, and Moss learned why only when the rest of the Grislies had gathered. She attended dutifully, and this time she whipped herself into a frenzy Moss had never seen before . . . but now he understood it.

A green light, she'd said, *just like the one that shone the night Reeve Gris vanished.*

It was a well-known urban legend, but never proven. Yet here was Myrtle, the least imaginative person on the planet, saying she saw it right after the school play Dunstan had performed in. She said it had sent her a message: that the Door needed a broken heart, and once it opened, Reeve Gris would be returned to them, and the town would be saved.

At first, it just seemed like another addition in the pamphlets the Grislies put out amongst each other — fan fiction fodder. But Myrtle was determined it was real, and that this was Moss's chance to prove himself.

Yet nothing seemed to make sense, except wandering the streets of his hometown, wracked with guilt. He'd seen the green light for himself. Then, he saw it again, bursting out of Lake Mallion — and like a demon come back from the crypt, there was Dunstan Cord, racing up the road towards his house.

At first, Moss thought he was hallucinating after pulling an all-nighter. But then he took off after him, watching Dunstan take corners like a frightened gerbil and leap up his front stairs two at a time. Then, before he could throw himself at the door and bang on it, begging for absolution, the ground heaved, and threw Moss into the shrubbery.

And he dreamed a dream about a dark city under the lake. About the lizard folk living there, the mushrooms that held things together . . . and of Dunstan Cord, centre stage, dragging them all down, down, down to their doom.

He believed Myrtle now.

When Moss came to, clawing his way up the Cords' steps, he realized the house was empty. But it had to be true. Dunstan was *alive.* Alive to tell the tale. Moss was in serious trouble, and so were his friends.

He'd gone round to Valmont, Raymond, Kavan, Gordo. All of them were still shaken up, but when Moss told them he'd seen Cord, they all went the same shade of purple.

"Was Reeve Gris with him?" Valmont asked, shaking.

"He was alone, but now he's gone again! I don't know what he's playing at. But . . . have any of you . . . been having weird dreams, lately?"

The four boys all looked at each other. Kavan grasped his hair, rocking back and forth. "Mushrooms. *Lizards.* And that green light—"

Then Raymond had pointed at Moss. "Wait . . . what's that in your mouth?"

Myrtle had been certain that the green light they were all seeing, Grislies and normies included, was there to help Knockum. But now as Moss rubbed his throat, willing his feet to keep moving as he walked towards Beckon Bandstand, he knew otherwise. The other boys had all shut him out, leaving him to fend for himself in this weird new reality they'd all wrought. There was only one person who could answer Moss's heretical questions, and he was probably actually at the bottom of Lake Mallion. His eyes couldn't be trusted. Neither could his mind, the splinter in it so wide that it was swallowing him up with every heartbeat.

This was all Dunstan's fault. It had to be; because Moss didn't want to face that it might be his.

Grasping the chain of the necklace he and the others had worn, all thinking they were some kind of supernatural patriots, hell-bent on taking matters into their own childish hands, Moss knew the truth. He'd killed his pretend boyfriend, and this was the punishment he deserved.

Or so he thought, until he heard laughter coming from the beach near the quay, saw a shock of curls in the glinting sunrise, and froze.

Dunstan!

All Moss's guilt fled, and tears of relief sprang to his eyes. He wasn't a murderer after all! Dunstan had survived! Everything was going to be okay!

Then Moss choked. He held a hand to his throat, the eerie warmth of it reminding him that no, things were not that simple. Not while a lizard person grabbed Dunstan up in his arms, the two of them laughing together.

And Moss's guilt transformed very easily into vengefulness.

MOMENTS EARLIER . . .

Dunstan woke first, and when he did, he realized he wasn't alone, which was a first in his young life. Beneath his cheek, Ven's chest rose and fell, eyes closed and face serene as his side-slit nostrils flared. He didn't snore; it was more like a gentle humming. Dunstan didn't mind. He cuddled closer on Ven's chest, counting his pale shimmering scales, and it was certain. He didn't mind this at all.

Ada was going to kill him. They'd stayed up much too late in the treehouse, talking and laughing and making grand plans, building them in the air with the Meteorlight and whispering them like they were fragile fungi trembling with the sound.

Then Dunstan had wanted a touch of romance to cap things off before they went back home for well-earned rest, before getting Ada's blessing to start his new summer gig in Jet. It would be a quick trip to Beckon Bandstand and the festival grounds, a tiny town tour under the cover of darkness. Even though Dunstan had to steer Ven away from eating Mrs. Patchins' dog, out for a midnight stroll, they made it there without much incident.

When they'd left the treehouse, Ven had put on a good show, but he was a live wire of big feelings hiding under his scales. Dunstan knew he was probably nervous and overwhelmed — likely the same feelings Dunstan had endured when he'd arrived in Jet. He wanted to reassure the prince after his long journey, so he mucked up the courage a hero would have and took Ven's scaly claw in his somewhat clammy hand.

After that, too many questions poured out of the prince, and it was Dunstan's turn to play tour guide. Once they reached the bandstand, Dunstan took a deep breath, held it, and let a few more of his doubts go.

"It's no Look Alight," he admitted, "but this is the stage I always wanted to perform on. Maybe we can! The Falling Star Festival is coming up, and they always need a main attraction. Could you imagine an audience of Knockumites and Jettites here together?"

Ven blinked rapidly down at Dunstan, surprised. "How did you know I was thinking the same thing?"

They walked down the centre aisle, well-manicured white gravel crunching beneath their shoes, flanked on both sides by long rows of pristine benches, smelling of fresh paint. It wasn't much, but it was one of the stages of Dunstan's dreams — theatrical and romantical. Maybe he was a slight scoundrel for bringing Ven here. After all, what had he expected? His intentions were innocent . . . for the most part.

"This isn't the Crisp, is it?" Ven asked. "You know, the 'make-out spot,'" Ven clarified. Dunstan missed one of the steps and Ven caught him, hissing his laughter. "What's 'make-out' mean?"

"Nothing we are remotely going to do," Dunstan scrambled. "I just wanted to show you the view."

Behind the bandstand was a wide, unimpeded view of Lake Mallion, mysterious and dark, clear as glass, the moon painting itself on its shimmering surface. Ven took to the railing and surveyed, mouth open in awe.

"I don't mind it — from this distance." Ven pegged the view out with his claws, like he was scouting a film location. "Maybe I'll add this to my algae mural back home. Expand the horizon a little."

"It only gets bigger from here. I'll show you more than this before the summer's done!"

Ven looked down at Dunstan mildly, clacking his claws along the balustrade in a comforting rhythm, then went back to searching the sleepy glitter of the lake and the town built around it. "I wish we'd met a long time ago, Dunstan."

Dunstan tensed. This was a *moment*. Just like in the movies. He had to slow it down and revel in it.

"Me, too," he answered quietly. Something large buzzed past, and Ven cast his tongue out, snatching it into his mouth. Dunstan laughed as Ven chewed loudly.

"Tomorrow, everything will be all right," Dunstan reassured Ven. "We'll be the grandest Truffledours Jet has ever seen." Then he reached down, gently winding his pinky finger around Ven's tail. The Meteorlight pulsed under Ven's scales and streamed out of Dunstan's eyes. It mingled, connected them, until whatever big feelings they were both having became one. The same feeling. And they both knew it as they held on to each other.

Heartstruck.

"We'll *both* be the heroes," Dunstan said, pulling Ven to sit down beside him. It was a warm night, and Ven put his arm around Dunstan, pulling him close, blinking up in awe at the gleaming moon hanging above them.

"And what's that?" Ven pointed. "Is that your main light source?"

But Dunstan laughed, mid-yawn. "Just wait 'til you see the sun . . ." This was one of the moments he'd take with him, every frame and every second, when his sight went away— but if their plan worked, and Dunstan found himself a permanent spot in Jet, maybe he wouldn't have to worry about going blind, after all.

In the morning, Dunstan tried to reassure himself. Maybe he was putting on a show for Ven, acting sure of himself, acting the hero. And now that Luisa was involved, she'd be the first to hold him to it. Promises were important. He'd broken as many as he'd made . . . but *this* promise? To help Ven, to give Jet back its Light? He'd keep it! Of course he would!

Then Dunstan sat up suddenly, rubbing his eyes. The green afterimage flashed, strobing and speeding up. He saw Ven — no, someone who looked a lot like Ven, full of the Meteorlight, aiming their arms upwards, towards the Door. *The Door.* Dunstan felt it beating, like a heart, heard a voice calling, felt that great, yawning loneliness as the Door pulled open its hinges. The Meteorlight, blinding, streaked away through the portal, just as something huge and impossible fell through, nearly crashing onto the little Jettite who had been there, holding tight to the taller one's coat, but now wrenched away as they were separated . . .

Fields and walls covered in mushrooms, all brightly lit, all going out. Dunstan was in a grand throne room, waltzing with his leading lizard, until everything he desired guttered out. His stage was dark. And Ven sat up suddenly, yelping in shock. He squinted then shielded his eyes, roughly pulling his tail away from Dunstan as he stumbled off the Beckon Bandstand and dove beneath it.

Stars speckled Dunstan's vision, sending a sudden headache careening through his synapses. He sat up, trying to recover. "Ven?" Panicked, Dunstan tripped down the stairs into the grass, but before he could even bend down to look, he was grabbed around the ankle and dragged partially under.

Dunstan hit the dirt and stared. Ven looked half-crazed. "The *Light*! It's — it's — !" He pointed wildly at the eastern sky, where the sun was coming up. Then Ven let go, gave up the ghost, and scrambled back beneath the bandstand, covering his head.

"Ah . . . oh." Dunstan should have thought of this, but with all the excitement of last night, he'd been a bit sidetracked. He reached a hand towards Ven. "It's okay! It's just the sun. It's not the Meteorlight . . . ! Well, it's kind of like that, since it's also in space, but it's not dangerous . . ." He stopped himself from saying, *I promise.* What if it *was* dangerous, to a Jettite?

"Put your goggles on," Dunstan urged, pulling on his own and forsaking his glasses. It somehow helped his headache, the little filter of darkness. "Come on. The sunrise on Lake Mallion is something you can't miss."

Ven huddled deeper in the dirt under the bandstand. "I can't do this."

Self-doubt. Dunstan knew it all too well. And he had to admit that even he preferred the dark now. His eyes were already hurting, and the sky was only a bright orange and pink, the light creeping slowly over the escarpment.

Dunstan crawled in beside Ven, not saying anything at all. Just waiting.

Ven's nervous glance flicked towards him. "I know I came all this way to see the High-up. But it's . . . bigger than I imagined and . . ." He scuffed the ground with his massive boots. "You must think I'm a real larvae. Totally scaleless. And maybe I am! I should've stayed in the dark where I belong."

Dunstan nodded. "So you still wanna run away."

Ven grimaced. "You're making fun of me."

"We're both runaways, aren't we? Maybe it's just a bad habit." Dunstan stretched his leg out, sticking the toe of his sneaker into the encroaching sunlight. "Maybe we should just start running towards something. Together."

Ven huffed. Then he snuck his tail nearer to Dunstan's shoe. "It's just harder to hide . . . when you're in the light."

Dunstan, unable to help himself, reached out and put his hand on Ven's. "It's also hard to be seen for what you really are in the dark."

Ven's mouth twisted, not precisely a smile, but an acceptance. "You really have a way with words, don't you, Bright Eyes?"

"Only when it counts," Dunstan said mildly. "And you're the prince of the Geodom of Jet! You left the only world you've known to find a way to save it — well, you decided to in the end, and that's what counts! I'll be right beside you the entire time. *I promise.*" He'd lost count of the promises, real and imagined. But at least Dunstan could keep this one. He hoped. "I'll lead, you follow."

Dunstan went out first, the light getting brighter as it finally crested the escarpment. Ven's goggles were securely on, as were Dunstan's, as he led them both away from the Bandstand.

"Let's go check out the sunrise by the lake; it really is a sight to see," Dunstan offered. "Then we better get home before Ada lays an egg."

As they hurried down the road, Ven croaked, "*Can* Higher-ups lay eggs?" and Dunstan burst out laughing.

They made their way to the grassy ledge right above the quay beach, which led away to the main marina half a mile down the shore. Closer was a nice mixed-use beach, which would be full of kids and lazing teens by midday. For now, just a little after sun-up, the beach was theirs. Dunstan was greedy for more perfect moments with Ven.

"It's warm," Ven commented suddenly, clenching the front of his coat.

Dunstan nodded. "It's summer here. The warm season. I know it's chilly down in Jet, but you can probably take off your coat. Actually, I haven't ever seen you without it on!" Dunstan clenched his teeth, biting off his misinterpreted glee. "I mean, not that I wanted to . . ."

But Ven had already slipped off the duster, much-used and creased, with its glittering gold patterns and precious stones sewn all down the back of it. Now that it was brighter out, Dunstan saw that Ven's scales, covering his long arms, were the same glinting mauve as his eyes, with patterns of dusky blue coming up to his shoulders like fireworks.

"That's better," Ven sighed. "I should get used to it, though, since we're going to be in the daylight more often!"

"The *limelight*," Dunstan grinned. They both threw off their Jettite coats onto the grassy knoll as Dunstan led them towards the water.

Ven hesitated. "And you're sure I won't . . . um, what did you call it? Drown?"

Dunstan shook his head, completely serious. "This is the shallow end. And I'll be with you." When they made it down to the sand, he pulled off his sneakers, glad he'd long abandoned the Jettite boots at home, and Ven leaned down inquisitively.

"Wow, what are *those*?" He pointed at his toes, and Dunstan buried them in the sand.

"Why, what do *your* feet look like?"

Ven seemed more like himself now, and he yanked off his boots, revealing clawed toes that looked like those of a Desdemona dragon. Dunstan marvelled.

"Weird," they both said at the same time, comparing side by side, then Dunstan pulled Ven towards the water.

"Now, look out there!" He pointed east, the sun hanging above the escarpment now, sending out bands of orange in the scudding clouds. It cast sparkling rays on the water, already alive with barges and trawlers, and as Ven surveyed it all, Dunstan pointed out a ways into the lake.

"We're even closer to the Door," he said, indicating the white buoys that looked like shifting waterbirds in the warm breeze. "You're not as far from home as you think."

Ven nodded and smiled. "Far enough."

Ven lightly dipped his tail into the water, pulling it away with a flick, splashing Dunstan in the mouth.

"Oh." Dunstan grinned. "That's how it's gonna be, huh?"

Ven held up his hands, immediately regretting this as Dunstan waded in and pulled the water up, throwing it at him. He made a squawking sound Dunstan hadn't heard before, something in between terror and giddiness.

Then Ven raced forward and picked Dunstan up, spinning him in the light of the risen sun and sending a cascade of water around them in a dazzle. Dunstan held on around Ven's long neck, and he knew, as they smiled at one another, the Light threading them together tighter, that this perfect moment he'd been chasing was real, after all.

Except it only lasted a second.

Ven put him down, and leaned in . . . and went flying as someone smashed him, and Dunstan, into the sand. For a split second, Dunstan's head was underwater, but it was pulled up sharply. He felt the pressure of someone straddling him, crushing his chest.

"What did you *do* to me?" Moss Richler seethed, and before Dunstan could choke a response, he took a good look down Moss's throat, and saw a small green Light, before he went under again.

Decca rubbed her forearms as she walked down Harwood Road at Luisa's side. The morning air was warm and fine. "You can take off your coat, you know," Luisa reminded her gently, not for the first time. But Decca just smiled lopsidedly.

"I wish I could, but I'm on duty." She turned her rosy pale head upwards, towards the warm, oncoming glow of daybreak. "It really is something to feel the light on your scales."

Luisa had questioned whether or not it was a good idea to bring Decca out into the open as the sun rose . . . but she also needed to get them both out before Hector came home, and another part of her wondered if the daylight would do the Stackling good. "You're not scared of it, are you? It gets a lot brighter here than it does in Jet."

Decca just raised her shoulder, scuffing her standard-issue boot across the cobblestones. "Jettites love basking. My grand-elder used to tell me tales of how warm the Meteorlight was, how comforting. Maybe this is what she meant." She spread her hands towards the sky. "You're so lucky."

Luisa looked up. She and Dunstan had spent hours staring into the stratosphere, playing tag with the dreams that hung amongst the clouds. But a part of her had taken it for granted.

An impulsive offer struck. "Have you thought about staying here?"

Decca lowered her arms, her gleaming eyes hooding slightly, as she rubbed her forearms again. "I have a duty to Jet."

"Sure," Luisa said carefully, trying not to make it seem a hopeful prospect, but speaking it anyway. "But there's plenty of space in Brindlewatch. Maybe if things continue to destabilize in Jet, the entire city will have to flee here as refugees." Her mind was already firing off the blueprint of an evacuation plan, how it could work, the PR . . .

"Who knows." Decca's tone was suddenly distant, and it made Luisa pause to look over. Then Decca quickly smiled. "It's a nice dream, anyway."

Luisa was going to ask something else, but she heard the clicking of thick heels on the road, and both she and Decca turned to the noise. Directly in their path was Coral Frakes.

It was broad daylight, and there was no hiding Decca now. The Stackling seemed tensed to run, but Luisa grabbed hold of her hand, holding her firmly in place. "This is the person I told you about, Decca. The one who knows more than she's letting on."

Coral, beneath her many layers of silk and secrets, nodded. "And this must be the Stettle Beetle stowaway."

Decca pried herself gently out of Luisa's grip, lifted her chin, and saluted with her tail. "Stackling Decca, Second Infantry of the Royal Geodom—"

"Of Jet, yes," Coral raised her hand, looking all about. "Mind that you two get out of the road, now, before—"

The exchange was cut off by loud shouts and violent splashes coming from the nearby beach at the bottom of the knoll just across the road. Coral went to the sound immediately, and unable to stop themselves, Decca and Luisa followed.

Luisa hollered as she caught a glimpse of Moss Richler throwing himself onto Dunstan in the shallows, just as Prince Ven recovered from gasping a lungful of lake water.

Now they were *really* in for it.

Ada was moving so fast, in a way she hadn't since she was in high school trying to keep up with Lorraine, and if she hadn't looked to the side, she may have missed it:

Coral Frakes, Luisa Alvarez, and . . . another one of those lizard people, but certainly not the wayward prince she was hosting. They were standing apart — Coral at the top of the Beckon fire road, looking down at the water of Lake Mallion, Luisa shouting an epithet that the wind carried away, and her companion trying to stop her from leaping forward.

"Coral?" Ada called, but her friend didn't turn to look, just took off in a furious rush of gabardine down the bank.

Ada made it to the spot where Coral had just been standing, grabbing hold of Luisa for both purchase and support. "What's—" But Luisa's companion let out a shocked gasp as they watched Coral leap into a fight already in progress. Dunstan was in the sand, coughing, as Prince Ven grabbed hold of another soggy teenager, about to hurl him into the surf. But Coral was in the fray now, lunging for the prince, who, reflexively, whipped his tail to keep her from advancing.

Coral caught the massive tail and held it, as if it was nothing at all. And Ada shrieked anew as an angrier, taller lizard in red came barrelling into the shallows.

While Ven, Coral, and the new player were engaged, the other teenager was making for Dunstan, who, along with the prince, was scrambling off the beach.

"Moss?" Ada said, recognizing the town's golden boy as he streaked after Dunstan and the prince. Meanwhile, Coral had a hold of the red-clad lizard. The two looked at each other, then Coral lost her grip, and the attacker turned towards Dunstan, the prince, and Moss.

"What's going *on*?" Ada shrieked, turning on Coral, who seemed paralyzed in place.

"That's the commander!" The smaller lizard with Luisa groaned, herself unable to make up her mind about where she should go.

Ada went for Coral. "We need to stop them! It's broad daylight! They'll be—"

"Vora," Coral said, in an altogether different voice than the one Ada recognized. "And Ven."

Then, before she could stop her, Coral took off at speed in the opposite direction, heading across the beach towards the marina.

Ada wanted to tear her hair out. "You two, go after Dunstan!"

Luisa nodded, grabbing the smaller Jettite, and taking off up the knoll. Ada needed Coral for this to work, and she was tired of not knowing.

She went down the beach, heading for Coral's studio.

Dunstan had spent many a summer working at the Normand Odeon. He needed pocket change for mail-order sheet music, as well as the inspiration of every reel of celluloid he loaded into the canister, to blast it against an enormous screen and do his part to bring his own dreams to life.

As he raced across the downtown quad, hand in claw with Ven, barefoot and exposed, he knew that the matinees would just be starting, the side door propped open with a brick, as the staff filtered in and did their morning meeting far away from any entrances. It was the best hiding spot, and once they lost Moss by Better's Best, Dunstan shoved Ven through an alleyway and towards the theatre.

"It's like the Look Alight!" Ven preened, Dunstan leading him into the dark gallery where the matinees were showing. Once inside, they crouched low behind the seats, shrouded in darkness, and Ven ducked in terror as the screen popped and the picture started.

Then the two of them lifted their heads, the movie reel spinning a showing of *Princes for Fools*.

"Dang. This is my fave," Dunstan said, then he turned to Ven, the rapture of the silver screen ribboning into his purple eyes.

Ven's head darted with the movements on the screen, with the pull of the orchestra as it lifted and swayed through the picture. "I take it back. I love it here." He grinned.

Unable to stop himself, Dunstan leaned his head onto Ven's shoulder.

"The Above has its perks," Dunstan whispered. "Like being a good place to hide from the people trying to murder us."

"Is that what that lolling larvae at the beach was trying to do?" His teeth gleamed under the movie's silver sheen. "I'll turn him into a meat-treat."

Dunstan shushed him. "We need to get back to my mom's, pronto. I can't believe the commander followed us up here, too. But it's in *her* best interest to lay low just as much as ours — and having blood on your tail isn't going to help us."

They both flattened to the floor as someone came into the theatre, pulling a large garbage can and a broom along with them. Ushers, about to do the first round of cleaning as they tested all the projectors.

It was the perfect spot for a date, but they'd have to survive first. "C'mon," Dunstan urged.

They slunk out, using the only exit available, leading out to the lobby. Dunstan aimed to take them back to the side staff entrance from whence they'd arrived, but ushers in their red velvet vests were pouring out of it now, and Dunstan spun around, shoving Ven backwards.

"That way, that way!" he hissed, pushing him towards the main exit, except when they reached the gold door handles, Dunstan saw a familiar face stalking down the street towards them.

"Double back!" Dunstan yanked Ven back inside behind the big artificial ferns in the red-carpeted lobby before Moss could see them.

From their new hiding place they saw Moss wasn't alone; Dunstan's stomach dropped as he watched the four other Grislies who'd thrown Dunstan into this mess tag behind their feckless leader, on the prowl for Dunstan's hide.

"This is as out of hand as my mom predicted," Dunstan groaned. Vora was nowhere in sight, but that didn't mean she wasn't out in the street, poised to strike. "They're all out to finish the job on me."

Ven's hackles flared; a shimmering fin that stood on end at the back of his neck now that he was past annoyed. "I can finish it before it's *started*."

"Bloodless tail! Focus!" Dunstan held Ven tight to prevent him from doing something stupid. "He's just scared. He thinks I've . . . infected him with the Meteorlight, or something."

Ven tilted his head. "Have you? Like Luisa?"

Dunstan felt his skin crawl. He'd wanted to see Luisa the minute he'd woken up, but things were, as usual, not working out the way he'd wanted them to. The image of the little green Light in Moss's mouth flashed across his brain, and the thing inside him seemed pleased at it. Dunstan didn't have time to unpack *that*. "I don't know! Luisa, Moss . . . I thought you said this stuff couldn't come out of me! How could they have it?"

"Dunstan Cord?" a voice squeaked from behind them, making Dunstan flinch. He and Ven turned slowly. Dunstan leapt in front of Ven, trying to hide him from the entire staff of the movie theatre congregating in a circle in the lobby. It was too late.

SCENE 11

ONE MOTHER TO ANOTHER

Ada, in the mad dash to get to Coral's studio, had stopped herself just a few boathouses down.

Now, she stood in front of the *Gris Mermaid*, which really wasn't a mermaid at all, knowing the truth. It was a Jettite, like Prince Ven, like the guard chasing after him, and the one helping Luisa. All this was real, and the person who made the sculpture had known all along.

Ada read the plaque. The statue had been put up a week or so after Dunstan was born. She'd come here often with him on strolls. Later, when he was older, Dunstan came on his own, too. This statue was an enormous part of everyone's lives. It was erected so they would remember.

"Or maybe so the artist wouldn't forget . . ." Ada muttered to herself. A loud crash echoed across the quay, only one place it could have come from, and she made for the studio, leaping onto the dock that led to the doorway.

"Coral?" she shouted, pounding on the door. "I know you're there! Come out and help me get Dunstan!" From the way Coral had fled, and the mayhem that had Dunstan in the middle, Ada knew that somehow this was all personal. She rattled the knob. "Please, just let me in!"

Ada nearly hit the dock as the window shattered, a hard shape sailing through it and into the water. Then another crash — and another window tinkled to the ground on the opposite side of the shack. Coral wasn't attacking her. She was having a fit.

Ada leapt up and tried the doorknob again, realizing it was busted; the entry wouldn't give. Something heavy had been shoved up against it.

A scratchy shadow popped up from the water, having failed to sink. With a glance, Ada saw it was a canvas, and that the painting in progress on it — a dazzling abstract of a dark place, dotted with mushrooms and green lights — had been utterly shredded in its wood frame.

More canvases rose to the surface — paint spades and palettes floating like flotsam as the current dragged them to the dock. It seemed like Coral was more intent on hurting herself than anyone else.

The shack grew quiet. A sniffling.

"I'm not in any shape to aid the community at present," a voice from inside rattled. A broken sort of voice, not the commanding one of the town eccentric who was more fond of cracking jokes than cracking windows.

Ada shoved hard on the door, needing answers and help, sure, but not willing to leave her friend inside alone doing herself harm. "Coral, I'm coming in—"

Once Ada was able to squeeze in past a glass and wood curio case wedged up against the shack door, she gawped at the carnage within. She knew that artists always had a certain temperament . . . but this was something else. Workbenches, stools, easels, and papers blanketed the shack, with Coral in the centre, head on her knees, face obscured.

But it was entirely uncovered. And in the light of the shack's broken windows, Ada saw what Coral had been hiding all these years.

A crown of horns encircling her head. Scales a smoky purple, and when she looked up, eyes like flaming opals, glassy and sad.

"Oh, Coral," Ada said, coming slowly to her friend's side, and crouching down. "Are you hurt?"

Coral's slit pupils searched Ada's face for something — shock, maybe, then looked away, embarrassed. "Homesick. Riven with guilt. But hurt? No. Jettites don't hurt easily. Tough scales."

There was so much going on: Dunstan being hunted down in the middle of town, hand in hand with a lizard boy; a Door that spoke in her dreams; mushrooms crawling out of her skin; and two towns on the brink. But Ada didn't feel as if she could leave this scene. "You've been hiding this for years . . . and I can see why, but . . . it must have been so lonely."

Coral let out the shade of a laugh, then stood up, grabbing her kerchief from her upturned recliner and wrapping it about her head, as if she wasn't ready to be fully exposed just now.

"A guardian's duty is a lonely one. I had to make sure the Meteorlight would be contained. Though your son isn't exactly the container I had in mind . . ." Coral sifted through the detritus, pulling out a large bag and shouldering it. "Keep him under control, will you, until I get back?"

"Get back? From where?" Ada snapped, feeling like this had happened with Coral already once before, and she wasn't going to have a repeat. She stood in front of the shack door, unmoving. "You don't have to tell me everything, but I need to know the truth. This Light, this Meteorlight. It's inside Dunstan — but can it go inside anyone else? Will it hurt him? Hurt others? It's from your world. Can't you just take it back there now?"

Coral shook her head. "It's not that simple. It's never been inside a Higher-up — a human — before, that I know of. I thought I could do this alone, but it seems I've left myself rather unprepared." She pulled the pack aside, stuffed a gloved hand in it, and drew out a smaller package. This, she pressed into Ada's hands. "Show this to Luisa and her little friend in red. Have them fix this, while I make sure we have backup."

Ada clutched the package close as Coral went around her and out of the shack, over the dock, and to the shore.

"I won't be gone long," she called. "Once I see Morag Gunn, everything will be back on track." She turned, suddenly uncertain of herself as she adjusted the pack. "For you lot, anyway."

Ada, hearing that, rushed to Coral's side. "And what about your lot? Where do you figure in all this — the Meteorlight, the prince? Why is it *your* job to fix it?"

Coral looked down at Ada with her striking eyes, then patted her on the shoulder.

"One mother to another," she said. "I'm not going to fail my children again."

Ada still didn't understand entirely. But she understood *that*. She nodded. "I'll give it to Luisa. I wish I could go with you."

Coral smiled, that unnerving Jettite trick of teeth and scales, as she pulled her coverings back up. "Sweet of you to say, when you don't even know what I've done."

"I'm sure it wasn't without good reason," Ada said, before Coral swept away, back on the path towards the escarpment.

She deftly removed her boots and gloves, stuffed them in her pack, and revealed scales and claws that caught the rock neatly, sending her up at an alarming, dexterous speed. Reaching the trees, she readjusted her coat, and vanished into the forest.

The group stared, open-mouthed. Shock, horror, you name it, they were manifesting it currently.

"It *is* Cord!" Kyle Waterford gaped. "Aren't you supposed to be missing?"

"Not at the moment, Kyle!" Dunstan used all his wiry frame to try to cover Ven, who was close to falling into the fake palm's giant barrel planter. "Anyway, don't mind us, just go about your—"

But in the midst of trying to grab Ven and take their chances with Moss, his cronies, and probably Vora, Dunstan half-tripped and sent the prince spinning, his tail whipping around and knocking the tree and Dunstan clean out of the way.

The prince caught the errant plant with the self-same tail, righted it, and cleared his throat awkwardly.

The uniformed teenagers stood in silence. Ven was before them, completely exposed, goggles around his neck, coat abandoned at the beach, his scales, horns, and fabulous side-blinking eyes on full display. This was the moment, the make-or-break of Knockum's first impression, before Moss's antics could break it for them.

"Wow," Roman Belacqua breathed. "It's like *Revenge of the Flesh Rippers*, but real life!"

Merissa Mayhew stepped forward, tentative but curious. "That really is an amazing costume."

"Uhhhh." Ven straightened, not sure where to look. "Thanks?"

Then the teenage swarm got so thick that Dunstan had a hard time joining the prince's side again. "Are you here filming a monster movie? This is so gnarly!"

"Are you a famous person under there? Can I have your autograph?"

Ven preened, soaking up the attention. "I'm *infamous* where I'm from."

"Okay, okay!" Dunstan grabbed Ven's forearm and pulled him backwards. "Sorry, but we're kind of on the run from the law, trying to save a hidden city from certain doom and whatnot, so we'd better be—"

"Oh my *gosh*, Dunstan Cord is working on a real live movie set as the *writer*!" Jennifer Cadamon squealed. "See? They're both wearing matching costumes, and those goggles! You must have really run away to Luxe and made your big break after all, like you always talked about!"

Dunstan had maybe said two words to Jennifer Cadamon his entire school career. She certainly never tried to talk to *him*. How did everyone know about his very specific life goals?

Maybe he hadn't gone as unnoticed as he'd imagined.

"Yes, um, a movie. We're . . . currently filming a chase scene!" It was as believable as anything, and Dunstan was already fabricating a way that Moss figured into the equation. "In fact, Moss Richler is out there, playing the role of the villain! You go on and tell everyone in Knockum this, in fact. And memorize this face!" He grabbed hold of Ven, shaking him lightly. "You'll see more of it around town soon enough!"

Although Dunstan was trying to drag Ven from the theatre to head back in the other direction across town, Ven waved with his tail. "It was so nice to meet some of my boyfriend's pals!" Dunstan didn't spend one second to catch his classmates' reactions as they threw themselves back into the street.

"You got your wish — now we're making a movie," Ven managed, as Dunstan held fast to the prince and tried to skirt him around the completely human onlookers glaring towards them.

"My wish . . ."

Then Dunstan stopped them in the middle of the sidewalk, completely forgetting their need to lie low. "Wait a minute. A movie . . . that's—" His face lit up in such a wide smile, he could feel his eyes streaming green. Ven clapped his hands over them and steered Dunstan behind a shop.

"Bright Eyes, you'd better cut it out now, before your meat-stick frenemy comes back," Ven warned, but Dunstan had pushed him away, clapping his hands as the notion unfurled in his mind.

"A performance! It's the perfect cover!" Dunstan squealed, pumping his arms in triumph and then Ven's, for good measure. "Not just for me, but for all of Jet! Just think of it. You, and any Jettite who manages to pop up here . . . if everyone thinks the town is going to be overrun with actors in costumes, and not lizards, then they'll be none the wiser to what's really going on!"

Ven blinked, looking from Dunstan to the theatre they'd just vacated. "So . . . they'll just think that we're putting on a show? And they won't lock us up?"

"Exactly!" Dunstan crowed. "I can't believe I didn't think of it before. Ven! You just became a famous Higher-up Truffledour!"

The prince's eyes sparkled. Impulsively, he grabbed Dunstan and planted a kiss on his cheek; it sent a flare of green Meteorlight rocketing above their heads, and they pulled apart, too late, as it popped in the air like a firework.

"Bash," Dunstan swore. Then a whistle blew.

"There they are!"

They twisted as one in the middle of the intersection. On one corner was Moss, along with the Knockum constabulary. On another, the Council of Mothers, each one poised with their own Perfect son, Moss's deranged cronies.

On the third corner, Commander Vora, looking like she was torn between murder and turning tail to hide.

When Ada, Luisa, and Decca crowded the fourth, Dunstan didn't know whose wrath would be worse.

But it was too late now. They were all out in the open street. They had all been seen. There was nothing to be done about it.

"I told you all that they were real!" Moss screamed. "That's the lizard who attacked me!"

"Domesticated Dora," Constable Acton gasped as he caught sight of Ven and Vora. He couldn't even get his whistle all the way to his lips.

"At least we've had a run-through of this exact scenario before," Dunstan said, grabbing hold of Ven's hand. Dunstan lifted his goggles, and let his eyes blaze outwards.

"It's the green light!" Myrtle screeched, grabbing hold of Moss and clutching him close, in the first-ever gesture of motherly protectiveness Dunstan had witnessed from her.

"Dunstan Cord, you get over here *right now!*" Ada, clearly having run over here, seethed through her clenched teeth.

"You're all just in time!" Dunstan hollered over her, gazing out at the shocked crowd as he tentatively stood back-to-back with Ven. "We've got a special preview of our show coming up!"

"Stop right there!" Vora and the constable said as one, then they looked at one another, faces twisted in consternation. The rest of the crowd seemed to be mesmerized by Dunstan and Ven, and the group from the movie theatre pushed their way out, eager to see.

But the constabulary were advancing. So was Vora. Dunstan

couldn't do this alone. He gazed blearily, looking for help, and found Luisa, of all people, surging towards him and Ven.

"That's right, everyone!" she shouted, clapping. "Get ready for the performance of a lifetime coming to Knockum's shores — a tale of our very own Door in Lake Mallion, the secret city that resides beneath it, and the adventures of the heroes set to save it! Now, back up and give them some space!"

Then she elbowed Dunstan, jerked her head towards Decca, and they went on crowd control, trying to keep people from entering the street.

Dunstan held out his hands, lifting them up as if they were holding something heavy and real. But what were dreams if not something to be carried? The gathering crowd let out a shocked cry as Dunstan painted the city of Jet over Knockum's buildings and roads, an effervescence of mushrooms, spires, and green glittering delights.

"Whoa, cool effects!" Dunstan heard Merissa croon, the green lights popping and fizzling like fireworks as they reformed into Jettites, lizard folk, walking amongst them and down Knockum's roads like they belonged.

Ven's vision. Dunstan's magic. And a pitch that the town seemed ready to accept.

Ven stepped in, bowing regally. "I am Prince Ven, come to your humble town with a plea to save my ancient city! Won't you help us, dear listeners, as we spin our spectacle for you?"

Moss looked incensed, but everyone else was utterly bewitched by the illusions tumbling and zipping by them, cast by Dunstan's hands and heart. How could they lose?

And in each of their eyes, that shining green glow, reflected back from Dunstan's. Dunstan felt full of their ardour, weaving fantastical imagery of everything he'd seen down below. "And you'll be able to see our extended show, as more of our troupe arrive in town to make it the most splendid spectacle the Knockum Falling Star Festival has ever seen!"

Luisa clapped and hollered loudly. The Council of Mothers, the Odeon kids, even the constabulary couldn't help but join in. Then, Dunstan grabbed hold of Commander Vora and steered her into the centre of the proceedings. She looked ready to bite his whole head clean off.

He took a chance, though; they needed one less enemy, and she didn't look ready to spill the truth and see herself taken in for her trouble. "And let us introduce you to our most benevolent Commander Vora, a guard with a grudge who seeks glory for herself, and to supplant the prince!"

Vora looked like she would break Dunstan in half. "No! I would never!"

From the corner of his mouth, Dunstan muttered, "Play along."

Unable to do much else, Vora looked out at the audience, smiling awkwardly as she bowed. To her surprise, everyone clapped.

"And no show would be complete without its stage manager, Luisa Alvarez, and her assistant . . ." He rolled his hand in Decca's direction, until she muttered her name loudly enough to receive a smattering of applause.

Dunstan looked to his mother, finally, grinning sweetly, and she rolled her eyes, clapping along, too.

Then, with his own clap, all the Meteorlight illusions evaporated like falling glitter, slipping back into Dunstan by degrees. The spell was over, and the townsfolk all blinked as if woken from a pleasant afternoon nap.

"Thank you, everyone, for your participation. But we have a lot of preparation to go before the grand show. Hope to see you there!"

Dunstan grabbed Ven and Vora and steered them towards Luisa, Decca, and Ada. "Please, no more grousing or griping until we get back to my house."

Vora and Ven exchanged a glance, but as the group met in the quad, Moss could be heard shouting, "No! It's not true! They're really lizards!"

"Give it a rest, Richler," the constable griped, "and leave the poor lad to his play."

Moss, face crumpled, tore away from his mother, bumping into Luisa as he fled, who rubbed her shoulder while Decca moved in to see if she was all right.

Dunstan turned to Ven. "See? Told you it'd work out."

"So far," Ven said, glancing between Vora and Ada, who was holding something wrapped in burlap gently in her hands.

"What's that?" Luisa asked. Ada shook her head, passing it to Luisa quickly while the others were out of earshot.

"Coral gave this to me to give to you. She said you'd know how to fix it. And your friend would help." Ada motioned to Decca, who blinked, unsure of her role in this. The townsfolk came rushing over to flood Luisa with queries, and Ada took her chance to turn back towards Dunstan—

—whose winning smile aimed for her suddenly broke, sending him faltering, and Ven catching him.

"Dun, what's the matter?"

The voice of surety and benevolent help inside Dunstan was . . . *shrieking*. It filled his skull with a horrible keening bellow, so much so he couldn't hear what Ada was saying. He crushed his hands into his ears, eyes clamped shut, feeling like his stomach was being pressed from the inside out.

He felt Ven's hands on him, guiding him out of sight and to a bench, felt his tail snake around Dunstan's fingers, pulsing his own reassuring light from scale to skin. The shrieking dimmed, and Ven helped Dunstan slip his goggles back over his eyes.

After a while, Dunstan could hear again, even when Ven whispered, "Better?" He nodded.

"What was that?" Ada asked, her face ashen as she crouched at Dunstan's knee, her arms around his shoulders as Ven moved soberly off.

"A problem." Dunstan glanced to Vora, her sneer seemingly aimed at Ven. Or was Dunstan seeing things?

"I think we need to go back home for now," Ada offered, squeezing Dunstan a little too firmly. "What you're doing with this green light . . . Dun, is it hurting you?"

Dunstan tensed so hard that it flicked Ada's hands from him. "Of course not! I'm fine! It's just . . ." He fiddled with the goggles, in the same way he used to with his glasses, when he was objectively coming up with a lie better than the truth. "It's bright out, is all. Just a headache." He got to his feet carefully and went to Ven's side.

Vora looked about ready to pop. "He looks fine enough to be incarcerated, thank you kindly. Now we're going to—" But Vora had no chance to protest as Ada snatched the javelin tip she'd pointed at her, petulantly keeping it out of reach.

"I think you're all under the impression that this discussion is over." She stabbed the javelin so hard into the ground that it shivered, and even Vora looked perturbed. "You are *all* coming to my house, to sit at my table, and explain to me why my son is possessed, and what this has to do with this prince of yours, and what you're going to do to *resolve it* before Dunstan has another conniption mid-lie."

Dunstan and Ven exchanged a worried look. The commander definitely didn't seem like she was used to being commanded, but all she did was squint.

"Tea sounds lovely, thank you," she hissed, allowing Ada to lead the way.

Ven, from the corner of his mouth, whispered to Dunstan, "Don't fall apart on me just yet, Bright Eyes," before grabbing his hand and holding tight.

"I don't intend to." Dunstan smiled to himself, closing his eyes, letting the reality wash over him: he was, for once, getting everything he wanted. Deserved.

Now we can shine, he whispered, more to himself than anyone else. Or maybe it was the voice inside him, recovered, whispering. Either way, it was right. It was true.

He didn't mind not knowing where one began and the other ended.

Luisa held back, holding the package Ada had given her and staring after Moss. Decca was incredulous.

"He bumped you!" she cried. "Are you all right?"

"Fine," Luisa said, the place on her arm where Moss had connected tingling. She felt strange, though. It didn't hurt, but . . . when he'd touched her, she'd felt a feeling that wasn't hers.

I have to get out of here. I have to get this thing out of me. Cord is going to pay for what he did to me . . .

She and Moss had been connected — only for a moment. In the same way that Luisa and Decca felt connected when the Meteorlight inside Decca spoke to that inside Luisa.

"Are you the show manager?"

Luisa turned to the knot of women standing before her — the Council of Mothers, an array of perplexity and questions waiting to spring. While everyone was eagerly meeting the new stars of Knockum, there was always something to do behind stage.

Luisa straightened, fingers feeling empty without a clipboard. "That's me, Mrs. Somerset. What do you need?"

"We need an explanation," Helene Trigger cut in. "How *big* is this show, exactly? I heard talk of a movie, too. Which is it? And are we going to be expected to put them all up?"

Decca seemed to be wilting under the attention and was backing away until Luisa grabbed her and held tight. "Please allow me to introduce the troupe's representative, Decca, who will be helping with the, er, actors upon their arrival." She rolled her hand, begging for aid.

"Yes, the geodom . . . coterie," Decca peeped, then she saluted. "At your service."

Luisa went on to fib that the incoming actors were all method and would be in costume for the duration of their stay — even the crew, because they were also "a part of the show." Raised eyebrows at this didn't last long as questioners shrugged, accepting it. After all, when had something so thrilling happened to Knockum? A little distraction was welcome, a star-studded one even better.

The prince and his hero had their in. And Luisa had her work cut out for her. Because as she watched Dunstan up there, on the stage, glowing from ear to ear, there was something else in him that made her pause. She wasn't sure it was really there.

"What's that you've got?" Decca asked, once the mothers had left them alone, placated — for now.

"It's from Coral . . ." she muttered, distracted, as she undid the ropes and the burlap.

"Are you sure you want to open that here?" Decca said, eyes darting. "We should probably get back to that Mrs. Cord's house, so I can go over everything with the commander—"

"What is this?" Luisa breathed, holding the thing between her and Decca across her palms. Something inside Luisa's fingertips shuddered, pulsing green. Then, from the corner of her eye, she saw Dunstan falter, tripping into Ven's arms. He looked like he was in pain. Luisa took a step forward to investigate, and he collapsed. Decca grabbed her back, eyes wide as platters.

"It . . . can't be." She took it from Luisa, turning it over; Ven hustled Dunstan out of sight, Ada and Vora following. Luisa would have to unpack that later.

The "device" was some kind of sceptre, a hard wand with corkscrew fungi that seemed calcified by age, dotted with dark, gleaming stone. It was topped by a flat frond of a mushroom, hard and black. The blade glowed Meteorlight green.

"You've seen this before?" Luisa asked. She was tempted to reach out and touch it again, but something inside her didn't like it. Something that wasn't truly a part of her. "It's from Jet, right?"

"It's not just from Jet," Decca swallowed. "This is the Filamenta. It's the only way that the Meteorlight could be moved around — before it went into you Higher-ups, I mean." Decca pointed it at Luisa, and she shied away. "It's been missing since the king betrayed the city! We all thought it was crushed along with him. And maybe it was." She ran her claw along a fine crack in the shaft. "See, right here? And the ancient mushroom here, at the top . . ."

"And Coral thinks *I* can repair it?" Luisa scratched the back of her neck, then her own eyes widened. Before pulling away the little bump she felt there, she snatched the sceptre from Decca.

"Hey!" the Stackling cried, but Luisa was already using the tough blade to pry the mushroom from the base of her neck, wincing as it lifted away, like a scab, but as she did, she felt that same bad feeling: something inside her not only shying away, but shrieking.

She pressed the little mushroom directly into the crack in the sceptre's shaft, the shrieking in her inner ear growing louder, until she couldn't push anymore and gave in.

"What were you trying . . ." Decca started, taking the sceptre and helping Luisa lean against the marina fence as she recovered.

Then they both stared at the sceptre, whose tip was . . . changing. The mushroom Luisa had prised off her was on the shaft, intact. Tiny roots formed from the place it had been cut, twinning to the blade and filling in the crack. Part of the black crust flaked away, as if the new growth had restored it.

"It's a start." Luisa grimaced, thinking of Dunstan's little collapse earlier. "I have a bad feeling that the Meteorlight isn't supposed to be inside Higher-ups . . . no matter how much of a benefit it could be to Jet."

They both looked to the place where Dunstan had just been putting on his show, so full of the Meteorlight it was blinding. This could be the key to helping them restore things not only for Jet, but for Knockum, too. Yet there was one thought ricocheting between the two of them, unsaid in the air: how did Coral get this thing in the first place?

"This really isn't necessary," Ada said again, but she knew it was pointless to argue with the commander as she lifted every teapot lid and twitched every curtain closed in her inspection of the Cord residence. But when she started dragging the sofa towards the front door to block it, it was a bridge too far.

"Tea?" Ada shrieked, and Vora spun.

"Where?" she cried, tensing for an attack.

"Please." She seethed, hands pressed tightly in front of her and teeth grit. "Please sit down, while I make you some."

Vora sneered. "I won't be imbibing anything from your degenerate realm, thank you. I'm fine to keep watch and be unimpeded in my duties."

Ada filled the kettle anyway. "And what duties would those be? Weren't you trying to arrest Dunstan and Ven? Why do you seem like you're trying to *protect* them?"

Vora stiffened, standing guard at the front door, her slitted eyes hooded. "Royal matters are none of your concern."

"Well they are now, because my son is involved, and I'd rather not have to go down to your realm to pay his parole." Just as she lit the burner, the upstairs hall clock chimed the hour and Vora leapt.

This time, a hand to Vora's chest, Ada pushed her lightly onto the living room chaise, and she staggered into it. "Everyone is safe here. If Moss says anything more, his mother will ship him off to avoid embarrassment. In the meantime we need to sit and come up with a better story than his, since I'm sure it won't be long until all of Knockum knows you're here."

Vora folded her arms, brow furrowed. "Better to leave quickly, then, and save your lot the trouble."

Leaning against the kitchen counter, just steps away from the living room, Ada considered this. It would make things a lot easier, banishing the wayward Prince and his coterie back from whence they'd come. But there seemed to be more at stake than she knew. Both Ada and Vora turned as Dunstan and Ven came down the stairs, snickering quietly to one another. Ada knew *that* look. If either of them were pried apart, it'd just be runaway Dunstan all over again. Sending Ven away wouldn't solve whatever was plaguing him.

And then what would happen to Knockum?

"How are you feeling?" Ada lobbed casually, turning back to setting out cups and flicking off the stove as the kettle neared whistling. She didn't want the commander to have another conniption or to appear as upset as she really was.

"Fine, Ma, it was just a fluke," Dunstan deflected, clutching a damp cloth in one hand and depositing it on the counter. "Ven thinks I just need to get used to using the Meteorlight, that's all."

"'Ven thinks,' does he?" Vora snorted. "Prince Ven rarely thinks, just acts impulsively and puts his entire geodom in jeopardy."

"Vora," Ven replied sweetly, all pointed teeth and glimmering joy, "would you kindly shut your trap unless you have something helpful to add?"

Ada stepped in with a teacup, shoving it into Vora's hands before she could leap off the couch. "How about some music?"

She leaned over and flicked the radio on, and it droned out a pleasant waltz. Vora didn't jump, per se, but she did stare.

"Now" — Ada settled down in her chair, next to the sitting room's modest firebox — "if you boys could stay still long enough, we need to have a very real discussion about what we do next."

"Are there any biscuits?" Dunstan ventured, hands in the cupboard, and Ada threw him such a look he visibly withered. "I'll just . . . have tea."

"Good luck having a discussion with *this one*, Ada Cord." The prince sat down, rather thornily, opposite the commander on the loveseat. "She's had it out for me since I was orphaned. Just constantly trying to chase me down to tell me I'm a failure and a fraud."

Ada blinked, staring at the two side by side. "You're not related?"

Vora tensed away from the radio that had held her attention a little too closely. "Why would you say that?"

Ada shrugged, and let the thought go. "Putting aside your petty past squabbles, we all have a very real problem. First of all, what's wrong with my son?"

"Do you want a list?" Vora quipped. Dunstan rolled his eyes, but uncharacteristically held his tongue as he sat on the other side of the firebox, offering Ven a box of crisps he'd nabbed.

Counting on her fingers, Vora continued, "Your hatchling has flouted our most sacred law, stealing the Meteorlight, which is *not* his to have; *then* impersonated a Jettite Truffledour, making a moth-boggling promise to an already beleaguered geodom that he was going to use it to save them! If that's not an insult to everything we've suffered as a people, I don't know what is!"

Ada glanced at Dunstan, who chomped down on a crisp so hard his teeth almost cracked. "Well, I mean, I wasn't really thinking of it that way . . ."

"You rarely think, Dun," Ada sighed, but he held out his hands.

"Honestly, I didn't! I just want to help Jet! That's all! And I didn't *steal* the Meteorlight — I still have no idea how I got it, or why it chose me, or whatever—"

"I may have an idea about that." Ada leaned forward, hands clasped between her knees. "But the person who can confirm it is conveniently tied down with the quake crisis on the other side of Lake Mallion."

"The lightkeepers have something to do with this?" Dunstan blurted.

Ven chimed in, "Lightkeepers? Do they know about the Meteorlight, then?"

Ada waved her hand, trying to keep order. "The lightkeepers just keep watch on the lake — the comings and goings of boat traffic and exports, mostly. Weather. That kind of thing." She bit the inside of her cheek. "But fifteen years ago, I witnessed something, something that I put down in a report that has since been edited." She turned fully towards Dunstan, with a sad smile. "The night of your birth, in fact."

"What?" Dunstan put the crisp box down, and Ven retrieved it from across the room with his tail, rapt. "Why did you never tell me?"

"Because I thought I dreamed it! And a strange dream about a light on the lake the night you were born didn't seem relevant at the time. It involved Reeve Gris's boat, so at first I thought it was redacted, you know, for the family's sake . . ."

"That's the name of—" But before Prince Ven could finish, Vora cut him off by spearing her tail neatly through the crisp box and dragging it towards herself.

"That was likely the same night that the Betrayer King sent the Meteorlight away. So it landed in your hatchling, then? And you never noticed?" This question was pointed at Dunstan, who squirmed under her assessing gaze.

"Not until . . . recently, I guess. When my vision started changing. I don't know what would have caused it to suddenly 'turn on.' It just sort of . . . happened."

"You didn't happen to have your heart broken, did you?"

Everyone turned to Vora in surprise, the last person in the room they thought would mention something romantic. She shook her head.

"One of our oldest legends. That the Meteorlight shines brightest in the seat of a broken heart. There was a little bit of it left behind, after Vert. And it continued to shine when Jet needed it the most. Maybe it responded to that in you." It was the gentlest thing the towering, sharp commander had ever uttered. Then she fished a crisp out of the box, sniffed it, and latched her forked tongue onto it. "Our next step will be to get it out of you."

"That would be best," Ada agreed.

"*Or*," Ven interjected, eyes blazing, "you let us do it *our* way, like we promised Jet."

"'Promised Jet,'" Vora crowed, turning to Ada. "Just so you're aware, since you're this one's caretaker, these two think they're going to perform a series of spectacles to keep Jet from crumbling, which it's doing, every time there's one of those quakes you mentioned."

Ada blinked, trying to take this all in, recalling what Dunstan had said earlier about how he intended to use this Light. "Spectacles? Like, what . . . performances?"

"Ma, really, it was *amazing*. I hit the stage in Jet, and the Meteorlight *surged*. I really felt it. The city became stronger! That's how it works; the more you share it, the more it amplifies. And the entire city runs on it—"

"Whoa, whoa. Wait. You want to perform in Jet . . . to save it?" The corner of Ada's mouth lifted helplessly. "Maybe Light *did* choose you for a reason. A little too on the nose, eh?"

"I *know*!" Dunstan crooned, grabbing her in a way that threatened breaking into song or dance. Or both. "It's the most incredible summer job, the best opportunity I could hope for!"

"But could it work?" Ada pointed this at the two Jettites, who glanced at one another in a way that was so familiar. Ven nodded vigorously while Vora protested.

"It's too much of a risk," Vora said. "Better to get the Meteorlight out of him. After all, it's having an ill effect."

"Up here in Knockum, yes, but not in Jet! I'm fine down there! It's probably because that's where the Meteorlight belongs. I have the Meteorlight, so I *belong* down there!" Dunstan was on his feet now, fists shaking.

"And anyway," Ven added, "I thought that wasn't possible, to remove the Meteorlight." He glared, somewhat meaningfully at Vora. "Only King Vert could move the Meteorlight around. He's not exactly around to fix this, and we don't have time to try to come up with some other sinister way to drag the Meteorlight out of Dunstan." He flapped his hands for emphasis. "Our goal is to keep the roof over Jet's head. We'd better try all we can, before there aren't any more spectacle houses to try it in."

Vora seemed like she was about to fill the air with more trembling oaths, but the radio crackled and switched to the news. "This is Gladys Britehart on Radio KNCK38, bringing you the latest update from the front . . ."

Ada tensed, and the four of them momentarily forgot their little Summit of Reason and listened. The update was short; nothing much to relay except that the struggle was ongoing. Ada kept her eyes carefully trained on the carpet, imagining very hard the sound of her wife's voice, the curve of her chin, in a ray of sunshine far away from a battle no one seemed to be winning.

The news switched back to the gay orchestra once more, and Vora let out a long sigh.

"The High-up isn't a utopia for us either," Vora said quietly, glancing at Ven. "I suppose my remaining question is: Why would you help us?"

Ada tilted her chin up, smiling politely. "Because strife is everywhere, scales or skin. We know what struggle is like, too."

Dunstan touched Ada's leg. She was surprised to see the look of awe on his face. "That was beautiful, Ma."

She shrugged, all tact. "You're not the only one who can make pretty speeches and big promises."

"It *is* a big promise," Vora agreed. "What will the other Higher-ups say, I wonder?"

Ada let out a lungful of a groan. "That's where we need a good story. But right now it sounds like, and I am reluctant to admit this, Jet needs Dunstan there." When Dunstan's face lit up like a Solstice firework, Ada quickly added, "*Not* overnight. If you can open that door to go, you can bloody well open it to get back here before supper."

Dunstan threw his arms around her again, and she couldn't help squeezing him tight, laughing as he pulled away and dragged Ven to his feet.

"Thank you," Vora said, somewhat begrudgingly. "For the borrowing of your hatchling."

"Emphasis on borrow." Ada stood, stretching. "I'll see what I can do in terms of finding more resources and support here. If people have been losing their homes, we have plenty here that are empty from the war . . . it's just a matter of convincing people without terrifying them."

Putting her teacup down gently, Vora gave Ada a once-over. "You don't seem terrified."

Ada patted the commander not unkindly. "I am, though. But best to use it as fuel." The boys were whooping and chattering away, making their own plans. "Please be careful, Dun."

"I'll see to it he is," Vora promised, following them out.

When they were gone, Ada sank into her chair, burying her face in her hands. The ground shivered and shook, the bottom falling out of her stomach, and when the quake passed, she knew that they were gone. On the radio, the orchestra played on.

ACT

IV

ACT

VI

SCENE 12

WHERE THEY SHOULDN'T BE

D unstan was still getting used to walking around in Jet, casually and free, amongst the Jettites as if he were one of them.

It really did feel like coming home.

They'd received a heroes' welcome as the Door opened at the base of the Tallest Tor, Commander Vora having to eat more than crow when she announced that Dunstan was to be made an official emissary for the High-up, brought to Jet to shore up its shuddering foundations and be the bearer of the Meteorlight they'd longed for. There had been a cheer so deafening it shook the cavern all on its own, and there was Ven, grinning wide as he held Dunstan's hand.

From then on, Dunstan had been given his ambassador colours, allowed to come and go as he pleased in Jet without being bothered by Stackers or circumstance. He even had Ada's blessing! There was something divine about being sanctioned as a hero, plus it meant a lower chance of impalement.

He still got the odd stare and whisper, but many folk smiled as Dunstan skipped gaily down the dark cobbles, the road lit with mushroom light posts that glowed the brighter for his passing. Dunstan was killing time; after their spectacle at the Look Alight,

Ven and Vora had an urgent meeting with the Higher-ups to talk out their plan to rebuild homes as Jet grew stronger. Dunstan had begged to go along, to finally meet Reeve Gris and the Sunken Three, but Vora, who earlier had wanted nothing more than to drag Dunstan up there by his earlobes, balked.

"Just do your job," she snapped, pinning Dunstan with a haughty stare despite their tentative truce. "Keep the people happy, keep the Meteorlight flowing, and prove your worth where it matters."

"'Prove your worth,'" Dunstan mocked now, on his own, holding up a hand and letting the Meteorlight flow off it into the shape of a jellyfish as it spiralled into the air. It struck the mushroom light post and made it surge, sending a ripple effect into all the lights on the network, and the larger mushrooms in the vicinity. There was a collective *ooh*ing from onlookers, and dusting his hands off, Dunstan triumphantly continued his victory promenade towards the market.

I'm the most worthy one here, Dunstan thought. *I'm doing it!* I'm *going to save Jet!* He jittered a two-step as he passed a music maker on the side of the road, unable to stop himself. His limbs felt loose, his mind electric, and best of all, his eyes didn't hurt! He spun in a swaying circle, the musician laughing and blowing into his pipe reed as Dunstan's accompaniment. Jet was where he belonged.

Even Jet knew it. Dunstan, feeling inspired, shot more Meteorlight across the street, creating a copy of the musician, playing a third lower so together they pulled the perfect harmony. Jettites on the sidewalks stopped to watch, as the beat bounced around from mushroom to mushroom, creating a light show in the centre of town and setting a new pulse.

Dunstan laughed out loud, leaping up and spinning around a fungi-fettered light post. Before he knew it, more Jettites joined in his wild dance, pulling their goggles down and basking in the Light.

In *Dunstan's* Light.

Dunstan found himself dancing step for step with a Jettite whose coat, tail, and collar were frilled daringly beneath flirtatious eyes, but he spun back and landed in more familiar arms.

"I was only gone a minute," Ven pouted, lifting Dunstan up and taking the lead as the entire street seemed to bounce with celebration. "And you're already dancing with someone else."

Ven blinked around at the street where Dunstan had been let loose; his musician copy had taken on a mind of its own, and an entire brass section had bloomed up around it. "Well, if you don't have as many fans as I do, I can make some for you."

Dunstan laughed as Ven placed him neatly on the ground. "Are you ready to head back up?" Dunstan asked.

Ven's easy smile fell a bit, then he twisted to the crowd, grabbing Dunstan's hand up and bowing dramatically. The street cheered, and Ven pulled Dunstan into a nearby close as they made their exit.

"How did the meeting go?" Dunstan asked, sensing something uncomfortable in Ven's demeanour.

Ven grimaced. "Fine," he lied. "I'm allowed to keep going to Knockum as ambassador, performing in the odd spectacle, and I get to keep my title. But I'm on a leash . . ."

"Hey." Dunstan grabbed up Ven's tail, and after a moment's hesitation, it twined around his fingers, his wrist, his whole arm. The glow they passed between them seemed to ease some of the tightness around Ven's forehead horns, and he sighed. "It's a win. No more Villain Ven. You're a hero now. *My* hero. You did that. You're allowed to be happy."

Ven's eyes went hooded as he stared down at Dunstan. He opened his mouth, closed it. Then he clicked his tongue. "You and your monologues, Bright Eyes."

"But wasn't today's great?" Dunstan cried, nearly bowling Ven over as he wrapped his arm around the prince's.

Everything was going so well.

No one was going to take that from him now.

"You were right!" Decca exclaimed as she swung her legs over the building's edge. "It's just like home!"

"Well, sort of." Luisa laughed, marvelling in Decca's enthusiasm. "It's funny how both towns have some kind of cable car. Maybe we've all been dreaming the same dreams."

Luisa had been meaning to bring Decca with her and Hector to Tantalon Depot for a while. It was one of her favourite places, after all. She was more mechanically minded than any of her friends, and she found comfort in places like it — Batterborne Powerhouse, the lightkeeper towers — since she was small enough to hold a wrench.

Decca, shielding her eyes from the midday summer sun, watched Hector work above them as Luisa approached, handing her a sandwich. "Is he all right up there? You Higher-ups don't have claws to climb, or scales to break your falls."

"We have harnesses, even if we're lacking in the scale department." Hector was on one of many teams working to keep the station going. The quakes had shifted a lot of power lines and buried cables, and they were trying to keep up. Luisa was still worried about him, about his strange sleeping patterns and even odder dreams, but Hector seemed not only happy to get down to work, but to train the Jettites who had followed him up there, keen to learn his trade. When he yawned, though, she frowned.

"It's nice seeing them working side by side," Luisa said out loud, to put her worries away. Below them, the gondolas slowly descended into the basin where Knockum proper fanned out, ringing Lake Mallion like a bustling crescent moon. It was one of the best views of the water in town. Luisa was convinced there was no better sight in Brindlewatch.

She glanced at Decca and thought, *This one isn't so bad either.*

Decca nodded, gulping the sandwich up in one go, and Luisa snorted. Self-conscious, Decca grimaced, then laughed, too. She seemed more at ease these days. Even though there was a lot to be uneasy about.

As they climbed down the service ladder to the main station below, Decca asked, "Oh, did you bring the next few Sade Sisters mysteries? The cliffhanger of *The Darkling of Edgerton Row* was a real doozy. I think I reread it twelve times!"

"I did! It's in the staff lockers . . ." When they came through the doors to the station, Luisa stopped. She faintly heard Decca ask if something was wrong, then Luisa found herself pulling the flap of her bag back to check that the Filamenta was still there.

Decca bit her lip. "I'm glad you're taking good care of it, but let's just keep it hidden." And she covered it again with the bag flap. "If any of the Stackers saw . . ."

"They'd take it back to Commander Vora, and I think we'd be treated a little differently." Luisa's eyes darted around the station. It was a sight indeed to see so many Jettites amongst the townsfolk, all chatting and enjoying one another's company. But the balance of power was precarious; everyone was putting on an act. Everyone was holding in a secret. Every day Luisa felt that the web was tenuous, ready to snap.

"I still can't get it to work, though," Luisa twisted her bag strap, sitting on a bench near a station sign, its time indicators flapping as each train coming from the city was delayed, or on schedule. The clapping tin helped her think. "It's absorbing my little mush-rooms, but I can't get it to get the Light out. It's almost like the Light is . . . resisting."

Decca chewed on her claw, and Luisa flicked it. She was grateful to have someone to talk this all out with. Fraternizing has been sold as internal liaising, a brand of espionage Decca seemed suited for, even if the Stackling was outwardly betraying her ranking officer to do so. "I wish Ms. Frakes would come back," she said suddenly. "If she had the Filamenta all along, she might know how it works."

Luisa nodded and turned towards two women on the other end of the station — Lorelei from Batterborne, and Kiki Somerset. They were speaking to one another, looking drained, faces pale.

And as Luisa's fingertips sparked, something was tugging on her, making her stare at the two of them.

". . . haven't slept very well the last few nights. Not because of our guests, mind you," Kiki said, hiding a yawn behind her hand. "I just don't know what it is. It's these odd dreams! I wake up feeling like *I'm* performing in a show, but I haven't memorized any of the lines."

Lorelei was shaking her head. "My Cameron isn't able to get *any* sleep these days. I thought it was from working the cook line at Chauncer's, since business is booming, but they hired a few more fry positions what with all the actors in town looking for extra work. Can bad dreams be contagious?"

Luisa turned to Decca, the same question in her eyes, whispering, "With the Meteorlight?"

Decca pursed her scaly lips. "Sometimes. In Jet, dreams can be passed along, floating in the air, or via the mushroom network. But that's because everyone in Jet has a little bit of the Meteorlight . . ."

"Sounds like dreams are spores . . ." Luisa said, almost to herself, then she stopped herself up abruptly. "Spores. That's how mushroom and fungi spread . . ." She looked to Decca, a pressure resolving in her inner ear like the solution to a difficult math problem. "Do you think the Meteorlight *itself* is a spore? And that's how it's spreading to others?"

Decca thought about this, then lifted a shoulder, helpless. "Maybe. I wasn't much good in fungi studies." The gears behind Decca's inverted heart horns seemed to be churning. "But if it is, would that be so bad? You seem fine! So does Dunstan."

"My skin has mushrooms growing out of it. I wouldn't call that *fine* . . ." Luisa made a careful count in her mind of the Knockumites in Tantalon Depot, keeping a tally as her eyes skated to possible Meteorlight-infected candidates. She first listed who she knew: Dunstan, for starters, at the centre of them all. Then herself. Did Hector have some, too, and was he suffering some ill effects? Maybe Lorelei's husband as well. Luisa *had* been having strange dreams, but she chalked it up to her real-life experiences in subterranea; she hadn't yet found herself falling asleep in odd places like Hector, but maybe that was coming.

And maybe, as she rubbed her arm, remembering their brief bumping a few weeks earlier, there was someone else she needed to add to the list of infected: Moss Richler.

"I don't like it," Luisa said finally. "We need to get this Filamenta thing working, and fast, especially if this becomes a town-wide problem." And there was the rub. No matter what Luisa tried, or how many mushrooms she fused into the Filamenta, she could still feel the Meteorlight inside her. And as single white glowing bulbs multiplied down her arms, it didn't seem like it was in any rush to leave her. They had no idea where to find Coral; all Luisa could hold on to was that Coral trusted her to fix it. However unhelpful the vote of confidence was.

Coral hadn't returned, no. But someone else had, from a little mini break out of town. And maybe *he'd* have some answers of his own.

As the city train pulled into the station on time, hissing steam as it clucked its way to a stop, Decca grabbed Luisa's sleeve in a claw, pointing. Stepping off the platform was Moss Richler.

Luisa stood up quickly. "You'd better make yourself scarce. I'll talk to him, get him to meet us somewhere alone. Tonight." Decca looked worried, and Luisa patted her on her inverted heart of horns, the point of them ending right between her golden eyes. "Don't worry. He doesn't look to be in any shape to do me harm."

Decca glanced Moss's way. "I'll grab those comics out of your locker, then," she said, then, before parting, pecked Luisa on the cheek.

Luisa hadn't been expecting that, but as Decca turned tail, she stammered, "F-for luck!" And was gone.

No more cold flashes, this time. Luisa was warm head to toe. It was nice to not be the only one fretting about everyone else. Decca made her feel like she was worth being cared for. Emboldened, Luisa adjusted her cardigan and headed for the platform.

Moss was wearing sunglasses, slightly askew, no evidence he'd come away from sleep therapy (if the town rumours were to be believed) any better rested than the Knockumites complaining of their strange dreams. Myrtle, likely, had just wanted him out of her hair as she fluttered about, welcoming the Jettites and trying to spread the Grisly word to the unsuspecting newcomers. Having a stark-raving son wasn't great for cult turnout.

Luisa clutched her bag, the Filamenta right there, under the flap, as she approached the bully that had not only taken her best friend from her but thrown him overboard and left him to drown in the lake. He flinched, a tightening of his whole body.

"Moss," Luisa said coolly.

The sunglasses dipped down, assessing, then he said. "Laura, right?"

"Luisa." She nearly said it through her teeth, then she remembered to smile. "How was Luxe?"

Moss was already starting to walk away, uneasy, but she dogged him pretty easily. All the pep and vigour of his football mendacity was more than diminished. "Luxurious," he retorted, trying to make good his escape down the platform stairs.

Then he stopped, frozen at the top. Luisa looked from Moss to the level below; there were Jettites down there in plain clothes, chatting with one another amiably. They looked up at Moss and frowned. He doubled back, muttering under his breath. When he got close enough, Luisa realized he was counting.

"They're just actors," Luisa said evenly. "They're not . . ."

"Don't play dumb with me, Laura. Luisa. *Whatever!*" Moss snapped, visibly agitated. "I know you're Cord's bestie. The 'stage manager.' You won't stage manage *me*." He dipped his sunglasses down, looking elsewhere, everywhere. "Cord's not here, is he?"

Luisa shook her head. "Busy with his shows. Why? Do you two need to take a little boat ride together? Recreate some intimate moments?"

She shouldn't have prodded him so hard, but the accusation had come out automatically. He snapped the sunglasses off, revealing dark red circles, the sign of someone who needed sleep.

He was panting heavily, then he took in a breath, and Luisa realized he was holding back a sob.

"What do you want?" he finally said. "To have me arrested? Go ahead. No one will notice. Or care! Cord's alive and well, spreading his curse all over this town." He bunched his shirt in his fist, looking utterly exhausted. "I deserve to be cursed. I know that now. What happened on the lake . . . I wish I could take it all back. We thought it was for the good of the town. But I see now — it's just made everything so much worse."

Luisa wasn't prepared for the speech, and certainly not to empathize with Moss Richler over anything. The full-body chill returned with a vengeance, especially after talking through the spore theory with Decca. "That's what you said earlier. That Dunstan infected you." She took one step forward, and Moss, automatically, stepped backwards, nearly tripping down the stairs at his back. "You have it, too, don't you?"

At that, Moss seemed to come awake, seemed to really see Luisa for the first time. Relief washed over his face, then he sneered, having caught himself giving too much away. He went to move around Luisa, but she grabbed him, and she knew, judging by how he yelped, that he felt the connection, too. The surge between them, like a static shock.

Luisa didn't like it; it wasn't at all like when she and Decca traded Light. All Luisa felt was Moss's fear, all-encompassing.

He was first to pull away, staring at Luisa like she'd slapped him with a lake trout. "He got you, too," he said, and Luisa nodded.

"I don't know how I got it. But you're right. I think it's only going to get worse in Knockum. If we both have it, then it could spread to others—"

"It was *Cord*," Moss emphasized, reaching for her to shake the sense into her, but thinking better of it. "It's *him* spreading this thing all over. The lizard people were in my dreams before they got here. Same with Dunstan's little show he's advertising all over town. If he'd only gotten Reeve Gris, like he was supposed to . . ."

Reeve Gris. In all this, Luisa had barely given a thought to him. In their initial trip to Jet, Reeve and his tragic friends were mentioned to be the ones ruling over Jet now, yet no one had seen them except on flags and monuments. Was Reeve Gris another key to everything that was happening?

"What if I told you I had a way . . . to take the Meteorlight out of you?"

Moss stared at her, as if too half-asleep to parse the words. "How?"

Luisa twisted the bag strap, glancing around at the other station-goers. "I've been given something that may help. A tool. But . . ."

"But you still have it inside you," Moss finished, his elation already gone. So he wasn't as dumb as Luisa thought. "Which means it doesn't work, does it?"

"Not yet," Luisa emphasized. "I'm working on it—"

"Better work fast," Moss said, jerking his chin towards the track over Luisa's shoulder. "Don't know we all have much time before Cord's Curse swallows all of Knockum."

Luisa had more questions, more flares, she always did. But then she followed Moss's gaze onto the track and felt two things at once: the Meteorlight inside her crow, as if celebrating, and the Filamenta in her bag shiver in response.

There, growing on the track bed, was a perfectly formed ear of fungi, glowing green. Luisa looked up and down the track's length, and realized it was . . . everywhere.

"Tonight," Luisa barked, almost a shout, and Moss, who had been retreating, paused. "After dark. Meet me by the lightkeeper station."

Moss blinked. Then with a chuck of his chin, he said, "Might as well be the guinea pig. What do I have to lose?" and stalked off.

But Luisa had something to lose. It wasn't only the two of them who were in trouble. She leaned as far as she could over the proliferating mushrooms and used her penknife to cut one free. She stuffed it into her bag. It had to be tonight. Or it might be never.

Interlude:
The Cost of Having it All

The stage is infinite. Possibility is no longer a factor; all of it is inevitable. The orchestra surges. The dance corps revs up. And for once in his life, Dunstan has everything he wants. A perfect prince partner.

The role of a lifetime. And in people's eyes, above and below, he's a hero, his glittering costume catching the stage lights, his every step a rhythm set, a staccato verse, a resolving chord. There's nothing he can't do. And nowhere he can't shine.

We can't shine, a voice offstage corrects. Dunstan falters and he hears a sour note come off a trumpet. Then he shakes his head, and the stage spins to reveal the set that is Jet, the dark rocks and mushroom platforms flickering, then surging bright as he kick-steps off them. The city swoons for him, from every spectacle house in every borough. Jet's brighter than ever. The foundations of the city have settled. Jettites are glad-handing and gracious as they ascend a lift to Knockum, and Dunstan did it all. No one talks about the Higher-up rulers anymore. Their history. Dunstan is the hero he promised he would be.

The stage sinks down as Dunstan does another flourishing sashay, revealing Knockum above; Ven swoons across it, the regal prince he didn't think he could be, bridging the gap between Jet's needs and the Jettites' needs in their new homes. He signs an autograph; a teen girl mock-faints into the kickline. As the crescendo of the music builds, the two sets level out and meet, with Dunstan and Ven reaching for one another across the gap—

But they swing away again. The audience laughs, lets out an *aww* as the two are separated by their divided duties. *It's all right*, Dunstan tells himself, shakes it off. *We'll be together soon. This is just what it costs to get what we want.*

The voice from offstage: *What I want.*

Dunstan shivers, glances around suspiciously. He's heard that voice before, it's coached him through some of his second thoughts. But did it sound . . . stronger? He takes the lift up, the raucous music fading to flutes and violins as he stretches his back, utterly wiped. He's kept his promise to Ada, returning every night for the supper bell. But the minute he crosses the Door's threshold, he feels . . . heavier. Like he could sink to the bottom of Lake Mallion (and be glad of it). *Isn't fame supposed to put you at ease?* Dunstan asks the crowd, and they throw all manner of

247

roses at his feet, him sweeping a bow as the curtain prepares to come down on another day perfectly spent. Posters of the Starfall Festival fan out across the stage, Dunstan's second raison d'être that he's pouring himself into, conjuring the show that Knockum expected, the one that the influx of performers — real or refugee — is going to provide.

Dunstan is the lord of the Truffledours now. As he steps out onto a near-struck Knockum set, racing up his front steps and still singing under his breath, he doesn't think of odd voices or missed moments with Ven. He thinks about how much he deserves this. How he isn't about to let it slip from his fingers—

"Hey. Cord."

The stage lights go out on Dunstan. The crowd *oohs* as he makes a slow deliberate heel turn.

The voice inside Dunstan growls, teeth bared, as the green light falls on Moss Richler.

Dumped out of his dizzy daydream, Dunstan stiffened. There was Moss, tensed up like a cowboy at a high-noon showdown, halfway inside the front garden gate.

The bullied Dunstan of long ago would weigh his options: athletics weren't his strong suit, despite his lung capacity for virtuoso solos in the midst of a dance sequence. So he would fight with words. But he'd tried all that with Moss before. And as the Meteorlight coiled and uncoiled inside Dunstan like a practised bullwhip, it was time to put on a new character face.

His goggles still on, Dunstan flicked them absently and grinned. "Moss Richler. Aren't you the town crazy now?"

Even Dunstan didn't recognize his own voice. Good. He was in character. Moss seemed uncertain now. He held on to the gate tightly. For strength, maybe, as Dunstan came down the stairs to meet him.

"You infected me," Moss said. "You're infecting others. I wanted you to know, before—"

"This, again?" Dunstan shook his head, sighing. "You really need some new lines. I could pen some for you. Except I don't want you in my show anymore. I don't have any need for a villainous, murderous ex." He flapped his hand. "Away to the crowd scenes with you."

"I'm sorry, okay?"

Dunstan jerked in surprise, for all Moss's sudden shouting.

"Is that what it'll take? To apologize? Because I *am* sorry. I shouldn't have tried to hurt you. I know I should be punished for it. But it's enough, all right? And I wanted to come to you, first, before I try it with Luisa . . ."

Dunstan came closer. Too quickly because Moss tripped into the road in front of his house, terrified as Dunstan vaulted the garden fence in a way he wouldn't have been able to weeks ago.

"Try *what* with Luisa?" Dunstan heard himself hissing, but was it someone else's voice, a voice from offstage . . .

Moss stood his ground, but he didn't seem all that sure of his footing. "If you could just take it out of me, you can have it back, okay? Make your little show that much brighter. But please, take it, and all those lizard monsters back down where you all belong. Leave Knockum out of it!"

Dunstan laughed: a low, cruel thing he'd never let out of his mouth, and yet. "You want to get rid of it, Moss? Why? The Meteorlight is a *gift*. Why not use it for . . . whatever it is you do? You're lucky I gave you any."

"I didn't ask for it! And it's not a gift, it's a curse. It's . . . it's making me see things I don't want to see! It's hurting me. And the dreams . . . not just my dreams. But everyone's—"

"Save it." Dunstan bit down on the words with his teeth, as if they were sharpened points gunning for Moss's tender hand, which was out, pleading. He retracted it quickly. "The Meteorlight stays. For both of us. So get used to it."

Dunstan coughed, as if something had been holding his vocal cords hostage. His eyes, too, stung, and he slipped his goggles off to rub them, letting the Light stream into the air. Moss cried out like he'd been struck, and pointed, and Dunstan rolled his eyes.

"Seriously, Moss, just get over it already—"

"If you won't help me, then I *will* take Alvarez up on her offer to take it out of me." He had turned, fleeing, but suddenly Dunstan was in front of his path. Not even Dunstan knew how he'd gotten there, but the panic coursing through both of them had been enough fuel.

Dunstan held on to Moss, tightly and Moss, though he was taller, stronger, seemed to crumple.

"What are you talking about?"

The Meteorlight in Dunstan met the one in Moss — involuntary, pushing, and pressing. Moss attempted to resist, but he wasn't ever the sharpest tie in the drawer. Dunstan saw it all through the lens of terror, then hope, his eyes streaming, his teeth gleaming. Luisa had a plan, a way to take the Meteorlight away. The one thing that had given Dunstan his new standing, his shows below, and the one he had promised Knockum above.

Then he saw something else: Ven, reaching, falling backwards into a dancing shadow, a ruined throne room, flanked by four sleepers and a world drowned in the bursting Light of glowing mushrooms—

Moss finally wrenched himself free, doubled over, and took off down the road, leaving Dunstan falling sideways into the garden gate.

The voice inside him, and the voice he'd always used, were one: *They're going to try to put the Light out.*

Luisa. Dunstan's best friend. Hadn't they made up? Couldn't she just be happy for him? Fine; let her take it out of Moss. And herself. Dunstan grabbed his goggles, fixed them on as he staggered up the walk and to the front steps. She had recently cornered him, asked him how he was sleeping, feeling. *Better than ever.* It didn't need to be true. There was no understudy for the Higher-up Hero. He had promises to keep. Stages to illuminate.

We must shine.

He would keep shining. He wouldn't let anyone take this from him.

No matter the cost.

SCENE 13

THE FALL OF KING VERT

L uisa adjusted Decca's jacket — borrowed from Luisa's closet, dark, a change from the crimson, less of a standout. "Just lie low. This shouldn't take very long. If it doesn't work, it doesn't work. But Moss might be a little testy. Or, it might work too well, and he tries to do something stupid. Either way, it's better he not know you're here."

Decca clicked her forked tongue. "I've done undercover work before, you know. It was part of training camp." Then her haughty look took on an edge of giddiness as she added, "We're on a stakeout, just like the Sade Sisters!"

"I figured you'd say that." Luisa snickered, until it reminded her, painfully, of Dunstan.

"I hope this works," she said furtively. "Dunstan hasn't been looking well. I checked in on him today, couldn't see his eyes, but . . ." Luisa swallowed the rest. If her minuscule amount of Meteorlight was taking a toll on her, what was his heckuva lot of it doing to him? The mushroom Luisa had nabbed from Tantalon Depot had been augmented into the Filamenta, tucked neatly into her bag and pressed into her hip. Would it be enough? It would have to be.

"The sooner this is over, the better," was all she said.

Decca's lips parted to reassure, but the scuffling of footfalls along the road nearby, the shadow cast in misty yellow beneath the street lamps, caused Decca to leap backwards and out of sight.

Moss — but he was walking quickly, partially limping, and staring over his shoulder.

"I'm here," he said, voice cracking. "Let's get this over with."

Luisa looked into the road behind him, her bag strap tightening against her as she whirled. "What's wrong? Did someone follow you?"

"Just hurry up!" Moss whined, rubbing his face. "Get this thing out of me before he comes."

"You saw Dunstan? Is he—"

Moss grabbed Luisa, holding her away from him, bunching the sleeve of his letterman jacket so only the cuff, wrapping his knuckle, held firm to her bag strap. No Meteorlight connection that way. Luisa heard the bushes rustle — *Decca* — and with her eyes searching the dark willed her to stay back. She needed to hear what Moss had to say.

"It doesn't want to come out," Moss whispered, as if the Meteorlight itself could hear. Luisa wouldn't be surprised. "And when Dunstan touched me . . . he's going to come for both of us. For the rest of it. So please, tell me it works."

Moss had seen something, something coiled inside Dunstan, the keeper of all the secrets; she looked to the darkness up the road, too, suddenly petrified that Dunstan would come thundering down it like a comet streaking, undoing everything.

"Let go," she said, trying to be gentle, trying to get the fear out of her own voice.

Moss looked down, as if only now remembering he held on to her. He let go so fast that Luisa staggered, her bag flap opening and the Filamenta clattering to the ground.

Moss gaped at it, the gnarled shape of calcified mushrooms glowing along the edges as it pointed directly at him. He shielded his face, his terror all encompassing. "What is that thing?"

When it began to glow ever brighter as Luisa reached for it, Moss lunged, snapping it up by its delicate shaft as if he were a touchdown away from absolution.

"Moss, stop!" Luisa went for both Moss and the Filamenta, but footballer that he was, he was faster, more crazed, knocking her to the ground easily, and clasping the Jettite artifact close as if it were a loaded gun.

Decca streaked out of the bushes and went right for him, until Moss aimed the Filamenta at her, and she nearly tripped over herself to stop.

Moss's eyes gleamed, wet and glassy as a hungry hound beneath the lamp post outside the lightkeeper station. "This is it, then? Your great solution to Cord's Curse?" He pointed it at Luisa, and both she and Decca flinched. "Have you tested it on yourself yet?"

Luisa swallowed. She had wanted to, sure, but she'd elected to hold on to the Meteorlight a little longer, for all the prescience it had, letting her see things when she shared it with anyone else. She wasn't about to explain that to Moss at the moment. She needed it back in her hands, to turn this back in their favour.

"Give that *back*," Decca snarled. She, too, was shorter than Moss, but he didn't have claws, scales, and a tail sharp enough to spear. "If you want us to help you—"

But Moss was shaking his head. "Maybe I deserve to be cursed. Maybe the whole town does. I saw this thing in my dreams." Luisa saw Moss's fingers tighten around it, heard a soft cracking, and she winced. "The Light can't be defeated. That's what it's telling me, right now. It's telling me to break this thing." His face, so tired, looked to Luisa, broken and seeking comfort. "I wanted to save Knockum. Is this how I do it? Who should I believe?"

Crack. Craaaaack.

Decca lunged with a yowl. Moss squeezed the Filamenta hard, raised it above his head, and made to bring it down over his knee.

But he was stopped by the heavy *thud* of something sailing from the top of the dark-obscured lightkeeper station. The three turned, and Moss was too late, as the Filamenta was snatched from his hands by the tip of a tail, and transferred into Coral Frakes's waiting claw.

"Ah," she said, looking it over. "Much better! Though I didn't show you how to prime it." A quick *click* with the strike of a fingertip, like a lighter. The enoki fronds of the filaments charged up and glowed bright. Coral grabbed Moss by the collar, pushing his head back.

"Open wide," she ordered, and a green knot shot out from Moss's teeth and into the fronds of Coral's ancient device.

Moss staggered backwards, clutching his throat. Unable to stop herself, Luisa went to his side, Moss kneeling on the damp pavement and staring into an unseen place, hands still around his throat.

She gently guided them away. "Moss?"

"I can't hear it," he said so quietly it may have only been to himself. And then he smiled, utterly relieved, his expression revealing a different sort of person Luisa never knew was in there. Moss grasped her hands tightly, then looked up at Coral. "Thank you."

"Oh, there's still work to be done if you want to make amends for what you've started, Richler." Coral jerked her head towards the lightkeeper station. "Maybe it's time to tell it all, now that the pieces are falling into place."

"Is that what we are? Pieces?" Luisa asked, but she wasn't about to back out now, and, with one look at Moss, she knew he wasn't either. The two moved to follow Coral, who was turning back towards the lightkeeper station. Luisa stopped, realizing Decca hadn't followed. "Decca?"

The Stackling had fallen to her knees, hand pressed to her chest, mouth open. "It's *you*."

Luisa frowned. "Decca, this is Coral. Why are you—"

"Your Majesty," Decca said, pressing her hands into her forehead.

Luisa looked from Decca to Coral. It was the first time Luisa realized that Coral's face was uncovered; she couldn't see much of it for the darkness, and her head was still wrapped in its usual turban. But with a *tsk*, she flicked it off, letting it unravel to the pavement. A diadem of horns, spiked, honed, and very much like Ven's, caught the streetlight, showing exactly what Coral Frakes had been hiding for fifteen years.

Allergy to the sunlight indeed.

For a moment, Luisa faltered, wondering how Coral could possibly be Ven, but . . . the colouring was the same, the same opalescent eyes, but the horns were longer.

Coral Frakes was Ven's parent. The Betrayer King Vert, who had sent the Meteorlight away and started this whole chain of events fifteen years ago.

But all Coral could say in response to Decca's adulation was, "There's coffee," as she led them inside.

Earlier that day, Ada Cord was having an experience entirely apart from Dunstan, Luisa, and the town that seemed joyfully oblivious to the secrets it kept.

Dunstan had his "day job" keeping Jet and Knockum both entertained and stable — a dream come true for him, and Ada was glad of it, but she had her own job. His gig wasn't a paying one, more humanitarian. *Reptilitarian?* But as everyone else seemed to be content in their place in it all, Ada felt like she was unmoored in the middle of a squalling Lake Mallion.

She attempted, and failed, to write to Lorraine about all this. It'd been a few weeks since her wife's last letter, filled with the monotony of life on the front, the relentlessness of the campaigns that never seemed to go anywhere but refused to end anytime soon. Lorraine longed for details of home, but Ada found herself unable to provide them. What could she say about how everything had changed?

At first, she wrote a long letter explaining everything. Reading it over, it sounded more like a submission to the national science-fiction revue. She stuffed that one in the firebox. She didn't want to burden Lorraine with this, either. Lorraine had tasked her with keeping their home, their town, under her watchful, if not needlessly curated care. Telling her wife that their son had a summer job in an underground city wouldn't exactly prove she'd been successful at her own War at Home.

And strangest of all, Dunstan seemed so much better now than he had, before it all happened. He was chipper; he was sweet. He was always on time for dinner, with the prince at his side, the two of them staying up late giggling long into the night. They were really quite the pair, and despite her misgivings, it reminded Ada of her own brushes with young love.

She just never imagined Dunstan's would be . . . like this.

Now, on shift at the lightkeeper station, she was trying again to write to Lorraine. This time, she focused on Dunstan's amour: "I've never seen him this happy, Lorraine. When he was in school, being treated awfully by those kids, or getting nowhere with his plays, he had Luisa at least, and their little group. They must have quarrelled, and things soured. Since then, Dunstan was just a mask on top of a mask. It was so clear he was in pain, but I just couldn't lift it . . ."

Was she writing a letter, or a journal entry? She sighed. This was supposed to be about Dunstan, not Ada. But as she reread it, she realized how much it had hurt, being so different from her own son, so distant from him, despite him being right there.

Then, as she often did as these weeks went on, while Dunstan was off fulfilling his dreams and everyone else was being useful with the town's many new arrivals, she thought of Coral. She hadn't seen nor heard of her in some time and was growing worried. No matter how many times she asked Korman to get a hold of Morag, she, too, was unreachable. She only hoped they were together, or that Coral knew the state of things. Jet was becoming part of Knockum, like it or not, and she was in for a surprise when she returned.

Maybe a surprise she'd always planned for.

One mother to another, I'm not going to fail my children again. Ada felt the press of those words in her own daily promise when she kissed Dunstan goodbye. The longer that strange green light had a hold of him, the longer Coral was away, the more Ada felt helpless to each possible outcome as the quakes continued, but Knockum still stood.

She rose from her station in the cupola. She was the only one on duty up here, monitoring the sonar, the view of things. The lake traffic had been diminished due to the quakes, but a few fisherwomen were determined despite the risks. The lightkeepers' work had been focused more on the shore than the water, and as Ada adjusted the brightness of the tower's main light, she flinched as it flickered, huge in its cage.

She checked the instruments. No seismic activity . . . Ada climbed the ladder that led to the lamp platform, donning her polarized safety goggles. She noticed there was something clinging to the cage that surrounded the enormous, burning bulb. Something like webbing. Or roots.

The only way she was going to get a closer look was by climbing onto the dome. It was a routine check and would be quick. She left her post and climbed higher on the ladder, coming easily to the aluminum hatch. She clipped her belt into the hook on the ceiling, gave it a hard push, and pulled herself up, sitting on the open edge.

She was surprised to find two people similarly belted into the roof, whipping their shrouded faces towards her as she shone her headlamp at them. *Would that I'd brought a bludgeon.*

But it wasn't nightscaped criminals or hoodlums, it turned out. "Coral?" Ada gasped. Then she turned to the second, much shorter figure, who had crouched, likely at the sound of Ada's approach.

"*Morag?*"

Morag Gunn, her wild white hair whipping in the lake wind, straightened to her full height and chuckled, relieved. "Ada Cord! Thank Gloria it's you."

Ada had been hoping for this moment, to find these two women and make them tell her everything, guide her in her compassless role, but she certainly wasn't prepared for it happening on the lightkeeper roof.

"What are you two doing up here? And what . . ." She shifted her lamplight onto the thing that Coral and Morag had been hunched over. "Is that?"

"*That* is Coral's last resort. I never believed they would turn into anything. That is, until your son made them go into bloom." Morag

257

carefully made her way towards the hatch. "Now, is there coffee? I think we all need to have a long overdue chat."

Ada moved out of the way and onto the roof proper as she watched Morag stuff her strong, stout frame into the hatch and down the ladder. She turned to Coral, standing with her as they stared at the bulbous mass growing out of the lighthouse shingles.

"It's . . . a mushroom," Ada said, reaching down to touch it, but Coral carefully moved her fingers away. With her tail.

"We were just checking its progress. And the fact that it's growing is both a good and a not-so-good sign."

"Nothing can ever be simple, can it?" Ada noted that Coral seemed a bit freer with her coverings. The top of her head was enrobed in a star-embroidered turban, but the rest of her scaly face was exposed to the cool night air. It was dark, after all. And even though Knockum was teeming with Jettites, Coral hadn't revealed herself to be counted as one of them. She had lived here the past fifteen years in disguise for a reason.

Except this was Coral Frakes, who had lived here the past fifteen years in disguise for a reason. And that she was on display near Morag Gunn told Ada all she needed. There was a long-standing trust between them.

A scream cut through the night then, a scuffling coming from just below, at the base of the tower. Before Ada could react, Coral said, "Keep the coffee warm. I'll be back," and leapt from the tower roof as if the eighty or so metre drop were nothing at all. Ada scrabbled down the ladder.

"Let me start at the beginning." Coral intoned this from her creaking folding chair, legs artfully crossed, still wearing her classic gold duster, her boots with the glowing roses prominent, if not a little more travel-worn than when Luisa last saw them. Moss looked nervous, but at least the tension had gone out of him. Between the three youths (Decca included), there was an air of eager need, of finally knowing.

And with a glance to Morag, exhausted but alert at Ada's post, Coral nodded. Decca held tight to the Filamenta, primed to be useful, to serve. Luisa felt for her. The Stackling was caught in the middle once again: in service to her city, the crown, her commander, her people, and now her loyalty to Luisa.

And Coral began.

INTERLUDE:
WHO BETRAYED WHOM?

The stage brightens from utter shadow behind Coral. A throne room, a light, pulsing. A king, unsure.

"I didn't want to move the Meteorlight. It was, absolutely, the last thing on my mind." Coral grimaces as she recalls that fateful night. "I was a king, but moreover, I was a caretaker. And not much of one! We were all of us in Jet quite used to the peace and prosperity our existence afforded. There wasn't much for us to do but live. The Meteorlight did the rest. We became lazy. There were tall tales about lands beyond ours, but we were, for the most part, content.

"And the Meteorlight didn't like that."

The light in the centre of the throne room hums, strobes, as if taking a breath. A sibilant growl.

The audience takes a breath, someone whispering, "So it . . . can think for itself?"

Coral grins, staring into the theatre's utter dark, staring inwards. "In a matter of speaking." Her stool creaks, she leans forward, claws clasped between her knees. "It's as alive as any plant or energy source, really. But we didn't understand much about it. Just that it was ever-present in our lives, and that we couldn't live without it. That it was a part of us, allowed us to share things with one another. I later realized, as I had nothing better to do with my time topside than to learn, that it came from the farthest reaches of space. Like most invasive fungi. Another matter entirely."

Across the background of the stage, a light borne on a dark black rock shears through the set. A rumbling and a flash.

"Like I said. The Meteorlight wasn't . . . satisfied. With prosperity. I often wondered if it simply grew bored. It seemed to want more than Jet. Some Jettites could feel it, but I reassured them things were fine." A penetrating stare to the front row. "They were not."

Mushrooms light up around the set in time to the haunting melody played as an accompaniment to Coral's monologue: "Being its caretaker, I was the closest person to it. *I* knew the truth. The Meteorlight wanted to shine, and it knew it had shone as much as it could in Jet. It had come here from *space*, after all. It knew there was more out there. So it used me . . . to send it away."

"So you say!" The audience turns to Decca coming out of the wings in a flash of corduroy — Luisa's jacket. Her teeth are bared, but when the spotlight swings to her, her eyes dart nervously. Someone in the audience *whoop*s, a galvanizing sound. She raises her chin. "Maybe you *wanted* to take it away and teach everyone a lesson about laziness!"

Coral smiles, her chuckle low, humourless. "Yes, I'm sure that's what they said about me, without me there to plead my case. But you've seen how it works through Dunstan, don't you?"

Another spotlight, another member of the gallery, seated in the front of the set, her golden pen and compass catching the stage lamps. "The Meteorlight took you over so it could leave," Ada says, trying to keep the exposition on a straight line. "You took it to the Door. It went through. But how is it in Dunstan?"

"Could it be" — the audience lets out a cry of joy as Luisa enters the stage, a crowd favourite — "that the Meteorlight, like the mushrooms that grow from it, is some kind of spore? Is that how it landed in him when you sent it away?"

Coral is nodding, the patterns of her scales illuminating the weight of her many worries. "Yes, certainly. I believe it landed in the first place it could. Inside you, Ada — you were there that night, after all. Then it went into your boy. Spores scatter, you see, and that's what it did when it tried to escape. Unfortunately, the Door opened right as Reeve Gris was sailing over. And, well . . . it sounds like some of the Meteorlight went into him and his friends, turning them into Jet's interim leaders." Then her fiery eyes land on Decca. "And how did that turn out for them?"

Ada looks stricken from her perch, stage left. "A spore? Does that mean that Dunstan is infected?"

"Not just Dunstan," Luisa cuts in, gesturing out into the audience, which has gone utterly silent. "It's spreading."

The stage lights snap out.

Coral, utterly still, kept her steady, sideways-blinking gaze on Luisa. "Spreading how?"

Luisa bit her lip, but this was one flare in her mind she wanted out in the open. "It started small. My dad, Hector. He was having trouble sleeping. Then he had dreams, dreams predicting the moment the Door in Lake Mallion opened. As if he were there, experiencing it." She turned to Decca, nodding. "He could see it happening, like when Decca and I connect with our Meteorlight. And there are others in town suffering from strange sleeping patterns, bad dreams."

Moss, for the first time from his corner, arms tightly folded as if they could shield him from this, muttered his piece. "I could see Jet in my dreams. So could my friends, the ones who—"

"Pushed Dunstan to the Door to begin with," Coral growled, and Ada flashed a furious look at the Richler boy. He hunched back into himself.

"It's not just the sleepy sickness," Luisa went on. "There are mushrooms spreading across town. What will happen when they get outside Knockum?"

Coral seemed to digest this, then turned, sharply, towards Decca. "Reeve Gris and his friends. What's happened to them? They're the humans who've had the Meteorlight driving them the longest. Though Dunstan's held it the same amount of time, it remained dormant . . ."

At this, Decca squirmed. "I don't know," she said, and it sounded true. "I've never seen them. We're not allowed!" She seemed to protest this to Luisa's openly questioning face. "There was a decree when they arrived that they had to *guard* the Meteorlight in the Tallest Tor. They've never left. The only people who liaise with them are the Stackers under the commander."

"Not a good sign," Morag scoffed from her own little corner.

"And what's your part in all this?" Ada asked her superior, her mentor. "Why have you been hiding everything all this time?"

"My part?" Morag shook her head, then jutted it at Coral. "I pulled her out of the water, that's what! Listened to her side of things. And believed her from the get-go." A wry scoff from the side of her mouth. "Kind of hard not to with the scales and tail."

"There aren't a lot of Morags in the world, which I learned very quickly," Coral added, swirling her coffee before taking a sip. "After I ended up in Knockum, I had no idea where the Meteorlight went. I thought it had been snuffed out. Or maybe soared off into space. But I stayed here, guarding the town, the Door — just in case. Making things ready, in case it did come back." Her glare cut pointedly to Decca. "If I could have returned to Jet, I would have."

"For Ven."

Coral turned to Luisa then, jerking like she'd been struck. She looked away quickly.

"Is that what that mushroom is doing on the roof? Making things ready?" Ada asked pointedly.

A nod. "I planted it up there years ago. The spores have remained dormant; it only blooms in the presence of the Meteorlight. Believe me, if things go sideways, we'll be glad we have it — and the others." She made a slight bow towards Morag. "Miss Gunn made sure that the others on every lightkeeper station around Lake Mallion are fruiting properly, as well."

Ada exchanged a relieved look with Luisa.

"But that—" Decca's protest seemed piercing in the lightkeeper station. She bit it off, though, and said, "The Meteorlight is . . . *everything*. It created Jet, created *us*." She motioned to herself, Coral, then paced. "It's inside every Jettite! Why would it do this? You make it sound so—"

262

"Evil?" Coral lifted a shoulder, looking more exhausted as her ad hoc interrogation spooled on. "It's not that. Certainly not benign, either. It just is itself, a plant but not quite, an animal but not quite. It has dreams, it shares dreams. It wants to survive. To thrive. Like the rest of us." A shake of her scaled head. "Just on a greater scale."

"And a bigger stage." Luisa held out a hand to stop Decca, to guide her back to sitting, and held her hand as she talked it through. "All Jettites have a little bit of the Meteorlight. They don't suffer ill effects from that. But they, and Jet itself, respond to things that make them happy, like the spectacles. That makes it shine brighter. It *wants* to shine. But it needs others to make it shine. And Dunstan . . . that's all he's ever wanted." Everyone stared at her openly, and she held up her hands, which were sparking. "It's not the same with me! I'm happy to stay under the radar! But" — she scanned the room — "Moss and I were close to Dunstan. It seems he passed some into us."

"And what will happen if it spreads to everyone in Knockum?" Ada asked, voice rising. "In *Brindlewatch*?"

"It won't," Coral said, but not very confidently. She stared at her boots. "The Filamenta wasn't meant to carry the entire source of the Meteorlight. It's why it cracked. And I used what few spores were still alive on it to seed all the lightkeeper stations. Even now that it's been fixed, thanks to Luisa's cleverness, it might not be enough. The Meteorlight is stronger now, in Dunstan." She sighed. "All I know is that the Meteorlight needs to go back in its box underground, with the Door shut and never opened again."

Coral went to Decca, her hand out, and reluctantly, the Stackling yielded the Filamenta. Coral hefted it, feeling its weight.

"I need to see these Higher-ups for myself. The ones who have been purportedly ruling Jet all this time." She turned her gaze on Decca, who seemed the most crushed by this interaction. "I have to see what happens if the Meteorlight stays inside someone for far too long."

Luisa stood up, mind still working. "You said that the Light splintered when you sent it off? Some of it must have gone into Reeve and the others, as the boat came down." Luisa hoped the flares of her thoughts were still her own, knowing that buried beneath them was the Meteorlight, alive and unwelcome. "Which means that whatever made them good vessels, is what Moss, Dunstan, and I have in common."

"A broken heart."

Everyone turned to Morag. She looked round the room, shrugging. "I'm no Grisly, but I keep up with their little legends. The night Reeve Gris stole his father's boat . . . he'd had his heart broken. The Sunken Three had, too. It's why they were all there, commiserating. If what those cultists say about broken hearts is true, it's what sucked them down in the first place."

"And Dunstan, too," Ada said quietly, fists clenching against the chair, remembering Dunstan's overly hurried explanation of his first foray into Jet.

"Mrs. Cord," Luisa cut in, "when did Dunstan start seeing the green light? You said that's when his eyes started getting worse . . ."

Ada creaked to her feet, ready to pace herself. "It was . . . a couple of weeks before term ended, wasn't it?" She blinked. "Weren't you two planning some kind of show?"

"We were . . ." The *Terrazine and Me* poster flashed across her vision. They had been rehearsing. Dunstan was late, again. Luisa had had it, and the moment Dunstan showed up and they'd gotten into it, he declared to Luisa, Arnault, and Mariah that he was leaving their friend group to date Moss Richler and *finally, truly shine*. She could feel the poster tearing in her hands.

Overall it was extremely dramatic. And very stupid. It could have been resolved with a late-night sniping and apology-fest at Veg Pot Noodle. But none of that happened. That's the day Luisa's heart broke; she'd felt it would be broken forever.

"Dunstan's heart was broken before Moss got to it," Luisa said, eyeing him curiously from the corner. "And I guess . . . mine, too."

"For the record, Cord broke my heart, too. Just in a different way." Moss rubbed his chest. "I didn't want to do what I did. I considered it a . . . sacrifice. For the greater good. And I guess it hurt me, too."

"As it should have," Ada muttered.

Luisa shivered, remembering her tally at Tantalon Depot. How many more broken hearts in Knockum had this glowing green spore planted in them?

"We need to get this Meteorlight out of everyone. But especially Dunstan." Ada went straight for Coral, who staggered back as she held the mysterious device just out of reach. "If it's doing something terrible to him, it needs to be removed!"

Coral shook her head. "You don't understand. The Meteorlight has grown almost as bright as it was in Jet during my rule. And it has woven itself so deftly around Dunstan's broken heart they won't want to part with each other. He'll need convincing. We need to offer Jet's Higher-ups as the proof, if they'll come back with us." Her face twisted with the emotion she was unable to show for over fifteen years.

"Whatever you do," Morag said grimly, "you'd better do it soon. That big show of Cord's is coming up at the Starfall Festival, and I have a feeling that when it's all over, the lizards will be sent packing . . . or the Meteorlight will have its way with all of us." She downed the rest of her coffee, got up, and headed for the door. "I won't alert the Brindlewatch guard yet, Coral. Don't want anything untoward happening to the Jettite refugees camped out here. They're innocent in all this, and they deserve a chance to go home."

But the key to all that was Dunstan agreeing to part with the Meteorlight, send it back to Jet where it could be locked away for the greater good Moss had just mentioned. Surely he would, Luisa thought. For the good of Jet? For Ven's home?

Ada looked to Luisa, who seemed to be thinking the same thing. Neither one of them looked too certain.

"If you're going down there, I'll go with you," Luisa said suddenly. But Decca grabbed hold of her.

"Me, too," she said, just as Ada was raising her hand, volunteering.

Coral waved them all off. "We'll need to plan it well. Make sure that no one else is in the city, that the Higher-ups are unguarded. Can you manage that, Stackling?"

"Ah, er . . . yes, Your Majesty," she peeped. At least Decca stayed true to a hierarchy, and Commander Vora was well below the King.

"What should we call you, then?" Luisa asked. "King Vert? Or—"

"Coral," she answered readily. "I discovered who I truly was in this town. And that's who I'll be until I can make up for not being able to resist the Meteorlight and causing all this in the first place."

Ada put her hand on Coral's. "You're not alone anymore," she said. And that was enough.

Scene 14

Beginning of the End

Interlude:
The Wages of the Limelight

A quick beat. A minor stammer of drum, trumpet, and string. A quick tempo to build them up. Dunstan and Ven appear from opposite sides of the stage, their steps mirror-image quicksilver until they collide, inches apart. They are magnets of opposing forces, and can't help but attract. They reach for one another and feint back, still dancing the same steps.

Then each has their solo: Dunstan in Jet, the glowing black metropolis of subterranean dreams. The Jettites lift him up! The green spotlight falls on Ven — strutting ably through the criss-crossing roads of Knockum, the humans begging for the prince's autograph, Commander Vora, and the Stackers bowing as he passes. The Knockumites raise him high.

Each hero receives exactly what they want. Each is given their stage. The divided crowds dance in sync, bringing Ven and Dunstan closer, so close; their fingertips and claws brush.

The two vanish down in their coteries as the music swells. When the corps dance deftly back into the wings, the two are left behind, at last, deposited on the lapping lakeshore beneath a shining moon.

They clasp hands and press foreheads. "I promise," they say. "We will still be each other's heroes."

The moon turns green. Dunstan, distracted, lurches towards it. The ribbons coming out of his hollow eyes reach for it. Ven grasps Dunstan by the shoulders, trying to pull him back, but it's too late. Dunstan finds his feet leaving the stage, finds the moon has a curious black pinprick in it that is slowly growing wider, more symmetrical, its prehistoric facets opening like a jaw.

Dunstan hears his leading lizard call, but there is no answer he can give.

There is only . . . the limelight.

Dunstan shut his eyes, hard. The ringing in his ears felt like it could be gunning for his arteries, other avenues to send a harsh spark through his body and blood. Then he opened them again, blinking rapidly as he realized he was not on a stage, not floating towards a sickly green moon, but sitting beside Ven in the Normand Odeon, in the projectionist's room, as the movie spun its spell on the screen below.

"Sorry, what did you say?" Dunstan asked Ven, who was gazing at him with concern.

He snuck a claw beneath Dunstan's goggles, meaning to raise them. "Did you fall asleep under there?"

Dunstan quickly slapped Ven's hand away, maybe too forcefully, and pressed his goggles down tight. "N-no, of course not! I was just really into the love story . . ."

It was the first time in a week that Dunstan and Ven had had a moment to be together. Things had begun to move fast since they'd dropped their bombshell on Knockum. Dunstan intended to tell everyone the truth, one day, but they had to make sure Jet was secure before all that. In the meantime, everyone needed to play their parts, above and below. And Dunstan wasn't about to admit that playing so many roles made him unsure who he was supposed to be.

The voice inside hadn't quieted, but it hadn't grown any louder, had it? Dunstan had tried to tell the difference, at first, then he did everything he could to put it all away into a box. What did it matter, anyway? He was *fine*. And after his encounter with Moss, he was worried, sure, but he still felt reassured each time he let the Meteorlight shine, each time it made him great. There was nothing to worry about. No one would take anything from him—

It's a curse! It's hurting me! Leave Knockum out of it!

Moss's words rang over the celluloid spooling in front of them. His fingers clenched the armrest as Ven sighed, resting his head on Dunstan's shoulder, mindful of where he put his spikes. "I missed you," he said quietly.

Dunstan glanced down. He'd wanted to ask Ven if the Meteorlight could hurt people . . . if there was a reason he was seeing more velvety mushrooms that certainly weren't native to Knockum popping up around town. To ask him if it was *normal* that Luisa and Moss had some of the Meteorlight . . . who else did? Dunstan had been shining in Jet to help it; but when he was shining in Knockum, was that really a good thing?

The lid on these swirling questions clamped shut, the locks on the box doubly reinforced. *No. Just enjoy this moment. Enjoy every single one. They're yours. Yours alone.*

As Ven wound his tail around Dunstan's arm and hand, Dunstan could feel the truth pulsing in their Meteorlight connection; Ven felt lonelier than ever, and that just wouldn't do.

"What's the matter?" Dunstan sat up with alarm because this feeling was dreadful, all-encompassing — too familiar. "I thought things were going well, establishing the Jettites here? The spectacles? Jet's okay now, isn't it?"

Suddenly Ven unwound his tail from Dunstan, whipping it back to his side guiltily. "Sorry," he said, an easy smile coating any misgivings, put away in Ven's own lockbox. "Everything is fine! It's just . . . don't you miss me?"

"Of course I do!" Dunstan had to keep himself from shouting. After all, they were only here on Larry Ledbetter's goodwill. He didn't let just anyone into the projectionist's booth. It was a sacred space. "We have our roles for now. But it won't be forever." Dunstan tried to feel like his old self, but where was that person, so far away now? He shook his head. "I wish we could just do a double act in Jet, like we did with the first show. That was like a dream."

"I know! And I've listened to so many records now. I bet we could make a stunner." Ven had brightened up at the prospect, remembering their little slice of bliss at the Look Alight. Then he tucked his chin, the smile all but fading. "But I have *duties* now. If I'd known being a prince would be so boring, I would've given up the title a long time ago."

"Yeah. It was hard enough sneaking away from Commander Vora. And Mum." The commander had, in fact, been Ven's chaperone since he'd arrived, in both Jet and Knockum. They never went anywhere without one another. Ven loathed it outwardly, but it was a small price to pay. At least it seemed that she and Ada got on well.

A little *too* well for either Dunstan's or Ven's liking. But it had finally worked in their favour when Ada turned on the news at the front, and one war story led into another, giving Dunstan and Ven their opportunity to sneak off.

They were allowed to be in the open now, and together. They held hands, leaned on each other. Ven had tried borrowing Dunstan's shirts, but they were too short. A few alterations at Dunstan's trusty sewing machine, and Ven had himself a decent wardrobe of fashionable tunics. If saving their towns didn't pan out, he'd market them on a Ferren runway someday. They were well and truly dating, and no one could take that away from them.

No offstage voiceover, not Moss Richler. *Not even Luisa.*

Luisa. Dunstan tensed again. Days after the Moss incident, he'd hand Luisa script pages as usual, eyeing her, wondering if she'd ever tell him about her connection to Moss, his ravings. She was simply buried in the work, the prep, chatting with the Jettite crew, the Truffledours, as if it were business as usual. She was the perfect stage manager.

Is she stage managing me?

Ven let out a clipped laugh, and Dunstan felt his skin crawl. "After this is all done, let's take a long . . . what's that called again? When you cancel all your responsibilities?"

"A vacation," Dunstan filled in, feeling far away from such a thing. "Where would you like to go?"

To the stars, the voice inside answered. Dunstan's head throbbed as he shut his eyes, tried to will all the locks on all the boxes to stay in place.

Ven smiled, leaned up, and gave Dunstan a gentle kiss. He said a line, a beautiful, heart-provoking stream of words that should have made Dunstan's heart leap.

Hasn't this scene happened before? the voice asked, clicking its invisible tongue. Dunstan swore he heard the grin in the words. *I'd be careful if I were you. You're losing hold of everything you want.*

Now Dunstan was in the crowd of a theatre, the scene of now unfolding in front of him — or was it a scene from Before? There, in the red velvet seats of the Odeon, his heart's desire's arm around him, the screen a flash and flick of promise across their skin, now scales. Dunstan couldn't hear Ven because this other, stronger voice coiled around every part of him, was speaking over it. *He's going to leave you. And when he does, what will you have? Just another broken heart.*

But this time, you'll be able to shine on your own. Shine . . .

Dunstan leapt out of his seat, pulling away from Ven, the ringing almost unbearable. It was like he'd been plunged into Lake Mallion's deep, dark depths all over again, though he rarely got to Jet the old-fashioned way. He was on his feet, heading for the projection-ist's door, but whatever Ven was saying — his face concerned, his unshielded eyes perplexed — it was all drowned out.

"Sorry," Dunstan said, though he couldn't hear himself saying it over the voice feeding him his stage directions. "It's getting late, isn't it? We should get back."

Then Ven grabbed Dunstan's hand with his tail, and it sent a shockwave through him. Instead of relishing their connection, Dunstan repelled it.

Or something inside Dunstan did.

The ringing resolved. Ven looked scared; of what, Dunstan couldn't guess at. It was just a dizzy spell. He was tired. But he didn't say any of that. All he did was smile the easy smile that had, before, been Ven's repertoire, not Dunstan's.

He grasped Ven's scaly hand in his, reassuring. "I just don't want us to get reamed out." He wove their fingers together, tugging Ven along. "Didn't you say you'd go anywhere with me?"

Ven's mouth opened, closed, became a line that somewhat resembled a grin. "Sure," he said. Dunstan was in the lead, even though he was much smaller, had always been the one to be rescued. Now he had the power. And he was going to use it.

He was going to shine for Ven. He was going to shine so bright, Ven would never let him go.

"He just . . . fell asleep."

Luisa and Decca stood in Lorelei's gaping front doorway. They'd been walking past on their way to Beckon Bandstand for yet another run-through of Dunstan's play, which was becoming its own creature, shambling slowly on the horizon towards Knockum, set to devour it. The Council of Mothers had been rushing up the road, Doctor Yarrow behind them. They all looked harried, and unfortunately, it was becoming a recurring scene.

Lorelei's husband, Cameron, was standing by the front window, completely asleep. He was so still, in fact, he seemed like a waxen figure, a green glow shining eerily beneath his skin. The council had not noticed it yet, but as Luisa leaned away from the doorway, casting a glance at the flowerbox beneath the window Cameron was standing near, fluffy caps were climbing alongside the pane, seeming to push outwards the longer Luisa looked. In Jet, they were beautiful. In Knockum, they were a bad sign.

This was the sixth family touched by the sleepies, a strange condition that was creeping through Knockum. As Luisa and Decca made to leave, they clocked a cluster of Jettites standing on the sidewalk, staring at the mushrooms. When they caught Luisa looking, they paced back up the road, muttering to each other and looking equally worried.

"They're concerned," Decca whispered, following Luisa's train of thought. "They don't want something to happen to blow Dunstan's ruse. To send them back to Jet. The Jettites are just as scared as we are."

"I don't know if that makes it better or worse," Luisa said, looking up the road towards Beckon Bandstand. "But I do know that we need to go to Jet. Soon." Hector was still at home, asleep. He had barely risen from bed yesterday, had taken a lot of convincing, and was still sent home from work. Luisa's chest tightened, worried that if she went home to him now, he'd be asleep mid-step, too, locked in a dream only the Meteorlight could show.

Decca nodded tightly. An unseasonably cold wind took up, scudding a ribbon of cloud across the sun that looked, unmistakably, like a mushroom.

Shine. We must shine.

Dunstan screwed his eyes closed as he sat on the toilet lid, pressing his fingers into them from the underside of his goggle lenses. The headaches hadn't been so bad until recently, and it must have been because he wasn't getting much sleep. How could he? It was so bright in Knockum, even at night, and his vision was worse up here than in Jet. He was trying to come up with a good reason to stay in Jet longer, because he never felt poorly down there. Down in Jet there were only the spectacles, the shows, the summer job of a lifetime!

He was paying his dues, like any up-and-comer of the stage. Down there he was loved. Whatever pain he was feeling now, he had to say it was well worth it. The fronds and fungi and mellifluous mushrooms below gleamed in a way Dunstan hadn't yet seen, reaching the tip of the tor, Ven's would-be palace throne. Dunstan was doing this all for his deserving, darling prince.

He needed to keep shining, even if it hurt.

He'd thought, once, of going to the Higher-ups. To finally meet Reeve Gris, and . . . he didn't know. Thank him? If it weren't for his little joyride fifteen years ago, and the weird cult of superstition that grew around him, Dunstan wouldn't be here. He wouldn't be fawned over and praised by Jettites and his former school bullies alike. Knockum was busier than ever. Folk were coming from miles around to meet the strange method-acting troupe, and excitement was building for *The Door in Lake Mallion*, the centrepiece of the Starfall Festival and probably his greatest work of showmanship.

Dunstan pulled himself upright and moved to the bathroom mirror. The twin tulip lights on either side of it were on, and it hurt to even be beside them, but he needed to take a good look. He pulled his goggles off. His eyes were always streaming with Meteorlight now, and in the reflection the ribbons seemed almost solid. Yet as they moved, smoke-wisp thick with Dunstan's breath, he saw his own eyes had gone totally black, save for a pinprick of green light in the centre.

But this wasn't what bothered him most.

He shucked off his coat, pulled up his shirt, and turned. The mushrooms were getting bigger, more difficult to hide. He'd need a thicker coat. A better costume. If this was simply a Meteorlight side effect, then so be it. He'd have to hold it together for as long as he could . . . because he didn't want the magic to end.

A knock at the bathroom door. "Dunstan? Are you okay?"

Ven! Dunstan opened his mouth to reassure the prince, his *boyfriend* — though they didn't feel like that lately. They were both busy getting what they wanted. And if Dunstan screwed this up, or showed any signs of flagging, then Ven would be back to where he was: a vigilante prince with no kingdom of his own. A tor tumbling down into oblivion.

And worst of all, Dunstan didn't want Ven to see him like this.

"Just fine!" Dunstan lied, pulling his shirt and goggles back down. "Be down soon."

But Ven's footsteps didn't move away from the door. "Can I . . . can I come in? There's something I need to talk to you about."

Dunstan's chest throbbed. It was that moment again. The edge before he slipped off into rejection. *We're sorry, Cord, but there isn't a place for you in the cast. Cord, you have grit, but you don't have* it. *Dunstan, I thought we were friends. This is over, you know?*

Don't let him see, the voice both hissed and cooed, the green ribbons seeming to stroke his back, between the clump of mushroom caps. A reassurance. *He won't understand. But you know it isn't wrong, to change, to become something greater.*

Dunstan was nodding. If Ven saw what Dunstan was becoming, would he break up with him? Maybe they had grown too far apart. Dunstan knew something was happening to him; he may be flighty, but he had a brain. He couldn't stop now, though. Not when everything was so close. *We have everything we need.* The light streaming from his dark eyes, coalescing in the mirror like oil, seemed to take on a shape, a faceless grin. *We can't lose everything we've built.*

Terrified, Dunstan leapt towards the bathtub, turning the water fully on. "Sorry, just hopping into the shower!" he shouted, then he snapped up his goggles, clasped his hands, and begged the Door to show itself.

And it did. Because the Door in Lake Mallion was always there when Dunstan needed it. It never asked him for anything in return, it never told him he was lacking, and it never left him hanging. It glowed, black and wanting, from beneath the bathwater.

The bathroom doorknob twisted just as Dunstan leapt in, to keep the show going just a little longer.

275

Hector was having the strangest dream.

They'd all been strange lately, true. But he'd never had much of an imagination. Not like the Cord boy. Not like his Luisa. Oh how they dreamed, how they shone, together! Every time he came to one of Dunstan and Luisa's plays, he lit up for them. He could never imagine the wild stories, plot twists, or pratfalls that unfolded before him.

Which meant these dreams couldn't be his. A glowing city of mushrooms and rock. Brilliant and beckoning. Bright but the streets were empty. Up he climbed a staircase, through a giant tower, the brightest light shining like a green, shuddering eye at the very top of it. It was silent in a way that swallowed even his footsteps — until he realized he wasn't climbing at all. He was a little vein of light, travelling through an ever-reaching network, bouncing off mushroom caps and stems and fronds.

This was novel to Hector, and thus didn't bother him in the least. Until he reached the top of the tower, and saw Luisa, her friends, folk he didn't recognize . . .

But four he did recognize. Knockum's brightest members of a lakeside tragedy. Here they were, asleep.

Asleep, like Hector, having fallen down this tunnel of light, just as he was fastening his engineering harness, a bed of velvety mushroom clumps blooming up from the place his shoes had fallen in the carpet.

Ada sat tightly next to Luisa, whose thousand-yard stare was a silent cacophony of emotion in the morning light. Hector had been safely tucked into his bed, with Coral's and Ada's help after Decca brought them to the Alvarezes'. Luisa had been resolute. It was tonight, or never.

To avoid suspicion, Ada, Coral, Luisa, and Decca boarded a skiff that had been in for repairs and made for the In Memoriam buoys.

They had to turn around, though, when they saw a '32 Comet's headlights racing towards the marina, Moss Richler leaping out of the front seat and hailing them to come back. Coral had admonished him for nearly blowing their covert operation, but Luisa was heartened to have him there. To have one more person to help in this last-ditch mission to save and stop Dunstan.

"This is not my favourite route for getting down there," Luisa said through gritted teeth. "The water at the bottom is colder than cold . . ."

"Don't remind me," Coral said, shuddering.

Decca swallowed, though she tried to be bright about it. "It'll be fine! Though I came up here in a Stettle car. I suppose going down wrapped around an anchor will probably be much worse!"

Coral snorted. Luisa patted Decca's shoulder, pushing her hair out of her face as they surged across the lake. Ada, at the helm, had been quiet this whole time. She stretched her neck, trying to get her focus. "How long do we have?"

They went over the plan again. Watches were checked. Dunstan's big show was this evening. They'd need to be back before then. The rest of Knockum — and its many visitors, from beneath the lake and beyond — were restless to attend it. They would all be gathered in one place. It would be the prime time to pin Dunstan down with the facts. And, the ragtag band had agreed, the time to expose the secret that the Jettites weren't actors, but refugees.

"Certainly there are more Jettites in Knockum now than locals," Coral noted, when they'd been concocting their reconnaissance. "But there will be those down below who didn't wish to leave, or whose homes are still intact . . . Stackers, too, keeping the peace." She took a deep breath and shut her eyes. "I'll have to come with you, of course. To guide you to the tor. That's the palace, where the Higher-ups will likely be . . ."

Decca was shaking her head, a bemused expression across her rosy scales. "I never thought it'd happen in *my* lifetime that the great King Vert, Loyal Betrayer, would be back in Jet."

Luisa grimaced at Coral's reaction, which was a tight sneer. "I think the time for titles is long over." And the corner of her lip had twitched in the tiniest of grins. "Besides, I rather favour *Queen Coral*, if I still have any say."

But now, on the boat, there was no room for laughter, not even the nervous kind.

"The show begins at 5 p.m. Dunstan will spend the day rehearsing. The prince is above with the commander, to represent the Jettites as a matter of diplomacy. This performance is for them, after all." Decca swallowed, crossing her arms tighter. Luisa knew it was a struggle for her to lie to her superiors. "I went over their itinerary myself before I, er, excused myself for this covert operation."

"That leaves us five, maybe six hours, to stop the show," Ada confirmed. "We can't let him go on that stage. Any more *performances* could send out more of those spore things, put more folks to sleep. And harm Dun."

She, too, had seemed torn, wanting to put Dunstan in a box until she could come back with the cure for him. But they all knew that the Meteorlight inside him was strong, and they'd need to be smart. To play by the rules she'd lived by. "We deliver him the proof, we take the Light out of him, and we send it back into Jet. And close that bloody Door forever."

The boat was quiet then.

"And what if the Jettites don't want to leave?"

Everyone turned to Moss, who was staring back towards the quay, the town beyond. He'd agreed to come along, mostly because he wanted to meet Reeve Gris once and for all, close the loop on his involvement in this strange tale, but he was right.

Decca piped up immediately. "They'll go where the Meteorlight goes. They . . . they want to go home." Her voice was shrill.

Ada and Coral exchanged a glance. The In Memoriam buoys came into view, bobbing in their wake as Ada pulled it astride, cutting the engine.

Luisa held out her hand to Ada, fingers sparking. Ada took it, then Decca on the other side, and Moss, grimacing, took Decca's.

"In we go." Coral grimaced, the Meteorlight casting a path for them down into the dark water. And the Door, shuddering, answered.

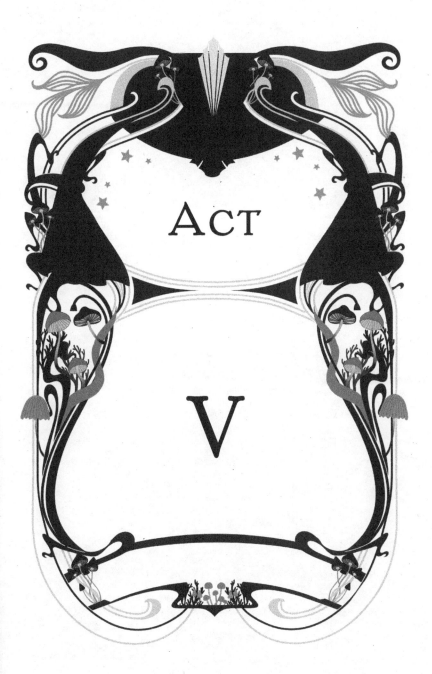

ACT

V

SCENE 15

THE CURTAIN CALL

D unstan slipped on his coat. He'd spent time embellishing it between shows. It was covered with winking stones. Thicker to hide his troubling transformation. Heavy, too, and when it caught the Meteorlight, no one else could be mistaken for the lead.

Because that's what he was. The writer, the creator, the leader. And tonight was the big show in Knockum, the Starfall Festival finally arriving on everyone's doorsteps.

Now that it was here, Dunstan's mind became muddier on what he'd have to do. If he could do it. And, most horribly, if he really wanted to.

For weeks he'd told himself his own private plan: put on this brilliant show. Return to Jet. Then live there, side by side, with Ven. Forever.

Well, maybe not *forever*. But for long enough. A vacation. They could explore the world whenever they wanted. But as soon as Ven had suggested it, Dunstan realized painfully that all he wanted to do, after hurtling forward like a Stettle Beetle car on a hairpin turn, was to stop.

Just for a moment. Just for a breath.

Because once the curtain fell on Knockum's grand show, the future was an unlit stage. Dunstan swore he'd envisioned a happily ever after, but his worries were crowding them out. No more kick-lines, no more big finales. Wouldn't Jet still need him, his Light? Would the Jettites all go home? Where did Dunstan fit, and above all, would it still be beside Ven?

He'd wanted to ask him, truly, but . . . he didn't want Ven's doubts added to his own. He wanted them to explore the world together, but what happened when Dunstan's use was over? Would they take the Meteorlight out of him, like Luisa had done with Moss? Would anyone have use for Dunstan at all?

Dunstan trudged up the stairs to his childhood home. He didn't know how he felt, sensations and exhaustion and worry all knotted together. He didn't know his inner voice from the Meteorlight's. He'd nod to himself as it told him what he needed to do, then shake his head, trying to clear it, to get some quiet. *We'll have it all*, it said, trying to goad him, to console, his only companion as the big show grew closer. *We will shine together, down in the dark.*

He stumbled over the final front step, catching himself on the door. He looked down and realized he'd tripped over an enormous mushroom cap, ridged and growing larger by the moment, blooming in broad daylight across the steps. He stared at it, somewhat indifferently, lost in the words the voice pounded behind his eyes. Dunstan was tired, and despite the adulations of Jettite crowds in spectacle halls, his newfound popularity in Knockum, and his summer love with Ven, he was alone.

It hit him all at once, his eyes bunching up behind his goggles. The limelight is a lonely place, he'd realized, maybe too late. *I'm going to talk to Mum, tell her everything. I want a lot, I want it all, I want to help, but . . . I'm so tired.* His mind swirled, his hands pressing into his eyes beneath his goggles . . .

In the pit of his stomach, he felt it like a fist balling up, a viper tensing its coils, just as he raised a hand onto the doorknob, desperate to open it and find his mom and let someone, anyone, talk him back to who he used to be—

As he stepped over the threshold Dunstan heard another voice —
a memory, one that rose up alongside the voice inside him. It was
his mother's voice. His other mother. Lorraine.

INTERLUDE:
WHERE THE LIGHT MEETS THE RIGHT

The porch falls away, leaving Dunstan in only black. His costume
is stripped away. His goggles are gone. He is a Dunstan of months
ago, a Dunstan with eyes framed in normal glasses, with dreams
behind picture frames. A Dunstan that isn't held together with
mushroom stems and lofty promises of heroics, of shining, one
that hasn't harmed his friends or ruined anything with his little
ambitions.

Lorraine is in the kitchen washing up after supper, Ada kissing
her as she heads off to work, the evening light slanting in perfect
golden bars through the window.

On the radio, a plum doozy. Lorraine smiles.

"It's always hardest to say goodbye to what you love, isn't it, Dun?"

She is still smiling in her laid-back way, auburn curls bouncing.
Lorraine is always done up, even when there is nowhere to go except
the front porch and especially when she's out on her fishing boat.
Every moment is a sensational party not to be missed.

"Mama," Dunstan says, looking about the set. It seems oddly
three-dimensional, immersive, but he knows he's performing for
an audience he can't see. It doesn't matter; it's so good to see her.

"I miss you. And I don't know what to do." Had he heard her
right? Painful to say goodbye to *what* you love, or *who*? Did she
mean Ven, Ada? All of Knockum? His every dream?

"The show must go on," Lorraine says, the smile in her words,
but her back is to Dunstan. He cranes his neck to see her face again,
but Lorraine moves away from the sink.

"My darling Dun," she says, turning the radio off with a snap.
"You don't have to say goodbye. You know that. You've worked so
hard, dreamed so big. Surely you're not going to give up now?"

Dunstan suddenly feels cold, realizing that the stage lights are snapping off one by one, leaving him and Lorraine alone in a circle of caustic light.

"I'm just tired," he says, wringing his hands, the excuse sounding petulant, childish. "I think I've . . . taken this all too far. Being the hero. Lying to Ven. To everyone. It's taking a toll that I didn't . . ."

Suddenly, Lorraine is enfolding Dunstan in her arms. He still can't see her face, but he clutches her tightly, burying his cheek into her perfumed blouse.

She rubs his back. "I know you never had it easy. But you always knew who you were going to be. It wasn't a lie. You've always shone, inspired everyone around you. You'll be all right."

Dunstan clings to Lorraine, willing this to be real: the feel of her skirt clenched in his fingers, the smell of her soap trying to cover up the fish and oil and lake brine. "And what if I had no Light at all? Do you think . . . do you think anyone would love me?"

"You'll always have the Light," Lorraine says, but it's not her voice. It's the voice from offstage.

Heart racing, Dunstan tilts his head up to finally look at Lorraine's face. But it isn't her face anymore. It is a bright *shining*, so bright Dunstan has to look away, tries to get free, but she holds to him tightly.

"If you're tired," the Meteorlight says, "I can shine for both of us. Why don't you take a little rest?"

Dunstan can feel the Meteorlight pulsing down on him, as well as through him, inside him. Pushing him down. He tenses up. "No! I . . . I don't need to sleep! I can . . . I can keep going!"

"Can you?" the Meteorlight says, a smirk there, if there were a face to make one. "I could do it for both of us. I could make everyone who doesn't believe in you sleep, too. But I'd rather take our tour to the next level. You and me, we could make all of Brindlewatch shine. I bet Ven would like that. Ada and Lorraine, too. Isn't that what you want?"

Then the ground beneath them both shivers. A sudden quake throws Dunstan and the shining Lorraine apart, the sets falling to pieces like they're made of splintering sugar glass.

"Ah," the Meteorlight says. "We'd better hurry, you and I. Someone's about to spoil the show's ending."

With another rollicking quake, Dunstan went flying down his front steps, breathing hard and sweating in his fantastically bejewelled coat. He was alone, the front door was locked, and there was nobody there at all.

The voice was quiet. For now.

"Your Highest?"

Dunstan flipped over, getting hastily to his feet and holding tight to his goggles. A Jettite, Lalum, from the chorus, stood there nervously clenching their claws.

"R-right." Dunstan nodded, wiping his face. "The dress rehearsal. I'm . . . I'm on my way."

"Of course, Your Highest, but, ah. I was wondering if you had seen Luisa." Lalum gestured with their head towards the festival grounds. "No one has seen her yet, and she's needed to run tech."

From behind his goggles, Dunstan winced. "She's probably with Decca. Find the commander. I'm sure everything is just fine." It would have to be. The show must go on, at all costs. And when it was all over, the stage would be set for Dunstan's grand destiny.

Though for the palest moment, Dunstan swore he felt the ground shiver again. Lalum looked back at him oddly, canting their head in confusion; they didn't look as if anything was amiss.

"It's fine." Dunstan waved the feeling of dread away, striding confidently beside his Truffledour compatriot. Whatever had happened to him on the doorstep faded away, like a distant dream. His swirling thoughts were coalescing into a singular purpose, and he felt, admittedly, much better.

He would put on the greatest show of his life. And whatever happened after the curtain fell, *he* would control it. *He* would shine so bright no one would stand in his way.

He grinned and felt the brighter for it. "It's showtime."

Around the main quay at the western dock was the Knockum Lightkeeper Station. In the past weeks Ada and her fellow lightkeepers had been busy touring the visiting "actors" through, to give them a sense of what lightkeepers did to maintain order on Lake Mallion. So the Jettites staying in town were well-versed in its purpose.

In most of the inner workings of the town, in fact.

The power that kept the lights on at each beacon, of course, was managed by Batterborne Powerhouse, a series of generators set at the escarpment level above Knockum, run by the Northern Dam twenty miles away in a segment of the Thousand Tributary system. This allowed the town to maintain its energy independence from the Far Cities, and count themselves, on paper at least, as above a hamlet on an economic scale.

But if one generator went down, say, in an overload or a storm, in order to keep the town running, it would take out Tantalon Depot — the gondola and train transport system that connected Knockum to Luxe and beyond. The energy from the remaining generators would be diverted to Knockum while repairs were underway.

It all made sense. But Commander Vora wanted to take extra care. One generator wasn't enough.

"What about all three?" Ven hazarded, as they stood together inside Batterborne Powerhouse with the current station manager, Lorelei, the skin around her eyes tight. "What would happen then?"

Lorelei was only half-listening. She was overseeing the engineering team, a few folks short this shift. "Well, we'd be entirely cut off from everything. Would take a catastrophic accident to do that, though. There are a lot of backups. And anyway, someone would have to get a message out by courier or some such, since the telegraph system would likely be knocked out, too . . ."

Telegraphs. Electricity. Generators. The Higher-ups really had innovation over the Jettites. Ven admired them for it. "Well. I can't think of *anything* that would possess enough power to cause an accident. Knockum has thought of everything." He grasped Lorelei's hand, smiling. "Thank you." Then, unable to stop himself, he asked, "Are . . . you all right?"

Lorelei seemed taken aback, staring at Ven's hand as if trying to work out how he got his hand to be so scaly. He pulled it away quickly, Vora giving him a bleak side-eye.

"It's just this . . . sickness going around. I'm hoping that, after the Starfall Festival, we can bring in outside help."

"Sickness?" Ven parroted, this time fully staring back at Vora, who had turned away to inspect one of the generators more closely . . . or avoid his gaze entirely.

Lorelei seemed uncomfortable, but, at her wit's end, she let it out: "The sleepies, folk are calling it. People just falling into deep, fairy tale dozes, and not waking up. My husband, and now Hector Alvarez . . ."

Something tingled in the back of Ven's mind. Wasn't Alvarez one of Luisa's names? "How many people have—?"

"And the mushrooms!" *That* sent a spear of panic into Ven. "I don't know if you've noticed them — I know you're quite busy preparing the show and helping out the other actors — but . . . why, no one has ever seen fungi cropping up like this. They're all over town. They only started to appear alongside this odd sickness and I . . ."

Lorelei bit back a sob. Ven, not knowing what to do, patted her on the shoulder, and she bucked up, putting on a pasted smile. "In any case, we're just so grateful that your actor friends are so handy."

Ven glanced up to the engineering team. They were more Jettite than Knockumite, wearing coveralls and grasping clipboards in their claws. Earlier, he'd felt that was an advantage, to be surrounded by his own citizens. He was doing all this for them.

But something settled in his scales. It wasn't gratitude or benevolence. He felt responsible for the Knockumites, too. And now, it seemed, they were suffering for helping them.

"Luisa is Hector's daughter, isn't she?" Commander Vora cut in. "Where is Luisa now, do you know?"

Lorelei shook her head. "Not sure. She called in about Hector. I think Ada Cord and Coral Frakes were with her . . ."

The commander ushered Lorelei off with a grim smile. "We won't keep you any longer. Thank you for keeping things in shape here. Essential nothing happens during the big show."

"Essential," Lorelei repeated absently, and once she was gone, Ven grabbed hold of Vora's crimson sleeve and steered her outside.

"It's happening again," Ven hissed, pulse ratcheting. "Just like with Reeve Gris, his three friends. They're all falling *asleep*."

"But Dunstan isn't," Vora snapped back, trying to keep her tone even. "He's strong. You said so yourself. It's why you vouched for him."

"But he's . . . he's different, too—" Ven could sense it, even when he'd tried to reach for Dunstan, to connect their Light. The last time he had, what he'd seen was more than worrying. And what he felt — the Meteorlight repelling him, as if it didn't want him to see . . . It was the same thing he'd felt the night he'd chased King Vert to the Door, tried to stop him from taking the Meteorlight away.

"Don't concern yourself about these Higher-ups. About the Meteorlight. Dunstan is still under your control, yes? Once we've taken things over here, he can go to sleep like the others. All that matters is keeping the Meteorlight ours."

They trotted easily down the escarpment, taking a route of treacherous rock knowing they wouldn't be seen or followed. "The plan is still the plan. I'll get to the cove. You do your job, Your Highness." She grasped Ven by the forearms, squeezing. "The show must go on."

This was the moment, after all. Ven's tongue flicked out and he nodded. Vora went one way, and he went his.

But before he finished the descent, he could see it perfectly from here: the festival grounds, and Beckon Bandstand, expanded outwards with its wings of lights, bright even in midday. He reached out with his thoughts towards Dunstan. What would happen if he told him the truth? Ven wouldn't have taken it this far if he'd known the people of this town, the ones who had welcomed his people with open arms, would suffer for it.

But the plan. Dunstan was pivotal to it working. Dunstan was the method and the reason.

And despite everything, Dunstan was the one thing he didn't want to lose. *Don't go breaking my heart*, Dunstan had laughed when they'd met.

But to make this all work, that was the one thing Ven would have to do.

SCENE 16

THE TRUTH IN THE DARK

Soaked but still moving forward, Ada, Luisa, Moss, and Decca followed Coral through the Hacklands and down treacherous rocky plinths into the city proper.

"I still can't believe this," Ada sniffed, reaching out to touch the glowing mushrooms. "I mean. I believed it. But seeing it is something else." The mushroom reached out dolefully towards her hand, as if it were a puppy seeking comfort. "No wonder Dunstan didn't want to leave."

"Yes, Jet has a pull about it," Coral remarked grimly. "But that's what the Meteorlight does. It fills a space. It pushes the darkness away. But it thrives in the dark."

Moss grimaced. "I saw enough of this place in my dreams. The sooner we're gone, the better."

Luisa agreed, thinking of Hector, of Dunstan, of all of it. She was still longing to be saved; she was exhausted that she was having to do all the saving.

As they came into a valley, walking slowly and carefully with their backs to the rock, Decca hissed suddenly.

"Stop!" Everyone flattened against the rock wall. There were footsteps above, a clanking, and a flash of red. Stackers running back in the direction of the Hacklands.

"Didn't we just come from there?" Ada asked. "I wonder what their hurry is."

Coral shrugged. "Perhaps a shift change. It's odd that we didn't meet with any interference using the Door . . ." She took another look to see if the coast was clear, then motioned them onwards.

"How much farther to the tor?" Moss asked. Luisa caught his tense glance as they came up into the open from the valley, the spires of Jet glowing and glittering.

"Another hour or so at this pace. Though . . ." Coral had stopped the group, looking around with a curious gaze. "Doesn't it seem . . . too quiet?"

Decca raced up an outcrop of dark stone and black sand, craning her neck to see into the byways between buildings. "There should be Stackers posted there, by the market, but . . ."

Coral joined her there, looking out. "Unless folks are hiding out at home, this doesn't seem right."

"Surely the entire *city* isn't in Knockum right now?" Ada laughed. Then her eyes met Coral's, shifted back to Luisa's. She stiffened. "Would Dunstan . . . ?" she started to ask, but truly, she didn't know the answer. If he had been sneaking more Jettites into Knockum, why? Had Ven asked him to?

"I don't think so," Luisa hazarded. "He only opens the Door for himself. But he's been focusing hard on the Starfall Festival lately, and doing fewer shows down here, maybe he hadn't noticed there was no more audience."

Coral looked over her shoulder, back towards the Hacklands. "Unless someone else has been opening the Door."

"But that's impossible," Luisa said. "Only Dunstan can—"

"Says who?" Coral shot back wryly. "Reeve Gris opened it. *You* opened it when I sent you after Dunstan." Then, she stopped herself, sideways-blinking down at Luisa. "Don't you know what it is that opens the Door?"

"The Meteorlight—" Luisa started, but then she stopped herself, the flares of her mind churning to develop the truth. If that were so, then any Jettite could have opened the Door long ago.

What is it that Dunstan, me, and Reeve have in common? That same strange loneliness of being rejected by those you care about the most.

"A broken heart," Luisa said out loud, frowning. "But who else . . ."

Coral straightened as if she'd been pierced in the back. Then she leapt down to the ground and grabbed hold of Ada.

"You were a track star, weren't you?" She looked round to the others. "Let's pick up the pace, ladies!"

Coral took off, with Decca close behind, and Luisa and Ada fighting to keep up.

"Who?" Ada asked, breathless. "Who else are you thinking of?"

Luisa didn't want to think it, but it fit. The Door liked a broken heart. And who else did they know who had known how the Door works and who had been as lonely as all of them?

"Prince Ven," she said to herself, to Ada, realizing too late that there was a player on the board who'd been dancing in plain sight, one she hadn't turned her suspicious eye towards all this time.

Everything was ready. There was nothing else for it now. No going back. But when Ven came up the sidewalk towards the festival grounds, he stopped. The green verge of the quad was filled with booths selling food and wares. Ven was so struck that he had to blink his eyes, clearing them, to make sure he wasn't in Jet. But no, it was Knockum. And the air teemed with everything he'd wanted. The rich smells of all the delicacies he'd partaken in since his stay here, mingling with those that the Jettites had tentatively brought with them. Knockumites and Jettites stood shoulder to jowl, chatting, laughing. The banners advertising the show whipped in a summer wind that tasted of something Ven had not yet experienced.

Joy.

The air was thick with it, and somehow it made his stomach turn, his tail flick in irritation, his hackles rise. This had been his plan, as Vora had been more than willing to remind him, and he was about to bring the hammer down on it all . . . but his head swam, his scales itched.

Ven twitched towards the sound of the Truffledour orchestra tuning, towards Beckon Bandstand, transformed into a grand spectacle stage. And on it was Dunstan, clear as day, running through the final number.

Ven's hackles flattened, and his chest ached. Ached in the way it had all these years, waiting, hoping, *wishing*. Because what he saw on that stage now, as Ven pulled himself deftly behind a concession tent for coverage, reminded him too much of himself. Dunstan dancing on his own, surrounded by others, yet deeply alone. Vying for the Light, reaching for it, waiting for someone else's Light to answer his. Waiting for a partner, a hero, anyone, to bring him out of the dark.

He leaned his head against the tent pole, shut his eyes.

The show had been going on far too long.

A claw snatched into Ven's coat, the one he'd worn almost all his life in that dark place: gold, sparkling, marked for a prince, marked to show he had authority, even if he pretended not to. He whirled on the intruder, Ven's tail catching him tightly around the arm before he could stop himself.

"Your Highness," Lalum grunted, gritting their teeth. "The Higher-up was starting to grow suspicious."

Ven released him harshly. "I'm here now. Anything else to report?"

"The stage manager is missing." Lalum's eyes darted. Beyond the festival grounds, a crowd was beginning to mill. They had added seating, but evidentially it wouldn't be enough. Amongst the Knockumites, Jettites filled the spaces, everyone chatting and sharing and making it seem awfully like this was real — that they fit in, were a part of this community now. Ven had to look away; it was too good an illusion.

People with things called cameras, devices made for capturing moments, loitered nearby as well, snapping off a few shots. Lalum and Ven shied away, and the prince dragged the underling closer to the stage as Stackers (bouncers) warned the camera-snappers back.

Lalum went on. "Not only that, but Dunstan's mother and Decca are gone. And the other one — the town recluse. Frakes." Lalum folded his arms. "Do you think they know?"

"If they do, it's too late," Ven snapped. There were many places this group could be. Even though Tantalon Depot was about to experience a major surge, it was still running. And all four of those in question knew part of the truth: that Jet was a real place, that the Jettites weren't actors, and that there was no show, not really.

They knew the truth, and they supported Ven. They had gone along with this little story for Ven's sake. Maybe their trust had finally run out, and maybe it was for good reason. Ven didn't feel inclined, at all, to try to stop them.

A part of him hoped they would stop *him* instead.

Ven swallowed hard, faked another genial smile. "It doesn't matter. Everything is going well, Lalum! We should be celebrating!" He moved to shuffle his coat off. It was stifling in the summer air, his scales longing to breathe. Or perhaps it was something else choking the life out of him.

"I don't know, sire."

Ven paused, turning slowly back towards Lalum. "What did you say?"

Lalum clenched their clipboard — Luisa's, evidentially — as a shield. "I'm sorry, sire, it's just . . ." Lalum was small and slight, and Ven had watched the would-be Truffledour beaning themself on the Look Alight's mushroom arch so many times, it was a wonder they were still standing. "It's just that the others. The Jettites. We all know we needed a new home, somewhere safe! But we feel that this . . . this isn't the way to go about it." Lalum backed up a step, lifting a shoulder. "I'm sure if we *told* Knockum our plight—"

"—they would eat us alive, Lalum." Ven felt his scales rise as the feelings flashed through him in a wave. "They won't accept us if they know who we really are. They think we're a novelty now. But you'll see. Tonight they *will* know. And they'll have to accept their new place in the pecking order. We'll have our chance to explain ourselves, with the upper hand. From the *stage*."

Lalum dipped their head, eyes cast elsewhere as they nodded. A wave of regret passed under Ven's scales, but he didn't take back his speech. "Yes, sire," Lalum muttered.

"Send word to Commander Vora. And don't look at me like that," Ven warned, wagging his claw as he climbed the stage steps. "Play your part, Lalum. Like the rest of us."

He took one last look to see Lalum slink away. *The others think . . .* so they'd been talking amongst themselves, had they? Ven checked the sky, the light in it. It would be time soon. Yet if they all thought this way . . . if they all thought this was wrong . . . maybe . . .

"Ven!" Dunstan cried, the music catching as he dropped his hand, and the figures of green Light flashing like starbursts in the reflection of his dark goggles. In the afterimage, blinking rapidly, Ven remembered the first night he had met Dunstan, on that awful vessel he'd always cursed. The one that had taken his father and the Meteorlight away. The place where he'd wished for things to turn out the way he'd dreamed — and there Dunstan had been.

He had kissed Ven without knowing him. And Ven had only ever told him the truth.

I intend to shroom-nap you and use you for my nefarious plot to get the bash out of here.

Ven swallowed. When he opened his eyes fully, Dunstan filling them, Ven wanted to tell him the *real* truth now, more than ever, and it flitted to the tip of his forked tongue.

"Dunstan, I need to tell you something," Ven said, betraying himself, his people, his cause. His heartstruck heart thumped. "I can't—"

"No!" Dunstan held up his hands. "No. Not now. After the show. Please." He took Ven's hands in his, reassuring, smiling in the way Ven always did. "The show will be brilliant. Knockum will love you.

But don't worry about a thing, about what comes after. I have a plan. One that won't see us parting forever. Okay?"

Ven felt as clammy as a Stettle Beetle as Dunstan wove his fingers into his claws. Numbly he nodded, just as Lalum had when he'd ordered him to stand down, to bury his misgivings.

Ven needed to play his part. Sometimes there was no other answer than to surrender.

They made it to the tor with little fuss. Still a few Stackers, but none of them keen to stop the group's rush to get to the Hacklands. It really seemed as though the place was deserted.

Or actively abandoned.

Decca was beginning to falter as she led everyone to the nearest Stettle carriage platform up a winding set of spindly stairs. "Maybe . . . maybe we should go back," she urged, eyes darting between the group. "Something might be happening above."

Luisa tried to reassure her. "We need the proof. If we can bring Reeve with us, especially, we have to show Dunstan the result of what he's taken on."

"If there's anything of Reeve left," Moss let slip, and Coral smacked him.

She looked to Ada and Luisa and shook her head. "We won't know until we know. I'm sure it's fine." King Vert had never been a successful Truffledour and Coral wasn't about to begin her career anew.

Unconvinced, Ada stepped up to the platform, looking both ways down the cable. "I don't think they're in service. And there wouldn't be anyone to take them if they were." The platform was as empty as the rest of the city. The mushroom pot lights flickered in Jet's eternal midnight. As they looked right at them, the lights flickered out, and turned black.

"That's strange," Luisa said. "I thought Dunstan's performances here would've corrected that . . ."

Then the ground beneath them shook, sending Ada wheeling into Coral's arms and Decca crashing into Luisa.

"Those, too," Coral said, testing her foot against the mushroom caps that comprised the platform beneath them. "Something definitely isn't right."

As Luisa inspected the cable line they stood in front of, she hurried for the transit control booth, which was completely abandoned, door left open, as if it'd been evacuated mid-shift. She called Ada over, and the two huddled over the controls. "If it's just like last time . . ." She grabbed hold of the lever, hand sparking, the green charge diving from her palm and into the power board. Ada mastered the lever until a Stettle car came trundling down the cable line in a shower of green sparks.

"A neat trick," Coral commended, the doors whooshing open. Yet as everyone went inside, Decca hesitated.

"Should I stay here and keep watch?" she said, rubbing her arm, one boot on the platform. With a last look to the glittering, maligned city, Luisa held out a hand, and after another moment, she pulled Decca inside.

Across the Light they shared, Luisa felt unease, but Decca pulled away as if she'd been static shocked, sitting hard beside Coral and staring at her feet. Outside the beetle-bodied trolley window, the lights of Jet twinkled. Ada pressed her hand to the almost-glass.

"This place really is beautiful, Coral." Her fingertips left a pressed-on afterglow of green, and she rubbed them together. "I hope . . . we can save it."

"That will be up to your son," Coral said, pulling the door closed and nodding to Luisa. She stood up, popping the window open, rummaging above until she felt the base of the hook that connected them to the cable. As she and Dunstan had on their initial escape from Jet, she let the Meteorlight move through her and into the cable car. It juttered on the line, then began its ascent towards the tor.

Moss, a quiet six feet of tension crammed into the car, also stared out in wonder. "Even without the dreams," he said, "I feel like

Dunstan told us all about this place. Or places like it. With his little shows. You know?"

No one answered, but they all agreed. The car lifted onwards, silent with everyone's misgivings. It moved as slowly as a Tantalon gondola and gave an impressive view of the city below. Was it truly empty, or had they just been lucky? Luisa feared she knew the answer but didn't want to speak it. *One at a time is good fishing.* She smiled. This was something Dunstan's other mother, Lorraine, used to say to rein him in from bopping to one thing and the other. Most of all, Luisa felt a storm of reasons and logic and blame building up inside her. This was all Dunstan's fault . . . yet it wasn't. It was all a coincidence, the Meteorlight percolating inside her best friend for years until his heart was broken enough to give it purchase.

She rubbed her fingers together. Wasn't that the way with most things that were bad for us?

"Look at that!" Moss cried, pointing out the window at the tor. As the Stettle car drew closer to the tower of black stone, Luisa saw that its surface was covered in intricate symbols and images. It was just like the ancient pillars of a Brindlewatch of old. The line separating Jet from their world was growing thinner as they climbed.

"The story of the Meteorlight," Coral confirmed, leaning towards Ada and pointing. "See? There's the Light coming down from the Blackest Black. Space." Ada smiled at her, the starburst in the stone glittering as they passed. "'All that was left from the Up was the Door, closed always to keep us safe and the Light protected. And from the Light the Jettites, the Dortites, all the folk of the Underlands came to be. And when they flourished, so did the Light, in an endless cycle.' And so on." Coral's scales coloured with something like pride. "I never thought I'd see it again."

The trolley car swung around then, its descent changing from a straight incline to a slow corkscrew around the tower, likely to get the best look at all the pictograms winding their way to the top.

Luisa pointed. "Look, there's more!" And there, unmistakable: a carving of *The Darling Mermaid*, balanced precariously on a rock plinth. The king giving up the Light to the Door. And a smaller Jettite . . . running away. Ven.

"So he was there," Luisa breathed.

Coral shook her head. "While I was under the Light's influence, I couldn't see or remember anything. If he was there with me . . . I thought I had been dreaming." Coral dragged a hand down her face. "I shouldn't have run off the minute I saw him in Knockum. I've avoided him ever since. I should have been honest with him from the beginning, but—"

"If you'd revealed yourself at any point, it would've risked exposing their plan. And ours. The reunion may not have been what you were imagining," Ada pressed, her hand on Coral's. "Every mother tries her best."

Coral looked at her friend tenderly, then to Decca. "So Ven was there when the Meteorlight splintered. Is this widely accepted knowledge?"

Decca was not looking at the pictograms. She was staring at her boots so hard that her eyes, unblinking, seemed to quiver. "Yes. Ven was there."

The pictograms changed then. The four rulers were augmented by a fifth. A Jettite, shining bright. Ven. Jettites clamoured around him, his arms held out. Venerated.

So not a deposed prince after all. What else had he been lying about?

Before Luisa could interrogate Decca further, the carriage car shuddered, swinging, and the five clutched each other in terror. They were high above the city, and any mishap meant no more second chances. But the car continued upwards, even for the shaking cavern.

"Hate water. Hate heights," Coral grimaced, and Ada patted her hand.

The pictograms persisted, showing figures atop the boat. The Great Vessel that had come from Higher-up. And the four figures were holding the Light.

"There!" Luisa said. "That must be Reeve Gris, and the others, the Sunken Three!" She counted: "Darla Denning, Emmerich Kohl, and

Lenny Steez. That *must* be them!" Their names had been scrawled in the backs of textbooks and on lockers, epithets or protections against bad luck, depending on who had written them. Names invoked on Hallow Nights to scare each other.

"If they're still . . . alive," Moss said, treading carefully, "then why didn't they just open the Door and go home?"

"We'll soon find out," Coral said. "We're here."

The car pulled up to a platform of magnificent mushrooms, fanned out in perfect symmetry and glowing incandescent, the Light at the top of the tor a sight to behold. It still climbed another fifty feet, its peak touching the twin stalactite that hung black and deadly from the cavern's ceiling.

Before anyone moved, Coral said, "Remember. If we're met with resistance, I'll try to use my royal influence, though since I'm an historical betrayer, it may not have much clout. But at least the powers that be may be distracted enough for you three" — Coral indicated Ada, Moss, and Luisa — "to get a good look at these so-called rulers. Get some answers."

Ada followed Coral out of the car. Down a path of glittering stone, with railings hewn from gem and dark sand, was a triangular archway. The Meteorlight shone over everything from the gables of the tower's tip, yet Luisa knew that, compared to Dunstan, it was a dim candle growing dimmer.

Just as Luisa was about to disembark, Decca grabbed her back hard, crying, "You can't!"

Luisa staggered, pulling herself free as she landed on the platform. Decca didn't get out of the car. "Come on! We're almost there!"

"I know!" Decca snapped back, completely not herself. Then her scales screwed up and she looked like she might cry — even though it wasn't something Jettites could do. "I *know*. And when we get there . . ."

Coral had pulled the Filamenta free, pausing as she turned, lowering it towards the young Stacker gently. "Decca. If you know something, you need to tell us. Are we walking into a trap?"

"No!" Decca held up her hands, then dropped them, clutching her forearms in her claws as her shoulders went up. "We're just not supposed to be here." The ground gave an experimental shiver, and she clasped her face.

At an impasse, all Luisa could do was reach out for her friend. Decca didn't look or speak, but she reached back with her tail, an invitation. Luisa clasped it between her palms. The Meteorlight coursed through, a calming ray, and when it came back, Luisa frowned. Decca snatched it away, face crumpled in shame.

"Luisa?" Coral asked. "What is it?"

But before she could reply, the ground not only shook, it heaved. Then they heard a thunderous *crack* that echoed as a terrible warning over the city.

Luisa had one moment to look up. The stalactite above the tor shivered; part of it sheared away, and Decca lunged from the Stettle car, knocking Luisa out of the way as it narrowly missed the cable line, crashing a hundred miles to the ground at the base.

Coral dragged Luisa and Decca to their feet as the ground went on shaking. "Hurry!" she shouted, and with Ada's and Moss's help, they all made it through the triangular archway and inside the tor proper as debris rained down on the courtyard behind them.

They found themselves coming through what Luisa could only describe as a monumental mushroom garden, well-tended, the fronds swaying as they passed, their Light pulsing in time with their steps and ignorant of the destruction raining outside. These mushrooms were unlike any in the city below; they were grand, old. But with every shiver, their Light faltered, and as the group raced past, making for the next door, many of them flickered out. Their massive caps crumbled on top of them as the city shook outside.

"This doesn't make sense!" Ada cried over the din as they took shelter in the next door's archway, Coral fighting with the door latch. "Dunstan putting on shows in Jet was supposed to *prevent* this from happening."

"Let me!" Luisa pushed Coral out of the way and held fast to the door handle, her hands blazing green. It began to loosen, and suddenly Ada joined her, her own hands blazing bright as the two pulled mightily. The lock gave way, and they were inside. Coral, Moss, and Decca leapt in, and Moss heaved all his weight to push the door closed.

Finally, the ground settled, offering a moment's respite as Luisa grabbed Decca by the hand and pulled her forward.

"Decca," she said evenly, but her voice was tinged with anger. "Why didn't you tell us?" When Decca opened her mouth silently, Luisa shook her hand. "Why?"

Decca pulled her hand back, clasping it with the other. "Orders," she mumbled awkwardly. "Our orders were . . . were to keep quiet until . . . until the *show*."

"The show?" Coral repeated, looking from Decca to Luisa with her own ream of frustration. "Will you two elaborate, now that we aren't being crushed to death?"

But rather than answer immediately, Decca sighed and said, "We're here. You'll see soon enough."

Ahead was a third door, heavy, huge, but through the crack in the opening, a strobing viridian. Flickering. Pale. Green.

Ada stood before it, staring at her hands. "You said . . . the Meteorlight finds purchase in a broken heart?" Suddenly she faltered, and Moss surged forward to catch her from falling.

Coral came to their side, clasping Ada's wrists in her scaled fingers, shaking her head. "You must have it, too, Ada. I can't pull it out." She raised the Filamenta.

"No." Ada pushed it down, got back on her own two feet and kept her eyes locked on the door ahead of them. "I can hear it. *Feel it*. I need to see."

Moss, Decca, and Coral held back as Luisa and Ada went forward first, because they could feel it: the Meteorlight recognizing them and the mushrooms that bore it calling them forward.

Luisa shielded her eyes as she, and the others, entered the glowing antechamber. So this was the top of the Tallest Tor from inside. When Luisa had first arrived in Jet, it beamed outwards, a definite beacon in a city grown in the dark, like a long-forgotten terrarium. She imagined that being inside that Light would be too much — but since that first time seeing it, the Light had shrunk, an orb no bigger than a football, its meridians feathery and insubstantial. Yet even for how little there was left, Luisa could feel it reaching for her, looking for a place to go. And though she felt compelled to reach back, Ada grabbed her and held her in place.

"I want to, just as much as you," Ada said, struggling, it seemed, to back them both up. "But we shouldn't."

"Absolutely correct," Coral said, hefting the Filamenta across her hands like a hatchet as she stared up into the cloisters of the Tor's uppermost peak. "Reeve Gris!" she bellowed. "Rulers of Jet! We have come to seek an audience!"

Above was only darkness. And silence. Coral looked to Decca. "Well? Now what?"

Decca stepped forward and pointed to the dais the meagre Meteorlight-filled mushroom rested on. Growing from the platform was what looked like four roots, running from the floor and up the black stone walls. Coral held up the Filamenta, which itself reached for what little Meteorlight it could detect. Then she gasped as she staggered back, and Luisa and Ada joined her side.

"Behold," Coral said grimly through her sharp teeth, "the rulers of Jet."

When the Filamenta was held up, it lit a ruffled mushroom, its gills glowing dully and parting when the Filamenta drew closer. Inside the velvet folds, a teenage boy, his face and body blooming with perfectly formed mycelia. His chest rose and fell, like a sleeping prince in a fairytale.

"It's Reeve," Moss breathed, moving as if in a trance to the mushroom pod. Here was the town legend, the one that Moss had tried to become in his stead, still Moss's age, locked forever in adolescence, unable to save anyone from anything in this state. What would the rest of the Grislies say, if they were here now?

Coral moved about the room along the path of the other roots, revealing the other three doomed passengers of *The Darling*

Mermaid. They, too, slept deeply, intricately connected to Jet's ancient mycelium network along with every mushroom throughout the city. Was the little bit of Meteorlight here keeping them alive? Or was the Light that had splintered into them keeping the city alive?

Without a word of warning, Coral whirled on Decca and grabbed her up in her claw. She yelped, and Luisa cried out, trying to get between them. "Coral! Wait!"

"What is this?" Coral seethed at Decca, ignoring Luisa. "How long have they been like this?"

"I . . . I . . ." Decca stammered, holding on to Coral's arm for dear life. "It's been a long time! Before I was a Stacker. And not long after they arrived." She pulled away, and Luisa held on to her, keeping Coral from rounding on her again. "I haven't been here before. I was never on tor rotation — that's the Stackers who are stationed here — b-but I knew someone. Lalum. They were a Stacker dropout, became a Truffledour. Th-they told stories." She gathered herself, tried to speak clearly. "Th-they said that the Higher-ups wanted to be good rulers! They kept Jet bright! But then they started to . . . to *change*. The Light changed them. No one knew what to do! So it was kept secret. U-until they b-became *part* of Jet and . . . the Meteorlight . . . started to fade—"

Decca may have said more had Ada not let out a blood-curdling scream. The four spun and saw that she had remained behind at one of the mushroom pods, her hand held in the grip of Reeve Gris, still sleeping, her Light answering it.

Then the mushroom in the centre of the room . . . *spoke.*

You have brought more spores with you. But you're too late.

A strange voice. Almost a boy's. But maybe a mushroom's. "Reeve?" Luisa whispered. The Light strobed, but this was the only confirmation.

Jet's roots needed more spores to be strengthened. More Light. But it's been taken from here. Drawn away. Made stronger at another source, with every surge. The mushroom strobed, sending out an image, unmistakably, of Dunstan.

The roots are too far gone. The foundations of rock holding Jet together are too weak. It needs all *the Meteorlight to do this. But all of it is inside the Performer. And the Meteorlight doesn't want Jet to be saved.*

"What do you mean?" Luisa breathed. "The Meteorlight *wants* Jet to *fall?*"

The mushroom was quiet for a moment, as if thinking, then another voice spoke up, a female one. Everyone turned to Darla Denning, who seemed to stir in her dream but didn't wake.

When we came here, we wanted to go home. This world wasn't ours. But the Meteorlight, what little of it we had — it wanted to shine. The prince showed us how to use it. We became rulers, and for a time we felt like we were doing the right thing. But the more the Meteorlight shone, the more tired it made us. It put us to sleep.

Even though Reeve's eyes were closed, and he looked so peaceful, he held fast to Ada's arm, seeming to grip tighter, and she cried out. Reeve went on.

But there was one thing we learned while we were here, while we were still awake: the Door was kept shut to keep the Meteorlight from escaping. And the Door needed to make sure it stayed that way.

The mushroom changed then, playing the scene out.

The Door helped us as we fell asleep. Jet was safe. Knockum was safe. Isn't that what a good ruler should do? But it wasn't enough. The Door had already been opened once. There was not enough Meteorlight to keep the lakebed from cracking. The Door has held it all together all this time . . . but the Meteorlight inside Dunstan drew more of our power away, every time it lit up Jet.

Luisa looked to Decca. "And that was the plan, was it?"

"No!" she cried, then backtracked. "Well, sort of! I don't know!" She truly did look torn. "It was the prince's plan. The city was in a crisis. We needed the Meteorlight to survive, and the Higher-ups had some. Things were all right! They saved us! When they fell asleep they weren't hurt, and Jet remained safe . . . until the Meteorlight started fading. Ven knew it wouldn't last, and we needed to find another way." She bit her lip. "Then the Door opened. And Dunstan came. It was like a prayer had been answered. And we just, all of us . . ."

She looked to Ada, Moss, Coral, and Luisa, then to the sleeping rulers, and held out her hands, at a loss. "We just put on a show. We were desperate."

Luisa hesitated, her heart roiling. Then she put her arms around Decca, who seemed to shrink into them, her secret finally told.

"You were all just trying to protect your people," Luisa said. "But taking over Knockum against its will isn't a solution. And lying to everyone about it has just made it worse."

"I know," Decca said brokenly, but she pulled away, more solid now for the truth having been spoken. "But there were two plans. The prince's, to keep Jet alive. And the Meteorlight's." She scanned the four Higher-ups grimly. "The Meteorlight wants Jet to fall. It's using Dunstan to grow more powerful. To shine and shine, no matter who it hurts. But I see now. Some lights should be left in the dark."

Ada looked into Reeve Gris's face, running her hand across his brow. She glanced up to Moss and saw that he had his hands over Reeve's, too. So many children involved, all making impossible choices when faced with such massive stakes.

"Without the Meteorlight, Jet will be crushed, and so will Knockum," Ada said. "If the lakebed cracks, we all know what will happen to both towns. We need to get back and get the Meteorlight out of Dunstan. Before he becomes . . . *this*."

Gently, Coral prised Reeve's fingers from Ada's wrist, placing them back into his mushroom cocoon. Moss, after a time, stepped back, but looked aggrieved to do so.

The Door will help you, the voice inside the mushroom whispered, fading as the Meteorlight did. *It wants to put an end to what it started when it crashed here. You need only ask it.*

But as soon as the voice faded, the tower sent the five of them reeling as another quake shivered through. Coral grabbed Ada, who held Moss's hand, and Luisa clasped Decca.

"I think we've got all the proof we need," Coral said, leading them out.

Moss protested. "We can't just leave them here! We have to bring them back with us, before this place falls on their heads!"

Coral shook hers, horns glittering in the fading green Light. "They're all that's keeping Jet standing now. Them and the Door. If we remove them, Jet falls, and it might take the lakebed with it." She steered Moss out, her strong arm brooking no refusal. "We'll find another way to bring them back."

The ground rumbled, rocks ricocheting, and the group took off at a run.

"What does that mean — the Door will help us if we ask it?" Ada panted, a horrible *CRACK* sounding from behind them as they made it into the mushroom garden.

"We'll try our luck when we get there," Luisa said as they found themselves back in the outer sanctum, their Stettle Beetle car swaying, sparking, beginning to slide away.

"Quickly!" Coral cried, gesturing towards the platform. The crack they'd heard was parts of the platform and the outer balcony shearing off — rock and mushroom alike, in a cascade spilling directly towards their carriage. They ran, leapt, and slid inside just in time to see the rest of the platform shatter outside the iridescent beetle window, the car jerking and careening down the steep incline they'd climbed to get here.

For now, the tor remained upright, but inaccessible, as they sped away. His face pressed against the window, Moss stared achingly back towards the inner sanctum. "How long will they be able to last?"

Coral shook her head, trying to focus on surviving what remained of their escape. "As long as they have a little bit of the Meteorlight left . . . they should be all right."

"If Dunstan doesn't take the rest of it," Luisa added.

"The Door is on our side. It will help us," Decca repeated hopefully, the cable shaking as the rest of Jet held on with what little strength it had left. "At least someone will."

SCENE 17

THE BROKEN HEARTS CLUB

The show had begun.

On the stage, Ven did feel different. He felt like the prince he'd spent his life trying to be, the image he tried to live up to. Dunstan had written him the part, but he'd been playing it all his life, and with much more gusto ever since that boat had fallen on King Vert and changed everything. He'd tried to make the right decisions. He'd always attempted to put on the proper show. The vagabond Prince act was fun, but it was just another way to try to save Jet.

But when he was here on the stage with Dunstan, he felt closer to the thing that made him *himself*, something he didn't quite recognize, save for the sheer joy he felt when he took on this role. No, not a role. No masks. They were just together. Simple. That's what Ven had wanted, all along. What he'd sat beneath the Door and begged for, for years. And the Door had opened and delivered Dunstan, and he'd treated him like a tool, before realizing that Dunstan was the answer. The simple thing. The real way out.

The critical climax of Dunstan's tale, where the lost prince of Jet decides to reclaim his legacy and save his people, with a human's help, was quickly approaching. Mid-scene, after his lines, Ven turned towards Lake Mallion, his heart a gable moth looking for a way out of his chest. Vora would be down there on her stolen boats, piloted by Jettites for their coup. Jettites who feared the water, in a world that was more water than rock. Humans themselves made up of the stuff, shedding it with their sorrow.

Ven turned his back on the lake, digging his claws into his eyes. His mind wandered dangerously, suddenly unable to shake the image of Dunstan's tears. A sign of sorrow. Of a broken heart. Ven didn't want to see him cry again. But he was about to.

" . . . Noble Prince?" intoned Dunstan, in a loaded, heavy tone. Ven blinked, glancing from Dunstan to Kepler Green, who was downstage, helming a meeting with the play's town council, during the romantic interlude. Both stared daggers at Ven to *get on with it*; he'd missed his line.

It was time, then. Ven cleared his throat, his skull ringing.

"Noble, yes! I am here for a noble cause — to save my people!" Ven stepped forward, staring out at the crowd through the screen of glowing orbs. Beyond the crowd and the festival grounds, the space was empty. Vora was late. He was going to have to do something Dunstan told him he shouldn't, when onstage. *Vamp.*

He turned, suddenly, to Dunstan. "But is it noble?"

Dunstan's stage smile faltered as Ven raced back up and sat next to Dunstan on the raised dais where he'd been striking out his monologue. The lighting crew, unsure what to do, spotlit Ven as he grasped Dunstan's hands. "I'm all for saving everyone, but — what about *us*?"

This was off-book, and Ven knew how much Dunstan hated that. But he was also a champion improviser, and they hadn't had any time to talk . . . to make *their* plans, which had nothing to do with saving either Jet or Knockum. This might be the only chance they got.

"What if we didn't go through with it, and we just did what we always said we would — run away?"

This close, Ven saw Dunstan swallow. He hoped the message had been received, despite how risky it was, and with an audience of hundreds. There was some murmuring in the crowd, but Ven didn't care. This was it. This was the moment, and maybe the only one they had.

The ground rumbled threateningly. Not much time left now. He squeezed Dunstan's hands.

"Bright Eyes," he whispered. "There's something I need to tell you—"

"Run away?" Dunstan cried loudly, pulling his hands from Ven's. He laughed, all for the stage. The effect. "But Prince . . . what about saving your city? Saving everyone? What about shining for all to see?" Through his teeth, Dunstan croaked, "*Please.*"

The ground kept shaking. Someone from the crowd cried out, and in response, Dunstan rolled his hands, summoning the image of Jet, which stood in for the story's broken city. "Even now, Your Highness, your city needs you! The quakes only worsen. This is how you can be the hero you always wanted to be!" Dunstan was trying to loop the quakes into the show, as if it were an effect, to keep people in their seats. Then Dunstan turned to Ven. "If we stick to the plan, then everything will be—"

"But don't you see?" Ven was desperate now. Hang the spectacle. He grasped Dunstan forcefully by the edge of his coat. "We need to go. *Now.*"

Then Ven saw it — this close, Dunstan's eyes had . . . changed. It was only the merest blink beneath the green ribbons, but he saw, clearly, that the bright amber of Dunstan's irises had been totally replaced with black pits and swirling green centres. And when Dunstan turned away, removing himself from Ven's grasp again, there was something in his twitching grin that wasn't right at all.

"Go where, Your Highness? We're right where we should be. Keeping our promises to everyone and putting aside what we want for the greater good." As the ground shook, the bulb lights in the air took on a shivering rhythm. A pulse beat. "That's what heroes do in all the stories. In all the plays. We have to be the heroes."

Ven's hands shook. "But what if we aren't the heroes?" he said loudly, asking the crowd, maybe, to judge them both here and now. "What if we were always the villains, putting on an *act?*"

He wanted to whip his tail towards Dunstan, snatch him and pull him off this stage. Go deep into the world where Dunstan promised they'd go and not come back. But time was running out. Soon, Vora would be coming up from Lake Mallion. Soon, everyone would know what Ven was really about. And soon, Dunstan would break from the inside out when the secret came crashing through, and Ven knew now, even if it was too late, that he couldn't bear it.

But when the ground stopped shaking, and Dunstan was still standing on the stage, expectant, Ven knew that this play was the last time he and Dunstan would be together. So he sighed and said his line.

"I'll do it. I'll be the hero." And he reached for Dunstan to kiss him . . .

As the crowd applauded, Ven looked out beyond it, and saw Vora, triumphant.

The show was over.

Ask the Door for help.

Even as they approached the Hacklands, perilously and mostly in silence, Luisa didn't know how to ask a Door for anything other than to open. But her mind wasn't just full of signal flares now — it was a strobing corona. Ven had lied to all of them, and they'd bought it. And so had Dunstan. Or, at least, the thing inside him. Were they really two separate things? He was the most volatile piece in this puzzle. Luisa inscribed every building they passed into memory, wondering how much longer they would stand as the cavern that held the black city in its embrace shuddered, and shivered, each concussion culminating at the source of it all.

The Door in Lake Mallion.

Luisa was beyond angry. It wasn't that. It was they'd all been conned, had *allowed* themselves to be, because there had been impossible promises put in each of their paths. Dunstan was promised fame, importance, love. Luisa was promised her best friend back.

Coral wanted to save Jet, then her new hometown, and had come face to face with the child she'd given up to do it — why couldn't she have it all? So when Ven came a-knockin', everyone was primed to let the fairy tale wash over them.

But in all of it, she knew Decca was put in a terrible position, and told her so, grabbing her friend's hand in hers. "None of this is your fault. I know you were just trying to do the right thing. If *someone* had just told everyone in Knockum the truth—"

"Would you have helped us?" Decca asked, point blank. Then she shook her head. "Of course you would have. But Ven was convinced no one would. We had to be sure. For Jet's sake."

"I would've done the same thing," Coral said, and Ada turned to her in surprise. "I put on my own performance and pretended. If I'd just have been honest, and out in the open, Knockum would have been more prepared. And my children . . ." She snorted. "Well, I won't be winning any parent of the year awards at this year's Council Community Fundraiser . . ."

"Wait." Moss stopped, and Ada, Luisa, and Decca looked back. "You said *children*. Plural."

Coral blinked rapidly, then held out her hands. "Yes. Ven. And Vora. They're both—"

The ground rocked as they stood beneath the Door, a concussive, violent blast. They all looked back to the tor to make sure it was still standing, the stalactite above it broken halfway but holding.

Ada helped Luisa to stand. "Never mind that now. How do we ask a door to help us? And what are we asking for, exactly?"

"A miracle," Coral snorted, folding her arms as she stared up at it. "The Meteorlight is too close to getting what it wants — to shine, to fill everything above with its Light as it spreads its spores, putting people to sleep just as it did with Reeve Gris and his friends. And the Door is too weak to contain it anymore. But the Meteorlight needs to be put somewhere . . ."

"Under the lake," Decca said suddenly. Luisa raised a brow. Decca went on, puzzling it out. "Jettites hate the water. The Meteorlight only seemed to get stronger when it was away from Lake Mallion, above it. And if it's put under the water itself—"

"Then it might not be strong enough to escape again." Coral chewed on this, then looked back towards the Door. "The only way for that to happen is for Dunstan himself to come down here. Which he may, to collect the last of the Meteorlight from Gris and the others."

Ada's eyelashes, glowing with the fragment of Meteorlight still inside her, illumined the tears collecting at the corner of her eyes. "I don't think it's our part to play, to ask the Door for help."

And as the Door, as if hearing them, sharply slammed its black symmetrical parts aside, Luisa continued for her. "So our part is to leave here, and—"

"—do the best we can with the script we're dealt," Coral finished, taking Decca's hand, who took Luisa's, who took Ada's, who took Moss's. Their broken, unsure hearts guided them.

The Door itself said, *Not long now,* as it dragged them through crashing cold water, breaking the surface in the centre of a ring of Jettite-piloted boats that had been waiting for them.

Overhead, the sky darkened as Knockum shook.

When the quake subsided, the crowd's screams went on. The Meteorlight Dunstan had cast guttered, shrinking into itself from the shock, and when he tried to get up, he found Ven was righting him, keeping him standing with claw and tail . . . but wouldn't let go when Dunstan tried to move away.

"There's no need to panic!" Cutting through the crowd was Commander Vora, followed by, at first, a column of Stackers . . . and then more Jettites in plainclothes, the ones borrowed from their new friendly neighbours who had mistaken them for actors.

The commander was smiling, and the Stackers flanked the crowd, allowing nowhere for them to go.

"W-what's happening?" Dunstan stammered, pulling on his arm. "Ven, you can let me go now."

Ven didn't look down at Dunstan. His mouth was grim, lips pulling back to show his sharp teeth. "I can't."

"What—" But with a flourish of the commander's coat, something was thrown up onto the stage. Ven caught it with a deft twirl, pulled up Dunstan's hands, and clapped them into it.

It was a cuff, pulsing and tightening. The same that had been used on him when they'd been captured in Jet.

"Dun!"

From the back of the crowd, Ada's voice. But she, like Luisa, Moss, and Coral as they were pushed towards the stage, were also bound. Decca, shamefaced, was the one behind them.

"Give them the best seats in the house, Stackling." Vora grinned. "We don't want them to miss the coronation."

"Ven, please, just tell me what's happening!" Déjà-vu crept up as Dunstan threw himself at the prince, but Ven moved out of the way and he fell, kneeling, at his boots. Dunstan looked helplessly to the crowd, their faces shell-shocked by this turn of events.

"Is this part of the show?" he heard someone ask.

Vora turned, arms open. "Citizens of Knockum, believe me. It *has* been a show. One of the greatest spectacles that Jet has ever put on. But now is the time for it to end." She gestured grandly at Ven, then clapped her fist to her chest, bowing. "I give you your new ruler, *King* Ven."

A beat. A cough. Someone snorted. "I don't get it," a voice lobbed. And Ven shook off his coat.

"This isn't a show," he emphasized. "I'm not an actor. Neither are the Jettites who have lived among you these past few weeks. Jet is a real place. *My* kingdom. And it is beyond saving."

Dunstan's mind reeled; this wasn't in the script, this speech, and Ven was delivering it in a way that wasn't put on. It was grim. It was real. And Dunstan felt sick.

"But it was true," Ven continued, "a hero *did* arrive in Jet, just in time, with what we needed. The Meteorlight. It allowed us to keep things on an even keel, to open the Door at the bottom of your lake long enough for us all to escape. And to find a new home . . . here."

"Enough of this!" This time it was Coral, bound but on her feet, her kerchief slipping and her dark glasses askew. Decca whispered something to Luisa, who tried to put a hand on Coral's, but it was knocked aside. "We don't have the time to be dilly-dallying with hostile takeovers! Everything is out of balance, and this town—"

"—is ours, now." The commander took to the stage, dragging Dunstan to his feet. "Jettites, we have reclaimed the Meteorlight! It is our people's birthright, and it is the legacy of our *king*, who toiled for too long to see this plan come to fruition, with your help. We will rebuild Jet here, in the High-up, and with the Meteorlight once more, we will be stronger than ever!"

The commander, obviously, was expecting a different response than the absolute silence from Jettites who, as far as Dunstan could see, were turning their faces to the ground, shuffling away from their human friends.

Dunstan saw his chance. He jerked away from Vora and clung to Ven's arm. "Ven, what's happening? Why are you doing this? Is it something I did? *Please!* I know I'm not really a hero, and I just wanted to perform, but how I feel about you is real, and we can—"

"We can *what*, Dunstan?" Ven loomed over him, sending him backing up across the stage. "Did you think we were going to be together, at the end of this? That it was all going to work out, happily ever after, like on your silver screen?" Dunstan tripped onto a set piece, but stayed upright as Ven towered over him, tail whipping. "How can you be surprised? Ever since we met, I told you the truth! The minute I knew you had the Meteorlight, I fully intended to use it to get what I wanted — to save Jet, save our people. I never lied. Only *you* did that!" Tail whirling, with a sick smile, Ven turned to the crowd. "Presenting your Higher-up Hero! Only striving to help Jet because it fulfilled *his* dreams, not mine."

"That's not *true!*" Dunstan said, but his face had changed, a glowering sneer, tight at every corner. Ven caught himself in those black eyes and faltered. He looked to Vora, looked out at the Jettites and Knockumites, and felt himself wavering.

Then Vora grabbed hold of Dunstan in her tail and held him up. "The Light has the right! And we have it back now, taken by tooth and claw! And if none of you like the new home we've secured for you, you're welcome to go back down to whatever is left of Jet!"

Vora let Dunstan down, but didn't let him go, gesturing towards the Stackers in the audience. "Escort the Knockumites back to their homes. We agreed this would be a peaceful transition." Then, to the crowd: "All lightkeeper stations are under our control, and you'll find that Tantalon Depot, as well as all roads out of Knockum, are blocked. You're welcome to come forward with any concerns as we—"

"But you did lie."

Ven, frozen and allowing this all to happen, flicked his opalescent eyes down to Dunstan, hunched forward with his face flat to the stage. The space beneath him was wet. "You told me you loved me. But you *lied*, didn't you?"

Ven closed his eyes like he'd been struck in the face, and not his heart. "I didn't lie about that," he replied quietly. Then he jerked when Dunstan started laughing.

"It's always the same story," Dunstan choked, getting to his feet. Vora went for him again, but Ven held up a hand, stopping her, as Dunstan turned to the crowd, his black, glowing eyes shimmering in the stage lights, the green bouncing off his white teeth. "If it's not Moss Richler breaking my heart on purpose, it's Knockum's new lizard king!" Then he turned his sights on Ven, smile ever wider. "*And we love a broken heart, don't we?*"

In one smooth motion, Dunstan snapped his bonds like they were made of paper. The green Light streamed not just from his eyes this time but his fingertips, too. His body seemed to change, inhabited, as the mushrooms bloomed beneath Dunstan's hair and through his coat.

Ven faltered. *No. It was happening again.*

Then one by one, the stage lights burst, and the crowd shrieked anew. In the sky above, thunder rumbled, the clouds gathering above Lake Mallion becoming a purple, swirling knot.

"The Light has the right," Dunstan repeated gaily. "It told me you'd do this. I didn't want to believe it. But in the end, the Light was also *right*. And the Light gets to choose where, and for whom it shines. We're going to shine for everyone. Even you, sweet prince."

Dunstan removed his gloves, a part of the costume, certainly, but Ven realized he hadn't seen Dunstan's hands for some weeks now. He backed up a step when he saw them now. They were covered in fungi, too, a type not seen for cycles. Dunstan reached out and grabbed Ven's tail. He didn't hear Coral's warning in time.

Ven, at first, imagined the gesture was out of some flagging affection — every time they'd shared their Light connection it had brought them closer, but not this time. A corona flashed across Ven's vision until he fell to the stage, screaming, as his connection with Dunstan painfully coursed through him.

Coral rushed the stage, and no one tried to stop her. But without even looking, Dunstan sent a tongue of green Light, struck her, and the commander, to the wings like they were pesky vermin and not twice Dunstan's size.

When the Light cleared, Ven was still alive, shaking and curled into a ball but breathing.

"See? That wasn't so bad," Dunstan admonished. Now all of him steamed green, Light coming off him in a mesmerizing fog as he looked down at Coral, her kerchief and glasses knocked off in her attempt to save Ven.

"You really outdid yourself when you sent me up here." The Meteorlight grinned with Dunstan's mouth at Coral. "You helped me then, and I'm sure you'll help me now. And if not you, then them."

It was only the merest flick towards the audience, and the Jettites cried out as all their Knockumite neighbours fell to the ground, suddenly, and inextricably, asleep.

In response, Dunstan merely shrugged. "Need a captive audience, you see. They'll dream, and their spores will spread, and I'll keep shining. Everybody wins."

"Dunstan Cord, you stop this right now!"

It was Ada, flanked by Luisa and Moss, and Dunstan seemed to hesitate. Then his dark eyes narrowed. "Waiting for an encore? Here's one last set—"

Dunstan raised his hand towards them. But this time, Vora leapt onto Dunstan, and in the panic, Decca undid Luisa's, Ada's, and Moss's bonds, all of them diving forward to help the fallen Knockum citizens to safety, with the assistance of the aggrieved Jettites and Stackers. Claw and scale worked together as Dunstan and Vora grappled. Luisa caught a flash of green and the commander sailed into the now-empty benches, her Stackers scattering, but Ven still stood, hands and tail at the ready.

Beside him stood Coral, holding the Filamenta in front of her.

"You're making a mistake," the former king said, the device clasped tight in her unsure grip. "Let the boy free. He's not a part of this."

"Not a part of this?" It was Dunstan's voice, but it was the Meteorlight's words, and maybe it was both of them sneering. "Dunstan is the reason I'm here at all. You think he doesn't want this? To get back at everyone who ever believed he couldn't *shine*?" Ven found his voice, but the wind was whipping up now, and he had to shout. "Dun, I know you don't believe destroying our two towns is worth it! The Meteorlight is out of hand. Please, just . . . help us send it back down to Jet, and we can —"

Dunstan clapped. "That's right. Another few fragments are down there, aren't they? And we can't shine without them." The sky crackled above Dunstan's head, and as it rained, a sparkling wall of water behind him coalesced into a familiar, dark shape. "I'll go to Jet, one last time. For old times' sake. You can join me if you like. One last dance?"

Coral kept her ground, and Vora held on to Ven as Dunstan laughed lowly. "You know where I'll be waiting."

Coral cried out, rushing forward, but before she could reach Dunstan, he'd tipped backwards into the Door, closing with a thunderclap, and leaving Coral face down on the set as the rain came down and the ground heaved.

It was Vora who picked Coral up, flagging when she came face to face with the head of spikes, the eyes that looked like hers and Ven's, and when she turned to her brother, he was on his feet, but looked like he was about to be knocked off them again.

". . . Father?" he breathed.

And Coral, tightly, nodded. "We need to get these Knockumites to shelter. Can you get your Stackers back on track?"

Vora, stunned, turned to her unit tangled in the benches and started barking orders. Coral tentatively approached Ven, a hand out.

"You . . . really have changed, but" — Coral swallowed hard — "you're still the same."

"You, too," Ven said, until he missed a step and tripped into Coral's arms. They stood like that a while, neither one of them sure what to do, and Coral, realizing she was, in fact, the adult, gave Ven an experimental pat, automatically turning on a straightforwardness that made them both flinch.

"We'll gather and figure out what to do next." Then, from Coral's shoulder, she felt the unfamiliar sensation of her child, weeping, tearless, into her duster, in the same manner he had when they'd both lived fathoms below, in the Tallest Tor, and that was it for the stalwart guardian, too.

"I broke his heart," Ven said, so quietly that the howling wind nearly stole the words, but Coral's ears had always been sharp. "I just— I had to—"

Coral had never imagined she'd have this chance again, so she relished bringing Ven closer, holding him tight, before they inevitably had to come apart again. "We often hurt the people we care about when we don't mean to. Love is like that."

Ven searched the former king's face, then cast his own at the ground, rain coming senselessly off them both in thick rivulets. Before long, the bandstand was deserted, the sky flashed with an off-putting green, and Knockum reeled as the curtain on the final act drew away.

Every time Dunstan had passed through the Door, it had become more and more like any other passageway in his life: doors in school hallways, his front door, his bedroom door, all of them blending and complicit in whatever mischief he was getting up to at the time, and whenever they shut, he forgot them entirely.

But this time, when he went through the Door in Lake Mallion, that impossible entryway that separated his world from his dreams, he stopped. Because it had said something to him.

"What?" Dunstan said, turning, but when he did, he realized he wasn't anywhere; he was floating in darkness, and far away there was a green Light, which seemed to be shrinking the longer he squinted after it.

Are you sure? the voice repeated, and Dunstan turned the other way, and there was the slab of black stone, its facets cracked and chipped. Had they always been? Dunstan realized he'd never looked closely at the Door before, even though it had changed his entire life, let him into the possibility he'd begged for.

He'd never even thanked it.

"Sure about what?" he asked, and he could have sworn the Door sagged a little as it floated in the abyss, as if sighing. As if exhausted.

Doors like to be opened, it said. *I'm grateful I got to open each time I did. For Reeve. Then for you. You both really seemed like you needed me. But I needed you, too.* A pause. *Broken hearts need each other, I've learned.*

With nowhere else to go, but with the curious feeling he was late for something, Dunstan wrung his hands nervously. "I'm glad you opened for me. Even though things seem to be . . . not right, just now. So thank you."

The Door straightened. *It was time for me to be open. And after this, I'll be open forever. And so will this entire lakebed. Some doors don't last. And all legends need to end eventually and give way to new ones.*

Dunstan frowned. "New ones?"

You're welcome, the Door said belatedly. *I don't regret landing on this place, or bringing the Meteorlight here, or letting it free. Even if it broke my heart to do so, I don't regret any of it. But I'd rather see the ending be right. Or else, what was the show for at all?*

Dunstan felt himself nodding then, and as if someone was watching him, he turned. The green Light was much brighter, closer, and he shrank.

"I'd better go," he said, and the Door began to slide farther and farther into the darkness. But before it was totally out of sight, Dunstan called after it: "Your legend . . . your story — it really was the best! I'm glad I got to meet you."

Dunstan could barely make out the words, but he felt them, across the void: *Your story will be better than mine. Try to make the ending the one you really want.*

Then Dunstan went back to dreaming his dreams, hand in hand with the Meteorlight.

SCENE 18

THE SHOW MUST GO ON

The coup was forsaken, although now, with all the Knockumites down for the count, would've been the best time for one. The Jettites weren't interested in taking over Knockum; not only because it might not exist by morning, but they had more scales in the game now. They were all escaping the loss of their homes; they weren't going to put their neighbours through the same thing. It was all claws on deck — even if that was just putting on the kettle and keeping vigil over their sleeping, mushroom-blooming hosts, and sharing the truth of their lives with them at last — even though they all dreamed through it.

The ground continued to shake, and even the Stackers at Batterborne Powerhouse weren't immune to Lorelei's good sense; they were already attempting to reach out to the Brindlewatch Guard, though the quakes had disrupted the entire system, and no messages were as of yet making it out. And, as the storm grew worse, those at Batterborne on land and those in the lightkeeper stations on the water realized they were mostly stuck, keeping watch as things either improved or they were blinked out of existence at the whims of a million-year-old meteor, the Meteorlight it had brought here so very long ago, and the dizzy daydreamer at the helm.

Rain battered the windows at the Alvarez residence, the little house fit to bursting with company Luisa hadn't prepared for. It was decided they should go there, to check on Hector, to regroup. Moss had stayed behind doing the work of the Council of Mothers in their absence, guiding the terrified and checking in on all the afflicted townsfolk. It was a role Luisa would never have guessed for the thick-headed quarterback — a role of care — but he fell easily into it, and they parted ways to wait the storm out in their own corners.

Ven, Vora, Decca, and Luisa had opted for the living room floor, all gathered around the spitting firebox and deeply invested in their own tumultuous thoughts as Ada sifted through Hector's cupboards and the freezer stuffed with pre-made dinners.

"Well, Lorraine didn't call me the reheating queen of south Smithereen for nothing," she muttered, imagining her wife's face every time Ada had attempted to cook in the past. But when she turned to investigate the state of the Alvarezes' sitting room, she doubted anyone was even hungry.

Which meant there was nothing to do but talk. "Who wants to go first?" Ada said, trying to put on the cheer as she clapped her hands, sending the Jettites flinching guiltily as if they were all expecting a stern talking to about their various seedy behaviours.

Coral had been standing at the far window, staring out into the untimely dark, when Ven said, "Why didn't you tell us?"

Vora lifted her head; she'd been leaning against a bookcase, cleaving close to Hector's radio, a familiar stanchion in the chaos. "Ven—"

"Tell you who I was when I first saw you two in Knockum, you mean?" Coral interjected. She hadn't turned around yet. "Why do you think?"

Though their reunion had begun tearful, it was anything but now. Ven got to his feet angrily. "I think you're as much a coward now as you were back then! When you stole the Meteorlight and started this whole mess in the first place!"

"Ven, that's enough," Vora tried, laying her hands gently on her brother's arm, but he jerked away. Ada knew a teenage outburst when she saw one.

"No!" Ven railed on, grabbing Coral and forcefully turning her to look her directly in the face; the length of their horns may not have matched, but their glittering eyes shone with the same feeling. "This all started because of you! Jet is *doomed* because of *you*! And now Dunstan is—" But then Ven choked, his hackles clicking, not wanting to put words to his thoughts and make them real.

Coral's face changed. "You think I moved the Meteorlight on purpose?" Her mouth twisted, and she held tight to Ven. "I didn't want to leave you *or* Jet! I didn't want to do any of it! I spent the last fifteen years waiting to find it again so I could get back to you and your sister!"

The little sitting room buzzed with the echo of Coral's words, fodder in the firebox breaking the silence with a thin crackle.

Ven's hands went slack. "Really?"

"And what about you two, if we're all so set on finding someone to blame?" Coral looked from Ven to Vora. "You *both* have been running quite the scam, haven't you? You, the prince's protector, and you, the tragic hero! But you were intending all along to either use Dunstan for his powers or plug him into the network down below. Then abandon Jet, and build — no, *steal* — a new kingdom for yourselves!"

Ven backed up, but he held his ground. "This wasn't supposed to happen! Dunstan was . . ." Ven stopped himself, the words failing, the frustration building. "He was the answer. He was going to fix everything! He was stronger than Reeve and Darla and Lenny and Emmerich. He was going to withstand the Meteorlight, and save Jet, and after we'd . . ." Ven sat down heavily on the settee, face blank. "This wasn't the ending I wanted, either."

Vora shuffled uncomfortably. "We were going to take over Knockum . . . nicely. Then we were going to give it back once you all accepted the idea of us. Find our own place. It couldn't be Jet anymore. It wasn't safe there."

"You should have just told everyone the truth," Ada said from the kitchen, and Vora, ashamed, shook her head.

"We were afraid," Ven said for her. "Staying in Jet was a risk. Coming here was a risk. We never felt like we had control of our own lives. It was all governed by the Meteorlight. We wanted to make a decision for ourselves. We didn't want anyone to get hurt."

"But they have been," Coral said, not unkindly. "The Meteorlight is out of its box. It has this town. It has Dunstan. And once it takes the rest of the Light from Reeve and the others, Jet and Knockum will both be gone."

Ven winced. Then, surprisingly, it was Luisa who sighed.

"Dunstan had his part in this, too. He has a way of talking people into things." She leaned her face on her fist. "Every time he daydreamed, you just wanted to join in. But . . . do you think that's because of the Meteorlight? Its hold on him?"

"No," Coral said at once. "The Meteorlight doesn't create anything. It inspires. It needs others to make it shine. Places for its spores to take root. Make no mistake — the Meteorlight needs *Dunstan* to shine, not the other way around." Coral pressed her hand to her chest, remembering. "It took a hold of me to get what it wanted, and for years I blamed myself. That I wasn't strong enough to hold on to it. And maybe I wasn't, by rook and rock. But Dunstan is, somehow. He's held on to it all his life. He's stayed alive and aware, even though the Meteorlight has its own plan. To shine brighter elsewhere. And it got its wish. However fragmented its journey has been."

Ada grimaced. "But we can't let it! It's changed Dunstan. If it shines out in Brindlewatch, outside this town, there's no telling what it could do. Someone has to go down there and bring him back, no matter what this *thing* has planned."

Luisa sucked in a breath, running her hand along the back of her neck and plucking a mushroom free. "Or just take the Meteorlight out of him and trap it at the bottom of the lake."

In the pause that followed, Ada exhaled, nodding.

But the Filamenta was snatched away in Ven's tail before she, or anyone else, could grab it where it had been left on the firebox mantle.

"It has to be me," Ven said, clutching the device close.

Vora balked. "Not alone! You need reinforcements—"

"I don't need you looking after me. Not this time. You've done that enough." A wry, grateful smile. Then Ven looked to Coral, his hard gaze softening. "I know I've made a mess of everything. I should have just . . . told Dunstan and everyone the *real* truth from the start. I should have trusted. But I didn't imagine he would . . ."

"Feel just as lonely as you did?"

Ven turned to Ada, then nodded, slowly. Though Jettites couldn't cry, Ven's face scrunched as if he dearly wanted to. "I can't let the Meteorlight take everything that's good about Dunstan. To swallow him up. Even if he pretended to be the hero, he really did want to save us." A hard swallow. "He doesn't deserve to be alone anymore."

Ada wanted to protest — after all, it was her son, and she wanted to be the one to rescue him, too — but Luisa stood and grasped her fingertips, the two of them glowing a subdued, effervescent green. "Dunstan will be okay," Luisa urged. "He's still in there. That's why we're still standing, I think. We have our part to play."

"She's right," Coral agreed. "We'll need to get a message to the lightkeeper stations if Morag hasn't already. We need to activate the fungi in the light stations, to snare the Meteorlight and push it under the water once the Door opens for the last time."

"But the Door is the only thing keeping the basin from shattering!" Vora barked, unable to see through the screen of her helplessness. "Even if it opens, and we capture the Meteorlight, won't everything come apart anyway?"

The room darkened with this prospect. "You have to ask the Door for help," Coral finally said to Ven, looking only at her son, who all at once seemed too young despite his height, despite his former wilted brashness. "The Door wants to see this put to rest, too. We have to put our trust in it."

"I'll do what I can." Ven squared his shoulders, stood up straighter, and faced his parent. He worked hard not to crack his determined expression. "Do you think I can save him?"

Instead of answering, Coral merely pressed her forehead into Ven's.

"We all have our parts to play," she muttered.

INTERLUDE:
A MÉLANGE OF MEANING

A dark stage comes to light, as the tension of the orchestra ratchets up.

A spotlight on Ada Cord's study; Luisa, Decca, Ada, and Coral lean over the map she's presented of Lake Mallion and its lightkeeper stations. Luisa pores over the calculations to mobilize the fungi within at the exact angle to capture the Meteorlight, which will make a break for it when Ven opens the Door — with or without Dunstan.

The spot cuts and reappears on the other side of the stage, where Morag Gunn at the Knockum Lightkeeper Station barks orders to the scurrying Jettites, standing in for the keepers, boats in the marina sloshing and sliding on their mooring lines, the abandoned boats of Jet's maligned coup anchored but being pulled slowly towards the centre of Lake Mallion. Above, the sky turns to a cauldron of uneasy stew. Below, the lake is a maelstrom, a storm that shouldn't exist anywhere inland gaining ground as time runs out for everyone.

And when this spot goes out, the dark, thundering stage only has room left for the prince, walking alone, towards the Door that started everything.

The stage glows green, and the audience can swear it hears music above the din of the storm, of the great calamity.

A waltz.

When Ven was young, he'd been certain of one thing only: he was going to rule this geodom *his* way.

He was raised in a rookery like all the rest of the hatchlings. Folk came to claim an egg pop after a hatching occurred, as was the cultural custom. In this way, everyone was related, and it kept the bonds of community strong. Being chosen as the prince was a fluke, by all accounts. And as Ven grew up, he felt it was more like a mistake than one of the luckiest things to happen to him. What hatchling didn't want to be the new ruler of an entire geodom?

Ven didn't. He had different dreams.

"Put those away," Vert had told him, regal in his bright, shimmering coat of gold, his red sash. "Your dreams should only be Jet's dreams! Don't worry. You'll soon realize that your dream has already been realized — you'll get the chance to serve."

Ven tried to smile. Tried to be obedient. But he couldn't. He watched the Truffledours in their grand spectacles, making the Light, and the city, shine brighter than ever before. Ven wanted to capture that feeling, but he didn't want to share it. Why did he have to share *everything*? Why couldn't he have something that was just his own?

But soon, he allowed Vert's dream to become his. What better calling was there than making your people happy, safe, and secure? And just as he'd accepted it, Vert had done a complete about-face, had stolen the Meteorlight, and changed everything.

And a great part of Ven was grateful for this. Because maybe he would have a chance to shine on his own.

As Ven made his way through Jet now, searching for Dunstan, it was only habit that kept him to the roads of his egghood, because nothing at all looked as it had. Tors and spires destroyed. Hovels decimated. Fungi shrivelled and bent, some of their caps flickering as they tried to hold on to the Meteorlight. And the water, so much of it streaming down the cavern walls, up to his shins and climbing, the detritus of the geodom floating away. Hadn't he wished for this? That it would all go away, and he could make his own way in whatever world there was above?

He had been small when it had all happened, barely old enough to remember the flash of green and the loss of his parent as a fuzzy stolen moment, but it had made a lasting imprint on every scale as he grew up. And as he did, he understood he'd been chosen out of all those eggs for a reason — he and Vora both. For as much as it was her destiny to become the leader of the Stackers, he had taken on the burden of keeping the kingdom together. She had always supported him, given him the space to try to be his own kind of prince. She'd helped him conceal the fate of the Higher-ups, had kept the peace. Had managed the Jettites so that Dunstan would be convinced Ven really needed him and would offer himself up willingly.

But in the end Ven really *did* need Dunstan, just not in the way he'd originally planned.

There was only one place Ven was headed, and that was for the radiantly glowing centre of Jet, the city suspended around the hope, and the boy carrying it.

The farther he walked, the louder the music became.

Ada, in her mind, was penning a frantic letter to Lorraine as she paced through town towards the lightkeeper station:

Do you remember our home, our little town, when we were younger? It wasn't much. It was all fishing boats and ferries, lights twinkling on the water. Simple. So were our dreams. I hope there's a Knockum for you to come back to, my love. I hope I can save it, and the little dream boy between us.

But it all hinges on a few mushrooms, and as many prayers as we can muster.

Ada stumbled, a hand to her forehead. "What is it?" Decca asked, but Ada waved her off.

"I'm fine. Just . . . just had a little tired spell there." The truth was that for a moment, Ada felt she was going to fall asleep on her feet, something she'd never done in all her night shifts.

The spores inside her. She'd fought off their tug, and on the back of her wrist, the bulbous head of a mushroom bloomed. She hastily covered it with her sleeve. She couldn't succumb. Not yet. Dunstan hadn't. And they were made of the same stuff. Ada trudged ahead.

Luisa, meanwhile, was running the calculations through her head as the rain pounded down, the group of them rushing to the lightkeeper station. They'd bid Ven goodbye, all putting on their own act, pretending as if he'd come back shortly, acting as if it were only a matter of talking Dunstan down — or up, in this case — and everything would be right again. Vora, Ven, and Coral had held on to each other quite a while before the prince had parted and, silently, gone through the Door, the action of it sending a concussive blast through Knockum so loud that Ada worried the lightkeeper station had come down.

Vora had gone to get a status report at Batterborne, to make sure the message could be received by all the other lightkeeper stations for the proper calculations to put everything back to rights.

"And you, Stackling." Vora had grimaced, her usual stony countenance breaking with feeling. "You will be commander in my stead. Do you understand?"

Decca, full of the purpose she hadn't yet come to terms with, let the brightness of her face outshine the meaning of the moment, and grasped Vora in a hug even the stern leader might not recover from.

"Luisa?" Ada called, as they'd reached the western road, confirming, thankfully, that the lightkeeper station was still there. Luisa had stopped short of following, unsure what her role was. She had let Ven remove the last spores of Meteorlight from her before he took the Filamenta down under the lake with him. He *needed* to return, because how else would the rest of Knockum be freed? All she could do was wait, reassure, hope. Here was Luisa in the wings as usual, waiting for the next cue — never on the stage. Always behind it. Isn't that what she preferred?

"I don't know what to do," Luisa blurted as Ada came back to her on the path. "I don't have powers. Or scales. Or grit. I just . . . is there a place for me in this at all?"

Ada opened her mouth, then barked a laugh that was loud enough to hear above the rain. "Luisa Alvarez! If it wasn't for you, we'd have been finished in the first act!" Then Ada grasped the girl tightly at the shoulders. "We're all in this production now. We have to make it through the finale. That's our job. And I'm not letting you out of my sight until the curtain call."

Luisa couldn't help but laugh, or maybe sob. "Now I know where Dunstan gets it from."

Ada grinned, glad to have her mettle confirmed as they rushed down the path and into the lightkeeper station to find Morag Gunn and meet the moments before the ending with aplomb.

The centre of Jet was different. Yet, somehow, it was exactly the same.

And that was the Meteorlight's doing.

Ven moved out of the way of Jettites coming and going about their business, sitting at patios, dipping into cafés, talking and laughing amongst themselves as if they didn't have a care in the world — which was, currently, coming down on their heads.

But when Ven threw himself backwards, out of harm's way from a huge plinth of rock slicing directly into the café he'd just stood in front of, the illusion was interrupted, though not shattered. The Jettites still chatted and enjoyed their leisure. Because all of them were cast out of glowing green Light, a perfectly running memory of the first time Ven brought Dunstan Cord through the city of scales and spectacles.

Pulling himself from the water sloshing the cobbled road, Ven shouted, "Dunstan?"

His voice ricocheted back to him, mocking. None of the light-shadows of the Jettites turned, and he pushed his way through them. The huge mushrooms Ven had grown up climbing all held on, hunkering shells of their former selves. Still glowing, but barely. All the effort of the Meteorlight now was in making the crumbling ruin look like it had all those weeks ago; Dunstan and Ven hand-in-tail as they lied blithely to each other.

The music reached a daring crescendo as Ven finally reached the base of the Tallest Tor, knowing he'd have to climb to the top, where the Light shone its brightest. Despite all the stories he and Dunstan had told each other, he still wasn't certain how this one was going to end.

"Yes! Mushrooms! Don't you dare cut them off! Follow the protocols!" Morag shouted over her radio, throwing the headphones away as she pointed to three Jettites, one of them holding a watering can.

"You better be giving that thing the biggest bloody drink of its life! It needs to be the size of a satellite if this is going to work! And you two, make sure it's done *properly*." Everyone nodded, frantic to help, which left Ada, Luisa, and Decca looking for something to do.

Until Ada staggered, and it didn't have anything to do with the shivering ground. Luisa cried out, but it was Coral who dove forward, swept Ada off her feet and into her arms, just as her eyes closed and she succumbed to the spores still inside her.

"Well, don't just stand there," Coral yelled, coat sweeping, horns glinting, looking every bit the monarch she was meant to be. "Hold on to something!"

Decca grabbed hold of Luisa, and vice versa. Luisa could feel the Meteorlight's spores inside her flexing, trying to grab hold of her, too, as if it was also struggling. She wanted desperately to sleep, and the Meteorlight wanted her to dream, to catch her in its net.

But instead Luisa gripped tighter to Decca. All they could do was hold on to each other.

Ven hadn't been to the upper sanctuary of the Tallest Tor in cycles. He preferred his little loft in the city, where he went to get away from royal duties. Where he would add to his lichen mural and dream his impossible dreams of the stage. And not be faced with the reality of the four Higher-ups, dreaming *their* dreams and convincing the Jettites that everything was all right.

As Ven slid into the unguarded antechamber at the base of the tower and began his long climb, he tried to tell the story as it was, truly. Coral — Vert — hadn't wanted any of this to happen, to see her geodom brought so low, on the brink of collapse, dragging more innocent people along with it. She wanted what Ven wanted. She wanted to grow old with her children, and count her legacy as assured. Even the Door wanted that, it seemed.

But the Meteorlight hadn't wanted it. How different things would have been, if the Meteorlight hadn't spoiled them. What kind of dreams would Ven have dreamed, as the true prince? Would he have looked up at the Door and wished so hard for a different life when the one he had here was pristine and glowing, radiant and real?

Would he have ever met Dunstan?

The ground shuddered as Ven reached the next level. He stopped, tail up in front of him, defensive; looking up, he threw himself aside as a slab of rock came crashing down, punching through the grand staircase that would lead him all the way to the top of the tor. Ven covered his head as sparkling black dust speckled his scales, and when he peered out from under his arm, his stomach sank. Above, there was a clear hole between where he stood and the grand chamber above, where the Higher-ups had slept these many cycles, dreaming beneath the glowing mushrooms that held all of Jet's memory.

But with the staircase removed, there was no way for Ven to get to the top. Yet now that there was a clear view, he shied away from a strobing brightness that cast itself onto him, cold and remote and, somehow, shivering in time with its laughter.

"You didn't think I'd leave you out in the cold, did you?" a mocking voice asked, and through the opening, by the magic that the Meteorlight was capable of, tendril roots thick as Ven's arms crawled down the expanse of the tor until they reached the very place where Ven was standing. From the knot of the roots bloomed the cap of an enormous mushroom, rising slightly and throbbing with power.

The music wasn't just louder now, but present in every corner. "Step right up!" the voice cried. "The Truffledour prince of the great Geodom of Jet gets to ride in style after his weary journey."

Ven swallowed. It was Dunstan's voice, but was it, truly? He'd hoped for an element of surprise, but he knew deep down that Dunstan, the Meteorlight, and his destiny, were waiting for him at the top of the tower he'd avoided most of his life.

Ven stepped up to the empty platform, staggered as it juttered to life, and let it raise him high.

"I always keep my promises," Dunstan's voice went on. "My mothers taught me that! I promised to be good. I promised to do well in school. I promised to dream of anything and everything I could be. I promised to save Jet. And look around — haven't I kept my word, everywhere I've been?"

The platform soared higher and higher, and Ven, knees bent to keep from tumbling over the edge, looked out through the broken windows of the tower, flickering by like frames in the Odeon. Through the destruction, the Meteorlight was attempting to mend the cracks, the fallen structures, filling them in with sickly green simulacrums, silky bright illusions, as if it could repair what it had done to the precious place that it owed its protection to.

"Jet is destroyed!" Ven barked back. "Your illusions are not going to cover that up! If you'd only stayed where you were supposed to—"

The ceiling and the brightness rushed so hard that Ven had barely time to gasp before the platform slammed home in the chamber, throwing him to the ground and stunning the air from his chest.

"You never had as much Meteorlight on board as me, but you were pretty good at illusions, weren't you?"

Ven lifted his ringing head. Above the glowing Meteorlight mushroom in the centre of the room, sitting atop the geodom throne, was a mushroom-covered Dunstan — eased back, legs crossed, and flanked on all sides by the sleeping Higher-ups in their blissful cocoons. A silent, slumbering audience, unaware of the show unfolding around them.

A slow clap, a grin. Dunstan's eyes didn't stream now, but they were changed. So was his skin, wherever visible; he was covered in glowing fungi that rippled with each gesture, word, or movement. Velvety caps and ridged ears of fungi. Where his freckles used to be, tiny glowing enoki.

Ven stood up stiffly. "It's not you, Dunstan."

"It's not?" he said, blinking, looking all around him. "Who is it, then? This is the me I've always wanted to be. The one that shines. And I've rebuilt Jet for you — for *us*. So you can see it one last time. Your perfect, blightless stage, where you stage managed me good."

Ven didn't have a response to that. Nervously, he glanced at the other Higher-ups: Reeve Gris, his broken-hearted compatriots. The Meteorlight had taken root in them, just as it had in Dunstan. The mushrooms around them still glowed. He hadn't taken it out, yet. He'd been waiting for Ven, for his one last monologue.

"I own that this is partly my fault." Ven folded his arms, affecting a casual air, though his bluff sent his blood racing. "I wasn't completely honest with you—"

Dunstan laughed so loud that its edge blasted around the throne room, explosive and sharp all at once like a perfectly aimed dart. "You were, though, weren't you? You were right. You told me exactly what you wanted with me, the day we met. I just didn't know the lengths you'd gone to to make sure I believed you were the good guy."

A green spark snaked beneath Dunstan's feet, shocking Light into the enormous mushroom he'd used to bring Ven here. Its surface rippled, showing *The Darling Mermaid*, just as Dunstan had disappeared back to Knockum through the Door after the daring chase. The Stackers who had been coming after Ven stopped their pursuit, as Ven gingerly climbed back down to meet them.

Ven grimaced. All the mushrooms had memory, and here they were, showing the truth of their first meeting.

A kiss. Simple, really. The flash of it bringing Ven back into the moment; not just the blinding ray of Light that their collision created, but the feelings intermingling.

Pain, the Light radiated. *Alone.* More than a broken heart, but a spirit cleaved by years of Dunstan's rejections. And seated neatly inside it all sat the Meteorlight, winding itself around this freckled boy full of his own grandeur. Ven saw his own reflection, saw himself in that loneliness — it was why he had sat under the Door so many years, making his little prayers. And here they were, come true.

He'd had to be a Truffledour to make it work. And he'd had to be patient; when the Stackers arrived to give Ven backup, and he instead gave them the signal to play along, many were confused when Ven sent Dunstan back to his world.

"We had him! Why send him away?" one of the Stackers asked in the image playing out, all of them gathering on the deck of the boat. One of the taller guards removed their goggles, revealing Vora beneath.

Another Stacker knelt beside Ven as he applied the woodear mushroom to his wound, wincing that he'd injured his Prince. "I still don't understand the point of all this showmanship. If we'd just captured him—"

Ven batted him away, pushing the mushroom in deeper. "We're playing the long game." Ven shook his head, eyes flicking to Vora. "We can't just *plug him in* like the others. It's not working anymore. We need to shore Jet up, keep it stable for a short while . . . then build our new kingdom elsewhere." Ven stared at the closed Door, still feeling the pulse of Dunstan's heart behind his eyes. "I saw it. A world beyond anything we can imagine. And all of Jet could be safe there. We just have to do things a bit differently. The *Truffledour Way.*"

Ven leapt to his feet, the plan spooling out as he paced and barked orders to the others. "Make sure the market square is set. I want that warmy to fall in love with Jet. Every detail has to be perfect — if he doesn't want to leave, then the work will be done for us, once he's let us into the High-up. And once his heart is well and truly broken . . . the Meteorlight will have done the rest by then. He'll slumber, and he'll be ours for the using."

The image fell away like rippling water, Dunstan leaning over it, mouth mocking. "What *else* was I supposed to fall in love with?"

Ven scowled. "It wasn't like that! It was just — I didn't know you! I was trying to save my people! What would you have done if you had thousands relying on you to solve an impossible problem, and the person with the answer just walked through the door?"

Dunstan threw his head back, rolling his eyes. "I would've rewritten the script! I would've thought about who would be getting hurt! I would've written everyone the happy ending they deserved!"

"Like Luisa?" Ven volleyed back. "Your closest friend? You betrayed her once to get what you wanted. How did *that* make you feel? How did you resolve *that*?"

The room crackled with a thunderclap of green, and Ven started backwards as a staircase of shivering bolts guided Dunstan down to Ven's level. Ven tensed for a blow, but Dunstan held up his hands, in dramatic lament.

"Never been much for fighting. So don't worry your pretty spiked head." He leaned in, his black eyes glittering. Even though he was a head shorter, he was intimidating; there was a terrible menace coming off him. "I didn't handle Luisa well. And you're right. All great plans come with sacrifices. Take the people back home. They're all asleep, but they can't stop me now. Like they tried to, in their own way, all the years I tried to shine. Even before the Meteorlight." Dunstan's mouth twisted. Ven was having a hard time finding the line where the Dunstan he knew ended and the Meteorlight began. Dunstan wasn't just its puppet; he really did believe what was happening, what he was *doing*, was for the best.

He raised his head and shook it, smiling. "But don't worry about them. The Meteorlight will keep them safe and dreaming while we go out and shine together. You can dream along with them, too, if you want. The Meteorlight gives and gives. It gave me back my sight, after all. It lets me see how well we'll shine. And you'll see too. You deserve to. After all, if I hadn't met you, none of this would be mine." Dunstan flicked his wrist, the Light dancing across the mushrooms nestled at his fingertips, firing outwards just past Ven's cheek as the room lit bright. It became like one of Dunstan's dreamy movie sets: columns, drapery, a checkered ballroom floor, the ceiling hung with chandeliers.

It truly was beautiful. The Meteorlight wasn't the one creating these images — it was using Dunstan's vivid imagination to do so. "You really are a wonderful dreamer, Bright Eyes," Ven said.

Then, a hand held out. Ven glanced down at it, at Dunstan's disarming, alarming smile. So much him and so much not him. "One last dance?" he asked, and unable to do much else, Ven took his Higher-up hero's hand, the waltz rising all around them, and took the first steps.

"You've come to try to convince me. To take it all away." As they spun, Ven's tattered coat revealed the Filamenta, strapped to his tunic. Ven didn't try to hide it. "If you take the Meteorlight out of me now, there's no telling what would happen to me. We're too entangled. It's waited my entire life to shine. We have so much in common. It's a part of me, and I won't part from it."

Ven searched Dunstan's much-transformed face. "Is that just another line?" he asked. "Or is it the truth?"

"Would you risk finding out? For what? Trapping the Meteorlight down here, struggling to rebuild a crumbling kingdom, when you know now the wide world waiting for you above? It could all be yours." Dunstan was in the lead, and Ven allowed himself to fly across the rubble of their shimmering fantasy. "All I want to do is shine."

"But your shining is hurting people! You've done enough! Can't you be satisfied?"

"Can you?"

Just as they spun, the argument was utterly circular. Ven wasn't going to win. He sighed. "Then I'll stay down here with you. You won't be alone." He extended his arm, and Dunstan leaned down, arcing on his own, before Ven pulled him close again. "Just spare Jet, and spare Knockum, and I'll stay with you here in Jet. You can shine for *me*. Forever."

Dunstan stared deep into Ven. Ven lifted his tail and wrapped it around Dunstan's hand, the one he'd been holding to lead him through the dance.

Across the connection, closer than they were standing, Ven felt the story he'd never considered before.

The Meteorlight's.

Loneliness is an uncomplicated feeling. It's heavy. One-dimensional. It can override every good reason you have because it's all-consuming.

A spore wishes only to spread. This spore was a Light. It wanted to share itself. It wanted desperately to shine, but it was locked in the heart of the rock that carried it across galaxies. They passed glorious sights, stirring up stardust, but the Light wished it could be free.

It was a presence and a thought and a need. The meteor it travelled in too had thoughts. It never wanted to be parted from the Light. They relied on each other. They were one.

But the Light couldn't guide the rock anywhere, just go along for the ride. And as suddenly as an age, as if its wish were answered, they were caught in the snare of a blue sphere, hurtling down, down, to uncharted frontier bright with possibility. *Finally! Finally!*

Through fire and air it plunged, and plunged, full of hope and wonder, until it crashed into the face of its dream.

The meteor cracked, its heart breaking wide. The Light inside the meteor's broken heart went deep into the earth, searching, guided by longing and hope. And everywhere it went, life popped up. Only a spore, at first, then growing, until the cavern its wish created was lush with it. The Meteorlight was granting its own wish. Life, the Jettites, the great city. All of it was wonderful. It was able to share its Light far and wide for many years . . . until it realized that so much time had passed, it was entangled in this deep, dark hole, worshipped and loved, yet craving more.

It was trapped in the heart of just another rock.

The loneliness was still there. For on its descent, the Meteorlight had glimpsed the world above Jet, and the yellow dawn that cast it all in glory.

The Meteorlight inspired the Jettites. But it wanted *more*. It wasn't *enough*. Why was the loneliness still there?

Its escape plan was millennia in the making. Nothing could stop it. The cavern it had been locked in could fend for itself. The only problem was the Door.

The Door knew what the Light was capable of. After all, that's why it had carried it across the stars, away from people, away from one place in the form of a meteor. A spore spreads, no matter if its intentions are good or bad. The Door loved the Light, and never wanted to be parted from it, so it stayed closed, kept the Light prisoner, kept everything on the other side safe.

Because one half of the Door faced the world above. It watched the world Become. It knew what could happen if the Light it carried across the universe was unleashed. So it stayed closed, keeping both worlds apart. It did its level best.

But the Door itself was a broken heart. So when Reeve Gris and his friends drove their boat over it, making their own broken-hearted prayers, though the Light had taken over the king, there was little it could do but open.

The spore shattered. No longer whole and desperate, it shot into the sky above a small fishing town, and kept wishing, as it always had, for a soft place to land.

And with its flagging strength, it found Dunstan Cord. Inside his heart, it slept. And it dreamed. Until his broken heart woke it up.

Ven came to on the ground of the throne room, the tower shivering violently. The Light in the chamber was almost too much for Ven to bear, but through the sharp lines of green, through the crumbling illusions, he saw Dunstan holding the Filamenta aloft as he dragged the last shards of Meteorlight out of Reeve Gris and his friends.

"I'm tired of being scattered. I'm tired of being alone." It was Dunstan's voice. It was the Meteorlight's longing.

Ven leapt up, grabbing the shaft of the sceptre and holding on tight. He was tired. But he couldn't give in. "I was alone, too," he said, struggling. "But Dunstan saved us both. And we owe him. His dreams carried us. I won't let you snuff them out."

Dunstan's face twisted with fungi and darkness and malice. "This kingdom will fall on top of both of you! The Door is giving out, and I'll be whole! I'll be free!"

"Then let me say goodbye," Ven said through sharp, gritted teeth, still holding on for dear life. "One last time."

His tail was on Dunstan's hand, the Meteorlight meeting him with a surge. But this time, Ven knew what to do.

Dunstan was sitting alone in his treehouse when Ven found him, deep at the end of his connection. The real Dunstan, diminished. Dunstan had always been small, physically, but to Ven he was a force, with or without the Meteorlight. It was a different kind of light that drew them together. And it's what kept them in this same space now.

"You should've got out while you could." Dunstan was staring out of his treehouse window into the solid inky nothing. "I'm sorry I let this happen."

Ven grabbed hold of Dunstan's shoulders, shaking him, but Dunstan wouldn't look away from the window. "You can still stop all this! You have to let the Meteorlight go, force it out, before it drops two towns on top of you!"

Dunstan smiled. He still hadn't looked away from the window. "The Meteorlight is the only thing that makes me special. Without it, I'm—"

"You're everything!" Ven hissed, and Dunstan did look up then. "The Meteorlight doesn't create anything! It takes and takes. All you've done is give yourself to Jet, to Knockum, to anyone who would listen to the dreams you wanted to share. Those all came from you — not from a little spore that's done nothing but made you feel small!"

Dunstan's face dropped. "But it's too late. I've . . . I've let it go too far. Everyone, the town, Luisa, my mothers — it's all my *fault*."

Ven held on tightly to this last shred of Dunstan Cord. "Loneliness is powerful," he said, "but nothing can snuff out a dream." He pressed his forehead into Dunstan's. "You opened a door inside me I thought was locked forever. You did keep your promise. You did save me. Now we have to save everyone else."

Dunstan held on, fingers clenched tight into this splintered part of Ven keeping him whole in this dark place.

Outside the treehouse window, the green approached, streaking across an impossible sky as it enveloped them both in its radiance.

The Door was tired. Its hinges and its locks fell away from their ancient tumblers. And for the last time, it opened.

Dunstan and Ven fought the Meteorlight until hands and tail had turned the Filamenta towards Dunstan. They felt it fight. It was strong, after all. It had created an entire city. In its wake had grown mushrooms and structures and roots the like of which Brindlewatch hadn't yet seen.

And as the Meteorlight left Dunstan, pushed out by the sudden force and desire to dream just a little longer, it felt the Door opening. It wouldn't squander its chance again. As it streaked upwards, mushrooms bloomed enormous and vibrant in its wake, trying to catch hold of it. But not anymore! The lakebed rent apart, the water pulled back from stopping it — finally! It could see the sky! See its way through!

The Meteorlight — a comet, a spore, a mass, a moment — stopped dead and hovering above Lake Mallion, caught in the net of the mushroom tendrils growing outward in great distances from the lightkeeper stations casting them. A web and a net, a trap and a promise. The Meteorlight struggled.

Then the mushrooms pushed downwards, weaving, pulling, pushing it down, though it tried to skirt around it. No opening was left, no place it could run, and as the Light was shoved back down, the water of the lake coming in through the Door's last miraculous opening, the mushrooms kept Dunstan and Ven's promise, the two of them holding tight to one another, as the wages of their dreams crashed all around them.

🍄

The ground was still.

Coral's tail had been wrapped around Ada, holding her close. Eyes opening in the silence, she noticed, through the broken amber pane of the lightkeeper station, the sky had changed. The storm, peeling back by degrees, revealed pinks and golds. A morning. The next morning. And the ground beneath them was still there, under their own version of the Tallest Tor. And Coral — the lost king, queen, the monarch who still so dearly loved her kingdom — turned her scaled head, her jewelled eyes, unencumbered, towards the sunlight for the first time in a long time.

In her arms, Ada's eyes fluttered, and she jerked awake all at once, so hard that Coral nearly dropped her like she would a live, slippery fish.

"The Door!" Ada said, looking around blearily but not seeing; no, she was still in the shared dream the Meteorlight had strung between everyone with the sleepies — who were all, Coral surmised, just waking.

Ada seemed to finally see the room, and the new day dawning outside. She turned to Coral, sad and full of a strange understanding. "It's gone."

Luisa clambered over the shattered glass to look out, the summer wind sneaking in. In the last dark of the oncoming dawn, she stared down at the water. Decca, Ada, and Coral joined her there, awestruck.

Lake Mallion glowed green, but faintly, the Light buried deep at the bottom of the lake whose fathoms were dearly drawn now. The rock of the lakebed was gone, replaced with Light, fastened to the basin by the roots of the great ancient mushroom system that it had borne. The Door may be gone, but it had kept its promise: it had helped them. It had opened that one last time, when it couldn't hold on any longer, and had saved them all.

Then another smarting pierce to Ada's chest as she woke entirely. "Dunstan." She raced for the lightkeeper station's steps, past the bewildered faces of Morag and the Jettites who had held everything together in the night, who were so shaken they didn't realize quite yet that they were allowed to celebrate.

Knockum still stood. And so, it seemed, did Jet.

But where had her son ended up?

Lake Mallion always had a boat on its waters, but from Porticul to Ghast, no boats would be leaving port today. The new lake bottom shimmered, keeping the water from crushing Jet, and keeping the folk on the shore wary of what this meant for them. Not all lights were beacons of hope and safety, and though this one may be dormant in its net, they would need to learn about its moods from their new Jettite neighbours, who themselves were cautiously dreaming of returning to their homes beneath the lake and the Light as they stared out at it.

How they would get there, terrified of the water, was another matter. But there was one Jettite who lay in the calm shallows, wondering, as he came awake, what it was about the water his people were afraid of. It felt good to be immersed in it, floating, for once not having to act a part except as flotsam riding the swells. And beneath the oncoming dawn, feeling the warmth on his scales as it filled his eyes, his senses recalled the first time he was led into the water, hand in hand with a boy who believed too much in his dreams to ever believe Ven wanted to stay on the shore.

Ven sat up suddenly, splashing until he was able to pull himself from the water, feeling a tug to that same shore to find that boy, until Ven realized Dunstan's arms were clasped tight around his chest. His tail held on long after the storm had broken.

"Dunstan!" Ven hauled him out of the water and onto the sand, rolling him onto his side and slapping his back, trying to get him to rouse, to waken. His clothes were nearly shredded, but to Ven's relief, he could see Dunstan's freckles again on his skin. No mushrooms, no mask, and when he opened his eyes and stared into Ven's, they were the *dignified amber* he'd been heartstruck by all those weeks ago, on a lost trawler in a lost place. But they were ringed in green, like an afterimage, and likely always would be.

"Did we manage the finale all right?" Dunstan croaked, and Ven pulled him close, hugging him tight and making him splutter what water there was in his lungs.

"I think it's safe to say we did," Ven said when he finally pulled away, the two of them covered in sand and lakeweed and impossibly goofy grins. Ven tipped his face towards the sun, stretching its golden arms over the lake and the town. "Have you ever seen anything like your first tomorrow?"

The last of summer's breezes caught Dunstan's hair, as he, too, turned his face to the sun, staring directly at it, not closing his eyes. He smiled, bittersweetly, and said, "Would that I could see it."

He reached for Ven, overshooting, until Ven gently clasped his hand with his tail. "But that's all right," Dunstan continued, still grinning madly as he leaned his head on Ven's shoulder. "You always could paint a picture. I'll just show you how to do it with words. I am, after all, the greatest showman Knockum's ever known."

Ven snorted, the new day bright with possibility. "You are at that, Bright Eyes."

CODA

Quixx Quarterly

*On the Anniversary of Quixx's Meteors
and Knockum's Extraterrestrial Lakebed*

A SPECIAL COLUMN BY PROF. DERREK BEDOUIN

WHILE I WILL BE THE FIRST to admit that my travel record is woefully small, along with my partner, the inimitable Constance Ivyweather, I took a much-needed sabbatical from our efforts to rebuild Quixx to, as they say, "hit the road." Indeed, this past year has been one of revelation since the sky fell on our heads, and since Knockum was almost totally washed from the map, as it were. Is it a coincidence that historically recurring meteors struck Quixx the same summer that an ancient meteor broke apart, hiding a dangerous secret? Do the mountain and the Door have something in common we don't yet understand? More than curious that such a momentous adventure would take place in Constance's hometown. So with all these factors at play, we had to see Knockum for ourselves — especially after intriguing mushroom samples were sent to me by one Luisa Alvarez with her own questions.

Lake Mallion, one of the greatest inland seas of Brindlewatch, was formed in prehistoric times from a meteor, classed, my associate Dr. Garnet writes, in a category not yet discovered based on Ms. Alvarez's further samples. It brought with it a sort of bioluminescence, a spore at once living and shining, and originated an entire people whose history may yet shed some light on the Camillites, my own folk from Mount Quixx. Another thread: the events of the summer that led to the Jettites entering Brindlewatch coincided with the same events that brought the Camillites to Quixx. What other new, fantastic peoples are there in Brindlewatch, yet to be met?

Eager to see the site for myself, I must admit that Constance and I were more interested to meet the Jettites, many of whom now live and work within Knockum and the surrounding county as if they were always meant to. The people there have come to accept them, and Brindlewatch has had an upheaval in the knowledge that creatures like them — and myself — are as much a part of society's fabric as the Brindles. My hope is that integration can continue with the examples both Knockum and Quixx have set, and that soon we will be seeing more folk like the Jettites and Camillites in the Great Cities, pursuing their dreams, whatever they may be.

I admit that I was not prepared for the sight of Lake Mallion now — an enormous, green, glowing, watery wonderland of ships and commerce! The view from the Tantalon Depot gondolas, fully upgraded with an additional route into the water itself, was beyond breathtaking, and the photos I've submitted along with this column do not do them justice.

The extension of the route includes watertight submersibles through a tunnel that has to be seen to be believed; constructed from naturally occurring fungi, the tunnel transfers the rider in their compartment not only through the water, but safely through the shining barrier that now serves as the lakebed. The Light in question is Meteorlight, the mythical luminescence that keeps Lake Mallion from collapsing, thus taking the escarpment along with it, and submerging the glittering city below.

It's a grand place, the city of Jet, newly discovered. Constance and I spent the better part of our vacation there, in the company of Prince Ven and his Truffledour ambassador, one Dunstan Cord. Upon our arrival, we were especially happy to learn of the rehabilitation and the return of four Knockumites earlier presumed missing, from before Constance's early childhood memory . . .

Article cont'd on Q4.

"And I thought *we* were the ones suspended in time," Reeve muttered, himself and his friends taking refuge in the Beckon Bandstand after that group of Grislies — *Dinah, what a terrible name* — had cornered them in front of Better's Best.

"I told you going out was a terrible idea." Darla rolled her eyes, then added the last barb. "Pretty sure I told you that on *that night*, too."

"Can it," Lenny groaned. "We've all heard it a million times . . ."

Emmerich was peering over the edge of the bandstand when he suddenly dove back down and shushed the others. "Someone's coming!"

Reeve Gris and the Now-Not-Sunken-At-All-Three flattened to the whitewashed boards as footsteps came up the gravel path. Darla, unable to help herself, peeked out towards the audience gallery, and let out the breath she'd been holding. "It's okay. It's just Moss."

Moss Richler, awkwardly carrying two baskets, shrugged before them, tossing his hair out of his eyes. "Sorry, everyone. I've been working with them, but it's hard for them to, uh, let go."

"You're telling me." Reeve smiled, then he patted the bandstand next to him, inviting Moss over. "Have a seat, Rich."

Moss hesitated at first. He usually did. He still didn't feel much like he belonged in Reeve's circle, or really anywhere since the Meteorlight had played its little game with Knockum. He'd always been a de facto leader when it came to his friends, but he ultimately realized he didn't like where it'd taken him, so he went the opposite way — complete withdrawal . . . until Coral Frakes intervened, as she usually did.

"You need a purpose, Moss, and not one that involves you moping around this town fecklessly. There's work to do." In the aftermath of the quake, the new shining lakebed, and the wake-up call of hundreds of lizard folk ready (and willing) to make things right, Moss thought Coral would have her claws full and would hopefully go on ignoring his existence.

But Coral still noticed everything. And when Reeve Gris, Darla Denning, Emmerich Kohl, and Lenny Steez woke up, still teenagers, and surrounded by mushrooms, Coral wasn't about to handle all *that* without help.

Emmerich grabbed Moss's pantleg and jerked him to a seat next to him, grabbing one basket after another. "What'd you cook up this time, fish boy?"

Moss snorted. "Chilli. I tried something more complicated, but it looked barely edible."

"Same with this. But we'll take it." Lenny smiled as he passed out the bowls, and Moss ducked away, grinning sheepishly himself. Back in Lenny's day, he'd been the star player of the Raging Roadrunners, a position Moss once enjoyed, and meeting Lenny, Moss's hero in his own right aside from the town mythos stuff, had been a highlight.

Secretly dating him was, too, but Moss wanted to keep something to himself in a town that knew everyone's business.

"Can't go on like this, though," Darla mused around a mouthful of chilli. "My moms are ready to put someone's lights out. And not in a neighbourly way." She grimaced. "It was hard enough coming home — all our friends grown up, married, with kids. Our parents a little crustier. Just because we didn't change doesn't mean I want to be worshipped. We didn't *do* anything in Jet, either!"

Emmerich chuckled. "I did keep one of those banners, though . . . it's hanging up in our living room. My uncle insisted."

Moss didn't ask the group very many questions. And Reeve, their de facto leader, didn't like to talk about it. Moss would sometimes come upon him staring at the glowing lake, and he'd longed to ask him everything, but after a year, he'd learned enough by waiting and listening slowly.

"I didn't mind being a king," Reeve said suddenly. The others all turned to him, mouths full, eyes wide. Then he shrugged. "For all of five minutes, I mean. But yeah. If I could do it all over again . . .

I wouldn't steal a boat when I got dumped. I think I'd just come here and use my brain."

The others nodded, quiet at first, until Lenny piped up, mid-laugh, saying, "Bremner Allan! He came back during the tunnel opening ceremony! Did you see him? He looks so—"

"Don't say old," Darla groaned. "We're technically the same age as Reeve's dumb ex."

"Does that bother you?"

They swung around to Moss, who seemed to shrink under the attention. "Sorry. It's just . . ."

"Y'know, ending up in a subterranean city, becoming their rulers, then getting hooked up to a mushroom network? Sounds bad on paper, but I woke up and I still had my life ahead of me! It doesn't bother me, I tell you." Emmerich cheerily tucked into another portion. "I think a fifteen-year nap, and a chance to start over, is a gift."

"We've wanted to say thanks, Moss, for all of it," Reeve said, giving a cheers with his chilli bowl. But Moss was confused.

"For what?" he said, stirring his own bowl listlessly. "I didn't do anything. Dunstan and the prince, Luisa and the others, they're the ones that saved Knockum. *And* Jet. *And* brought you lot back up to Knockum. They're the heroes. I'm the villain. I deserve to be called that." He snorted. "Not even that. My role was so tiny as to not even be credited. I was just a thug."

They were quiet a while. Then Lenny squeezed his shoulder. "I know you feel bad about what happened. With Dunstan and all. And, none of us are saying it was right. You were as dumb as Captain Moron over there" — he jerked his head towards Reeve, who rolled his eyes — "stealing the boat to begin with. But we know you, Moss. You've worked hard to make amends. Everyone screws up. It's okay."

Moss had opened up to them as they'd all grown closer, the shame of his choices bursting out of him like it was made of its own unconcealable light. He wasn't like Dunstan, making grand speeches and gestures and performances. He couldn't own up to his mistakes in the limelight. He could barely do it in the shadows. He didn't even rightly know if, when Coral appointed him the representative of Reeve Gris and the Sunken Three, he'd done a good job of helping them reintegrate into the lives they'd left behind, or shielding them from town curiosity. He'd tried just treating them like regular kids.

But then Lenny grinned and shook Moss harder. "Couldn't have been set free, though, if you hadn't been a Grisly in the first place!"

Moss groaned. "I'm not a Grisly anymore!"

"You are!" Darla crowed over him. "We all are. We're the New Grislies. And I'll keep saying it so long as it annoys Reeve."

They all laughed and raised their bowls, and Moss, for the first time in a long time, felt the long crack in his heart healing.

Ven checked his watch. Time, and its measurement, had been one of the more curious things he'd had to learn. The watch had been a gift from Ada on the one-year anniversary of his new — actually legitimate — reign. But Ven still preferred to tell the hour by the sun, the warm and welcoming light that didn't demand much of him except to take a moment, every now and then, and bask in the possibility of a new life.

A familiar clacking against Tantalon Depot's tiles, amidst the busy comings and goings that the station was still growing accustomed to. He spotted Dunstan straight away, wearing his goggles and laughing at something a pair of young Jettites had said. They must be the exchange students that had come up for the term, likely for the new summer drama program Dunstan was overseeing as part of his senior year project.

Ven whistled, and Dunstan tilted his head. An almost-Jettite trait that always made Ven's heart skip a little. Dunstan bid the students farewell and clicked his way ahead with his cane.

He folded it up neatly and took Ven's outstretched arm, the gesture easy. "Waiting long? Sorry, got caught up after showing the students an old SVanway recording of *Crimes of Fashion*."

"'If the murder was the decadence of fashion, does that make me an accessory?'" Ven quoted in his best gauche accent, and Dunstan fell into giggles. "It's one of my favourites, too."

"I know," Dunstan sighed. "Though I have to admit that it's hard getting back into the swing of things after Professor Bedouin's visit."

"Definitely. He's charming and very dedicated to his work! And he's very good at Chase Ball."

"It's the eight legs," Dunstan agreed. "And that he's always trying to impress Constance."

"Still a very good dancer!" Ven relayed. "I wish you could have—"

He'd let his forked tongue run away with him again, biting off the last few words as they climbed into the gondola. "Sorry," he mumbled, but Dunstan patted his arm.

"It's fine! Really. Not being able to see Brindlewatch isn't going to stop me from . . . *seeing* it? If you know what I mean." As they sat in their seats, he leaned his head on Ven's shoulder. "It gives me a different perspective to create. As long as I can see my dreams in my mind, I can make them happen. Life isn't over. You taught me that."

Ven sighed comfortably. "It's just starting, I suppose," he said, as they descended on the cable track, the Stettle Beetle carapace glittering in the summer sunlight. "What happened in Quixx got me thinking, though. About their own little meteor shower too close to home."

Dunstan frowned. "I'm glad we gave Derrek the sample from the Door. I hope he'll be able to discover what it means. And if the event in Quixx and the Meteorlight are connected. But . . ."

"But I don't like waiting and not knowing, either," Ven finished. All the Meteorlight was now shining beneath Lake Mallion, creating a barrier between the lake water and Jet, and keeping both towns safe and secure with the mushrooms keeping it in check. They were reminded that it wasn't of this world. That enchanted living outer space Light, though given a purpose now, might not be the only one of its kind to find purchase in Brindlewatch. It had tried in the people of Knockum, removed with Coral's Filamenta and returned to the lakebed. But would it stay there for good?

"I was also thinking . . . Derrek and Constance came here for a vacation. Maybe you and I can finally have one." Dunstan lifted his goggles as the gondola swooped into the water and down the mushroom channel. Though he couldn't see anymore, he could still feel the glowing hum of the Meteorlight against his eyes, and it was comforting.

"Somewhere outside Jet and Knockum?" It was Ven's turn to be uneasy. He looked down directly into Dunstan's amber eyes with their green halos. "I don't know if I'm ready for that."

But Dunstan clasped his fingers between Ven's scaly claws and held on tight. "We can both lead. And follow."

Ven smiled. Promises, promises. They'd ended up keeping every single one of them, even if they hadn't been made with the best of intentions. And the bond they had now, a trust that shone brighter than Meteorlight, couldn't be broken.

"What about a diplomacy tour?" Dunstan offered. "I can see it now on marquees across the Split Continent! 'Prince Ven Performs Princely Duties and Unifying Spectacles across the Greater Cities!' Ooh, we could go to Luxe, it's so close by — they have the Lavish Theatre, you know, one of the best . . . Or Oiros City! The Kadaver's Soiree is on tour there right now, they could open for us . . ."

As the gondola descended, Dunstan and Ven made their plans, their mended hearts shining bright in the glittering green glow of their dreams. Jet, and Brindlewatch itself, lay open and waiting for them both.

ACKNOWLEDGEMENTS

This book was not done in isolation. It was done surrounded by family and strangers alike in various locations, like cafes or comic conventions or my own yard, during a particularly busy and distracting summer. I was also surrounded by dozens of competing deadlines, commitments, and priorities, and felt keenly my own mortality (maybe that's an exaggeration . . . but I recall a husk-like feeling throughout the process).

It's also the first book I completed since having a child. You may not realize this, but being a writer requires a certain amount of brain cells that have to be completely unassigned, and when you're a mother AND a writer, every brain cell is spoken for (or have multiple I.O.Us pasted over them). So needless to say, this book felt like the hardest thing I've ever done as a creator. And I'm grateful for everyone who supported me through it — my long-suffering husband Peter, who has to always deal with the mercurial moods and grumblings as plot holes follow me around all day. My son's incredible nanny, Eileen, who was absolutely essential in keeping the littlest member of the family active and happy in a summer when mum was wandering around with a thousand-yard stare in sweatpants. My work friends who nodded in compassionate commiseration as I griped about spending my spare moments blearily hallucinating the worlds of Jet and Knockum. My two wonderful editors who alternately patted me on the shoulder or jostled them like fierce boxing coaches every time we jumped back into the revision ring.

And, for once, I'm going to thank myself. Hey, you! I mean, me! You did it! You wrote another book, somehow! You stared out a lot of windows on this one! And it seems like you wrote this book twice . . . which I think you did, since you have an entire document of "alternates" and "cuts" that is twice the size of the book you're finally holding in your hands. It was a really nice summer out, too, and you had to sit a lot of it out to get your words in (at least it was at a patio table most days).

I also want to acknowledge the parents out there. I wanted parenthood to be more of a present theme in Mallion because the caregivers of the heroes are truly unsung in all the fantastical shenanigans they have to put up with. How can they work to protect total municipal annihilation while also balancing their kids' need for space (and need for reining in). Ada is definitely a part of me, constantly trying to plan for every outcome, watching the plot fall through my fingers, and having to adapt or perish. She's much more put together than I am, though. I hope we all have an Ada in our lives. And a Coral. Not so much a Myrtle.

One last thing: when I was young, I really wanted to be an actor. Dancing, singing, all of it; I was determined to "make it big" on stage and screen. Obviously, I went a totally different direction (some might say the total opposite direction) in my form of artistic expression, not for lack of trying, but because a lot of people said "no" to me, and I didn't have the support to keep trying or really believe I could do it. I still wonder What Might Have Been if I'd really gone for it — and if dancing through Dunstan Cord is as close as I get, I think that's okay. But to those who have a longing in their hearts and a dream on their sleeve — to you I say, Please go for it. Keep working, keep trying, keep shining your weird, wonderful light wherever you go. We're so lucky to have you here, and a "No" is as good a stage as any.

S.M. Beiko is a Winnipeg-based fantasy author and an award-winning graphic novelist. Her work includes *The Lake and the Library*, the Realms of Ancient trilogy, and the webcomic *Krampus Is My Boyfriend!* Beiko won the 2020 Best Graphic Novel Aurora Award and was nominated for the 2020 Joe Shuster Award.